HEARTS OF OAK

BERYL KINGSTON

AGORA BOOKS

ABOUT THE AUTHOR

Beryl Kingston is the author of 30 novels with over a million copies sold. She has been a writer since she was 7 when she started producing poetry. She was evacuated to Felpham at the start of WWII, igniting an interest in one-time resident poet William Blake which later inspired her novel *The Gates of Paradise*. She was an English teacher from 1952 until 1985 when she became a full-time writer after her debut novel, *Hearts and Farthings*, became a bestseller. Kingston continued writing bestsellers for the next 14 years with titles ranging from family sagas to modern stories and historical novels. She currently lives in West Sussex and has three children, five grandchildren, and ten great-grandchild.

ALSO BY BERYL KINGSTON

HISTORICAL FICTION

A Time to Love

London Pride

War Baby

Hearts and Farthings

Kisses and Ha'pennies

Two Silver Crosses

A Stitch in Time

Avalanche of Daisies

Suki

Gates of Paradise

Hearts of Oak

Off the Rails

Everybody's Somebody

THE EASTER EMPIRE TRILOGY

Tuppenny Times

Fourpenny Flyer

Sixpenny Stalls

THE OCTAVIA TRILOGY

Octavia

Octavia's War

The Internet Revolutionary

FICTION

Maggie's Boy

Laura's Way

Gemma's Journey

Neptune's Daughter

Francesca and the Mermaid

NON-FICTION

Lifting the Curse

A Family at War

HEARTS OF OAK

BERYL KINGSTON

This edition published in 2019 by Agora Books

First published in Great Britain in 2010 by Robert Hale Ltd

Agora Books is a division of Peters Fraser + Dunlop Ltd

55 New Oxford Street, London WC1A 1BS

Come cheer up my lads 'tis to glory we steer
To add something more to this wonderful year.
To honour we call you, not press you like slaves,
For who is so free as the sons of the waves.
Heart of oak are our ships; heart of oak are our men,
We always are ready.
Steady, boys, steady.
Well fight and we'll conquer again and again.

David Garrick
1717-1779

CHAPTER 1

Admiral Lord Nelson, hero of the Nile and darling of the nation, was leaving Portsmouth. It was one o'clock on a fine September afternoon and the air was shore-side busy, pungent with the smell of spilt beer and gutted fish, and boisterous with the cheers and shouts of a surging crowd of locals, who had gathered in the narrow streets of Spice Island, to escort him from The George to the jetty and bid him farewell. His barge was ready to carry him out to his flag ship, its crew sitting to attention with oars raised; the entrance to the harbour was full of small ships waiting on the calm water to salute his departure; but for the moment, as he walked down the steps by the bathing machines, he was dramatically and obviously alone, his handsome face pale and withdrawn under his black bicorne hat, that pitiful empty sleeve pinned to the breast of his blue jacket, scarlet sash bold as blood across his chest, white breeches and white silk stockings immaculate against the sea-stained wood of the steps.

"Such a fine good man," Molly Simmons said to her neighbours, as they struggled to keep their footing on the slippery cobbles, straining forward for a last look at their hero. "I means for to say, when you think what's ahead of him, poor soul, off to fight them pesky Frenchies, no wonder he looks peaky. They say 'twill be a fearsome battle. This could be the last time he sets foot on English soil, think a' that. I means for to say, the last time we shall ever see him again."

"Don't talk morbid," Lizzie Templeman said sharply. "You don't know what's to come no more than any of us."

"Quite right," Mary Morris agreed, frowning at Molly. "No point meeting trouble half way. If 'tis coming, 'tis coming, and we'll face it when we must, that's my opinion of it. Meantime I'll trouble you to keep *your* opinion to yourself."

Molly had seen her mistake as soon as the words were out of her mouth and now she regretted them, remembering that Lizzie Templeman had a son in one of Nelson's ships. "Time goes on, that's the trouble," she apologised. "You sort a' loses track." And she tried to make amends for her clumsiness by saying something complimentary. "Seems only yesterday we was all at your Jem's wedding. Such a pretty wedding. All them flowers an all."

It had been a pretty wedding, Mary thought. She and Lizzie had made sure of it. A pretty wedding, a good match, and everything starting off so well and now look where they were. There was no sense in the world.

IT HAD BEGUN on a quiet evening in March when no one in her family was expecting it. The wind had been blowing all day, which had been a fine thing because it had dried the laundry beautifully, and now the wash was indoors, folded up and put in the baskets and standing in the corner of the kitchen ready to be ironed, and she and Marianne were setting the table for supper. Marianne had made the bread that morning and it had turned out well, so she was feeling pleased with herself too, because you can never be sure with bread, and Pa and her brother Johnny were back from the yard and had washed their hands and were sitting up to the table waiting for the stew to be served. A quiet, ordinary, humdrum sort of evening. A time for taking their ease after the hard work of the day.

When they heard the knock on the door, Mary sent Johnny to answer it without very much interest. It wasn't usual to have callers at that time of night, but the neighbours were always popping in and out for one thing or another. She was rather surprised when he came grinning back into the kitchen with young Jem Templeman following behind him. A handsome creature young Jem, with those thick, dark curls all over his head and those fine, dark eyes and that easy way of walking and he was looking particularly well that evening in a red shirt that looked as though it was new made.

"An' what can we do for you, young man?" Mary asked, stirring the stew. "Laundry, is it?" Most of her callers came carrying bundles of dirty linen and she was always ready for trade.

"No," he said. "Nothin' like that, Mrs Morris." And he gave Jack Morris one of his bold looks. "Fact of it is, I come for to ask Mr Morris a favour."

"Then 'tis wheels," Jack said, because he was always ready for trade too. "Is that the size of it?"

Jem grinned, showing his nice white teeth, and Marianne watched him admiringly. He really was very handsome. "No, sir," he said. "'T'en't wheels neither. As a matter a fact…" and then he lost confidence for a second and hesitated, for, despite his bold appearance and his easy smile, he was more unsure of himself and more easily put down than anyone would ever know, or he would ever admit.

"Well come on then, my sonny," Jack Morris said, laughing at the hesitation. "Sit 'ee down an spit it out. We don't bite."

"Well then," Jem said, sitting on the nearest chair and gathering his courage, "'Tis like this here, sir. I come to ask your permission to come a-courting."

The words had an impact like a bomb exploding. It would have been hard to tell which of them was the most surprised. Young Johnny's eyes were as round as saucers at the thought that anyone should want to court his sister, Mary was beaming fit to split her face and Marianne was blushing with disbelief and pleasure. She could feel her cheeks turning red. He couldn't mean her, surely to goodness, not when he was so handsome, and she was so plain. Because she *was* plain there was no denying it. It was a private sorrow to her. When she was little, she'd watched the fine ladies driving about Portsmouth in their carriages or out shopping in the fine new shops, and she'd thought how tall and superior they looked with their haughty faces, all those long noses and big eyes an' all, and their fine clothes and their white hands, and she'd wondered if she would grow up even half as pretty. But she hadn't, of course, although she'd watched the mirror every day. She looked what she was, the daughter of a wheelwright and a laundrywoman, short in stature, plain in feature, altogether ordinary, with nothing about her to catch the eye. Her legs were too short and her face too dull, with little grey eyes and a blob of a nose, and she wore hemp and linsey-woolsey and her hands were always red-rough with soda and scrubbing. They were red and rough at that moment. And yet, she was the only one he could mean, and he was looking straight at her and smiling. My dear heart alive! she thought.

Her father was the first to recover. "Well now," he said, "as to that, 'twill need some consideration."

"I finished my apprenticeship last week," Jem told him. "I'm a master carpenter now, master carpenter an' cabinet maker, what's a good trade. I means to set up a workshop hereabouts, which should make me a good livin'. Which bein' so, I needs a wife to help and support me, like. So what I means for to say is, I been watching your Marianne in church, ever since I was 'prenticed, admiring her like an thinkin' about it, an I've talked it all over with Ma an' Pa, what's agreeable to it, an' now I'd like your leave for to come a-courting."

"My stars, Jem Templeman," Jack said, laughing again. "You don't beat about the bush."

The laughter was encouraging. "Is that yes or no, sir?"

"Well as to that," Jack said, "you'll have to ask our Marianne."

Jem turned towards her and looked directly at her for what seemed a very long time, half bold, half hopeful, but not saying anything, while she tried to catch her breath, for really, he'd taken it quite away. But when he spoke, he was splendidly proper.

"What do 'ee think, Miss Morris?" he said. "Shall we walk out after church on Sunday?"

She accepted his offer at once before he could think better of it. "Yes," she said. "I would like to."

So that Sunday they walked out of the town and into the countryside, she in her Sunday best and he in his new red shirt and, after a long silence during which they both wondered what he was going to say, he told her all about the work he was going to do and how he was going to hire a workshop and how hard it had been being apprenticed and what a long time it had taken. "Seven years from start to finish, what seems for ever. I was fourteen when I began." And she listened and marvelled to think that he would confide in her. She might not be the prettiest girl in town, but she knew how to behave.

It was quite a relief to him that she listened so well and said so little because he'd been awake half the night wondering how this courtship would begin. Wanting a wife was simple. 'Twas what everyone did. You got to a certain age, you found yourself a job, you settled down, you looked around and found a wife to cook for you and mend your clothes and share your life, bed and board sort of thing. Even to think of it was a pleasure. Bed and board. What could be better? 'Twas just the persuading of her that was the problem, for, if he was honest, and he prided himself on being honest, he really didn't have the first idea how to go about it. He'd seen plenty of courting couples walking out, naturally, hand in hand, or with their arms about each other, or kissing in quiet corners, but he didn't know how they'd managed to get the whole thing started. What were you supposed to say? And what if you said the wrong thing? But now, they'd taken their first walk together and he hadn't said anything wrong and it had all gone well. She'd listened, and she seemed to like him, and she'd certainly approved of what he'd said. When he escorted her back to her parents' house at the end of it, he was smiling with satisfaction. "I will see you next Sunday," he said.

Now that he'd discovered how to talk to her, the next Sunday was easier. He told her all about his master, Mr Henderson, and what a stickler he was. "Allus had to be the best you could do. Take your time, he used to say. Take your time an' then you won't spoil the wood. Very partic'lar about that he was." And she listened again. On the third Sunday, he told her about his parents' pie shop and what hard work that was. "Which is why I made certain to have me a trade." And she listened again.

By the time they'd been walking out for a month, Marianne felt there wasn't much she didn't know about him except whether he loved her, although she assumed he must do, or they wouldn't be keeping company and that was now such an established thing that her neighbours were beginning to talk about it. It disappointed her that there'd been no love talk between them — and surprised her, too, for her friends were always telling one another what nonsense men talked and she'd been quite looking forward to it — but maybe that would come later. For the moment, it was enough that he'd singled her out and they were known to be courting.

Then one evening, he arrived at her house with a bunch of daffodils and without saying a word, thrust them into her hands. Now that's a deal better she thought, lifting them to her face to smell them. Flowers were known to be love tokens. Everyone said so. And this is my first. My very first. She thanked him kindly and found an old jug to put them in, arranging them prettily and smiling at him all the time. And when he suggested that they should take a turn about the town, she went with him happily.

It was a balmy April evening and because she was so grateful for the flowers she put her hand in the crook of his arm as they walked along and gave it a squeeze. Now, she thought, we shall have some love talk, surely. He might even propose.

"Where are we goin'?" she asked.

His answer was rather a surprise. "To Mother Catty's," he said. "I got something to show you."

So they walked through the alleys to Mother Catty's lodging house, which was a small narrow building, where the amiable Mrs Catty plied her trade as local nurse and midwife and let out her rooms to augment her earnings. The door was ajar, as it usually was, so they walked into the hall which was very dark and smelt of cabbage and old shoes, and Jem led the way up the staircase, taking care to avoid a broken tread, up one floor, up two, until they reached the top of the house, where there were two closed doors giving out to a small landing.

"Here we are," he said, and opened the nearest door with a flourish. "This here is our room, what I've took for us." It was a wonderful moment. Our room, what I've took for us.

It was a small square room with a shuttered window looking out over the backyard and a fireplace with two trivets. There was nothing in it except for a brass bedstead with no mattress, an empty coal scuttle and, standing in rather splendid isolation in the middle of the room, a brand-new chest of drawers, smelling of new wood and varnish.

They stood side by side with their hands on the wood. "I made this," he told her proudly. "An' 'tis the best thing I ever done. What do 'ee think?"

"'Tis a fine piece," she said, and meant it, for she could see what care he'd taken with it.

"I shall furnish this place with everything we could want," he told her and walked about the room showing her where the furniture was going to be put. "A table and two chairs under the window, don't 'ee think? An' some shelves here for our pots and pans and so forth, an' a washstand in this corner, where 'twill be neat an' tidy. You shan't want for nothing, I promise you."

It wasn't exactly love talk, but it was the next best thing. My home, she thought, standing in the middle of the room and gazing round at it. My own home, where I can have a table an' chairs of my own an' a washstand an' a chest o' drawers...

"So we'll call the banns, shall we?" he said.

That wasn't exactly a proposal either, but she said "Yes" at once. Now, she thought, he will kiss me. She did so want him to kiss her, or put his arms round her, or even do some of the exciting things that married folk were permitted to do. She didn't know what they were, because she'd only heard them spoken about in hints and whispers, but the whispers had been too breathy and the hints too sly to leave her in much doubt that they were pleasurable. She lifted her face towards him, ever so slightly but enough to show that a kiss would be welcome. Oh surely, he'll kiss me now, she thought.

But, to her great disappointment, he didn't. "Good," he said. "I'll arrange it on Sunday."

HER FATHER ROARED with laughter when she told him. "He don't let the grass grow under his feet, that young man a' yourn," he said. "I'll say that for him. So when's the wedding?"

"He's arranging it on Sunday," Marianne told him.

It was arranged for four weeks later, in the week after the banns had been called for the third time and, as her mother was quick to tell her, it would mean a lot of work in so short a time. "He could have give us a bit more notice surely to goodness," she said.

"He wants it settled," Marianne tried to explain, and then

blushed because that made it sound as if he was in a rush to get her to bed and that wasn't the truth of it at all, although she wished it could have been. "I means for to say, now we got the room an' all, an' he's makin' the furniture an' everything." But it upset her to think that she'd be making extra work for her mother. "I know 'tis a lot to do," she said, "but I'll help 'ee with it."

"I daresay Lizzie Templeman will make the pies," her mother said, "bein' it's her trade, an' we can manage the custards atween us. But then there's bedding to get. You'll need a mattress and blankets and a couple of pillows at the very least. Goose feathers, I think. They're the best. I daresay your Aunt Min will make 'ee a bedspread. It'll be a bit of a rush for her, but she does 'em lovely. And then you'll need a new gown for I can't have you married in rags. That would never do. We'll go to town this afternoon and chose the material."

Preparing for a wedding was really quite exciting, even if there hadn't been any kisses. They chose a length of sky-blue cotton and set to work that evening cutting it out and basted the pieces together. When Jem arrived to ask her to come out for a walk, he grinned to see how busy they were.

"I en't sure I can this evening," Marianne told him, biting the thread. "There's rather a lot—"

But her mother was taking the cloth away from her. "You go, child," she said. "'Tis a fine evening an' the walk'll do 'ee good."

So they walked. But even then, there were no kisses because he was so busy telling her about their new furniture. "I got a fine set a shelves made for our pots and pans," he said, as they headed off into the fields. "I shall put 'em up tomorrow an' you can come an' see 'em."

"Yes," she said. "I would like to." He was so excited about all this furniture she could hardly say anything else. And it *was* good furniture. There was no denying that.

So the banns were called, and the pies and custards were made, and her dress was stitched and ready, and the flowers were ordered, and, the night before her wedding, she and Jem went to Mrs Catty's to put the final touches to the room that was going to be their home.

It really was a very fine room now that everything was done. The little wooden table he'd promised stood beside the window with two chairs set beside it, the shelves he'd put up were full of pots and kettles and dishes, for all the world as if they were part of a dresser, and the chest of drawers was set against the wall and full of their clothes, all neatly folded away. There were coals in the scuttle and a salt pot and two candlesticks on the mantelpiece and the trivets on the hearth were polished shiny ready for use. And dominating the room, the high bed stood waiting, all neatly made up with its two goose-feather pillows and its thick straw mattress and the cotton counterpane her aunt had made for her, spread cleanly over it all. My home, she thought, enjoying the sight of it and tomorrow I shall start to live here. I can't wait.

She looked so happy standing there that Jem was almost tempted to kiss her. But he thought better of it. He'd controlled himself admirably all these weeks for fear of doing the wrong thing and 'twas only a matter of hours now and then they'd be man and wife and nothing they could do could possibly be thought wrong. There'll be time enough for kisses tomorrow, he thought. I can't wait.

CHAPTER 2

It was a mad, glad day, the sun so bright it dazzled their eyes as they stepped from the stone-dim calm of St Thomas's church, the sky as blue as forget-me-nots and full of rollicking clouds, a crazy west wind blustering the town into a frenzy. It trembled the great sails of the anchored fleet as they hung slack to dry, whipped the skirts and coat tails of the wedding guests so that it was all they could do to walk upright, and blew Mary's straw bonnet right off her head, hat-pins and all, bowling it along the church path as if it were a bundle of chaff.

Marianne walked at the head of the procession, holding Jem's warm arm with one hand and her now rather battered bouquet with the other, feeling dizzy with triumph and happiness. The wind pinned the long straight skirt of her new gown tight against her striding legs, defining every curve of belly and thigh, and even though she knew it was probably immodest to be revealed so clearly, she gloried in it, because she could see that Jem was admiring her.

No more plain Jane for me now, she thought, as she struggled on against the wind. 1 left all that at the church door. Pa can't call me Pudden no more. I'm Mrs Marianne Templeman now and Jem loves me, I'm certain sure, even if he en't said so yet. And tonight, he would kiss her at last, when the dancing was done, and the guests were gone. Oh, she couldn't wait!

But there was a wedding breakfast to be got through first and it had taken a deal of time and a lot of hard work to prepare and Ma and Mrs Templeman said it was the best spread they'd seen for years so she knew she was going to enjoy it. She was too excited to do proper justice to it but she sat at the centre of the long trestle table in the mariners' hall and blushed to be called "Mrs Templeman" by her father and "my good wife" by her dear Jem and drank so much ale it made her head swim and did her best to eat what she could of the pressed pies and cold meats, and the melting jellies and custards that were set before her.

Jem made an excellent meal. "My dear heart alive," he said, when his second plate was clean, "That was a feast an' no mistake. If you feeds me half as good as this, gel, we shall live royal."

"Be a bit of a job," she said, half amused and half alarmed. Did he really expect her to cook pies and such? "Bein' we only got the one room. You can't cook pies without you got an oven."

"An' that reminds me," he said. "I'm off outside to water the roses, my lover. All this ale do make water somethin' chronic. Follow me out in a minute or two. I got somethin' to show 'ee."

"What?" she said. "What you got to show me, Jem?"

"Follow me an' you'll see," he said, winking at her, and he pushed his chair back, stood up and ambled towards the door, explaining to his friends as he went. "Got a few roses to water."

"Don't drown 'em," they called. And he was gone.

Marianne felt self-conscious sitting by herself at the table with everybody looking at her. Being the centre of attention had been lovely when he'd been sitting beside her because they'd all been looking at him, naturally. It was different now she was on her own. How long's a minute or two? she thought. Maybe I should count 'em. But that was silly. They must be up by now.

"'Scuse me," she said to her father, who was sitting on her left-hand side. "I got to go an' water roses an all."

"You drunk too much ale, gel," her father laughed. "You an' your Jem are a pair. The privy's out the back."

And very smelly it was with all the use it was getting. She was glad to get out in the air again, even if it did smell of fish, and even if it was still blowing her sideways. She stood in the yard, smoothing out the creases in her skirt and looking for clean spaces to tread in on her way back to the hall, when she was suddenly grabbed from behind and her husband was holding her so close, she could barely breathe.

"Good gel," he said. "Come on. We got a bed waitin' for us."

Her throat was so full she could hardly breathe at all. "D'you mean now?" she asked.

"Now as ever is," he said.

"What about the weddin' breakfast?"

"That's finished."

"And the guests. Shouldn't we go back to...?"

He turned her in his arms and kissed her full on the mouth while it was still open, pushing his tongue in as if he were taking possession of it, exploring and thrusting. It was such a surprise and so pleasurable she could feel her flesh leaping in answer to him. "You comin' back wi' me or en't you?" he said.

So she followed him through the alleys to their room, where everything was neat and new and waiting for them. My home, she thought, where I'm goin' to live an' Jem's goin' to love me an' we're goin' to be so happy together an' he's goin' to kiss me. She knew he was going to kiss her now. Oh my dear Jem, she thought, turning towards him.

But then all thought was stopped because he had her by the shoulders and was pushing her backwards onto the bed, talking to her in a hot, thick voice, that she hadn't heard before. "Oh my lover, I waited so long..."

She was expecting pleasure, now that she'd been given a taste of it, and lifted her mouth eagerly for kisses, but he was pushing up her skirt and fumbling at his breeches and he'd got his face jammed against her shoulder and didn't seem interested in kissing. Maybe he'd kiss her in a minute. But he didn't. He was pulling her legs apart, roughly and with both hands, grunting "Come on, my lover, come on," and then he was suddenly pushing something inside her, something hard and hot.

"Ow," she said. "That hurts."

But he didn't stop. He went on pushing it in and out, hard as iron, lying right on top of her and grunting, "Come on. Come on."

She tried to wriggle out from under him, but he weighed too much, and he was pinning her to the mattress. She tried to push him off, but he paid no attention. He just went on and on, and the stabbing was getting more and more painful, sharp and stinging as if he was cutting her.

"Please, Jem," she gasped. "Do stop. You're hurtin' me." But the words were disjointed as if he was pushing them out of her chest and she wasn't sure he could hear her with all the grunting he was doing. She grabbed hold of his shirt and tugged it. "Please!"

He gave an odd sort of groan and stopped moving. For a second, they both lay still, then he put a hand on either side of her, propped himself up and looked down at her. "What's the matter with 'ee?" he said, and he sounded cross.

"You was hurtin' me," she told him.

"No I wasn't," he said, and now there was no doubt that he was angry. "That don't hurt. That's love, gel. What you was made for." How dare she say such a thing! He wouldn't hurt anybody. It wasn't in his nature. She was making it up.

His annoyance made her stubborn. "I don't know about all that," she said. "I only know you was hurtin' me."

"You're just a big booby," he said, trying to speak more kindly. "That's how it is. I never hurt nobody in my life. Make your mind up to it and don't go a-sayin' things."

She struggled out from under him and stood by the bed,

pulling her skirt down. It was bunched up around her waist and most uncomfortable. Then she noticed that there was a trickle of blood running down her leg. "You've made me bleed," she said. "Now say you haven't hurt me."

He was so cross he could hardly contain himself. Fancy saying that when he'd just been loving her, and he'd made the effort to speak fair to her. Didn't she have any modesty? Standing here with the blood running down her legs saying such things. He fastened his breeches, buttoned his red shirt, ran his fingers through his hair, returned to normal in the usual way. She was still standing there in the middle of the room staring at him. "Now what?" he asked, irritably.

"I shall have to take my dress off, or I'll stain it," she said.

Oh what a nonsense, to be fussing over a dress. "Do as you please," he said. "'Tis all one to me. I needs a tot a' rum. I'm off out." His disappointment was so dreadful he simply couldn't stay with her a moment longer or he'd be shouting.

She was struggling out of the dress, pulling it over her head, blinded by the folds of cloth. "You won't go without me," she pleaded, her voice muffled. "Jem…"

But he'd already gone.

Tears pricked into her eyes. How could he be so unkind? she thought, as the tears rolled down her cheeks. When we're just married an' all. Were all men like that? Maybe they were. How would she know? But there wasn't time for speculation. She had to clean herself up and make herself tidy. What she needed was a clout and the only thing she could think of that might answer was the old chemise she'd put in the chest of drawers that morning. She'd planned to wear it as a nightshirt, but it would have to do. At least her scissors were in the drawer too, along with her pins and needles, so she wouldn't have to tear it with her teeth. She cut two long strips from the hem, one thick enough to make the clout and a thin one for the cord. Then she folded and knotted until it was ready, set it on the bed, and poured a little cold water from the ewer into the wash basin. It took a while before she was satisfied that she was clean and protected and by then her tears had dried and her thoughts were steady. I'll have to think of some excuse for being away so long, she decided. I can't just walk back into the hall and say nothin'. They'll wonder. Unless Jem's back before me and he's made excuses.

But when she walked back into the hall there was no sign of Jem and her guests instantly set up a catcall. "Where you been then, you bad gel? As if we didden know?"

"Oh en't you the sly one."

"An' what you done with that husband a' yourn? Wore out I shouldn't wonder, poor feller."

She could feel the blushes burning her face and knew they were enjoying her embarrassment. Why do they have to be so coarse? she thought, looking away from them. "He's gone to get more ale," she said, offering the first excuse that came into her head. "He'll be along presently."

"An' how long was he, my lover," one of his friends asked slyly. "A good ol' length, I'll wager. Was he long enough for 'ee? Or did 'ee want more."

"Leave the wench be," Mary Morris said, coming to the defence of her child. "Unless you wants somethin' a' yourn cut short." Which was greeted with a roar of delight.

"Well said, Mother Morris," they called. "You got his measure an' no mistake."

Mary sat down beside her blushing daughter. "Where *has* he gone, Marianne?" she asked.

"To get a tot a' rum, so he said."

"He's a man for his liquor," her mother said, "which is no bad thing in the ordinary run of events. It shows manly. But he'd best get back sharpish now, liquor or no, for here's the piper come an' no groom to lead the dance."

"If he don't come back I shall lead it with Pa," Marianne told her. "I aren't a-waitin'. 'Ten't kindly to keep us waiting." But she couldn't help wondering where he was.

HE WAS SITTING in the snug at The Dolphin with a third tot of rum in his hand talking to two new friends. He'd come slouching in, feeling aggrieved and frustrated and altogether out of sorts, and they'd greeted him from the chimney corner, calling him "My ol' lubber" as if they'd known one another for years and asking what he fancied. He knew they were seaman, the cut of their jib told him that, and so did their weathered faces and imposing beards, and in the normal course of events, he wouldn't have taken any notice of them, seamen being what they are. But this wasn't the normal course of events. He needed company and a bit of sympathy and they were there to offer it. So he told them he could use a tot of rum, "Thank 'ee kindly" and they ordered it for him straightaway and pulled up a chair for him to join them.

"Women, is it?" the older of the two asked, as the rum was laid before him. His eyes were as dark as his beard and he looked decidedly mischievous. "Tom Kettle's the name and this here's Peggy."

"On account a' me leg," the younger man said and swung a thick peg-leg up onto the table so that Jem could take a look at it. "Work of art is that," he said, patting it. "Ship's carpenter done it for me arter the Nile."

Jem examined the object with professional interest. "Turned on a lathe," he said. "Very handsome. He done a good job with it."

"Now dang my eyes," Peggy said. "There speaks one what knows. You wouldn't be a carpenter yourself now, by any chance?"

Jem admitted his trade, with some pride. "I would, sir. Not that it's done me much good. Served me 'prenticeship, so I have, seven years man and boy, carpenter and cabinet maker. I been a carpenter's mate for six months. I bought me tools. I thought to be a master carpenter with work in the neighbourhood, an' a wife an' family an' all. Found me a wife, nice quiet body — I went out my way to find a quiet one — nice quiet body what ud cook an' clean an' so forth, an' then what happens?"

His companions were agog for more.

"Married her this afternoon, as ever is, what you'd think she'd be pleased about. But no. She give me such a tonguing, you'd never believe. An' here's me thinking what a nice quiet body she was. I had to get up an' leave her. Couldn't take no more of it."

"Well now, my ol' lubber," Tom Kettle said, "It just might be your luck's a-turnin'."

"Not much chance a' that, sir," Jem said glumly. "Like I told 'ee, I married the wench. Mores the pity."

"A parlous error," Tom Kettle said. "Never wed 'em, that's my advice. Bed 'em but never wed 'em. Howsomever, the deed's done you say."

Jem was maudlin with drink and feeling sorry for himself. "More's the pity," he repeated. "I made my bed, as they say, an' now I shall have to lie on it."

"Not," Tom Kettle said, tapping the side of his bulbous nose with his forefinger, "necessarily. Have another tot an I'll tell 'ee what I have in mind."

The rum was ordered and delivered, and all three men drank, Jem morosely, the sailors happily.

"Now then, my lubber," Tom Kettle said, "what I have to put to 'ee is this. How would 'ee like a job what 'ud take 'ee far away from this harridan a' yourn an' pay you good money to boot?"

"I'd like it very well," Jem said. "Onny it don't exist. Like I told 'ee, I've made my bed an' now—"

"An' now, my lubber, you must join the navy an' be a ship's carpenter, what is an honourable post for any man, an' well paid, an' leave your troubles behind you. Tha's what you must do. Stands to reason."

Jem's reason was now so fogged with rum he could barely think. "Must I?" he asked.

"My stars yes," Peggy said, supping his own rum. "See the world. Good shipmates. Women a-plenty an' no questions asked. Good grub. Good pay. Good prize money, when the time comes. Grog a-plenty. Tha's the life for 'ee. Take my word for it, you'll never find a better."

"Well... I don' know about that," Jem said, his voice slurred. "Tha's a bit of a compli... condi... compli-nation... cation, I means."

"Simplest thing in the world," Tom Kettle said. "There's my warrant, d'you see?" And he waved a piece of parchment in front of Jem's unfocused eyes. "All you got to do is say the word, sign your name on this ere paper which we got all ready an' waiting for 'ee, an' you're a free man. What could be simpler?"

Put like that, what indeed? "A paper you say?"

"Just sign your name, my lubber," Peggy said, leaning towards him. "Or make your cross. An' you're a free man. Show that harridan a' yourn who's boss."

There was something cream-colored lying on the table, with a pen and an ink horn beside it. Now where had *they* come from?

"Sign it," Peggy urged, "an' you're a free man."

"Now, d'you mean?"

"Now, my lubber. What could be simpler?"

To Jem's addled brain, it looked prodigiously difficult. But he made a supreme effort and, after three false starts, signed his name at the foot of the page.

He was startled when both men gave a bellow of delight and slapped him on the back.

"Welcome aboard, shipmate," Tom Kettle said and stood up.

"Are you goin'?" Jem asked.

"We're all goin', my lubber," Tom said, and hauled his new recruit to his feet.

Jem found it surprisingly hard to stand and for a few seconds, he swayed and tottered, trying to control a sudden dizziness, knowing he was very drunk, while his two companions supported him on either side and waited until he was fit to move.

"Come on then," Tom Kettle said, steering him towards the door.

"Where to?" Jem asked.

"Why to sea, my lubber. I got a tender all ready an' waitin' for 'ee. You're in the navy now."

CHAPTER 3

Mrs Marianne Templeman was still waiting in the mariners' hall. The dancing was over and done, the piper had been paid and gone away and most of the guests had gradually drifted off too. Now, sitting alone at the long table, she was beginning to worry. What if he'd drunk himself silly and was lying in the gutter somewhere? It would be her job to get him home, being his wife, she knew that, but how would she go about it? She felt cross with him for treating her so. It wasn't kindly. Not on their wedding day.

"Shall you come home with us?" her mother asked, joining her at the table. "We got to be out the hall in a minute or so, Mr Jones says. He'll tell your Jem where you are."

"Thank 'ee kindly, Ma, but no," Marianne said. "I think I'll go back to Mother Catty's an' see if he's there."

"An' if he en't?"

"Then I shall go an' find him. He can't have got far."

"Try the inns," her mother advised. "If he went for ale, he's like to have stayed. You know what men are when they're in drink. Daft as ha'pence, the lot of 'em."

It was sound advice, but which inns? There were so many and none of them particularly welcoming to women on their own, unless they were whores. They let *them* in soon enough on account of they brought trade. Ah well, she thought, I shall just have to try them all until I find him.

The wind had dropped a little since the afternoon and the sun was warm on her shoulders. She wrapped her shawl around her nevertheless. It wouldn't do to look too grand. Not when she was walking through the streets on her own and certainly not if she had to go trawling the hostelries.

The room was exactly as she'd left it, the bed tousled, the dirty water pink with blood and gathering scum in the pail, what was left of her chemise lying on a chair. As there was no urgency if he was just out drinking, she changed into her work-a-day clothes, tidied the place up and carried the pail downstairs to empty it in the privy. Then, feeling virtuous, she set off on her search. There were drinking houses a-plenty down at the Point, but they were rowdy places, so she decided to give them a miss for the moment and try the inns in the High Street, which served a better sort of customer and was nearer to hand.

It was also impossibly crowded — with carriages and post chaises blocking the road, porters trying to trundle their carts between them and a motley collection of mongrel dogs, jumping and barking at everything that moved. Not the easiest place to go searching, she thought, as she dodged through the melee and over the cobbles, but she pushed her way through with her usual determination, avoiding the dirt as well as she could. She did so hate to get manure on the hem of her skirts.

The first place she came to was a coaching inn and it was noisily busy because the last coach of the day had just arrived, the horses were being uncoupled and led away and the yard was full of travellers and their luggage. It took her a very long time before she could catch the eye of a potboy and then the idiot didn't know who'd come in that afternoon.

"We've had all sorts," he said wiping his forehead with his cap. "'Tis all Oi can do to serve 'em, never moind remember their names. What do 'e look loike this feller a' yourn?"

But although he recalled plenty of men with curly hair, they being "two a penny hereabouts", none was wearing a red shirt. "That I would ha' remembered, bein' broight loike."

The next inn along the road was The Duke of Buckingham and nobody had any recollection of a man in a red shirt and told her to be off out of it when she persisted. It was the closest inn to their room in Highbury Street and she'd had hopes of it. But now she came to look at it, it was a deal too grand for her Jem, all those great ships' timbers and all. Nothing daunted, she crossed the road to Peacock Lane and tried the modest inn on the corner. No luck, although at least they were civil. "Try The Dolphin," the pot boy suggested. "They been busy today." So she tried The Dolphin.

"Jem Templeman," the barman said. "He's one a my reg'lars."

"Has he been in?"

"In an out. You won't see him again in a long time."

She thought he was joking. Men had such odd ideas about what was funny. "I'd better," she said, "seem we was married not three hours since."

"You never was!" he said, plainly surprised. "I means for to say. Three hours since. Well I never."

"So where's he gone?"

"He's been pressed, gel. Gone to sea. Of Peg-Leg an' Tom Kettle took him. You could ask 'em if they was here. They'd tell 'ee. Half seas over he was. They was darn near carryin' the feller. Like I said, you won't see him again in a long time."

She felt as if he'd hit her in the stomach. He couldn't have gone to sea. Why would he do such a thing? He had a good job, a good wife, he was settled. It was his wedding day. Seaman went to sea, or men who needed work. Not Jem. "You're pullin' my leg," she said.

"No, my lover. 'Tis true as I stand here. I seen it with my own eyes. He's gone to sea. Him an' half the world. They're all off to sea today on account a' we're at war with France again, d'ye see? Admiral Lord Nelson come down at one o'clock, all in a great rush. He was aboard the *Victory* by ha past three. Thirteen-gun salute there was. I wonder you didden hear it. Made enough noise. There's been midshipmen roundin' up their crews all day, an' luggage comin' an' goin', provisions bein' took aboard, an' I don't know what-all. Given a fair wind, they reckon to set sail tomorrow, so I'm told."

"They may go when they please," she said fiercely, "but he'd better come back home sharpish. Tha's all I got to say on the subject."

And she left the inn in a furious temper. It blazed her to the quayside, which was as busy as she'd ever seen it and so full of carts and carriages it was all she could do to squeeze between them to get to the water's edge. Livestock of all kinds was being taken aboard, pigs by the dozen, driven and squealing, goats bleating, chickens squawking in crates or being carried two by two and upside down with their heads puzzled and swinging. Everywhere she looked people were carrying provisions or manhandling furniture, sides of salt beef, sacks of flour, hogsheads of beer and crates of wine, sea chests and great chairs, bureaux and tallboys, and pushing among them, a variety of tradesmen were shouting their wares and swearing at the competition. Two hired coaches packed with sailors had collided in the middle of the road, and were now firmly locked together, to the delight of the seamen who were traveling on top and had a ring-side seat. The noise and stink of it ail were overpowering. How am I s'posed to find him in all this? Marianne thought. 'T'would take a month a' Sundays so it would. But he had to be there somewhere. They couldn't have took him aboard ship already, surely to goodness.

There was an officer sitting on the nearest bollard smoking his pipe and obviously waiting for someone or something, so she decided to ask him.

"If you please, sir," she said, "could you be so kind as to tell me where they put the new recruits? Ones what've just joined, I mean."

"Aboard ship I daresay," the officer told her, adding rather brusquely, "What's it to you?"

She bristled against the rebuke in his tone. That would have to be corrected and double quick. "If you please, sir," she said, maintaining her politeness, "he's my husband, sir, an' he's left his tools behind what he'll need on the voyage."

His tone softened. "Don't you fret your little head about tools, my dear," he advised. "We've tools of every description in the navy. The Admiralty sees us well provided. He'll find all he needs when he's aboard."

So that was a wasted effort. She thanked him and pushed on through the crowd. Who would know? There must be someone. What was it the barman had said? He'd been took by a man called Tom Kettle — she remembered that — and a man with a wooden leg. Very well then, she'd look for a man with a wooden leg. But even as she made her decision, she saw three men with wooden legs directly in her line of vision, all busy carrying things and none of them looking the least bit welcoming. Nevertheless she tried them all. "If you please, sir, could you tell me if you've met up with a man called Jem Templeman today?"

The first man grunted and looked cross, the second told her to be off out of it, the third turned his head towards her so abruptly that the sack he was carrying caught her on the shoulder and nearly knocked her off her feet. She recovered her balance quickly, but not quickly enough to scold him for his carelessness. He was already deep into the crowd and wouldn't have heard her even if she'd yelled at him. It made her feel disheartened to be so roughly treated but she went on searching. What else could she do?

An hour went by and then another, tolled implacably by the church clock, and she still hadn't found him. Bum boats arrived at the quayside, were loaded to the gunnels and set off again, oars creaking; a longboat eased alongside to collect the lounging officer; another squawking cartload of chickens was trundled across the cobbles; there were one-legged men wherever she looked. And it was growing dark and cold.

She felt miserably weary to have searched for so long and with such a will and found no trace of him. She walked across to the bollard the officer had been using as a seat and sat on it herself, heavily. I won't go home till I've found him, she thought. If it takes all night, I'll find him come the finish.

"Ain't you found that feller a' yourn then?" a voice said above her.

She glanced up into the speaker's face and found she was looking at one of the local whores. She was an amazing sight, seen close to like that, her cheeks rouged red, her curled hair dyed the colour of straw, her teeth much browned and decayed, her titties pushed up so high by her stays that they tumbled out of her bodice as she leant forward. My stars, Marianne thought, what would Ma say if she knew I was talking to one of these? But the woman's face was kindly, and she looked concerned.

"No," Marianne said. "I en't an' that's the truth of it."

"I been a-watchin' you," the woman said, "between times like. I knew you was looking for someone, the way you been askin'."

"'Tis my husband," Marianne confessed.

"Ah!"

"We was married this afternoon an' now he's gone to sea an' I don't know where he is."

"He's a hard-hearted wretch wherever he is," the whore said, trenchantly, "to leave his wife on their weddin' day. I never heard the like. You're well rid of him, you ask me. Find yourself another what'll treat you better."

Marianne was annoyed to hear him blamed so roundly, particularly as it was exactly what she'd been thinking herself. "I didn't ask you," she said hotly. "You en't to speak of him so. You don't know the ins and outs of it."

"Easy on, my lubber," the whore said, amicably. "Keep yer wool on. I meant no harm."

"I reckon he's been press-ganged, poor man," Marianne said, speaking her thoughts. "It don't make no sense for him to up sticks an' go, not like that, an' not on his weddin' day."

"'Tain't legal to press 'em, not no more," the whore told her, sitting down companionably beside her. "'Tain't allowed."

"Allowed or not, I reckon they done it," Marianne said. "He wouldn't go without tellin' me goodbye for a start. He'd ha' come home an' said goodbye, at the very least. No. He been press-ganged, you see if I en't right."

"No way a knowing though, is there, my lubber?" the whore said, and she stole an orange from a street trader's passing tray and hid it in her skirt, so neat and quick he didn't see the going of it. "'Course they got ways an' means without pressin' 'em. They gets 'em tipsy fer a start an' then they signs up without seein' the meanin' of it. They could ha' done that. Tom Kettle's a dab hand at that sort a' trick."

The name blazed light into Marianne's memory. "Tom Kettle?" she said. "Do you know him?"

"Not professional as you might say," the whore told her. "We works the same inns d'yer see, so I sees him around. He's been mighty busy today, I can tell 'ee that though. He ain't been out the Dolphin all day to my certain knowledge, an' that wooden-legged feller's been up an' down to the quayside all afternoon, sendin' 'em off."

"An' one of 'em my Jem," Marianne said. "Do you know where he was sendin' 'em? Oh please say you know."

"Well as to that, my lubber," the whore said, "I got no idea. There's twenty ships an' more in the roads. Could ha' been any one of 'em. He works for several captains, that I do know. I just seen 'em go." She pulled the orange from under her skirt and began to peel it. "Have half?" she offered.

They sat in the declining light and ate the orange between them, two young women in a world of men, while candles were lit in the drinking houses behind them, the last of the bum boats was loaded and went creaking off into the channel, and the great distant ships grew ghostly in the half light.

"All those ships," Marianne said miserably, "an' he could be on any one a them. How would I know?"

"Beats me, my lubber," the whore said. "I reckon you'd have to join the navy to find out for certain."

But of course, Marianne thought. It was the obvious answer. She was never going to find him on the quay because he wasn't there. And she was never going to find anyone who knew where he was. They were all too busy with their own affairs. She would have to join the navy and go after him. It was the only thing to do. I'll borrow Johnny's breeches and his old shirt, she planned, an' I'll put my hair in a plait the way the sailors do, an' then I'll go back to the Dolphin an' find that rotten old Tom Kettle an' join the navy myself. So help me if I don't. I en't a-goin' to be no deserted wife, with everyone laughing and pointing and mocking, not if I can help it.

"Thank 'ee kindly fer the orange," she said to her new friend and stood up, shaking her skirts to rights.

"You off then?" the whore said, sucking the last segment. The juice ran down her chin, glistening in the fading light.

"Yes," Marianne said, "I do believe I am."

WHEN SHE GOT HOME, the house was full of noise and laughter for her parents were in the kitchen and obviously had company. It took no time at all to sneak into the back bedroom and find her brothers breeches, which still lay across the end of his truckle bed where he'd thrown them when he changed clothes for the wedding. His shirt was ready to hand too. That was in a crumpled heap on the floor. She changed quickly, plaited her hair and tied it with a length of string he'd been using for fishing. Then she crept past the kitchen door, as quietly as she could so as not to alert her parents, and strode out of the house, newly masculine and full of determination. How easy it was to walk in breeches. She hadn't realised how much skirts got in her way until that moment. It was a pleasure to stride along the road.

The Dolphin was as crowded as it had been in the afternoon, but this time Tom Kettle was there. He was easy to find because he was making so much noise and, besides, he was sitting next to another seaman who had a wooden leg propped up on the chair in front of him.

"Tom Kettle?" she said. There was no need for politeness or preliminary. She was a boy now.

"Who wants ter know?" Tom Kettle boomed.

What was she to call herself? She could hardly say Marianne. "I do," she said.

"An' do you have a name, my lubber?"

She had a name in that instant. "Matt," she said. "Matt Morris."

"Well now, Matt Morris, what can I do for 'ee? Since you're so almighty keen to see me."

"I wants for to join the navy," Matt Morris said.

"A bold lad, bigod!" Tom Kettle said. "Well now, Matt Morris, you come to the right shop. D'you have a trade by any chance?"

"No, sir."

"What is your father?"

"He's a wheelwright, sir, but I don't intend for to follow him. I wants a life a my own. I'm willin' to learn."

Tom Kettle was satisfied that he'd seen the reason for this enlistment. Many's the boy had joined the fleet to escape an unwelcome trade. "Then so you shall, bigod!" he said.

Two minutes later, Marianne was a member of His Majesty's

Navy, the recruitment papers signed with her new name, and countersigned by her new friend Tom Kettle, all, as the gentlemen himself declared, ship-shape and Bristol fashion. It was the easiest sovereign he'd ever earned.

A tot of rum was ordered, and she drank it with outward bravado and inward misgiving, surprised to find how quickly it made her head spin. She was patted on the back by Tom Kettle and thumped between the shoulders by his friend Peggy and told she would steer to glory and return in a month or two with her pockets full of silver. Then since they were being so friendly, she asked them whether they remembered enlisting a man called Jem Templeman.

"Fine feller," Tom Kettle said. "Joined this afternoon, didn't he, Peg? You took him to the quay, didn't cher?"

"Then you know what ship he's on."

"Well, as to that," Tom Kettle said cautiously, "I couldn't say." It was bad policy to tell anyone where his enlisted men had gone. Some of 'em had left debts behind and some had all manner of troubles. This one was being chased by a harpy of a wife if he remembered correct. "We just delivers 'em to the captains, like we'll do for you. 'Tis the captains what sends 'em on to the ships."

Marianne tried not to look disappointed. But it didn't matter really, for she'd find him soon enough once she was afloat. Now it was just a matter of saying goodbye to her mother and father and then she could be aboard and off on her search. "Could I just cut off home for a while?" she asked. "To say goodbye like?"

In the normal run of events, Tom Kettle would have sent his new recruit to the press room and kept tight hold of him until he could get him aboard, but this lad was so eager and earnest he let him go, advising him to be on the quay by nine o'clock sharp, "or we shall cast off without 'ee."

So Marianne went back to her parents' house to break the news to them. Her appearance in the kitchen caused quite a stir.

"My dear heart alive!" her mother said. "What do you look like, gel? What have you got on?"

"She's got my breeches," Johnny said. "That's what she's got on. What you playin' at, Marianne? I thought you was a married woman, not one a' them actor fellers."

"I'm an actor feller from this day on, Johnny," she told him and explained. "Jem's joined the navy an' I don't know where he is, except he's at sea."

Her mother was so astonished her jaw fell. "Joined the navy," she said in disbelief. "He can't have. Not on his weddin' day. I never heard the like. What's got into him? 'Ten't natural."

"Well he has," Marianne said. "The barman at The Dolphin seen it. Only he don't know what ship he's on. Nobody does. I been lookin' for him ever since I left you, Ma, an' I've tried an' tried, an' I can't find no one what knows where he is or where he's gone or anything. Except he's in the navy. So I've joined the navy too an' I'm goin' after him to find him."

The announcement caused absolute consternation. "You've took leave of your senses," her father said. "Gels don't join the navy. That's for the likes a' young Johnny here. 'Tis only boys they wants, not gels, so let's have done with it an' no more silly talk."

"'Ten't silly talk, Pa," Marianne tried to explain. "He's my husband. Where he goes I got to go."

"But not to sea, gel," her father said. "You can't go to sea. 'Tis out the question. I forbid it. Gels don't go to sea."

His heaviness made her stubborn, as it always had done. "There's no point goin' on about it," she said, "an' you can't forbid it, for the deed's done. I've signed the paper an' I'm going to sea. I just came back to say goodbye." And she put her arms around her mother's neck and kissed her. "I'll be back as soon as you know it," she promised. "With Jem alongside a' me. You'll see. Wish me well."

"Don't you do nothin' of the sort, Ma," her father said. "She's makin' a terrible mistake. You just tell her so."

"What would be the good a' that?" Mary said, sadly. "Would it stop her goin'?"

"No, Ma," Marianne said. "It wouldn't. Nothing's going to stop me now. I've made my mind up. I can't stay here an' be laughed at. I got to go—"

"I shall go straight down to that quay an' tell 'em you're a woman," her father said. "That'll stop you."

Marianne was beginning to feel horribly irritated. Couldn't he see she'd made up her mind? "No it won't," she said, speaking directly to her father. "An' I'll tell you for why. It won't on account of I'll just go straight back first chance I get and sign up again with a different name. Won't make no difference at all except I won't come back to say goodbye, I'll just go. I don't belong to you no more, Pa. I belongs to Jem."

He threw his hands in the air with exasperation. "We've just give you the best weddin' a gel ever had," he said, "all that food an' all, an' the piper an everything. Don't that count?"

"It's got nothin' to do with the weddin', Pa," Marianne said. "I'm goin' on account of it's the only way to find him. Can't you see that?"

"You're an ungrateful, wicked gel," her father said. "That's what you are. An' I allus thought you was such a good little thing. Well, how wrong I was! This is downright rank disobedience an' you'll be punished for it. You mark my words."

Marianne decided to ignore him. "You wish me well, Ma, don't you?" she said, turning to her mother. It meant a lot to her to have her mother's blessing.

"I do, child," her mother said, putting her arms round her. "I think you're making a terrible mistake, mind, but I wish you well with all my heart. I truly do."

"Then I'll be off," Marianne said, being brisk about it because she was suddenly too close to tears for comfort. "There's my weddin' ring. Look after it for me. I'll send 'ee letters when I can get hold of pen and paper. I can't promise many of 'em, sea travel bein' what it is, but I will write. You can depend on it."

Then she left them, striding quickly away from the house and along the dark alley towards the quay, her chest aching with tears. Wherever you are, Jem Templeman, she thought, you're causing me a deal of grief.

Jack Morris was still fuming. "And what are we going to tell Lizzie Templeman?" he said to Mary. "We shall look a fine pair of fools."

"We'll tell her the truth," Mary said. "That's what we'll do. That her blamed fool son's run off to sea, what's the most foolish thing I ever heard of, and our Marianne's gone to sea after him to find him."

"An' I allus thought she was such a quiet little thing," Jack said. "I can't think what's got into her."

"An' I can't think what's got into him neither," Mary said trenchantly. "An' if he was here I should tell him so. He needs a piece of my mind, wherever he is. Blamed fool."

It would have pleased her to know that he was lying in a miserable heap on the quarter-deck of the frigate *Sirius*, feeling extremely sick and extremely sorry for himself. He was soaking wet, his head was pounding, someone was making the devil of a racket grinding and thumping, it was dark, and the ship was rolling from side to side, sloshing his innards about like water in a pail. Why was he on a ship? Hadn't he just got wed? He had a faint recollection of a marriage service and walking away from a church with Marianne hanging onto his arm, and there'd been a wedding breakfast with plenty of ale. He remembered that. But as to what had happened next, it was as if the events had been punched out of his head.

"So you're back in the land a' the livin', are you, my sonny?" a voice said. "An' not afore time. Look lively."

Jem opened his eyes and squinted up at the speaker, a thickset man with a formidable beard and massive shoulders, holding a lantern so that they could see one another. "Where am I?" he said.

"Where are yer?" the man mocked. "Why, where should you be, you dunderhead? You're on the *Sirius*, that's where you are, which is the best frigate afloat, so think yourself lucky. The eyes an' ears of Admiral Cornwallis's navy we are an' don't you forget it. Now you got work to do. Look lively."

Jem did his best to stand up. "Had a skinful," he explained.

"Sick as a dog you was," the man said, grinning at him and showing a mouthful of very white teeth. "We had to throw you in the scuppers, my sonny, and wash you down or you'd ha' stunk the place out. My name's Mr Turner and I'm the master carpenter on this ship, which means to say you're my mate, so you do as I say. At all times. Understood? Right then, my sonny, pick up your gear an' follow me. We're wanted in the galley."

There was a carpenter's bag standing on the deck by Mr Turner's feet, so Jem picked it up as he was told and did his best to follow the man, which he did very unsteadily, for the motion of the ship was throwing him about so much that he could barely keep on his feet. But at least he knew the galley was the ship's kitchen and at least he had some tools, so he wasn't surprised when they arrived on a lower deck in a low-ceilinged room full of sailors, and he found himself standing beside the biggest cooking stove he'd ever seen, with a table lying upside down beside it.

"First job, fix the table," Mr Turner said, and turned to the cook, who was another stolid looking man, with a wooden leg. "This here's Jem, Charlie," he said. "I hope you got some good grub fer us tomorrow. I didn't think much a tonight's. Load of ol' cagmag that was."

"Onny the best for you, Mr Turner," the cook said, lifting the lid on a huge cooking pot and inspecting the inside. "You know that. So what about this 'ere table then?"

"Jem'll do it," Mr Turner told him. "Give him enough light. I'm off to inspect the hull. I shall be in the walk if you want me." And he marched away, his lantern bobbing before him.

"Needs a carpenter does that," the cook complained, but he was talking to the air.

"I *am* a carpenter," Jem said. It was making him cross to be talked about as if he wasn't there. "A master carpenter."

The cook was lighting more lamps. "Well, we shall see, shan't we?" he said.

Yes, Jem thought crossly, you will. I'll make sure of it. And, as soon as the lights were ready, he set about his task. At first glance, the table looked as though someone had hit it with a hammer. One leg was so badly split it would have to be replaced. Where did they store the wood?

"Got a job on, aintcher?" the cook said with obvious satisfaction. "Wasn't stowed proper, that's the trouble. Took a bashing in that last storm."

"If you can tell me where they keep the wood, I'll make it up as good as new," Jem promised. And although he had to suffer the ignominy of being led to the store by one of the ship's boys as though he was an imbecile, he made an excellent job of the repair. The cook said it was ship-shape, damn his eyes if it wasn't, which was obviously high praise. But then the bell struck four times and the sailors who'd been cleaning and stowing pots while he'd been turning the new leg, gave their utensils a last rub and their cook a farewell nod and were gone.

"Time fer shut-eye," the cook explained. "They got to be up after the middle watch to get the fires going or you won't get no grub come eight bells."

"I could do with some grub now," Jem said. "I'm starvin'."

"I daresay you could, my lubber, but supper's all over an' done with long since, so you'll just have to do without."

"En't you got no bread?" Jem asked hopefully. "Chunk a bread 'ud do me fine. Stave off the pangs like." And he looked for a bread bin.

"We don't keep nothin' lying' around," the cook said, interpreting the look. "Not in a galley. You ought ter know that. Or ain'tcher never been ter sea afore?"

Jem packed his tools and admitted his ignorance.

"You got a lot to learn then," the cook said.

CHAPTER 4

I t didn't take Marianne more than five minutes to discover
that life at sea was going to be extremely difficult. When she'd
rushed off to enlist, she hadn't thought any further than her anger
had taken her. It had all seemed very simple then. She wasn't
going to stay in Portsmouth and be mocked by her neighbours, so
she would have to find Jem and make him come home. That was
all there was to it. Now, and a bit late, she realised that there was a
going to be a very great deal more to it. For a start, she was going
to have to learn to live a completely new kind of life, as a man
among men, and according to their rules and regulations, what's
more, for everything on board was regulated. And it was all as far
removed from her life at home as it could possibly be.

There were so many people aboard, hundreds and hundreds of
them, seamen and marines and ship's boys and officers in a
variety of uniforms, and all of them telling her to look lively and
jump to it. And as if that wasn't enough, they kept ringing bells,
incessantly, day and night, and everybody seemed to know what
they meant, except her. Not that she had time to ask because she
was rushed from one thing to the next. For the first few hours, she
lived in a state of obedient bewilderment. She was shown where

to buy her sailor's slops, which, according to the purser, was "on tick, bein' as you ain't earned nothing yet" and bought a canvas "ditty bag" as well to store her things in; she was given a place at the mess table on the gun deck and told never to sit "nowhere else"; she was shown where the heads were and told to piss over the side "when you'm a need of it" — as if I could! — and when her first shift was finally over, she was told to sling her hammock between the guns like the rest of her watch was doing and was mocked when she tried to climb into it, which was a great deal more difficult than it looked.

It was a miserable, worrying night. She wanted to pee but there was no sign of a chamber pot, not that she could have used it if there had been, and she wasn't at all sure she could find the heads in the middle of the night. The bells rang, her companions snored and farted and ground their teeth, and at daybreak, when she'd finally fallen into an uneasy sleep, she was shouted at and told to show a leg and wake up and look lively. And then, when she opened her eyes, a new problem pushed into her head to worry her. How on earth was she going to change into her sailor's clothes without being seen? There were half-naked men stepping into breeches and pulling on shirts and waistcoats and jackets everywhere she looked and no possibility of any privacy. In the end, she changed her breeches while she was still in the hammock and contrived to sit with her back to her messmates when she put on her shirt and jacket. By the time she was dressed, she was out of breath and her heart was beating most uncomfortably, but the change had been made and she was wearing the same sort of clothes as all the other seamen, the same striped breeches and the same duck cotton jacket, with a black straw hat on her head and good stout shoes on her feet, looking the part even if she didn't feel it.

The day progressed in a series of embarrassments. She felt as if she was in a foreign country surrounded by men speaking a completely foreign language, she understood so little of what they were saying. And it annoyed her that she had to be taught the simplest things — how to stow her hammock "roll um up tight like that see", one of her messmates told her, "now pass um through the hoop, now give um seven turns, six en't a bit a good, 'tis seven or nothin', and then you can stow um in the netting"; how to scrub the deck with a holystone and flog it dry with a length of rope — this by a saucy boy who couldn't have been more than twelve and made a point of mocking her whatever she did. You wants your ears boxed, my lad, she thought, as she worked. I been a-scrubbin' floors all my grown life. I don't need no whippersnapper a-tellin' me what to do. She had no idea what the time was, nor how long she'd have to work before she had something to eat, but she daren't ask because that would reveal her ignorance of those interminable bells. By the time the decks were scrubbed white and the brass fittings had been polished and the rails wiped clean, she was so hungry her stomach was rumbling and aching.

But eventually the bell sounded eight times and work seemed to be over for a while and everyone headed back to the gun deck. Now she had to be shown how to lower the table and benches from the beams and set them ready for breakfast and then she was told to retrieve her spoon from her ditty bag. "An' look sharp about it or 'ee won't get nothin' to eat". After that, they all waited while the mess cook, who was a tall man with an imposing black beard, ambled down to what he called the galley but was actually a huge stove at the far end of the deck and returned with a steaming dish of porridge which he called skillygalee. Why do they have to have different names for everything? Marianne thought, watching his hands as he served them their portions, dollop by dollop. It was a bit lumpy, whatever it was called, but it was hot and filling, and she was glad of it and ate it greedily.

"Now then, young feller-me-lad," the mess cook said, "when you can stop filling your face for a second, you en't told us your name yet, what you should ha' done long since."

She stopped eating, aware that they were all grinning at her, and told him her new name. "Matt Morris."

"Well now, Matt Morris," the mess cook said, "I'm Johnny Galley, which was Johnny Galloway afore I come aboard but is Galley now on account of I serves the grub, which don't 'ee forget or 'ee'll starve to death, and this here is Abram, and that there is Henry and that there is…"

She nodded at them in turn, her head spinning at being told so many names all at once. But they seemed friendly and the man called Henry leant across the table to talk to her. "You'm new aintcher?" he said. "Teks a bit a' getting used to, does the sea."

"Aye, it does," she agreed. "'Specially them bells. I can't get the hang a' them at all."

"Three watches," Henry explained. "Eight hours each, from noon to noon, one watch on, one watch off. Bells every half-hour, reg'lar. Two lots of eight bells in each watch, one rung after the first half-hour's gone by, two on the hour, three on the next half-hour and so on. 'Tis all eights aboard ship, d'you see, being there's twenty-four hours in a day."

It seemed simple, put like that.

"Next time you hears eight bells," Henry said, "'twill be the end of the morning watch. An' when 'tis the end of the forenoon watch, 'twill be one bell an' the bosun's mate'll play *Nancy Dawson* an' then you'll know 'tis dinner time."

The bells were ringing again. No time to ask any more questions for that was obviously the signal for the mess to be cleared, dishes wiped clean with a rag and stored in racks against the ships side, spoons packed away in ditty bags, the table and benches raised and hung in the beams out of the way, while Johnny Galley carried the serving dish back to the stove.

Now what have I got to do? Scrub the lower decks apparently. They likes things clean, she thought, as she scoured with her holystone along with all the other boys, and it occurred to her that the ship was still at anchor and wondered why they weren't moving.

If I'm to find my Jem, she thought, 't'will have to be when we'm all in port on account of I can hardly swim out to all the ships in the fleet, even if I could swim, what I can't. I'll go ashore first chance I gets an' ask all the sailors I meet till I find him. Sweat and determination flowed together. Oh I shall find him, no matter where he is. I've made my mind up to it. I shall find him an' we'll go home together, and everything will be all right again. He's got to be in one or the other of our ships and from what I seen this morning, there can't be more than a dozen of 'em. I wonder what work they've set him to do.

IT WOULD HAVE SURPRISED her to know that her husband wasn't in her own part of the fleet at all but several leagues away leaning over the rail on the quarter-deck of the *Sirius*, which was making speed towards Brest. A few minutes before, he'd been hauling on a rope to lift the sails as the ship changed tack, now he was talking to his new shipmates and doing absolutely nothing at all.

"I thought I was a carpenter," he complained, rubbing his new blisters. "Never thought I'd end up manning a rope an' that's the truth of it."

"Step aboard a frigate, my lubber," the nearest man said, "an' you're a jack of all trades. I'm a gunner by trade, but we does what needs to be done aboard a frigate accordin' to the watch we're on, an' that's all there is to it. Fighting ship is this. You'll get to ply your trade presently, bein' 'tis the forenoon watch."

Jem thought of the great guns, resting heavily against their blocks and wondered what it would be like when they were fired. "D'you ply your trade in the forenoon too?" he asked.

"No, my lubber," the gunner told him. "Guns is fired off after supper. As you'd ha' heard last night if you hadn't ha' been tiddly. We seen you in the scuppers, didden we, boys? You'd had a fair of skinful hadn'tcher."

"Yes," Jem admitted and suddenly remembered everything about it in painfully vivid detail, Tom Kettle plying him with rum and roaring with laughter, pies and pressed meats covering the table at the wedding feast, all those pretty little jellies and custards.

"What brought you to sea, then?" the gunner said. "You aint a reg'lar. That I *do* know. Not by no account. Name a' Tom, by the way."

"Pleased ter meetcher," Jem said. "Name a' Jem." Then he paused. He could hardly tell them the real reason, although he remembered it well enough this morning. It shamed him even to think of it. He could feel her pushing him away, telling him to stop, could see her standing in the middle of the room with a trickle of blood running down her leg, saying he'd hurt her. What a thing to do to him! He could feel his anger rising at the memory of it. Was it any wonder he'd run away to sea? "Nagging wife," he said, eventually. "Couldn't stand her no more, so I upped and went."

"My stars!" Tom said. "I wouldn't like to be you when her family catch up with you. We had a marine aboard once, done the self-same thing an' when he got back home again her brothers up an' took a horse whip to him. Nearly had his eye out."

"They'll have forgot all about me by now," Jem said, assuming a bravado he didn't feel because the story had made him wince. "Bad penny, they'll say. Good riddance to him." He could almost persuade himself he could hear their voices. "Sides, I shall come back with a pocketful of silver. En't that the size of it?"

"So they says," Tom grinned. "That or a peg-leg. There's no tellin' if we fights the Frenchies."

"Are we going to fight the Frenchies?"

"If Admiral Lord Nelson had his way, we'd be fightin' 'em tomorrow," Tom said. "Trouble is we can't find the beggars. They give us the slip every time."

"Run away, d'you mean?"

"Every time. No sooner they sees his flag a-flyin' than they're off."

"That's why we'm off to Brest," another man said. "To see if we can find the beggar. That's our orders, d'you see. To find the beggar."

"Right then, my sonny," Mr Turner said from behind him. "We got work to do. Follow me."

Jem was beginning to get the hang of keeping his balance as the ship rolled beneath him, and knew he had to bend his knees to accommodate the movement. He followed his new master in his new lurching way, across the gun deck, down the gangway and into a narrow space between the hull and the bulkheads. It was dark and cramped but it seemed to be where he was going to work.

"Bungs," Mr Turner said.

Jem had no idea what he was talking about, so he waited.

"We could be in the thick of it when we reach Brest," Mr Turner said. "There's no knowing. They could skulk away an' hide, which they been doing long enough in all conscience, or they could come out an' face us. Any which ways I likes to be prepared. So good stout bungs is what we need. Like this one here." And he traced the outline of a large round plug of oak that was firmly embedded in the hull. "If we're in heavy seas an' we gets holed below the waterline, d'you see, we needs to plug like lightning. I likes to have a good stock ready an' waiting."

They lurched to the storeroom down in the hold and made bungs for the rest of the afternoon, large ones for cannon balls from 32 and 24 pounders, "In case we meets a man a war", smaller ones for 18 and 12 pounders, "In case 'tis a frigate". Jem worked doggedly and quietly, as he usually did, but as the minutes passed he became aware that his master was watching him with approval and, after a while, they began to talk in the desultory way of men engrossed in their work.

"This'll be your first trip I'm thinking," Mr Turner ventured.

After nearly a day aboard, Jem knew the correct way to answer. "Aye, sir."

"A lot to learn, I don't doubt."

"Aye, sir. But I'm a quick learner."

"You're a good worker, certainly," Mr Turner said. "I'll give you that."

They worked companionably until eight bells were rung and not long after that a single bell sounded, and he could hear a piper up on deck, playing a familiar tune. Mr Turner put his tools away and headed back to the gun deck. "Grub an' grog, my sonny," he said, rubbing his hands together. "Pint a' rum and water does wonders for the spirits."

And so it seemed to do, for after the meal, which was ship's biscuits and a generous helping of salt beef boiled to a stew, they were all in splendid humour. None of them was on watch so they had the afternoon to themselves and could do as they pleased. Some took a needle and thread from their ditty bags and sewed ribbons into the seams of their shirts and trousers, some used the time to smoke a pipe or chew a wad of tobacco, and a group from Jem's mess gathered round the ship's story-teller for a yarn and were soon chuckling and laughing. But Jem sat apart and watched. He needed to get his thoughts into some sort of order and it was the first time since he'd come aboard that he'd had the leisure to do it.

He couldn't understand how all this had come about. Nobody joined the navy on their wedding day. It was unheard of and it didn't make sense, especially to him, for he'd got himself a good job and a room to live in and he'd made all the furniture for it. He was set up. But he knew he must have signed papers and been enlisted, or he wouldn't have been brought aboard and be sailing into a sea fight now — if that was what they were doing. He was sure Tom Kettle was at the back of it even though he had no recollection of anything between being plied with rum in The Dolphin and the moment when he was woken, tight as a tick and drenched with water. He struggled to remember more until his brain was aching, and, in the end, he gave up. It was no good thinking. He was here, he had food in his belly and a job to do, and he'd be paid at the end of it, royally so Tom Kettle had said. He did remember that. In any case, he could hardly walk away from it and swim home, even if he wanted to. As the yarn went on and the laughter grew more raucous, his thoughts became more and more muddled and, after a while, he found himself wondering what would become of Marianne without a husband to support her and pay the rent. She'd treated him very badly, there was no doubt about that, but he couldn't help feeling responsible for her. When all was said and done she was his wife, no matter how badly she'd behaved. She'll go home to her father I daresay, he thought, trying to ease his conscience. She'll be looked after there. And for a moment he pictured her, sitting by the fire in that crowded kitchen, helping her mother with the mending, the way he'd seen her when he first came visiting, that thick hair escaping from her cap, her face scowling with concentration, her hands busy.

IN FACT, that thick hair was swinging behind her in a long fat plait, and her hands were as busy as they'd ever been, but she wasn't sewing, and she wasn't scowling, she was climbing the rigging of His Majesty's Ship *Amphion*, buffeted by the wind so far aloft, soaked by a brief shower of rain and enjoying it hugely. The *Amphion* had lain at anchor in St Helen's for the last twenty-four hours waiting for Admiral Lord Nelson to make some decision or other, and now the decision had been made and they were under sailing orders and Marianne had been sent aloft with the other boys to unfurl the mainsail. If she looked down, she could see the captain on the quarter-deck looking very grand in his splendid uniform with his epaulettes glinting like stars. And there was the *Victory* with Admiral Nelson's flag flying from the mainmast. This is more like it, she thought. Now we can sail off to the nearest port and I can start my search.

A strong north wind blew them south into the Channel; there were several more squalls of rain; the distant coast looked grey and foreign and, for a day at the end of May, it was unseasonably cold. She was quite glad when eight bells sounded, and it was time for a bit of warming grub, which was peas and plum duff and very tasty, although the grog still made her head spin.

"En't got yer sea legs yet, have 'ee my hearty?" Johnny Galley said, as she staggered from the table.

"Never mind legs, Johnny Galley," she told him. "'Tis your grog what's knocking me sideways."

At which her messmates gave a roar of delighted laughter and the nearest thumped her on the back. "Wait till we gets to the Bay a' Biscay," he warned, grinning and showing a mouthful of brown teeth. "That'll knock the legs from under yer."

She didn't like the sound of that at all, but she certainly wasn't going to let him know it and answered him back boldly. "That'll take more than some of sea to knock me off my feet, I can tell 'ee." At which, she was applauded and thumped between the shoulder blades again until her back was quite sore.

When she was woken for her next watch, the English coast had disappeared, and they were on their own in a grey pitching sea with storm clouds louring overhead and no sign of land or life.

"Is this the Bay a' Biscay?" she asked her messmates, when the morning chores had been done and they were sitting about their table sustaining themselves with steaming bowls of skillygalee.

"Lord love yer, boy," Johnny Galley said. "It'll be three, four days afore you sets eyes on that. We'm still in the Channel, my sonny, onny on the French side, which is to loo'ard, d'you see, where we'm blockading the beggars. We'm headin' for Brest this time, to meet up with the Channel Fleet."

One of the other ship's boys instantly set about enlightening her further, counting off the beleaguered ports on his fingers, "We got 'em penned in all along the Channel," he told her. "Boulogne, Dieppe, Cherbourg, Brest, Lorient."

"Stow it, clever-clogs," Johnny Galley said, cuffing him about the ear. "We knows you knows. You won't look so clever come the Bay a' Biscay, let me tell 'ee. You'll be hanging over the gunnels with the rest of us then."

If he's trying to worry us, Marianne thought, he's making a good job of it. She didn't like the sound of hanging over the gunnels at all. "Are we joining the blockade then?" she asked.

"No, my lubber," Johnny Galley said. "We'm to meet up with Admiral Cornwallis by the Black Rocks, what's the admiral of the Channel Fleet."

By now, Marianne could see that this man liked to be the purveyor of information aboard and would take as many questions as she liked to ask, so she asked the next and obvious one. "Where's the Black Rocks, Mr Galley?"

"West-north-west of Brest, my lubber. Where else would they be?"

THEY ROSE out of a heaving sea, black as their name and looking decidedly treacherous. But there was no sign of a fleet or a flagship, and no sign of a port, nothing but a single frigate with all sails furled, rocking on the swell and waiting for them.

"*Sirius* is that," Johnny Galley told Marianne, when she and the other boys climbed down onto the deck again after reefing their own sails. "I sailed on her one time. She belongs to the Channel Fleet. Been left here with news for Admiral Nelson, I shouldn't wonder, although they did say we was to be meetin' with Admiral Cornwallis."

The *Amphion* creaked and rocked as the rest of the fleet gathered and waited. The rocks glistened in the rising sun. Small waves slapped against their bows, spinning droplets of white spray across their newly scrubbed deck. A brazen pathway widened across the dark water. And presently, a longboat put out from the frigate and was rowed across to the *Victory*, where her captain was piped aboard. Then another headed that way, and another, as the captains gathered, and the last of them was their own Captain Hardy, who set off with a highly satisfied expression on his face, doffing his hat to his watching crew.

"Now they'll talk," Johnny Galley said, "and then we shall know where we'm to go next, I daresay." Six bells was ringing. There was no more time for leaning over the gunnels and watching the fleet. "No peace for the wicked," he said, grimacing at Marianne. "There's work to be done, my lubber."

She supposed that there was and knew she would have to do it, although she would have preferred to stay where she was and go on watching. There was always the hope that one or other of the ships would drift close enough for her to see the faces of the men on board. Jem could be out there, riding the self-same waves as she was, or rowing one of the captains out to the *Victory*. And how would she know if she couldn't see him? It was very frustrating. But you'm at sea now, she told herself, an' you'll have to do as you'm told an' put up with it.

CHAPTER 5

Admiral Lord Nelson took breakfast with his captains and lieutenants in the gilded stateroom of the *Victory*. The cook had excelled himself that morning with a pair of roast ducks as well as the usual ham, eggs and kidneys and there was a great quantity of toast and strong coffee besides, so his guests ate well, but the Admiral was abstemious, as he invariably was when there were matters to be decided, and only took a poached egg and a single rasher of ham.

Captain Prowse arrived from the *Sirius* with news that there was no sign of any movement in or out of Brest and a letter from Admiral Cornwallis, which was an apology for having sailed before they were able to meet and explained that it was because he had a rendezvous at sea with the other ships of the Channel Fleet, "there being no other cause which would have prevented me from meeting my old comrade in arms." The graceful compliment made Nelson smile, but Cornwallis's absence presented him with a problem. The last orders he'd received before he left Spithead were that he was to meet Cornwallis at the Black Rocks and hand over the command of the *Victory* to him and how could that be done if the man was somewhere in the Atlantic? If he'd been at the meeting, they could have come to an amicable arrangement and he could have kept the *Victory*, for he was sure Cornwallis was well provided with ships of the line and had no particular need of her, whereas he would find it hard to do without her.

The problem of obeying the Admiralty's instructions in these altered circumstances was discussed over the roast duck and the ham and kidneys. Several of the captains at the table thought that finding the admiral in the Atlantic would be an almost impossible task, given that he could be anywhere along the French coast and given that the wind was freshening and changing direction.

"If it blows from the North as it did when we left the Solent," Captain Sutton pointed out, "we shall be hard put to it to sail in any direction but southerly, leave alone conduct a search."

"Nevertheless," Nelson said, "difficult though it may well be, that is what we are duty-bound to attempt, if we are to follow Admiralty orders as officers and gentlemen. I have no desire to hand over this ship, for I tell you plainly, when I fight the French, as I fully intend to do, no matter how far and how long they run, I would rather fight them aboard the *Victory* than on any other ship of the line. However orders are orders and, as I said, we are duty-bound. We will search until dusk, gentlemen, and then rendezvous again and reconsider our position." It was a compromise but one that might turn out for the best with a contrary wind blowing.

It blew strongly all through the day, but his fleet battled against it and searched wherever they could, without news from any quarter or sight of a single sail of any description. When they returned to the Black Rocks at the end of the allotted time, they were exhausted but no further on than they'd been when they started.

"If I am to be at Gibraltar to take command of Sir Richard Bickerton's squadron and to meet with Governor Ball," Nelson said, as he and Captain Sutton stood on the quarter-deck surveying the return of the fleet, "I cannot delay any further. I shall transfer to the *Amphion* this evening and sail on with Captain Hardy. I leave you to continue the search. If you have not found Admiral Cornwallis after six more days, you must return to Plymouth for further orders. On the other hand, if you find him and he has no need of the *Victory*, which I am confident will turn out to be the case, you are to follow me with all speed. I have written letters to cover both eventualities."

THE NEWS that the *Amphion* was to be Nelson's flag ship provoked a mixed reaction aboard. Some of the crew agreed with their captain that it was an honour to be chosen, others complained that it would be "all spit an' polish from now on" and predicted that they would all be harried "from here to Sunday". Nevertheless, the dog watch turned out in style to line the decks and cheer their Admiral as he was piped aboard, for whatever else they might think they were all agreed that he was a fine good man and the only one who could find them of Frenchies and make 'em come out and fight.

To Marianne, his arrival was exactly what she needed. She'd been tetchy with impatience while they'd been searching the empty sea. It had all been such a waste of time for how could anyone find one little ship on all this water? It wasn't humanly possible. Now they could get on with their journey and she would soon be in Gibraltar and could go ashore and find her Jem. She'd started to learn the language — or some of it at least — found her sea legs, discovered a way to dress without attracting attention and now she wanted to get on with the real purpose of her voyage.

"Soon be in Gibraltar, eh, Mr Galley," she said, when the great Admiral had gone to his quarters and they were all dispersing.

"You got the Bay a Biscay to contend with first, my lubber," he said. "Don't forget that."

But she'd learnt a few sailor's superstitions by now and knew that the way to deal with a potential hazard was to make a bargain with Fate. If she could get through this bay without being sick, she would find Jem. And in the event, the dreaded bay, was no more of a problem than the Channel had been and a great deal calmer. The sea was a deeper blue than she'd ever seen it and the waves were longer, rolling them onwards in smooth inexorable swathes of water, but there were no storms, the wind blew fair and the sun shone like a blessing. The clothes they'd washed in sea water the day before, were dried and ready to be worn by the time church was rigged on Sunday, and from then on it was all plain sailing and their voyage south continued without let, hindrance or incident. Johnny Galley said he'd be blowed if he'd ever knowed such a crossing and swore their new shipmate was a good omen, and their new shipmate grinned and agreed with him. The only thing that puzzled her was where all the other ships had got to and why they weren't all sailing together the way they'd done when they left Portsmouth. Eventually, she asked him.

"Gone a-searching with the *Victory*, my lubber," he said. "We shan't see them for days yet. Don' 'ee fret about 'em. They'll catch up with us later."

That wasn't the answer she wanted. "How much later, Mr Galley?"

"How should I know?" Johnny Galley said. "You'll have to ask the Admiral, you wants to know a thing like that. Get an' eat yer figgy dowdy an' don't ask so many questions."

He was looking quite cross, so that's what she had to do. But her thoughts were spinning with frustration. What if they hadn't caught up by the time the *Amphion* reached Gibraltar? She couldn't put her plan into action if theirs was the only ship in the harbour. Oh come on do, she urged the empty seas. Show a sail for pity's sake. But two days later, they were traveling east, just out of sight of the Portuguese coast, still making good speed but still alone, and her shipmates said Gibraltar was just a few leagues away.

And then just as she'd given up hope, the look-out called, "Sail ahoy!"

There was instant activity on the quarter-deck. Lord Nelson and Captain Hardy had telescopes to their eyes, several midshipmen stood eagerly about waiting for orders. But they were looking the wrong way, surely. The fleet would be following them, and they were training their telescopes on the seas ahead of them. Oh, now what?

It wasn't long before they all knew. The ship they were watching was a brig, small, two-masted, low in the water with the weight of her cargo and French. They were catching up with her fast and were going to take her. The excitement on board was palpable for this was a chance to earn some prize money. A brig was fair game and could be carrying valuable cargo.

Marianne was surprised to see what an easy capture it was. The little ship put up no resistance at all, hove to obediently so that the *Amphion* could come alongside, and surrendered her cargo without argument.

"Fortunes a' war, my sonny," Johnny Galley said, as they settled to supper. The brig had been stripped and was now sailing behind them towards Gibraltar. "They're lucky they was took by a British frigate accordin' to the articles a' war. If we'd ha' been pirates wed ha' killed 'em, every man jack."

Which all very well, Marianne thought, but where's the fleet? That's what I wants for to know. Where's the fleet an' where's Jem?

HE WAS in the middle of his first sea fight too and enjoying it hugely. During the last few days, he'd listened to his shipmates bragging of death and glory and been none too sure how he would react when he came under enemy fire himself, but from the moment all hands were piped and the gun crew began to clear the decks for action, he was lifted into a state of such triumphant excitement he wanted to shout and cheer. He didn't do either, of course. There were too many other things to attend to. But the joy of being in action was as strong as any emotion he'd ever felt in his life. It was three parts terror, he couldn't deny that, but the remaining seven parts were sheer bloody-minded exhilaration.

Their enemy was a French frigate that had appeared over the horizon just before six bells in the morning watch and, instead of taking flight, as they'd all expected, had sailed straight and aggressively towards them.

The gun crews were growlingly delighted. "Want a fight, do she?" they said, grinning bravado at one another. "Well she's come to the right shop, this time. We'll blow her out the water, shan't we, boys? Ho, there'll be money in this."

Once the decks had been cleared, Jem and Mr Turner went below to the orlop deck taking their bungs with them.

"I doubt the beggars'll hole us," the carpenter said. "We're a deal too low in the water for that, but 'tis a heavy sea and I likes to be prepared."

By that time the entire ship was prepared and prickly with tension, as if the very air was bristling. Bare feet pounded on the decks above their heads as the powder monkeys carried up shot, they could hear orders shouted sharp and quick, seven bells clanged, then there was a sudden lurch as they went about, turning broadside to their prey, and after that several long seconds when nothing happened at all. Jem held his breath until his throat ached and his heart was beating so wildly, he was afraid Mr Turner would see it throbbing under the cotton of his jacket and tried to cover it with his hand. When the cannon were fired, the noise was so sudden and so shattering it made him jump. The air was instantly full of smoke and stink and unfamiliar sounds. He heard the whistle of approaching shot, the roar of the guns' recoil, another set of thunderous explosions, another growling recoil, and then an unexpected cheer, which startled him almost as much as the first broadside had done. He wished he could be up on deck and could see what was going on instead of being stuck below in the darkness. And, as if in answer to his thoughts, Mr Turner spoke to him out of the gloom.

"They've never took her so quick," he said. "Nip up atop an' take a look-see. Only don't let anyone catch you. We're supposed to keep to our stations."

It was easy enough for there was sufficient smoke swirling between the decks to give cover to a dozen men and once he'd inched out into the daylight, he discovered that all eyes were fixed on the spectacle of their vanquished enemy. She was shot to pieces, just as the gunners had predicted, her sails torn, her main top-mast broken, her rigging trailing like ribbons. It was, as one of the powder monkeys was happy to tell him, just enough damage to disable the beggar but not too much to prevent her making good prize money.

"You're ships carpenter, aintcher?" the boy said. "We made work for you an' all then. Once we've took off their supplies an' brung 'em to order an' so forth, you'll be shipped across to put all to rights again. You see if I ain't right. Then she can sail with us when we moves on, what we got ter do on account a we got ter find the Admiral."

At supper that night, after the frigate had surrendered and been given a new Master, and Jem and Mr Turner and three topmen had been shipped across to make the necessary repairs, the crew were given double rations of grog by way of celebration. By the time Jem swung drunkenly into his hammock, he was so full of rum and the euphoria of a difficult job well done, he felt as if he'd won the battle all by himself. What a life this is! he thought, as the sea rocked him to sleep.

The next day they made sail to re-join the fleet and find

Admiral Cornwallis. There wasn't a man aboard who didn't feel confident of success.

"We could find a needle in a haystack if we set our minds to it," Tom said to Jem. "What with our signals an' all. An' as to them Frenchies, they can eat as many frogs as they like but, when it comes to fightin', they ain't a match fer us an' never will be. You can see that now can'tcher, my lubber? Once Lord Nelson can tease 'em out a harbour, what he'll do sooner or later on account of he's set his mind to it, we'll blow 'em out the water, you just see if we don't."

To Jem, standing there on that British deck, on the last day of May, in the warmth of the summer sunshine, it all seemed perfectly and predictably possible.

THE *AMPHION* ARRIVED in Gibraltar late at night on Friday 3 June and dropped anchor in Rosia bay in the darkness. Marianne was off watch and fast asleep, but the grinding of the anchor chain woke her at once. We're here, she thought. At last. Now I can start looking for him. They're bound to send the boats ashore for fresh water and provisions. Stands to reason, all the food we've ate a-coming here. Very well then, I shall get aboard the longboat one way or another — they're bound to need hands and I can turn mine to anything — and once I'm ashore, I'll ask everyone I meet. On which happy plan, she slept again.

And was woken at four bells to a crushing disappointment. There were no other British ships in the bay. Not a single one. As she scrubbed the decks with her holystone, she kept a weather eye out for new arrivals, but none came. Admiral Lord Nelson went ashore to meet the local worthies, looking very grand in his full dress uniform, and at eight bells, they were piped to breakfast in the usual way, but they dined on their own in the empty calm of the harbour with the great brown rock rising above them like a citadel and a blue sea lapping their timbers, as gentle as a cat, and no more British ships arrived to join them. Where were they all? Even Johnny Galley couldn't tell her.

"Still searchin', I shouldn't wonder," he said. "They'll catch up with us sooner or later. You ain't afeard being on your own, are yer?"

"No," she said boldly. "'Course not. I was just a-wonderin' where they were."

The boats went ashore to pick up fruit and water. Captain Hardy inspected the ship. And then there was nothing to do but wait for the Admiral's return. The forenoon watch passed peacefully, they were piped to dinner, which was a very leisurely meal, and then left to their own devices for the rest of the afternoon watch. The sun was so warm it made the watch on deck lethargic. They basked, smoked their pipes, gossiped, told stories, and waited.

And then, just when Marianne was half asleep, the longboat put out to fetch Lord Nelson back and two British frigates breezed into the harbour. She was very cross. What a useless time for them to arrive, she thought, when the supplies are bought and aboard and the Admiral's coming back and there's no reason for anyone to go ashore. If they'd put on more canvas, they could've been here the same time as us.

"Stir your stumps, you great lazy lump," a midshipman said, as he marched by her, trim in his uniform and full of importance. "Haven't you any work to do?"

It took her an effort to pull her mind round to what he was saying. "What?"

"What?" he echoed. "What d'you mean *what*? What sort of word is *what*? Here's the Admiral been hard at it since first light and you think you may lollop about the decks doing nothing. Stir your stumps, my sonny, or you'll know the reason why." And he walked on feeling pleased with himself.

Stupid puppy, Marianne thought, glaring at his back. Giving

himself airs! If I'd met him on Spice Island afore all this, I'd've cut him down to size in two shakes of a lamb's tail. But there was no time to feed her fantasy because eight bells were sounding, and it was the start of the first dog watch and there was work to be done.

It began as soon as the Admiral had been piped aboard. The two frigates sent a boat across with mail for Captain Hardy and the Admiral and were sent orders by return that they were to guard the straits. Not long afterwards the *Amphion* weighed anchor. Captain Hardy and Admiral Nelson stood on the poop deck to guide their departure and Marianne Templeman busied herself on the deck below and watched them, wondering where they were all off to and how long it would be before they got there.

She got her answer at supper time. "Malta," Johnny Galley said. "On account of we got to meet up with Sir Richard Bickerton's squadron what's there a-waitin' for us, seemingly."

He was in a good mood, so she ventured to ask him how long it would take.

"As long as it needs, my sonny," he said. "Our Nelson's in no partic'lar hurry, d'you see, on account of he wants the *Victory* to catch up with us. We shall have to wait an' see. Patience is a virtue at sea, so they say."

In the long days that followed, the *Amphion* made very slow progress through the Mediterranean. It grew hotter by the day, there was very little wind and the coastline they passed was interminably the same, long and brown and silhouetted with odd foreign-looking buildings, brown as the shoreline with bulbous domes that caught the sun and sharp narrow spires that looked like needles.

"Mosques," Johnny said, when Marianne asked him what they were. "Where the Musclemen goes to pray."

Who were the Musclemen?

"Heathens," Johnny said, "what you don't want to have nothin' to do with. Very nasty there are."

"Well I en't surprised they're heathens," Marianne said. "Livin' out here in all this heat. 'Tis enough to turn anyone heathen." The sweat was running down her back and her jacket was sticking to her, as if it had been glued. "Is it always as hot as this?"

"We're a deal further south than we was, my sonny," Johnny told her, "an' 'tis high summer, what's always hot in these parts. Take yer jacket off if it's plaguing you."

But she couldn't possibly do that, so she shook her head and looked away from him.

He laughed at her, showing his broken teeth. "Go on, boy," he teased. "Don't be shy. You wouldn't be the only one."

Which was true enough, for there were ships boys all over the ship scrubbing the decks and climbing the rigging in their shoes and breeches, their bare backs turning brown before her eyes. In fact, as the hot days passed, there were only two others, as far as she could see, who kept their jackets on. And just as well, for she wouldn't have liked to be the only one.

She took to working as close to the other two as she could, feeling she wouldn't be quite so noticeable if they were near and, after a week of it, she began to notice things about them, which set her to wondering. The way they walked for a start, and the way they laughed, which was almost a giggle sometimes, and the way they talked to one another, heads close and confidential. And now she came to look at them, the shorter of the two with his blue eyes and his soft fair hair was too pretty to be a boy. What if they was women too? Wouldn't that be a thing. Not that she could ask them, in case they wasn't. But she wondered more every time she saw them.

And then one morning, the shorter of the two suddenly spoke to her. "Aincher warm?" he said.

"Boiled alive."

The boy gave her a knowing look. "Why don'tcher strip off that jacket?"

The question embarrassed her. It was altogether too direct. If they were women, it would be all right, but if they weren't she could be open to teasing or even worse. "'Cause I don't want to," she said.

"On account of you got somethin' to hide," the boy said. "That the size of it? Like us maybe. We got things to hide, ain't we — Jack?"

The odd emphasis he'd given the name made Marianne sit back on her heels and look at them, the holystone idle on her hands. Now she was almost sure she'd been right.

"You got somethin' to hide an' all 'ave yer — Matt?" the boy said. "Somethin' under yer jacket maybe. Or a pair a' somethin's."

"I might have," she said. "An' then again I might not."

The boy called Jack gave her such a wide grin there was no doubt what they were talking about. "We knew you was a woman," he said. "We been watchin' you fer days. What's yer real name?"

Now it was possible to confess because she knew it was safe and that they wouldn't tell. "Marianne," she said.

"I'm Peg," the boy told her. "An' this here's Moll. This your first ship? Use yer stone, the lieutenants looking."

They scrubbed assiduously, their jackets damp with sweat.

"I thought I was the only one," Marianne admitted.

"No fear a' that," Moll said. "There's lots a' women in the navy. You'll see. Only we has ter keep it dark, on account a' Nelson don't like women aboard ship except for that Lady Hamilton, what's a right bad lot if you ask me, great fat lump."

"Hush up!" Peg warned. "He's a-comin' our way."

In the next two days, they spoke to one another whenever they could. They were all on the same watch, so it was easily done, and, as the heat increased and tarpaulins were put up to give the live-stock some shade, there were corners to hide in. They shared tips on all sorts of things — how to wash themselves without making their shipmates suspicious, how to use the heads without being noticed, the best way to get their clothes clean in sea water.

"It's a lark bein' ship's boy," Moll said, "but you has to look slippy with every mortal thing. We'll show 'ee come next wash day."

As the breeze inched their ship nearer to Malta, their confidences grew. After a week Marianne confessed that she'd joined the navy to find her husband and told the story of their wedding — leaving out the more intimate details for modesty's sake — and the peculiar way he'd disappeared. Like her, they had no doubt he'd been pressed.

"Stands ter reason," Moll said. "He'd never up an' leave you, not on your weddin' day. That ain't nat'ral. You ask me, they got him so drunk he didn't know what he was doin'. That's the sort a dirty trick they plays. We've heard that story over an' over, ain't we, Peg?"

"We'll find him atween us," Peg said, patting Marianne's arm. "Very next port a' call we'll all go ashore and we'll ask every jack tar we finds. It shouldn't be that hard, being ship's carpenter an' all. Look chearly, my lubber. We'll find him."

Their sympathy was so cheering and warming — and womanly. Oh, it was good to have friends.

CHAPTER 6

By the time the ship arrived in the grand harbour at Valetta, the three girls were staunch companions. And, true to their promise, Moll and Peg contrived to get ashore on the same bum boat as their new friend. After they'd showed willing and helped to load the fruit, the three of them asked permission to explore the town together and went swaggering off through the hot streets like the rolling jack tars they were. As Moll said, "We ain't got the whiskers, my hearties, but we got the style." They also had the chance to question any sailors they met on the streets and the quayside, but there were very few of them and none was any help. They said they worked in the dockyard and they knew that Sir Richard Bickerton's squadron had been at sea for more than a month and was expected to meet up with Lord Nelson somewhere off the coast of Italy. But that was all. And there were no other ships of the line in harbour expect their own.

Marianne was cast down. "Why don't they come into harbour same as us?" she said. "They must need supplies, same as we all does. Stands ter reason. So why are they all at sea?"

"They're looking fer the Frenchies," Peg explained. "Can't fight the beggars if we can't find 'em. An' our Lord Nelson's set his heart on fighting 'em."

There was a sudden outburst of cheering from further along the street. "That'll be him," Moll said. "I'll lay money on't." And she set off at a trot towards the sound, leaving Peg and Marianne to follow the swing of her pigtail.

It *was* their hero, riding in a two-horse carriage looking very handsome in his full dress uniform with his medals glittering in the strong sunshine, smiling as the crowds pushed and cheered beside him, waving their hats and kerchiefs and telling one another what a fine good man he was. The three girls elbowed with the best and managed to get to the front of the crowd as the great Admiral was driven into the sun-blanched courtyard of the Governors palace. They were so close they could see every line in his face, the edge of the scar just visible below his hat, that fine full mouth poutingly determined even when he was half smiling.

"If anyone's a-goin' to beat the Frenchies," Moll said, "he's the man to do it."

"He's got ter find the beggars first," Peg pointed out, "which ain't the easiest of things seein' how slippy they are."

"Well I hope he *don't* find 'em till I've found my Jem," Marianne said. "That's all I can say. I don't pertick'ly want to be aboard when he's starts a-fightin'."

Moll laughed at her. "He won't ask your permission, my lubber," she said, as the carriage disappeared into the courtyard. "Nor nobody else for that matter. Well that's that then. We seen him. Now let's see the sights."

They explored the town for the rest of their watch, admired the fine lace that was being offered for sale in the fine shops, lusted after the sugar cakes in the baker's, told the beggars who followed them to "sling their hooks", decided they didn't think much of the cathedral, which Marianne declared, "a gloomy sort a' place" and were impressed by the number of carriage folk who were driving about the streets for all the world, as if they were members of the London *ton*, with fine horses high-stepping before them and footmen standing impassively behind them.

"They makes money hereabouts," Moll observed.

But Marianne wasn't listening. She was standing in front of a small dark shop gazing through the dusty window panes at the goods on display, the long quill pens and the neat bottles of black ink, the red sticks of sealing wax and the cut paper arranged like a half-open fan. She had one hand resting on the sill, but she wasn't even aware that it was there because her mind was in a turmoil of sudden guilt, remembering her mother and how stricken she'd looked when they said goodbye, and her own passionate, forgotten promise to write to her. And here I've been all this time, sailing the high seas and having a fine old time and never giving her a thought, poor Ma.

"Do 'ee think they'd take coin a' the realm hereabouts?" she asked her friends. "Bein' foreigners like?"

"You could ask 'em," Moll said. "No harm in tryin'. What sort a' coin you got?"

Marianne fished in her pocket for the silver thrupenny bit she carried about with her.

"Is it one a them cakes?" Peg wanted to know. Her mouth was still moist at the memory of them.

Marianne enlightened her. "No," she said. "What I wants is pen an' ink an' such, like those in the winder. I promised my ma I'd write to her."

Her friends were most impressed. "My stars!" Peg said. "Can you write then?"

"Yes," Marianne said, "I can, an' I should ha' done long since onny I forgot all about it. Poor Ma."

They pushed her into the shop at once. "Come you on then," Moll said. The sooner the goods were bought, the sooner they could see her at work. It wasn't every day of the week you could watch someone writing a letter.

But the shopkeeper had no intention of taking their English

money, even after he'd bitten the thrupenny bit to make sure it was sound. He spoke to them sternly in his own language and it was clear he meant no.

"What's the matter with the fool?" Marianne said in exasperation when they stepped out into the sunshine again. "My money's as good as the next man's. Don't he want a sale?"

"That's foreigners for yer," Moll said. "Blamed fools the lot of 'em. Ain't got the sense they was born with. I should try the purser if I was you. I bet he's got pens an' ink an' all sorts. The captain's always a-writing letters. If we gets back sharpish you can ask him afore the end of the watch."

Which they did, all three of them together.

He gave them his calculating stare. "It'll cost you," he said.

Marianne was equal to bargaining. She'd done plenty of that back in Portsmouth. "How much?"

A price was agreed and noted in his book to be docked from her pay. Tuppence three-farthings for a pen "you'll need to sharpen it mind", a small quantity of ink in an ink horn, three sheets of paper "good quality is that", and a stub of sealing wax. She took them down to the gun deck at once and, after settling herself against the nearest cannon, put pen, inkhorn and paper between her legs and stooping forward composed her first letter home.

Dear Ma

    I hope this finds you as it leaves me, being as I am well. We has plenty to eat abord. I am in the Meddytranium abord a fiiggit, what is a fine ship & the eyes & ears of the navy. We hopes to find the Frenchys soon.

Then she ran out of inspiration.

"Ain't you writ a lot," Peg said, admiring the lines of writing. "I never knowed such a scholar. Read us what it *says*."

But at that moment, the bells sounded for the end of the

watch, so she had to roll up her letter and stow it away in her ditty bag with the rest of her purchases.

"I'll add some more another time," she said. "An' read it to you then."

"Pity you can't write to that husband a yourn," Peg remarked, as they parted. "You could tell him where you are, an' then he could find you. He must be missing you somethin' chronic, poor man, new married an all."

Marianne wasn't interested in a letter that couldn't possibly be written. She was wondering how long they would stay in Valetta and hoping it would be a good long time, so that the rest of the fleet could catch up with them and she could set about searching in earnest. "Our Nelson won't want to move on yet awhile," she said to her friends. "Not if he's a-waiting for the *Victory.*"

But she was wrong. Nelson was in a hurry to be off. He was enervated by the heat and impatient to retake command of the fleet and, as always, he made a rapid decision. He would stay in Valetta for thirty-six hours. Then he would head for Naples. There was precious little wind but they must make shift and do the best they could.

MARIANNE WAS ANNOYED to hear that they were moving on, when she'd hardly had any time at all for searching; after all they could have stayed where they were and waited for the rest of the fleet to catch up with them, but she didn't mind the lack of a good wind. It was cool under the tarpaulins, and a slow progress meant more time for gossiping with her friends in between setting the sails and gave her a chance to add a few more words to her letter. After a few quiet days in the sun she became philosophical. Valetta had been a disappointment to her, she had to admit, but she knew there would be other harbours and other opportunities. Sooner or later, she would find her man. It was just a matter of waiting.

"Patience is a virtue at sea," she said to Peg, as they climbed the rigging together to put out more canvas to catch what little wind there was. And she was pleased by her new wisdom and her forbearance.

She enjoyed her passage through the Straits of Messina too. There were so many merchant ships to see, many of them very heavily laden, some smelling of spices, all manned by the strangest looking crews, and when they were negotiating the narrowest part of the channel, a collection of small boats appeared on the eastern shore and rowed out towards them until they were alongside. Within minutes, a horde of extremely dirty boat people were swarming aboard, grinning and nodding and all talking at once, with basketsful of fruit and flowers for sale. Marianne had never seen lemons and oranges so big and, as they were cheap, and these traders were happy to take English pennies and ha'pence, she bought a clutch of them. They made juicy eating.

"This is the life," she said, as she and her friends sat in the shade and gorged themselves.

"It don't suit Lord Nelson," Peg observed. The Admiral was on the poop deck talking to Captain Hardy and frowning at the traders.

"He looks cross," Marianne said, peering round the tarpaulin at him.

"That's on account of he don't know where the Frenchies are," Moll told her. "Like you an' that Jem a' yourn. He'll have a different face on come the fighting."

As usual when her shipmates talked of the battle to come, Marianne felt a shrinking in her belly. "En't you afeard?" she asked.

"No point being afeard," Moll said. "Leastways not yet awhile. What's to come will come they say. I'll face it when I has to."

"An' if the worst comes to the worst," Peg said, "we can always jump ship an' go back to bein' women again." Despite her blue eyes and her pretty face and an intriguing air of vulnerable fragility, she was as shrewd as any man aboard and much tougher than she looked.

Until that moment it hadn't occurred to Marianne that her gender might protect her. It had been something to change and discard, that was all. Now the thought of reassuming it to avoid a battle swelled into a happy fantasy.

"I can jest see 'em, a-searchin' for us," she said, "an' askin' if anyone's seen us and we standin' in front of 'em, bold as brass in our skirts and caps sayin', 'What was you a-lookin for? Three ships boys? No we en't seen three ships boys. Not nowhere about'."

The other two began to giggle. "No we ain't seen 'em," Moll echoed. "Oh that's rich. My stars if it ain't. I can jest see us a-doin' that."

They were enjoying the joke so much they didn't notice the arrival of Johnny Galley until he was standing right in front of them. "En't you got nothin' better to do," he said, "except sit here a-cackling? You sound like a pack a' silly wenches."

He was looking straight at Marianne as he spoke and, for the long fraught second as she held his gaze, she was seized by panic, her heart thumping and her breath tight in her throat. He knows, she thought. Oh my dear life, what will he do? Fortunately, eight bells were sounding the end of the afternoon watch so he grinned at her and moved on and the moment passed. But after they'd eaten supper and the guns had been tested and she was rolled up in her blanket snug and sleepy in her hammock, the moment came back to trouble her. Her secret was out. What would he do about it? If he told the lieutenant, she'd be put off at the next port of call and then what would happen to her? I was as happy as a sand-boy a-sittin' there eating them oranges, she thought, an' now 'tis all gone topsy-turvy again. I must make sure I works extremely hard an' does every mortal thing they tells me to. Then it might right itself again.

The days passed, the ship progressed, and nothing was said.

Perhaps she'd been imagining things. That was possible. Wasn't it? In any case, there was work to be done and there was no point in worrying about something that might not happen. For the moment, it was enough to work and sail and see what sights there were to see. One day, they passed a French town which her shipmates said was called Monaco. It looked a calm sort of place out there in the distance and there was no sign of any French ships. But three days later, there was considerable excitement when an English fleet appeared on the horizon. The signallers were instantly set to work to relay a message, which they had to flag up twice but which, after a long wait, was eventually answered. They had found Sir Richard Bickerton and his squadron.

To see all those great ships breasting the green waters towards them, all sails set and flags flying, was a moment of unexpected pride to Marianne. I'm part of the British fleet, she thought, what's a-goin to see off the Frenchies and end the war. And even if it meant being part of a battle, in that sun-dazzled moment she was almost glad of it.

Johnny Galley sidled up beside her. "There's a sight for sore eyes, my lubber," he said, squinting at the fleet, "what we've waited for long enough in all conscience. That there at the forefront's the *Gibraltar*, what's Sir Richard's flagship. Eighty guns she carries an' as fine as ship as ever sailed the sea. I wouldn't like to be a Frenchy if she was on my tail. An' behind her, d'you see, that's the *Renown* and the *Superb* and the *Belleisle*!

He was in high good humour and bushy-bearded with information and, as he seemed to have forgotten his suspicions, she asked him questions.

"Those two little fellers are sloops," he told her, "what are uncommon useful to have in a fleet. An' there's a frigate a-followin' up to leeward. See her? An' that there is the *Agincourt*, if I'm any judge."

"I suppose Nelson'll leave us now he's got a proper flagship," she said. "I mean, he won't stay aboard a frigate when he can have a man-a'-war, now, will he? Stand ter reason."

"Well, as to that," Johnny said, leaning towards her confidentially and speaking right into her ear, "'twill be fine thing fer us if he does, for then there'll be a cabin to spare for my old mate the carpenter, what I means to make use of." And he suddenly put his head into her neck and kissed it.

She was caught up in such a confusion of feelings she didn't know what to say — shock at his boldness, embarrassment in case someone was watching, fear because he *did* know and there was no gainsaying it now, horror that he was treating her so when she hadn't given him any reason, but, over and above them all, an instant and undeniable pleasure. She was still shaken by it when he lifted his head, looked straight into her eyes and winked, and then she felt herself blushing and had to turn away to try and hide the tell-tale colour. It didn't work.

"There y'are, my lubber," he said, hugging her about the waist — only briefly and more of a tug than a hug but that stirred her too. "'Twill be a fine of thing. You mark my words. A bit a' pleasure in our lives."

She found her tongue as he walked away. "No," she said. "'Tis out the question..." But he was striding off towards the companionway and wasn't listening.

My dear heart alive, she thought, now what am I going to do? I can't take a lover. It en't possible an' anyway I en't that sort. I'm a good respectable woman, that's what I am, an' married to Jem, what I been searchin' for all this time, an' I don't belong to no one else. He shouldn't ha' come after me like that. An' specially onboard ship. 'Tis too dangerous altogether. What if we was caught? 'Twould be a floggin' matter. Anyways I don't want a lover. I got enough to do looking for Jem without that. But, try as she might, she couldn't pretend she wasn't tempted. He'd stirred her as much as Jem had done on that distant wedding day. And that wasn't right, but that was the truth of it. Oh, my dear heart alive.

Orders were being piped. There were sails to furl, an anchor to drop. No time to think or worry. The great ships were gathering about their Lord Admiral. Soon longboats were being put out and rowed across bearing messages and mail, to return a few minutes later with invitations to the captains to dine that evening. The ship was hot with activity as fowls were caught and killed and a goat was slaughtered, leaving a pool of blood to be scrubbed clean by the ship's boys, and below decks, pies and puddings were baked in the great oven, to the usual accompaniment of roars and shouts and a great deal of clanging and banging. It was all wonderfully exciting, even to someone as troubled as Marianne.

Supper was rushed because the watch had to be prepared and ready to pipe the guests aboard. Johnny Galley grumbled about it all through the meal. "We shall be sick as dogs, you mark my words, boltin' our food. 'T'en't wholesome took so quick." But Marianne enjoyed the commotion and the sight of all those fine uniforms climbing aboard lifted her spirits like sunshine. It was as good as being back in town when the gentry were taking the air. She knew there was no hope of finding Jem on any of the ships in this squadron because they'd all been in the Mediterranean long before he'd left Portsmouth. But the sight of them riding the waves around her, gave her hope that sooner or later, they would meet up with Nelson's fleet again and then she *would* find him. She hadn't solved the problem of what she was going to do about Johnny Galley's advances, but she *would* find Jem. Meantime, she'd just have to keep out of Johnny's way as well as she could and hope that Nelson would stay aboard.

Had she known it, that was precisely what the great admiral was telling his guests at that very moment.

It was always a pleasure to him to entertain his captains, especially when so many of them were old and trusted colleagues, like Hardy and Sir Richard and Captain Keats, and especially when they came bearing news of the thorough search they'd been undertaking. The French fleet was thought to be in Toulon and frigates had been sent to San Fiorenzo, Genoa and Leghorn to test the truth of the reports and to discover how many French troops were there and how they were being deployed. Others had been despatched to look out for an enemy squadron rumoured to be approaching the Mediterranean either from the West Indies or from Brest.

"We are not very superior in point of numbers," Nelson told his captains, "so we must keep a good look-out, both here and off Brest. If I have the means I shall try and fight one party or the other before they form a junction. Is your squadron in good repair?"

"The *Agincourt* has sprung a leak," Sir Richard told him, "so she will have to return to Valetta for repairs, but otherwise we are sea-worthy."

"Are you well provisioned?"

"We need fresh water and meat and fruit."

"We will send the sloops to the Bay of Rosia and Barcelona," Nelson decided, "to buy bullocks and oranges and lemons and such fresh greens as they can find. What news of the *Victory*?"

"She is in the Mediterranean," Sir Richard said, "but more than that we cannot say."

Nelson made his final decision of the evening. "If that is the case, it is clear she is returning to join us," he said. "I shall, therefore, stay aboard the *Amphion* with Captain Hardy until such time as we meet with her. More wine, gentlemen?"

THE NEWS that their admiral was staying aboard spread around the *Amphion* at breakfast the next morning. Marianne, watching Johnny Galley out of the corner of her eye, was very relieved. It would give her a few more days to think what to do about him.

Her friends on the other hand, knowing nothing of his advances and nothing of her indecision, told her exactly what she had to do and urged her to do it at once.

"You must finish that letter to your ma," Moll said. "An' get it all signed and sealed an' give it to the purser. There'll be a packet boat sent, you mark my words an' if you don't look sharp, you'll miss it."

It was good advice, so she took it as soon as she could, crouched by the gun in the half-light with her pen clenched tightly in her fist and her tongue between her teeth. At first, she couldn't think what to say. She couldn't tell her mother she'd got a suitor — she'd be horrified — and it would be cruel to say they were heading for a battle, that would just upset her and all to no purpose because it could all be over by the time the letter arrived. In the end, she simply said they'd met up with another fleet, that the oranges in Italy were as big as a pig's bladder *"An' that sweet you woudden beleave"* and that she hadn't found Jem yet. *"However I shall go on a-trying, you may depend on it!"* Then she signed her name with a pretty flourish, wrote her mother's address in bold letters, used her sealing wax for the first time and took her missive to the purser, who promised to put it in the mail sack, "This moment as ever is."

Then there was nothing for any of them to do but wait and see what would happen next.

They waited for three weeks, while the admiral grew visibly more impatient, pacing the decks with his telescope to his good eye scanning the horizon for the first flicker of a sail. It was the end of the month before one appeared but to everybody's great relief — except for Marianne — it *was* the *Victory* and following behind her was the rest of the fleet.

There was an instant surge of activity. The admiral's sea-trunk had to be packed and ready by three bells in the first dog watch, and so had Captain Hardy's because it appeared that he was going to take command of the *Victory*. A new master arrived to take his place on the *Amphion* and to dine with Captain Hardy and the Admiral at the end of the forenoon watch. Instructions were sent out to the fleet at regular intervals throughout the day. Two frigates were given orders to watch Toulon, the *Sirius* was sent to escort Captain Keats to Naples, a sloop was sent to carry the mail to the packet boat. The sea frothed with activity. By 5.30 that afternoon, the Admiral was packed and gone and minutes later, his old flagship gave him a nine-gun salute to mark his return.

"I never knowed a man so quick," Moll observed, as the guns roared their welcome. "When he's set his mind to a thing 'tis all you can do to keep up with 'un."

But Marianne was wondering about the carpenter and his cabin. There seemed to be a lot of activity in the direction of the wardroom. What if he really *was* going to get a cabin? And what if he let Johnny Galley have the use of it? What would she say if he asked her again? And, more to the point, what would she do? She was surrounded by ships of the line and Jem was bound to be on one or other of them, so she ought to have been thinking about how she could get ashore and ask after him, but her mind was stuck in the dilemma like a wasp in treacle and couldn't move on or out to anything else. My dear heart alive, she thought, what am I a-goin' to do?

CHAPTER 7

It was a bright calm day when the *Sirius* arrived in Naples and the long, curved bay was still as a millpond and blue as the sky.

"Nelson's love nest is that," Tom said to Jem, as the two of them stood by the rail chewing a quid of tobacco and enjoying the scenery. The ship was at anchor, sails furled and under orders to stay in the bay and show the flag, so for once there was little to do. "And that there mountain's a volcano, name of Vesuvius, what spits fire and rock all over you, if you so much as look at it."

Jem was impressed. "I hope it won't go spittin' fire while we'm hereabouts," he said. The mountain looked peaceful enough under the blue sky, but he'd heard enough stories about the power of a volcano to view it with respect and was surprised to see that there was a pink and white building nestling against the lower slopes. "People live there seemingly," he said.

"That's there's a monastery, so they say," Tom told him, spitting his own stream of fiery tobacco into the blue water below them. "Monks d'you see, an' there's no accountin' for monks."

The water lapped against the hull, rhythmically, soothingly, as gentle as a lullaby, lick, lick, lick. The two men turned their heads to spit in unison and returned to their chewing, ruminatively and with considerable contentment. "This is the life, eh, shipmate?" Tom said.

"'Tis a curious place," Jem said. "I'd like to go ashore."

"No chance a' that," his friend told him. "You heard what the lieutenant said. We're to stand prepared at all times. 'Tis a fearful place fer fightin' seemingly."

It certainly looked it, for there was an ancient fortress beside the harbour made of stone with round tessellated towers and arrow split windows, and along the bay, the houses looked like fortifications too, as though they'd been built into a cliff face. They were pitted with cavernous doors and windows, black against the sulphurous yellow of the stones, and strung about with rickety balconies, where the washing was hung out to dry and old women sat in the sun, smoking their pipes.

"That there," Tom said, pointing to a grand red villa facing the bay, "is where Emma Hamilton lives, what is Nelson's light a love, an' a saucy baggage by all accounts. That there's his love nest. He had a palace of his own somewhere hereabouts, I couldn't tell you where, but that there is his love nest."

All this talk about love nests was stirring some unexpected emotions in Jem Templeman. It was making him remember his own love nest for a start, that he'd paid for fair and square, and furnished so handsomely. The memory of it was so sharp it was making him yearn to see it again. And yet he'd walked off and left it without a second thought. He couldn't think how he'd come to be so foolish. Even if she *had* scolded him — which she had, there was no denying that — he didn't have to run away and join the navy. That was a coward's trick and, now that he had time to consider it, he could see it. I lost my rag, he thought. That was the trouble. There was no patience in me in them days. And now here he was, miles from home standing by a ship's rail feeling homesick. Because that's what he *was* feeling. Homesick and ashamed of himself for being so stupid.

That evening when supper was over, he was at a loss to know what to do. He couldn't just sit about and mope. That would be foolish, and he'd been foolish enough for one lifetime. Eventually, he decided to join Tom along with the rest of the watch as they gathered round Old Amos, the story-teller. At least a tale would pass the time.

"Did 'ee ever hear tell of that of admiral what Lord Nelson hanged?" Amos said. And when heads were shaken and lips licked in anticipation, he beamed around at them and settled to entertain them. "'Neapolitan prince he was," he said, "'asides bein' admiral, name a Prince Carry Cho-lo, or some such. Anyways, he were a prince an' an admiral, like Oi said, an' he come a-fightin' the King and Queen a' Naples what were personal friends of our Lord Nelson and Lady Hamilton, what Oi don't doubt you've heard of. An' ol' Admiral Nelson he weren't havin' none a' that. No, sir, not he. So what do he do, moi hearties? Why he sets straight out to capture the man. What he done in two shakes of a lamb's tail, bein' the best admiral what ever sailed the high seas. So what happened then, moi lubbers?"

They didn't know and said so.

"So what happened then was he put this Carry Cho-lo on trial for treason, tha's what he done, an' he found the beggar guilty in no time at all. An' that afternoon, that very afternoon mind, he put out to sea and he hung the beggar on board his own ship, swung him from his own yardarm so he did, until he was good an' dead. Tha's what he done. An after that they cut him down an' put stones in his pockets an' threw him overboard into the bay an' watched him sink. An' they all said that was the end of him an' a good riddance to bad rubbish." Then he paused for a few seconds to let the drama of the story sink in.

"Now," he went on, in a confidential tone, "you might think

that was the end of the matter. Most men would. Stands to reason. But if they did, moi lubbers, they'd be wrong. Oh my dear life. They *would* be wrong. So what happened next? you ask. Well I'll tell you. A few days later, Lord Nelson was a-givin' one of those there parties of his, what he gives for all the lords and big-wigs an' all, out here in the bay on his flagship. An' they'd just about come to the puddin' and they was all half seas over an' laughin' an' enjoyin' theirselves when a great cry went up. Oh a fearsome hullabaloo. Yellin' an' shriekin' an' all sorts. So they rushed out on deck to see what it was — as anyone would. An' there was the fleet hung about with sailors, all up in the riggin' like monkeys they was an' all pointin' at the sea an' yelling and shriekin' fit to make yer blood run cold. An' there, out in the bay, standin' bolt upright in the water and movin' straight towards them, was that of Prince Carry Cho-lo, dead as a doornail with his eyes open and his long hair a-trailin' in the water, looking straight at Lord Nelson like an avengin' spirit come back for justice. Now what do 'ee think to that, moi hearties? Like an avengin' spirit, he was, come back for to haunt Lord Nelson with his eyes open an' his long hair a-flowin' on the tide."

"My dear heart alive!" Tom said. "I wouldn't ha' liked to ha' been Lord Nelson."

"Nor me neither, moi hearty," Amos said. "For 'twas an omen a' bad luck whichever which way you looks at it. What Oi hopes we shan't have cause to regret when we comes to fightin' the Frenchies."

Several of his hearers crossed themselves and said "Amen!" Fighting the Frenchies would be bad enough without having a curse on you.

"I didn't like the sound a that at all," Tom said to Jem when the group dispersed. "Do you think it really was an omen?"

"No, I do not," Jem told him. "I don't believe in omens. I think we makes our own fortunes with our own behaviour." And he should know.

"But you can't tell, can 'ee?" Tom said sombrely. "I means for to say, there's some uncommon strange things happen at sea. Downright unnat'ral some of 'em. There's a feller aboard seen a mermaid once, so he says. Singin' to him she was, right out at sea, with long green hair an' everythin'."

"You don't believe *that*, surely?" Jem said. A drifting corpse was one thing, a mermaid quite another.

"You never knows, my lubber," Tom said. "You never knows." Then he laughed. "'Twould be a rare of thing to write home about."

His words stirred Jem's conscience for the second time that day. He hadn't sent a single letter home since he enlisted, and he knew he should have done. 'Twas just that writing was such a fearful thing, all that struggle with pens and ink and such, and not knowing what to say nor how to spell it. Anyway, they'll've forgot all about me by now, he thought, trying to quell his conscience and failing. I'll write tomorrow. That's what I'll do. Tomorrow as ever is.

MARIANNE'S LETTER was delivered to her mother's house on a warm easy morning in September. It wasn't exactly an undivided blessing. To start with, it took far too long to scrape together sufficient money to pay for it, and then, when it was finally put into her hands, there was no one around who could read it for her and that was an anguish that made her chest ache. She'd waited so long for this promised letter, and now here it was, and it was useless. She put it on the kitchen table and stared at it for a very long time, but apart from the signature and the word "pig", which didn't seem at all likely, the handwriting remained inscrutable despite her most earnest scrutiny. Eventually, she picked it up and took it down the street to Lizzie Templeman's to see what she could make of it.

"Well, now," Lizzie said, pursing her lips and assuming a learned expression, "I en't exactly what you might call a scholar, not in the true meanin' a' the word, not in the way a scholar might take meanin' from it, but I'll see what I can make out. 'Twon't be all of it, mind, there bein' a parlous lot a' writing." She paused and studied the letter, narrowing her eyes in order to see it better. "That there is *I am well*," she said, pointing at the words. "That there is an *I* and that says *well* and that there says *fine ship*, what you would expect a-comin' from a sailor, what she is now if you comes to think about it."

"What's that great long word in the middle?" Mary said, pointing at *Meddytranium*.

"That'll be where she is, like enough," Lizzie said, "but don't ask me to pronounce it. I can't be doin' with foreign words. English is bad enough in all conscience without that."

"That word there is *Jem*," Mary said, suddenly discovering it. "What does she say about *him*? Can you read that bit?"

"*I en't found Jem yet*," Lizzie read, surprising them both by her fluency. "Well, that don't surprise me. I never thought she would, not in the middle of an ocean."

"If anyone can find him, she will," Mary told her stoutly. "You can depend on it, Lizzie. She's made up her mind to it."

"I'm sure she will if she can," Lizzie said. "She's a good gel. Always was. I hope they're looking out for her on that ship of hers. My Jem can look arter hisself, great lummox that he is, but she's jest a slip of a gel."

"Only they don't know that, do they?" Mary pointed out. "They think she's a boy, so she'll be treated accordin'." Her face was crumpling with distress, tears dropping from her eyes. "There en't a day goes by I don't think of her, wonderin' how she is an' if they're treatin' her fair. Not a single day. I looks on her weddin' ring and I thinks and thinks."

"Don't take on so, my lover," Lizzie said, putting a comforting arm round her friend's bowed shoulders. "She's writ you a good long letter, which you got to admit, shows she's thinkin' of 'ee, which is a sight more than Jem's ever done for me. Don't fret. She'll be home in no time at all, you see if she en't, with a poll-parrot on her shoulder most likely."

But Mary's long control had been breached and she had too many tears to shed to be comforted. "Treated like a boy," she wept, "and she was always such a dear, good gel. Treated like a boy. And they say there's a great sea battle a-coming. What if she's caught up in that? She could be killed."

"There's no point thinking about battles," Lizzie said practically. "If 'tis to come, 'twill come and there's nothing we can do about it. Never trouble trouble till trouble troubles you. That's my way a' thinking."

"Treated like a boy," Mary wept. "My Marianne, all on her own in some horrible sea at the ends of the earth, an' treated like a boy."

It would have surprised them both to know that the *boy* was being treated very well. The *boy* was being courted.

JOHNNY GALLEY SET about his courtship in his usual way and after careful preparation. First, he helped his old shipmate Mr Ferguson to move back into his cabin, and praised him for a first-rate carpenter who should never have been moved out of it in the first place, then he threw out hints that he might like to make use of it "now an' then like if occasion were to arise, if you was agreeable", and to his great delight, he'd been given permission, after being told he was a dog, "damn my eyes if you ain't". After that, everything being in order, he set about enticing his ladylove.

At first, he tried larger portions of skillygalee, plum duff and spotted dog because he knew she was partial to them. Then he suggested to the cook that he'd found a fine lad to help out in the galley "from time to time like" and, after waiting for a day when a north-west wind was blowing fit to chill her bones, he took her to work there for part of her watch. It pleased him to help her into one of the privileged positions on board and he felt protective to be taking her out of the teeth of a gale — but better than both those things, it would give her an excuse to be somewhere else, in case her mates took to wondering where she was once their affair was underway. However, being wily in the arts of seduction, he didn't say anything nor make any advances yet awhile for fear of alarming her. Steady as she goes, he said to himself, as he watched her scoffing her skillygalee, smiling as she lifted the spoon to her mouth. She'll come round to it. They allus do.

Meantime, pushed on by Nelson's determination, the fleet was hunting the French and since the *Amphion* was no longer his flagship, she was back on duty as a frigate and had plenty to do. They were continually on the move, to Rosia bay to buy citrus fruit and fresh meat, to various watering holes to fill the leagers, to Toulon because the French fleet were rumoured to be lurking there and, whenever the weather allowed it, round and round the islands of Minorca, Majorca, Sardinia and Corsica keeping a sharp look-out from dawn to sunset and never seeing anything beyond fishing boats and other ships of the line. The weather was bad that autumn and often against them. There were days when they worked the ship hard from sunrise to sunset and made so little progress it wasn't worth the effort, and worse ones when they couldn't move at all but had to furl sails and sit it out until the storm blew over.

Marianne took it all philosophically. She was never seasick, she didn't mind hard work and the visits ashore gave her the chance to start searching again. Not that it did her any good, for the sailors she met on the quaysides told her to a man that they'd never heard of a carpenter called Jem and that their carpenter had quite a different name, although one old feller did venture that the sea was full of fleets and full of ships "being as the Admiral's keeping us all on the look-out" and asked what port he'd sailed from.

He was the first man to show any interest, so Marianne told him.

"Ah," he said. "Portsmouth. Then if he ain't with Admiral Lord Nelson, he'll be with Admiral Collingwood like as not, what's a fine admiral to serve, or with Admiral Cornwallis a-guardin' the Channel, what they been doin' these many years now. Could be anywhere from Land's End to Alexandria an' that's the truth of it. Why do 'ee want to find him? Owe you money, does he?"

"He's a relation."

"Well if that's the case of it, my sonny, I'd give up looking for him if I was you," the old man advised, "on account of you'll never find him in a month a' Sundays. 'Tis like looking for a needle in a haystack, searching these waters. I knows. I done it many's the time. An' we knew who we was lookin' for, what you don't seemingly."

Stupid old fool, Marianne thought angrily, and she gave him a brief nod for politeness' sake and left him. What does he know of it? And she stalked back to the bum boat, feeling cross. If I means for to find him, I shall find him an' he can say what he likes.

But by the time she was back aboard the *Amphion* again, she was beginning to feel downhearted. She'd asked so many people at so many harbours and she hadn't found one who'd even heard of him. An' I *must* find him, she thought. I can't stay aboard much longer. Not with Johnny Galley knowing and paying court the way he is. All those extra portions were very welcome, especially when she'd been working hard, and so was being taken off to the galley to work in the warm, but they were love tokens for all that and she knew it and was worried by it. If he followed them by making advances and talking about that cabin again, she didn't know what she was going to do about it. If only life wasn't so complicated.

Then three things happened in quick succession that changed

her feelings and her opinions. First of all, the wind dropped and then it disappeared altogether leaving the ship becalmed, her sails hanging slack and idle in the empty air, the sea flat-calm and with a dull metallic sheen like the surface of a mirror.

"Now what do we do?" she asked her two shipmates as they stood by the rail, gazing out at the motionless sea and the rest of their fleet lying becalmed to port and starboard.

"We sits tight, my lubber," Moll said, "an' we takes our ease an' we waits for it to blow again."

"And when will that be, think 'ee?"

"Who can tell?" Moll said. "There's no way a knowin' with that of wind. Could be tomorrow. Could be a week. We has to wait an' see. One good thing though, 'twill give us a bit a peace and quiet. We shan't be for ever up an' down the rigging settin' them ol' sails."

Them old sails hung empty-bellied well into the forenoon watch under a sky as white and ominous as death. Marianne found the stillness eerie and she was chilled to the bones without her usual work to keep her warm. She wished someone would strike up a tune to cheer them but old Robbie Norris, who had an accordion and usually provided them with jigs and hornpipes in the afternoon watch when they were at rest, was perched on the capstan playing a doleful shanty which, in her opinion, wasn't doing any of them any good at all. She glowered at him, sitting there so mournful-like with a mist gathering round his woolly cap. A rare thick mist it was too, twirling and wreathing about him some giant white snake, more like a...

"My dear heart alive," she said to Moll, "there's a fog a-comin' on."

"'Tain't a-comin', my lubber," Moll told her. "'Tis come."

Within seconds, the ship was swathed and dank with it, decks and gunwales oozing moisture as if they were sweating, sails and sailors insubstantial as ghosts in the sudden gloom and no sign or sound of the sea at all.

"I can't be doin' with this," Marianne complained, shivering and hugging her jacket to her chest in a vain attempt to keep warm. "I hopes that ol' cook's got some good hot grub for us come noontime."

"What you'll see, my lubber, when you gets to the galley," Johnny Galley said, materialising out of the fog, first his chest bulging towards them, then a fog-dewed beard and the dark folds of his breeches, and finally his head, shoulders and boots. "Look lively. I en't got all day." Marianne was glad to go with him because at least the galley would be warm, and she followed him cheerfully. It wasn't until they'd edged down the companionway and were sidling through the gun deck carefully avoiding the sleeping bulk of the cannons, that she realised they were heading in the wrong direction.

"Where are we goin', Johnny?" she asked. "This en't the way to the galley."

"Ask no questions, be told no lies," he said.

"That's all very well," she said. "I needs for to know."

"Well then, you knows now," he said. "We're here."

They'd reached the door of a cabin, he was opening it, sneaking inside, catching her hand and pulling her after him. No, no, she thought. This can't be happening. But it was. He was kissing her neck and pushing up her jacket to fondle her breasts.

"No, Johnny," she said, trying to struggle away from him. "I can't."

He took her face between his hands and held her still, grinning at her. "Why not, my lubber? Tell me that. An' don't say on account of 'ee don't like it 'cause I knows better. 'Tis writ all over 'ee, so 'tis."

And it was true. She did like it. She could enjoy it if… "I'm married," she said. "I'm a married woman. It en't right."

He dropped his hands, threw back his head and gave a great roar of laughter, showing those uneven teeth. "All the better," he said. "Wives is the best. They know what's what. An' who's to miss a slice from a cut cake, as they say?"

"I got a husband, Johnny."

He pretended to look round the cabin. "I don't see him."

"He was pressed," she explained. "I come into the navy for to find him."

"What you en't done."

She defended herself stoutly. "Not for want a' trying. I been ashore every port we come to, askin' an' askin'."

"We got an hour," he said, pulling her towards him. "Come six bells Mr Ferguson'll be back with the rest of the mess. There en't a soul to see us — not that they could with this fog to hide us — there's no one to stop us. No one'll know, an' I never see a gal so ripe for lovin' as you." And before she could open her mouth to protest again, he kissed her long and languorously.

Her mind was still thinking "No. Don't. I mustn't…" but her senses were stirred and singing. To be kissed so and held so was a pleasure beyond anything she could remember. It was so warm and enfolding and loving. And it felt so right.

He was kissing her neck and stroking her titties with his thumbs and murmuring, "You'm the prettiest gal I ever seen."

"I en't pretty," she said. "I never been pr—"

But her protest was kiss-smothered. "Prettiest," he said, when he raised his head, "an' softest an as ripe for love as a peach a-waitin' to fall." What she would do soon, surely to goodness, when he'd been so sweet with her.

"Well…" she said, still dubious. "I shouldn't really, Johnny." But he was right. Nobody would know, 'specially in all this fog. Jem was far away, and he'd probably forgotten all about her by now and she *had* tried to find him, what no one could gainsay; she'd gone out of her way, trying and trying, and anyway he'd run away from her on her wedding day, which was cruel and that was the truth of it. And he'd hurt her, which was cruel too. And anyway there wouldn't be any harm in it. Just this once. It would have to be just the once, that was all. "You wouldn't hurt me, would you, Johnny?"

"Hurt 'ee!" he said, black eyebrows raised in surprise at the very idea. "Lord love your pretty eyes! I shall pleasure 'ee."

"Well," she said. "I shouldn't really, I knows that, but maybe…"

He unbuttoned his trousers.

CHAPTER 8

Fog obscured the ship for the next four days to Johnny Galley's immense satisfaction. Now that he'd caught his little light a' love, he had no intention of letting her go and fog gave him the perfect excuse to tease her into the cabin again. Next morning, he togged himself up in his best waistcoat, tied a clean kerchief round his neck and gave his beard a trim and a good brushing. Then, choosing his moment, when he knew she would be at leisure, he prowled the quarter-deck until he found her with those two stupid mates of hers, gave her a conspiratorial grin and told her she was needed in the galley, "What's the best place for 'ee in this weather, if you ask my opinion on't."

The grin and the opinion were both wasted, for Marianne had been awake most of the night regretting what she'd done and worrying about it until she felt quite sick. Now she was feeling very unsure of herself, ashamed that she'd given in to him so easily, ashamed that she'd been unfaithful to poor Jem, even ashamed that she'd enjoyed it. And she *had* enjoyed it, rather to her surprise. She'd enjoyed it very much. "What if I was to say no?" she said.

"Orders is orders," he told her.

That's true enough, she thought. So she had to get up and follow him down the companionway. And, of course, they weren't going to the galley, as she knew perfectly well. She would have to tell him this couldn't go on, she really would. But she couldn't argue with him out on the open deck where anyone could hear. It would have to wait until they were on their own. So she followed him into the cabin.

It was dank with fog, even in that little enclosed space and she was horribly aware of him, standing there so close to her with his beard bristling. She sat on the bunk and took a deep breath to sustain her. "We can't do this, Johnny," she said.

He sat down beside her, being very calm and perfectly reasonable. "You don't have to do nothing unless 'ee wants to," he told her. If this bird was to be well and truly limed, he'd have to catch her softly. "All you got to do is tell me what 'ee wants. 'Tis all in your own hands."

"I'm married," she said.

"Aye, so you are."

'T'en't the right thing to do."

"Well now," he said, smiling at her, "as to the rights an' wrongs of it, there's a deal to be said on either side. 'Tis my opinion of it, we've earned a bit a pleasure in our lives, what with bein' at sea all this time, an' workin' all hours, an' the fog an' all. Don' 'ee think so?"

She didn't know what to say, for their talk seemed to have tilted into an odd direction. But as he seemed to be waiting for an answer, she supposed she had to give one. "Well," she said, "we does work hard, there's no denyin'."

"Only got to look at your hands to see that," he said, and he took one of them and stroked it gently with his thumb.

She didn't pull away because he was being so tender, but she didn't speak either, partly because she didn't know what to say and partly because even this little touch was so pleasurable.

"My dear heart alive!" he said as if he'd just thought of something. "Was 'ee afeared a' bein' found out?"

"No," she said. "You wouldn't tell no one, would you?"

He pretended to be upset at the very idea. "As if I would. You can't think as bad a' me as that."

"No," she said, feeling sorry to have upset him. "I don't. I know you won't tell."

"No one needs for to know," he said, putting his arm round her shoulders in a comforting way. "I means for to say, we got this place to ourselves, all hid away an' snug an' warm an' a-waitin' for us when we needs it. Private like. What could be better? Asides which 'ten't no one's affair but our own. We en't upsettin' no one. 'Tis a secret atween us. Private like." Now if he were to turn her a little — gently does it — he could kiss her cheek. "Our little pleasure what we've earned and what don't do no harm to a living soul. What could be wrong wi' that?"

She tried to turn her head away from him, struggling to think of all the arguments she'd been rehearsing during the night, but he was moving too and before she could think he'd caught her and was kissing her with a sudden passion that took her breath away.

"You'm the prettiest thing I ever did see," he said. "'Twould be a wicked waste not to love 'ee."

"I'm married," she tried.

"All the more reason," he said, sliding his hands under her jacket.

"I wouldn't want to do nothing what 'ud…" she began. And was kissed silent, this time at such length that she began to kiss him back. She simply couldn't help it.

"'Course not," he said, unbuttoning her breeches and gentling her down onto the mattress. "Prettiest thing I ever did see."

He was careful to keep his expression gentle and his hands slow but inside his head his thoughts were roaring. You'm limed my lover, you'm limed.

MARIANNE SLEPT WELL THAT NIGHT, eased and tired by so much pleasure and very nearly convinced that Johnny was right. The chaplain would have had a very different view of it, she knew that, and so would Father Peter what married her back in Portsmouth. 'Twould be all adultery and the ten commandments if they was to hear of it. But they never would hear of it. She'd make sure of that. And besides, they hadn't been doing any harm, 'twas all private and 'atween theirselves, the way Johnny said, a private pleasure, that's all it was. Just a private pleasure.

After that, there wasn't any point in worrying or in arguing about it either. She'd given in twice, so why not a third and fourth time? Or a fifth? Soon, she couldn't remember why she'd worried at all. It still made her feel guilty and even a bit ashamed when she was alone and had time to think about it, but that wasn't very often, and it *was* a pleasure and, what's more, it got better every time.

There was only one trouble and that was that the weather got worse and worse. The fog was blown away by a strong north-wester which rapidly became a severe storm, which meant they had hardly any time together at all. And the first storm was followed by a second that was even worse. It grew progressively colder and more impossible to make any headway. After four weeks of it, the old hands began to grumble.

"High time we was took into port," they said. "Ol' Lord Nelson don't never mean for us to stay at sea all winter. 'Ten't nat'ral. He won't have a ship what en't plumb crazy come the springtime if that's how he means for to go on."

"Quite right," Marianne said. "We done enough for one season, surely to goodness." If they were in port they wouldn't have to work anywhere near so hard and there'd be more time for pleasure. "He can't mean for us to sail all winter."

But that was exactly what he did mean, as he told his dinner guests some days later.

The latest storm had finally subsided, and he'd invited his captains to dine with him so that he could praise them for all the efforts they'd been making. After the meal, he was sitting at ease, twirling the stem of his wineglass between his finger and thumb and watching them with his one clear eye, when Captain Keats ventured the question that all of them wanted to ask.

"Are we to winter at Malta, my lord?" he said. And when Nelson regarded him steadily, he added, "Should we not endeavour to save the ships from this inclement weather?"

"Were I to winter in Malta I would undoubtedly save the ships," Nelson admitted, "but if I am to watch the French, which I am determined to do, I must be at sea, difficult though that might be. At present, the French fleet is still in Toulon, as you know, and shows no signs of coming out, but I tell you, gentlemen, were we to head for Malta, as I know you would prefer, you may depend upon it they would come out at once thinking the coast clear and we would lose them."

His captains were disappointed, but they didn't say so. They knew they couldn't argue against his determination. But it would be a hard winter if they were to be at sea all the time.

"We are parlously short of water," Captain Keats said, offering the one practical reason for getting ashore even for an hour or two.

"As I am aware," his Admiral said. "I've a mind to try the Maddelena Islands since they are the nearest to us at this moment. Captain Ryves visited them in the *Agincourt* last year and speaks highly of them. We will leave two frigates to watch Toulon and pray for a fair wind."

What they got, despite fervent prayers, was a wind so foul that although they struggled against it for four days, working their ships hard with their top-sails double reefed, they only made seven leagues progress and sustained so many split sails that they were quite beleaguered. Nevertheless, because their need for water was now extreme, Nelson decided to press on even in the teeth of the gale and they struggled to make what headway they could for another four hard days, finally limping towards Maddelena on the eighth day, totally exhausted and thoroughly dispirited. But what they found there almost made up for their struggles for it was an almost perfect harbour, set in a small bay, secluded and beautiful and, best of all, with the decisive advantage of two entrances.

The next morning, while the bum boats were heading off to fill the leaguers with fresh water, the Governor of Maddelena came aboard the *Victory* to welcome them to his islands. He was given a nine-gun salute and was immensely pleased to be so honoured and, after he had breakfasted with the Admiral, he declared himself delighted to accept an official name for the harbour.

"We will call it Agincourt Sound," Nelson said, after the ship of the line that discovered it. "And we will stay here until the storm has blown itself out."

Marianne didn't care what it was called as long as they could stay there out of the weather and preferably for a good long time. Her arms were still aching after the struggle of the last eight days. I'll ask Johnny, she thought. He'm bound to know.

"We'm to stay here a day or two, seemingly," Johnny said. "An' not afore time."

"Only a day or two," she said. "'Ten't much Johnny."

"A day or two all nice and snug and cosy-like," he said, "and Mr Ferguson with plenty to keep him occupied and no storm to toss us from pillar to post, like it's been doin' this last eight days. I means for to make the most of it."

"I shall have to go ashore from time to time like," Marianne warned him.

"Just so long as it en't our time like," he said, and grinned at her.

She went ashore that first morning, and on every single

occasion the bum boats set out. Her shipmates were most impressed. "He might be a strip of a lad," they said, "but he takes his turn handsome." But, in fact, she was driven by a guilty conscience and a need to find her Jem that was greater than ever, even though there was nothing much she could do if she *did* find him because they could hardly jump ship on a little island. This time, she tried to be more methodical and not only asked if anyone knew of him but made sure she'd found out what ship they were sailing on so that when she got back on board, she could write the names down on a sheet of her notepaper and put a tick beside them. By the afternoon of their third day, when she'd asked the water gatherers from sixteen different ships, she was beginning to have second thoughts about the old man in Rosia Bay. He could have been right. She could be looking for a needle in a haystack. It certainly felt like it. Or he might be in a different fleet altogether and God knows where that might be. And yet she *had* to find him. She couldn't just sail about enjoying her new pleasures and forgetting him. That wouldn't do at all.

THE *SIRIUS* WAS in Valetta along with the rest of Admiral Collingwood's fleet, sheltering from the storms while they took in supplies and Jem and his shipmates were sprucing up for a night on the town. They had pay in their purses and clean clothes on their backs and, despite the chill of the weather, they were hot for liquor and women.

"This is the life, my lubbers," Jem said, as they swaggered towards Strada Stretta, cockily square-shouldered, secretly moist-handed and with the rolling gait of seamen newly arrived ashore. "My stars! Look at those titties over there!"

The whores were out in force, strolling their temptations before the newest arrivals, the British fleet being a good source of trade, and the one that had caught his eye was plumply luscious and well displayed.

"Drink first," Tom said. "Women'll wait. I got a thirst on me like one a' them there camels in the desert an' I knows just the place for to quench it. Step lively, my hearties!"

It was a small, dark bar half way down Strada Stretta, rush-lit and floored with sawdust ready for spillage, and it was crowded with whores and sailors, who greeted the new arrivals with a cheerful roar and made room for them on the benches. The wine was cheap and plentiful, there was an accordion playing and there were women on offer wherever they looked.

"This is the life!" Jem said.

He was still saying it two hours later, although not quite so clearly, for by then his words were sloshing about in his mouth like sea in the scuppers and he wasn't entirely steady on his feet. But he'd had a first-rate evening, drunk more wine than his belly could withstand and staggered out into the street to spew most of it up again, found two accommodating women to satisfy the itch, danced the hornpipe on the table to roars of approval from his messmates and generally made a happy fool of himself.

It wasn't until he was roused at six bells the next morning that he realised that the evening hadn't been quite the success he'd imagined. He had a roaring headache, it was bitterly cold and worse, as he discovered when he'd struggled out of his bunk, his purse-strings had been cut and his purse was missing.

"The lousy, rotten, thievin' whore!" he said. "She's nicked my money. Every last farthing."

Tom was scratching his head and yawning. "There's more where that come from," he said easily.

"No, there en't," Jem wailed. "She's took it all. Every last farthing."

Tom stared at him. "You don't never mean for to tell me you took all your pay to a whorehouse."

Jem nodded miserably.

"More fool you then," Tom told him. "That's all I got to say to 'ee. I never heard such folly." But then the conversation had to come to an end for a midshipman had appeared and was shouting at them to stir their stumps.

Jem sloped off to his duties, inwardly cursing himself for being a fool and he went on cursing all through a long and tedious morning. "I tell 'ee, Tom," he said, when they sat alongside each other eating their midday meal, "I wish I'd never took the shillin' and that's a fact. I was a blamed fool then and I'm a blamed fool now. I'd ha' been better off stayin' at home, wife or no wife. Least a wife don't steal your wages."

That provoked a roar of laughter. "If that's your way a' thinking, my lubber," old Josh said, spluttering into his grog, "you'd best think again. Women are all the same. Take my word for it. That wife of yourn'll be the same as all the others. She'll have the coat off yer back afore you can blink."

"No, she won't," Jem said, stung into defending her. He'd given her a black name in all conscience, but she wasn't as bad as all that. "She might have a tongue in her head — that I won't deny — but she's an honest woman. I'd stake my life on it. She en't a thief."

"They're all the same!" Josh told him. "You mark my words. Nary trust a one a' them."

"'Specially whores!" another man said. "They puts one hand down yer breeches while the other one's a-nicking your purse. 'Tis the same the world over."

Jem sighed heavily. "So 't'would seem," he said.

Tom grinned at him. "Well, you know now don'tcher, my lubber," he said, and raised his tankard in mock salute. "Down the hatch, shipmate. Drink up and look chearly. Worse things happen at sea."

Jem drank his grog and ate every last mouthful of his figgy dowdy and was partially cheered, but the irritation niggled in his mind for days. Hard work and distance had muddied his memory and it was sometimes quite hard to remember what Marianne looked like. He could remember her hair, good, strong, thick hair it was, the colour of a ship's rope. If he closed his eyes, he could see it clearly. And he seemed to recall a blue dress and a strong wind whipping it tight against her belly as she walked, and if he strained his mind, he could see her hands hard at work in her father's kitchen, sewing or sweeping or setting the table, but the rest of her was a blur. It rather upset him, for after all, she *was* his wife when all was said and done. Howsomever, what was done was done and whether or not he could conjure up a picture of her, one thing he was quite certain about: she was a hardworking honest woman. She would never have stolen his money or cheated on him in any way. And for a yearning moment, he wished he could see her again.

"High time we was sent home to Portsmouth," he complained to Tom, when the wind had changed direction and they'd finally been given the order to set sail from the harbour. "I'm sick a' this winter, going all on and on. He must send us home soon, surely. We can't stay at sea all year long.' Ten't nat'ral."

"Don't get yer hopes up," Tom warned. "He'll stay at sea until we fights the French and that's all there is to it. We shall see the winter out, you mark my words."

·

CHAPTER 9

There was a snowstorm blowing, flakes swirling thick as goose feathers from an obliterated sky and blown into impenetrable swathes by the force of a fearsome gale. Marianne had seen plenty of snow falling during her childhood and until that moment she would have said she was well used to it and had never been much affected by it, but it had never been anything like this. There was no peace or prettiness about this fall, no gentle descent, no distant hills to receive its silent cover, no muffling and calming silence. This snow was cold, cruel, all-enveloping and absolutely terrifying for, beneath its chilling fall, the sea rose into the biggest, blackest and most terrible waves that she had ever seen. They mounded one after the other and reached such heights that they were taller than the mainmast and they fell upon the ship with a dreadful roar and such power, it made the timbers shake and groan.

When the first one grew before her disbelieving eyes, Marianne screamed with fear. She simply couldn't help it. She knew this was the most dangerous place for a ship under sail — they all knew that — that the wave was falling straight towards them and that if it hit them, they would be lost. She was frozen to the deck with terror and watched as the wall of water fell upon the struggling ship with a roar that filled her ears and stopped the blood in her veins. There were people all around her struggling with the capstan and hauling on the ropes, but she couldn't move, not even to obey orders. It wasn't until Moll ran past her and hit her between the shoulder blades and yelled at her to "Look chearly!" that she was pulled out of her trance, turned to and began to work with the rest. After that, she worked automatically, obeying orders and not stopping to think, and then it gradually became clear to her that there was a pattern to what they were doing and that the pattern could save them if they held to it strongly enough, and that calmed her fear.

They were running before the wind with the mainsail half reefed, the way they usually did in a storm and with a fore-top-mast stay-sail and a fore-top-sail, to prevent her from yawing and to lift the bows. The top-sails could take what little wind there was in the trough of the wave and that gave them the chance to manoeuvre the ship into position to ride the next roller so that they weren't struck in the stern and turned sideways on, which, as they all knew, would put them in danger of taking the next wave broadside on and being broached. It was taking all their captain's expertise and every straining ounce of their combined and desperate energy to do it and each new wave was a palpable threat and a renewed terror. The ship bucked under every impact, shuddering like a frightened horse, but they were staying their course and outwitting the force of the wind.

Time passed, the waves grew, taller and taller, mounding and descending one after the other, inexorably. The struggle continued. There wasn't a single member of the crew who wasn't cold and exhausted, but they worked double watches, no matter what state they were in. If the ship's bells were sounded, nobody heard them; food was prepared, somehow, and served whenever and wherever it was possible; they snatched whatever sleep they could when they were off watch; the snow fell as if it would never stop and the storm showed no signs of abating.

"How long's this goin' on?" Marianne said miserably to Moll, as they crouched on the gun deck eating what they could of their cold figgy dowdy. "It's been more'n a day an' a half now."

"No way a' knowin', my lubber," Moll told her, wearily. "'Tis a storm, so it is, an' you knows what *they're* like. One minute blowin' fit to take your breath away and the next swirlin' off to torment some other poor beggar."

"Well, I wish this one 'ud swirl off," Marianne said. "Damn my eyes if I don't. I can't be doin' with storms at sea."

"Nor me neither," Moll said. "Only we don't have much choice in the matter."

"How long till spring? Tha's what I wants for to know," Peg said. "It can't go on like this for ever. I've forgot what the sun looks like."

Marianne wiped her calloused hands on her jacket. "I hates the winter," she said, "an' I hates the sea, an' I wish I'd never joined the navy an' that's a fact, which I never would ha' done if it hadn't ha' been for that blamed silly husband a' mine, what I hates too. Goin' off an' getting' tiddly an' leading me into all this. Blamed fool!" She'd forgotten how earnestly she'd been searching for him, forgotten how she'd vowed to find him. Now her mind was stuck with the knowledge that it was his fault she'd been fighting a storm and was frightened out of her wits. "If he was to appear afore me this minute," she said. "I'd spit in his eye, so I would, husband or no husband."

"I don't know about you two," Peg said, "but I'm for some shut-eye. I'm dead on my feet an' that's a fact."

They slept fitfully, despite their exhaustion, stirring to shift and shiver even though they were wrapped in their blankets. But they woke in total darkness to the sound of eight bells and an encouraging change in the movement of the ship. It was the end of the middle watch, the morning watch was about to begin, and the storm was abating at last. When they reported to their various stations, the snow had stopped falling and they could see the sky and the horizon again and, although there was a strong sea running, the waves were white tipped and manageable, and the order was being given to put on more sail.

Breakfast was quite a cheerful meal and it became a celebration when Johnny Galley arrived with the news that they were heading for Maddelena again, to take on supplies and fresh water, so he said, and to make some necessary repairs, particularly to the sails, which had suffered a lot of damage in the high winds.

"Not afore time," his messmates said, nodding their approval, and one of them added, "I hopes we stays there till springtime an' has ourselves a proper rest, what we've earned in all conscience. I don't hold with sailin' in the winter. 'T'ent nat'ral."

"Try tellin' the Admiral," Johnny Galley said, and winked at Marianne.

And that's another thing, she thought, looking up at his bold face. We en't had a minute to ourselves for weeks an' weeks. An' that en't nat'ral neither. We needs our pleasure to keep us going. She was irritable and angry, torn by too many muddled emotions, still feeling the fear that had shaken her during the storm, ashamed of herself for being cowardly when her shipmates had been so stalwart, guilty for taking a lover when she was a married woman, angry that she'd been such a fool as to join the navy, annoyed with herself and the world and everything in it, the winter, the storm, the incessant cold and particularly that great stupid lummox she'd married. If it hadn't been for him, she would never have taken the shilling in the first place. It was all his fault. Well, I hopes he's been caught in that ol' storm too, she thought, wherever he is. 'Twould pay him out, so it would, an' serve him right, leavin' me like that.

⁓

IN FACT, he was in Valetta again. The *Sirius* had been transferred to Admiral Collingwood's fleet and had been lying at anchor in the harbour for the last two days and, far from paying him out, the storm had done him a good turn. They'd come through it well enough, all things considered, with just calloused hands and aching bones and two ripped sails to show for it, but it had thrown Mr Turner into a fever, which nobody could understand but which was real enough. For two days after the storm died down, the carpenter lay in his cabin with his eyes closed and the sweat pouring down his face, groaning and suffering, and when the surgeon came down to inspect him, the diagnosis he made was immediate.

"He is a deal too ill to remain aboard," he reported to Captain Prowse. "We must send him to the new naval hospital as soon as we come to harbour. They are better placed to deal with such fevers."

Captain Prowse agreed. "Make the necessary arrangements," he said. "Mr Turner must be cared for. Fortunately we have another carpenter aboard."

Five hours later, Mr Turner was wrapped in a blanket and carried down the gangplank like a large damp parcel by four of his shipmates and lifted into a Maltese carriage and driven away to the naval hospital and, as soon as he was gone, Jem Templeman was promoted to Mr Templeman, ship's carpenter, at a handsome rate of pay. At the end of his next watch, he moved in to the luxury of the carpenter's cabin.

He was inordinately pleased with himself. "Ship's carpenter," he said, admiring his black curls and his weather-browned face in Mr Turner's little shaving mirror. Maybe he should grow a beard. 'Twould be fitting to his new rank and easily done. "'Tis an ill wind that blows nobody any good," he told his reflection happily.

The wind had been blowing in just the right direction to speed them into Valetta and for more than a week, it blew in just the right direction to make it impossible for them to leave. None of the captains was particularly anxious to return to the trials and storms of the Mediterranean and Admiral Collingwood was happy to give his crews time to rest and recuperate. He would have stayed in the harbour for the rest of the winter had it not been for Nelson's strict commands that the seas should be patrolled. As it was, he delayed for as long as he could and only set sail again when the wind was in exactly the right quarter. By that time, Mr Turner was struggling with the second recurrence of his fever and in no state to re-join the ship, so it was decided to leave him behind until their next visit.

Nobody on the lower deck was the least bit surprised to hear it. A seaman's life was transitory at best and usually short, as those who had lived through a battle were only too well aware.

"I allus knowed we'd sail without him," Tom said. "Stands to reason with a fever. We don't want no fevers aboard an' all of us breathin' the same air. 'T'ent healthy. 'Sides, we got a good ship's carpenter in of Jem." He was proud of his shipmate's promotion, even if it meant they wouldn't mess together. "He'll see us all right. An' Mr Turner'll be better when the spring comes, you see if I en't right. Make a world a difference will the spring."

Old Josh growled. "If it ever comes," he said, wiping his beard, "which I got my doubts about. You ask me we're stuck with a long winter an' more storms, I shouldn't wonder."

But his pessimism was misplaced. Spring came in its old dependable way, with a sudden waft of scented air to lift their spirits and a gentleness of sunshine to dry their sails and their slops.

"Although what good it'll do," Josh grumbled, as they skimmed through the green waters, "I can't say. Now we shall have the Frenchies out of harbour an' a fight on our hands."

"You'm never satisfied," Tom teased him. "Tha's your trouble."

"Tha's on account of I knows what's what," Josh said. "They'll be out, you mark my words."

But three weeks went by and the sun grew stronger and the

sea remained peaceful and there was no sign of a French sail, although they patrolled all the most likely places and kept a weather eye open as long as there was daylight to see by.

"'T'won't please Lord Nelson," Jem said, when he and Tom met up in their leisure time to chew tobacco and gossip.

"Can't do much about it though, can he?" Tom said. "If the beggars won't come out an' fight, they won't, an' that's all there is to it. He'll just have to exercise some patience like the rest of us."

NELSON'S IMPATIENCE was as strong as a storm, but he did what he could to curb it by keeping himself busy attending to the care of his men and his ships and, as usual, found plenty to do. He sent for his secretary at first light and kept him busy all day, writing letters at his dictation, and in private moments, he wrote to Emma telling her how much she was missed and how dearly she was loved, glancing up from the notepaper from time to time, to gaze at her picture on the cabin wall.

My heart is with you, he wrote, cherish it. I shall, my best beloved, return — if it please God — a victor; and it shall be my study to transmit an unsullied name. There is no desire of wealthy no ambition that could keep me from all my soul holds dear. No! It is to save my country that I sail for so long.

Every forever, I am yours, only yours, even beyond this world.

CROUCHED on the deck of the frigate *Amphion*, Marianne was spending her leisure time composing letters too. She'd written three long epistles since that first difficult composition and had grown so accustomed to the sight of her handwriting spreading across the page, and so used to the business of finding suitable things to say that she'd become quite fluent. She'd described the snowstorm in some detail, naturally, and told her mother what mortal peril they'd been in and how close they'd come to being broached and how bravely they'd struggled through it, bragging a little, like the sailor she was. When she read it through to Moll and Peg, she was afraid she might have bragged too much and added a postscript to reassure her poor mother that no harm had been done.

Howsumever you en't to worry on my accounty dearest Ma. 'Tis all plain sailing now. We skuds along all chearly like with narry a care in the world so long as them old Frenchies don't come out for to give us aggravation which they en't shown no sines a doing this many a monthy which long may it continew.

Then she hid the letter in her ditty bag to wait for the next packet boat, feeling pleased with her endeavours. She hadn't said anything about her search for Jem, but she supposed her mother would understand that you can't go looking for people when you're in the middle of an ocean — even if you wanted to. She was a sailor now and must live her life according. Except for the times she spent with Johnny Galley.

The plain sailing continued, to everyone's relief. The French continued to skulk in the harbours to everyone's relief except the Admiral. It looked as though they were going to sail round and round the Mediterranean all through the spring, just as they'd done all through the winter, without a shot being fired.

The warm days passed without incident. March breathed into April and April eased into the warmth of May. There was nothing for the crew to do but work the ship, carry messages for the Admiral, eat their meals and take their ease. Which Marianne and Johnny did most happily. But then, just when they weren't expecting it, everything changed. Late one easy afternoon a frigate sailed into view and it was flying the one signal Marianne didn't want to see: *The enemy is at sea.*

There was instant and ordered activity aboard the *Amphion* and the four ships of the line that were sailing with Nelson when the order came. The frigate was despatched to spread the news to the rest of the fleet, which was patrolling the seas around Corsica and Sardinia, and the five ships put on sail and made all speed to the southern coast of France.

Marianne obeyed orders with the rest of the crew, climbing the rigging and setting sails and doing whatever was required of her, but her mind was numb with disbelief and she worked mechanically without being aware of what she was doing. They couldn't be sailing towards a battle, surely to goodness. Not after all this time. There was no sense in it. How was she to jump ship when she was out in the middle of the Meddytranium? More pressingly, where could she hide if the Frenchies started firing their cannon? She kept an eye open for Johnny, but he was on the lower deck among his fellow gunners, clearing the decks for action, and had forgotten all about her. She looked for Peg and Moll, but they were kept as hard at work as she was and didn't have time to talk or even look at her. She wanted to howl because she was afraid but howling was a waste of time and she knew it. And once they'd relayed their message, the ship made steady progress towards the enemy, its bows cleaving the green water clean as a knife and making the spray rise with a hiss, its sails cracking like a cat-o-nine-tails in the strong wind. This can't be happening, she thought, over and over again. Please, God, don't let it happen. I'll never commit adultery again, I promise, if You'll just make it not happen.

As the hours passed and their progress continued, she grew calmer. If they had any sense, the Frenchies would get out of the way and go off and hide somewhere, the way they'd been doing all these months. They might have done it already, for all she knew. We might get to the French coast and find it empty of any ships at all, the way we done so many times. Anything was possible.

But the French ships were waiting for them and although their gun ports were still closed, there were so many of them and they looked so formidable under full sail and with their colours flying that she was afraid all over again, her heart thudding against her ribs and her mouth dry. She stood by the rail and counted them, watching as they shifted and manoeuvred — eight men-a'-war and six frigates. Oh my dear heart alive, she thought, 'tis fearsome odds. There's fourteen of them an' only six of us. We shall be blown out the water.

The officers were shouting orders again and there was a rush to obey them. The ships had to change tack and form a column and prepare for action. The decks were sanded and sprinkled with water; nets were carried up from below and hung across the upper deck and the quarter-deck to prevent injury from flying splinters; the bosun and his mates were puddening the yards; the loblolly boys were setting barrels of fresh water by the masts and the scuttlebutts and carrying empty buckets down to the orlop deck where the surgeon was preparing his table and sharpening his knives, the marines were stationed in the gangways and in the tops; there were powder monkeys everywhere, carrying shot of all kinds and the captain was on the quarter-deck in his full dress uniform, silk stockings, gold lace and all. The battle was almost upon them. There was no time to stop, no time to think, no time to breathe.

And then, just as suddenly as the preparations had begun, they came to a halt. The French ships were on the move, their battle line breaking, they were turning north, sailing towards the harbour, disappearing section by section, lower decks, upper decks, mast after mast, yard after yard, staysails, topmasts, colours and all, until they were lost under the horizon and the sea was clear of them.

Below decks, the gunners were cheering as though they'd won a victory and were mocking the yellow-bellied Frenchies' for cowards; the powder monkeys were wiping the sweat out of their eyes and looking pleased with themselves; the captain was scowling because they'd lost an opportunity and he knew how annoyed the Admiral would be, but Marianne was limp with relief because she'd been spared a battle.

Peg was at her side, staring at the empty sea. "Well, what d'you make a that?" she asked.

"'Twill be something to write home about," Marianne told her. "Shows what cowards the Frenchies are. I knew they'd cut an' run."

"'Twon't please our Nelson," Peg said. "You mark my words."

"I can't help about Nelson," Marianne said. "It pleases me." And she wondered what Johnny would think of it.

"That's Frenchies for you," he said, when they met in the cabin the next day. "Lily-livered the lot of 'em. Why are we wasting time talking?"

Later, as she was getting her breath back, she remembered that she'd promised not to commit adultery any more. It was a nasty moment and it made her feel horribly anxious, because it had been a solemn promise, almost like a prayer, and even if it hadn't been a prayer, it was a serious bargain with Fate which was just as binding. She ought to have remembered it, not gone ahead and forgotten all about it. But she *had* forgotten about it and she had gone ahead and now it was too late. She lay very still and quiet, thinking about it. Maybe it wouldn't matter that much. After all, it wasn't the sort a' promise anyone could keep, not really, not when you came to think about it. It was just something you said in the heat of battle. Wasn't it? People said all sorts a' things in the heat of the battle. But she *had* said it and she'd meant it at the time. She remembered that clearly. Oh my dear life, she thought, what can I do about it now?

"Time for 'ee to cut off," Johnny said, giving her shoulder a shake. She was looking uncommon dreamy and it wouldn't do for her to fall asleep.

She stirred herself. "What?"

"Back to duty," he said.

CHAPTER 10

Portsmouth was in the grip of invasion fever that summer and, like so many of her neighbours, Mary Morris was irritable with anxiety.

"We shall all be killed in our beds," she said, ironing furiously. "That's what'll happen to us, you mark my words, every blamed one of us. Killed in our beds and I don't know what else besides. It fair makes my blood run cold to think of it. 'Tis no earthly use you pullin' a face an' sayin' 'No you won't'. Why d'you think they're building watch towers all along the coast, an' pilin' up beacons — you've only to look up an' you can see 'em on the heights — an' sendin' soldiers, an' I don't know what-all? If that don't mean an invasion's a-coming I don't know what does."

"They done that last year," Jack Morris said, smoking his pipe and trying to be reasonable, "which you got to allow, an' nothin' come of it."

"Last year was last year," Mary said, pushing her damp hair out of her eyes. The kitchen was hot with steam and hung about with sheets and towels and pillow cases, dripping from the racks on the ceiling, ironed and airing before the stove, piled damply into laundry baskets on every inch of floor. It had been a bad day for drying clothes and Mary was weary with too much work, her hands sore and red, her back aching fit to split in half. She held the iron towards her cheek and sighed. It wasn't hot enough to use any more. She stooped to set it on the trivet and took up another one, straightening her back before she set to work again.

"This year, last year, I can't see no difference," her husband said mildly.

"Tha's on account of you en't a-looking in the right direction," Mary told him crossly. "There's all the difference in the world. He wants for to be emperor seemingly. Tha's the difference."

"Who wants to be emperor?"

"Boney, that's who. Wants to be emperor. Lizzie was tellin' me just this very afternoon."

"Well then let him," Jack said. "Tha's my opinion of it. 'Ten't none of our affair."

"How can 'ee talk such nonsense?" Mary said, her cheeks hot with work and exasperation. "If he wants to be emperor then he wants an empire. Stands to reason. You can't be an emperor without an empire. An' where's he goin' to get an empire from? You tell me that. Why he'll come here for it. That's what he'll do. We're to be his empire. 'Tis as plain as the nose on my face. He'll come here with his cannon an' his soldiers an' his great ships an' he'll walk all over us, you just see if he don't, an' we shall be his slaves. So don't you tell me he en't comin', for I knows better."

"He won't come to Portsmouth," Jack said. "Not with all our ships hereabouts."

"'Course he'll come to Portsmouth," Mary said. "'Tis a port. Where else would he come? 'Tis just the very place. An' where's Lord Nelson when we needs him? Gallivantin' in foreign parts, that's where he is, when he ought to be in the Channel, keeping watch, which would bring our Marianne back home again, where she ought to be an' which he should ha' done long since. She got no right to be gallivantin' in foreign parts. That's my opinion of it. Fourteen months she's been away, I'll have you know. Fourteen months an' another winter comin' on. It's enough to worry anyone sick."

"She's writ to 'ee," Jack pointed out.

"Four letters in fourteen months," Mary said, bitterly, "an' the last one all about some battle she could ha' been caught up in."

"Which she never," Jack said, with heavy patience. "The Frenchies cut an' run. I remember you an' Lizzie readin' it out."

"An' what if they hadn't?" Mary said. "She could ha' been blowed to bits. 'Ten't right, a bit of a girl in the middle of a battle. I don't know what the world's a-comin' to, I truly don't. Girls at sea, where they never ought to be in all conscience, an' Boney comin' for to invade us."

It was too much for Jack Morris. He'd never been able to stand her outbursts, and this was a bad one. If the Frenchies were going to come, they'd come and all the talk in the world wouldn't stop them. "I'm off out," he said, standing up and reaching for his purse on the mantelpiece. "Time to wet the ol' whistle."

"Oh that's it," Mary said angrily. "Run off, I should. Turn your back. That'll stop ol' Boney, I don't think!"

But he was already opening the door.

He never faces up to anything, Mary thought mutinously. 'Tis the most aggravating thing about him. And I knows I'm in the right. They wouldn't be putting up all those great towers and building beacons and recruiting troops if they didn't think there was like to be an invasion. 'Twill be no earthly good runnin' off to wet his dratted whistle when the soldiers are at the door. God save us all. What are we to do when the soldiers are at the door?

SHE WAS CERTAINLY RIGHT about Napoleon's imperial ambitions. His invasion fleet was ready on the other side of the channel with over 60,000 fully armed troops primed and under orders. And preparations for his coronation were well in hand.

In July, the French fleet in Toulon fired off their cannons to celebrate his "historic decision" to be crowned. And the next morning, not to be outdone, Nelson gave orders for the British fleet to fire an even bigger salute to mark the sixty-sixth birthday of King George III. But, when the smoke of these belligerent tributes had drifted and dispersed, nothing was changed. The French fleet was still safely tucked away in the harbour and although Nelson watched and waited, straining his remaining eye with constant observation, they showed no signs of coming out again. He, too, was anxious in case England should be invaded, for he knew how real the threat of a seaborne invasion could be. It only needed a fair wind and the slightest lapse in the watchfulness of Admiral Cornwallis and his fleet, and the French could be on the beaches. But the weeks passed and became months as he prowled the French coast, waiting and watching, and there was no news of an invasion, which was a relief, but no hope of the battle he was determined to fight either, which was an endless irritation.

"This is an odd war," he complained to his captains, when they were gathered about his table on a quiet evening in October. "Not a battle! We've been at sea for seventeen months, and many of us haven't set foot ashore in all that time. Bonaparte means to be crowned an emperor, thereby showing his overweening pride, and yet his fleet still hides in Toulon and can't summon up the courage to come out and face us."

They agreed with his opinion of their opponent's cowardice and one or two of them were encouraged to ask whether they were going to spend another winter at sea.

"If they won't come out and face us in good weather," Captain Hardy said, "are they like to do it in bad?"

"According to our spies," Nelson told them, "Bonaparte is considering opening peace negotiations with Mr Fox."

"Is it likely, do you think?" Hardy asked.

"It is impossible to guess at the state of mind of a putative emperor," Nelson said, wryly. "But should it turn out to be the case we shall doubtless be recalled, and the decision will be made for us. More wine, gentlemen?"

News filtered through to them slowly as autumn chilled into winter. The dreaded invasion didn't come and letters on the last vessel to arrive reported that the weather in the Channel was so bad that it looked as though it would be postponed until the spring. There were no peace negotiations, but Napoleon gave no orders to his fleet to engage their waiting enemy either, so the sea patrols continued. They were now well into their second winter at sea and they seemed to have reached a stalemate, which showed no signs of being broken. After such a long fruitless wait, Nelson was at a low ebb, frustrated and depressed and, as he was now beginning to admit, not in the best of health.

During the long dull days he wrote letters — to Emma, lovingly and often, to suppliers with detailed instructions of the goods he needed, and, after giving it thought for several days, to his physician, who was the one person to whom he could speak freely about his health and the miserable state he was in and could be told that he was wondering whether he ought to ask for a few months' leave.

Although I am ready to die for my country, he wrote, *I cannot see that allowing myself to degenerate into a helpless invalid would benefit anybody.*

He reported that his stump was a better predictor of the coming weather than any barometer and that although he was obeying instructions and wearing a green shade over his eyes for protection against the glare of the sun, *I can every month perceive a visible (if I may be allowed the expression) loss of sight.* In short, he admitted that his health was poor and that he was troubled to be in such a wretched state when he needed to be in full possession of all his powers when he faced the coming battle.

Finally, after thinking about it for several weeks, he wrote a courteous request to Viscount Melville, the new First Lord of the Admiralty, to ask for leave of absence *for the re-establishment of my health* and to suggest that Bickerton was capable of commanding the fleet *in the present conditions.*

Then there was nothing to be done except wait for a reply.

What arrived was a cutter with letters from his spies in Gibraltar, reporting that Spain intended to throw in its lot with Bonaparte and declare war on England "within the month", and secret instructions from the Admiralty that he was to dispatch two frigates to intercept a Spanish treasure fleet which had sailed from Montevideo and was currently off Cadiz and bound for Ferrol.

"Two frigates are insufficient," he said to Hardy. "We need greater fire power if we are to take a treasure fleet. Send a message to the *Donegal* that she is to proceed to Cadiz with four."

The *Donegal*, which was a ship of the line and carried eighty guns, duly put on all sail and proceeded — accompanied by four frigates. And one of the four was the *Amphion.*

MARIANNE WAS QUITE PLEASED to be sent aloft to put on more sail. She'd been feeling just a sight too queasy for the last week or so, retching and heaving at the least movement of the ship, and being kept busy would take her mind away from her sickness. It annoyed her that she was being seasick. She'd always been proud of withstanding the sea no matter what and now here she was spewing with the rest of 'em.

Peg said there was no accounting with seasickness and rubbed her back when she passed her hanging over the stern, but Moll was thoughtful.

"'Ten't like you, my lubber," she said, when she found Marianne crouched against the capstan recovering from a particularly miserable bout. "You was allus fit as a flea."

Marianne felt too ill to answer her and they were being given orders, so the moment passed. But it was a nuisance and she had to admit it.

Now, as the *Amphion* sped through the green waters with a fair wind to fill her sails and all hands hard at work, she felt quite herself again. 'Twas idling what made me sick, she thought. That's all. And she wondered what they would do when they met up with the treasure fleet. It would be quite an adventure.

The four ships of the treasure fleet hove into view just outside Cadiz, travelling at a stately pace and heading towards the harbour. The gunners were soon at action stations with Johnny Galley among them. Not that they would be called on to fire off their cannon. She knew that. Johnny had explained it to her, not long after they'd set sail. "We'll show 'em our guns," he'd said, "an' they'll do as we tell 'em and hand over the gold. That's the style of it. Then we'll share out the prize money and go home rich as lords." And he'd grinned at her and gone below to the gun deck.

It didn't work out quite as he'd predicted. The Spanish ships hove to right enough, as soon as they were accosted, but they didn't show a white flag. They lined up ready to do battle.

Marianne was horrified. They couldn't be going to fight, surely to goodness. Not against a ship of the line. But there was no time to think about it, for commands were being given. They were to change tack to line up in opposition and she was being ordered up into the rigging. She knew that was just the place where they'd be aiming those great guns of theirs, but she did as she was told and looked chearly about it, climbing quickly and working as neatly as she could given that her heart was thundering in her chest and her hands were shaking. When she looked down, she could see the enemy gun ports opening, the mouths of their cannon glinting in the sunlight. My dear heart alive, she thought. What if they fire on us now?

They fired while the thought was in her head, with a roar that hurt her ears and a great deal of black smoke that spread from their gun ports like clouds, but their aim was poor, and the shot fell well short, each one hitting the water with a splash like a fountain head. She was down the rigging and had reached the deck before she was aware that she was moving. Then everything happened at speed. The *Donegal* opened fire with an even mightier roar from her forty great guns. Smoke swirled across the deck of the *Amphion* so that for a few seconds, Marianne couldn't see what was happening. Then there was another frightening roar and one of the Spanish ships exploded before her eyes, shooting flames and debris high into the air. It was so powerful and so dramatic, she was impressed despite her fear. And then it was all over. The other three Spanish ships were running up white flags. I been in a battle, she thought, an' I've come through an' I en't been blowed up an' all those people on that ship have. Poor souls. Then she was sick.

She went on feeling sick while the longboats were sent out to gather up their haul and bring it back to the *Donegal* and the three Spanish ships sailed off towards Cadiz, defeated and denuded of treasure. Supper than night was a celebration, but she felt too queasy to do justice to it and she was still feeling sick the next morning when they re-joined the British fleet and their captains were rowed across to the *Victory* to report to the Admiral.

"I never knew the likes of you," Moll said, when the three girls were using their holystones and Marianne was pale with nausea. "If weren't for the fact that you en't found him, I'd ha said your husband was the cause of all this retching and spewin'. Last woman I seen who was as sick as that was in the family way."

"Well, I en't found him," Marianne said quite crossly, "so you're wrong." But she could feel her heart shrinking with a new kind of alarm. What if that's what it was? People *were* sick when they were carrying. She'd seen some of 'em. And she an' Johnny had been living like man an' wife for a good long time, she couldn't deny it. And then there was that promise she should have kept and never did. What if this was a punishment for not keeping her side of the bargain? It could be. Now she came to think on it, she hadn't seen her courses for an age. Not that that signified, for they came irregular and always had. But what if Moll was right? It didn't bear thinking about. No, no, she thought. I can't be carrying. I won't be. An' I won't think about it neither. Moll could be wrong. 'Tis a fool's game to sit about moping, when it's something what might never happen. Best thing to do is just get on with things the way I always done an' not go thinking too much. I'll write to of Ma, first chance I get, an' tell her about the battle, that's what I'll do, and how I seen a Spanish ship blowed up to smithereens afore my eyes. My stars but she'll like that. 'Tis a rare of tale to tell and 'twill brighten up her life considerable. They has a dull ol' time of it in Portsmouth. But worry niggled in her mind and kept her awake at night no matter what she did.

NELSON TOOK the reports from his captains more easily than they'd expected. He smiled benignly upon them as they sat round his table eating the breakfast he'd ordered for them, urged them to eat hearty and told them he hadn't thought to see the Spanish put up a fight any more than they had, adding, "But such are the fortunes of war."

"They won't take kindly to losing their revenue," Captain Hardy remarked, cutting into a good stout slice of ham. "We must expect reprisals."

"According to our spies," Nelson told him, "They are likely to declare war upon us within the month. However 'twill be of little consequence to us whatever they decide to do. They have a considerable army by all reports, but their fleet is small and ill prepared."

"Do we know how many French ships are presently in Toulon?" the captain of the *Donegal* wanted to know.

"Our most dependable sources tell us there are eleven of the line and eighteen frigates," Nelson told him. "And would they were at sea."

There was a general grumble of agreement. They'd been playing cat and mouse quite long enough.

"Here's to our victory," Hardy said, raising his glass. "May it be granted to us soon."

Sitting there in his familiar stateroom among his admirable captains, Nelson was regretting his decision to ask for leave. He felt he had been unwise and precipitate. But the deed was done, the request had been sent and now there was nothing he could do except wait to hear what the Admiralty were going to do about it. He hadn't said anything to his captains, naturally — leave was a private matter — although he'd written to Emma, telling her he would be home to spend Christmas with her at "our beloved Merton". Now with December imminent and the weather unpredictable he was beginning to think they wouldn't meet again until the New Year.

MARIANNE'S fifth letter was delivered to her mother on Christmas Eve and because it was very long and had a lot of words in it that they couldn't make head nor tail of, she and Jack took it down to The Dolphin to ask the landlord if he would be so kind as to read it to them. It was read aloud, once to them and once to the assembled regulars, who all thought it was a fine thing.

"Blowed to smithereens," they said. "My stars! That'll show 'em. You got a fine gel there, Mrs Morris. Good as a boy she is, any day. What a tale she'll have to tell when she comes home."

It made Mary feel quite proud to hear such praise being heaped on her absent daughter, but it didn't stop her worrying.

"I can't see why she don't come home now," she said to Jack, when the two of them were back in their kitchen again, full of ale and warm with their neighbours' approval. "She's done enough for 'em in all conscience, bein' in a battle an' all, which you can't deny now. That *was* a battle an' no mistake. They ought to send her home soon, surely to goodness. They can't keep that great fleet at sea for ever, now can they? I don't want her in any more battles. She's only a gel when all's said an' done."

"She en't a gel," Jack contradicted, cleaning his pipe over the stove.

"She's a woman growed, an' a married woman, don't 'ee forget, an' if you ask me, she'll go her own way an' beggar the consequences, the way she done when she took the shillin' in the first place."

"Aye," Mary sighed, "so she will, but what way is it like to be? That's the question. What way is it like to be? She en't found Jem an' she can't stay in the navy for ever and she must come home soon, surely to goodness. 'Tis all such foolishness."

CHAPTER 11

With an irony that certainly wasn't lost on him, Nelson's long-awaited letter from the Admiralty arrived just after dark on Christmas Day. At any other time, he would have welcomed the news it contained, for his application for leave was granted and could be taken *"at such time as was convenient"* and his suggestion that Bickerton could take over command during his absence was accepted too. But it had come too late. His watchful frigates had just sent him a message that the French fleet in Toulon was embarking troops, so he knew that they'd had orders to come out and give battle at last and that after waiting so long he was about to see action. There was no possibility of taking leave now. The hour was too pressing. He set the letter aside, gave orders to Hardy to put on more sail and sent his remaining frigates with messages to the fleet to tell them to make preparations. Within an hour, he was in sight of the enemy coast.

It was a clear night and he had a good view of the harbour, even with his inadequate eyesight, but it was plain that the French fleet were amusing themselves by sending up night signals and they showed no signs of sailing out of the harbour. He watched for an hour or two as blue lights were burned, and rockets soared into the night sky, then, since nothing else was happening, he gave orders that a close watch should be kept and went down to his cabin to rest and prepare himself for battle.

THE *AMPHION* SET off on her errand before he was asleep. Marianne was woken at eight bells by the speeding rhythm of the ship and knew she was under full sail. Being four in the morning, it was still completely dark, and the rest of her watch grumbled out of their hammocks to light lanterns and tell one another they hoped there was some good warming grub to look forward to come breakfast. But Marianne was quiet.

During the last few weeks while the *Amphion* had been sent on one errand after another, hunting without success for any Spanish ships they could find and keeping a look out for any change of activity on the part of the French, she'd been observing some very worrying changes of her own. At first, she'd tried to dismiss her growing belly as a sign of greed. She enjoyed her food too much. That was what it was. But the weeks passed, and she ate no more than usual and certainly with less appetite and her belly went on growing. Now she was as sure as she could be that Moll was right and that she was carrying a child and she was so caught up in panic and shame that she hardly knew what she was doing. She went about her duties like someone in a dream, sitting back on her heels at thoughtful intervals with the holystone idle in her hands. The lieutenant of the watch had to speak to her quite sharply. But to hear someone say, "*Look chearly; boy. We ain't got all* day", was so inappropriate that it made her feel hysterical. She wanted to laugh and scream and lift up her jacket and show him her belly. She couldn't, of course, so she took her feelings out on the deck, scrubbing it as hard as her diminished energy would allow. Little do 'ee know, young cock a' the walk, she thought, keeping her head down and not looking at him, I en't a boy. I'm a woman grow'd — an' growin'.

But what was she going to do about it? She couldn't stay on board much longer or someone would notice. If they'd only put into the sort of harbour where merchant ships were like to call, she could jump ship, buy herself a skirt and a bonnet and find a passage home — providing she could scrape together enough money to pay for it. But how much would it be? And which harbours were likely? And what sort of ship would be prepared to take a passenger? She'd learnt a lot about life at sea, but she hardly knew anything about life ashore. I shall have to tell Moll and Peg, she decided. They been in the navy longer'n me an' one or other of 'em will be bound to know something. Not that she had a moment to talk to them that day. They were all kept too hard at work, changing tack and unfurling sails, as the *Amphion* hunted for one of Admiral Collingwood's ships so as to deliver Lord Nelson's message.

They found one at the end of the first dog watch, when the three girls were supposed to be at rest and were sitting by the mainmast taking a breather. She was a frigate and she was sailing out of the straits of Messina.

"The *Sirius* is that," Johnny Galley said, coming up to stand before them. "An' as sweet a ship as you're ever like to find. I sailed aboard her one time. As sweet a ship as you're ever like to find."

"Is she one a' Collingwood's?" Moll wanted to know.

"She is, an as sweet a ship as you're ever like to find."

"Aye, so you keeps a-sayin'," Moll said.

"En't you got work to do?" Johnny said, and skipped out of her way before she could kick out at his legs.

"Blamed fool," she said, when he was out of earshot.

Marianne looked across at the *Sirius* and sighed.

"You'll find him one day," Peg said. "You see if you don't."

Marianne sighed again. "I wasn't thinkin' a' my Jem," she

admitted. "I've give up thinkin' of him long since. I don't reckon I shall find him now. He could be anywhere."

"You got a face as long as a wet week," Moll said. "If it ain't Jem, what is it?"

It was a good moment. There was no one around to hear what they were saying. They were all too busy looking at the *Sirius*. "You know what you said about me bein' sick an' all," she said. "Well, you was right."

"I knew you was carryin'," Moll said. "Only had to look at 'ee to see that. So who's the father? It's that Johnny Galley, ain't it?"

Marianne felt so miserable she could only nod.

"How could 'ee've been so foolish?" Moll said. "You might ha' knowed no good 'ud come from that one. Love 'em an' leave 'em is Johnny Galley, an' he won't be a blamed bit a use to 'ee now."

Peg was much more sympathetic. "What will you do?" she asked, blue eyes concerned. "You'll have to jump ship, won't you? 'Course. An' if you've got any sense, you'll do it first port we come to. Gibraltar maybe. There's ships a-plenty in Gibraltar what 'ud tek 'ee home. Or in Malta, only we don't seem to go into Malta nowadays. We allus stay at sea. 'Twould do for 'ee if we did, only we don't. Anyways, you can't stay in the navy. That's a certain sure thing. Cheer up. You can jump ship easy. We'll look after you. Least you ain't being sick no more."

It wasn't much comfort to Marianne, for a swollen belly was more obvious than sickness. But at least she now knew the sort of ports she ought to be aiming for. "Thank 'ee kindly," she said to Peg, and did her best to smile. I should ha' stuck to looking for Jem, she thought, an' not gone along with Johnny. I should ha' kept my promise an' that's the truth of it. But love was sweet, there was no denying it. If only it didn't lead to trouble. An' I did try to find him. I tried an' tried.

~

JEM HAD RUN up on deck as soon as the *Sirius* hove to and he and Tom were standing by the rail chewing tobacco, enjoying a spot of idleness and watching the *Amphion* as she rocked on a grey swell a few hundred yards away. Her longboat was being rowed across with its message and Tom was entertaining them by guessing what it was going to be, each guess being more preposterous than the last.

"We're to set sail for the West Indies," he said.

Jem laughed at him. "With the Frenchies in Toulon?"

"Well then, we're to have double rations a' grog an' double pay till the end a' the voyage."

"Double rations a' grog could be likely. I'll grant 'ee that. But I en't sure about the pay."

"Well then, 'tis orders for us all to go home for the New Year. How would that suit?"

Jem made a grimace. "It'll be a deal more serious than that," he said. "An' what's more serious than going home, pray?"

"Not goin' home," Jem told him.

He sounded so decided about it that Tom was intrigued. "Don'tcher want to go home?" he asked.

Jem shrugged his shoulders. "Not particular. There en't nothing for me there. They'll have forgot all about me by now." Then, because thinking about it was making him feel uncomfortable and homesick again, he changed the subject. "Look at them three idle great lumps a boys," he said. "Sittin' by the mainmast. See 'em? They been there ever since we hove to. En't they got no work to do?"

"We're as bad," Tom pointed out, spitting a long stream of tobacco into the sea. "We been a-standin' here since we hove to."

"That's different altogether," Jem said. "We en't boys."

They weren't going home either as they discovered as soon as they set sail again and the news that the Frenchies were out was spread from station to station. It caused a predictable stir and much bravado. "We'll blow 'em out the water, won't us, boys? 'Twill be a battle an' a half."

Jem wasn't at all sure how he felt about being in a major sea battle. He was a bit too well aware that the *Sirius* could be blown out of the water just as easily as a French ship. Not that there was anything he could do about it. They were all locked aboard with no hope of escape and they must sail on and accept their fate, whatever it was and however soon it came.

THE GREAT FLEET gathered despite the fact that the weather was foul and made progress difficult; the ships took on supplies — but never once from a place that was any use to Marianne — and made sure they had plenty of water and lemons, for a battle is thirsty work; the gunners fired their cannon every first watch, timing and improving their speed. They ate well and drank deep and waited. But it wasn't until 19 January when the *Victory* was in Agincourt Sound, that the *Active* and the *Seahorse* finally arrived, flying the signal they were all waiting to see. *The enemy is at sea.*

"Now," they told one another, "we can get on with it. 'Tis just a matter of finding the beggars."

It was the worst possible time of year for tracking down an enemy fleet. For a start, there was a gale blowing up from the west-north-west, so that leaving the Sound was difficult. The entire fleet knew that a passage through the Straits of Bonifacio was impossible and that they would have to manoeuvre through a narrow and dangerous passage between the Biocian and Sardinian rocks. But they set off in good spirits following the *Victory* and keeping a weather eye out for the light at her stern. As darkness fell, she burnt a blue light and another ten minutes later and fifteen minutes after that, the fleet was clear of the Straits and the hunt had begun.

Marianne worked automatically, obeying orders but not

thinking about them. If they were hunting the French, they'd hardly be likely to take shelter in any sort of harbour now, and once they found them she would be in the middle of a battle whether she would or no. Her mind went round and round like a rat in a trap, but for all its scrabbling anxiety, she couldn't think of anything she could do.

"Cheer up, my hearty," Johnny Galley said, when they gathered for their dinner. "Don' look so down. We got good work to do."

"Blow 'em out the water, so we will," her mess mates told her.

She didn't answer them, for what could she say? She just sat amongst them and ate her plum duff and thought what fools they were to be talking so loud and bragging so much. And the ship plowed on towards the battle, dragging her fear and anxiety with it.

Next day, a storm blew up and they were hard put to it to make any progress at all. It battered them mercilessly for the next five days as they struggled to stay upright under storm staysails, and by the time the wind finally dropped, they were all tired out. But they were still no further on and they hadn't seen any sign of the enemy.

Nelson was in a fever of impatience, writing in his journal that he had *"neither ate, drank, or slept with any comfort"* for the last five days. He was miserably seasick, as he usually was in rough weather, and torn by the knowledge that he might have made the wrong decision when he gave the order to head for Sardinia. His spies had sent him two contradictory reports, one that the French fleet was heading towards the southern end of Sardinia, and would then proceed to Naples, Sicily and Egypt, the other — which was acknowledged to be mere rumour but was nevertheless a rumour strong enough to be reported — was that they had received orders to evade the British squadrons that were blockading Cadiz and to head west across the Atlantic to the French arsenal at Martinique. Sailing to protect Naples or Sicily or Egypt, meant that he had left the way clear through the Straits of Gibraltar, but if he'd stayed to guard the Straits, he would have left Italy and Egypt open to attack. Like so many decisions at sea, it was fraught with difficult possibilities.

The next morning, the *Seahorse* returned to the fleet, flying the signal that she had something to communicate and when Captain Boyle came aboard, he reported that he had seen an enemy frigate off Pula. The weather had been so thick he hadn't been able to follow it, but it was sailing in the expected direction. It was a sign, but, as Nelson was well aware, not a particularly strong one. One frigate was not the same thing as a fleet especially as the French admirals used their frigates as scouts and messengers in exactly the same way as he did. Nevertheless, he acted on the information and dispatched two of his own frigates to Palermo and Malta with letters to Sir John Acton and Admiral Ball to warn them of the situation. Then he continued his pursuit, dividing his fleet in two, sending the *Donegal* and two attendant frigates to the southern coast of Sicily and taking the rest of the fleet through the Straits of Messina himself.

MARIANNE CAME up on deck as the *Amphion* entered the Straits and the first thing she saw was a great mountain shooting flames into the air.

"My dear heart alive," she said to Peg, who had followed her up on deck "They've set fire to the mountain."

"No they ain't," Peg said easily. "Stromboli is that. 'Tis a volcano and that's what volcanoes do. There's another one up Naples way. Smokes like a chimbley."

"Never mind Stromboli," Marianne said. "'Tis an ill omen, that's what's *that* is. A blamed ill omen, all afire like that. 'Tis a-showin' us what's like to happen when we meets the Frenchies, an' the sooner we gets away from it the better 'twill be for us." The sight of it was making her shiver.

It took them quite a while to negotiate the narrow passage because it was crowded with small boats and the wind was contrary. They had to work the ship hard to make headway, but she kept an eye on the fiery mountain all the way. Oh, if only they could put into a port and she could jump ship.

And then, when they were through the channel and in clear water and she was beginning to put the horrid image from her mind, Johnny Galley came striding up to her to tell her she was wanted in the galley. She followed him, hoping it really was the galley and not the cabin, but he took the wrong direction as soon as they were down the companionway.

"No, Johnny," she said, stopping by the nearest cannon and putting her hand on it to steady herself. "I en't in the humour."

"'Course you're in the humour," he said, looking back at her and winking. "I never knowed you when you wasn't. Come on. We en't got more'n a minute or two." And he went striding off towards the wardroom.

She followed him although she didn't want to, and she knew it was a foolish thing to do. But she was in the most peculiar mood, heavily aware of her swollen belly, full of fear, resentful, irritable, prickling with superstition, the image of the mountain filling her mind with fire.

He opened the door and shoved her into the cabin. "Now let's have no more nonsense," he said and pushed up her jacket. Then he paused and looked at her belly. "My stars," he said, "You put on some weight, en'tcher? No wonder you say you en't in the humour. I shall have ter cut your portion." But he was joking, and his face was full of delight at the sight of her. That rounded belly was giving him the itch most pleasurable.

She was stung to a sudden and quite bitter fury. "Never mind put on weight," she said pushing his hands away. "I'll have you know, that's your weight I'm a-carryin'."

He was unbuttoning her breeches. "What you on about?" he said. "You en't never a-tellin' me 'tis my fault you'm so plump."

"Well, if it's not your fault," she said, "I don't know whose fault it is."

The understanding of what she was telling him took several seconds.

Then his face darkened into an ugliness she hadn't seen before. "Now look 'ee here," he said, "you better watch your mouth if you're goin' to say things like that. If you'm in the family way 'tis none of my affair. Make your mind up to it and don't go sayin' it is. You could have me flogged you say things like that."

"Don't you care what you done to me?" she said, appalled at his unkindness.

"I en't done nothin' to 'ee," he said. "Nothin'. Understand? An' don't you go a-sayin' I have, or I'll take a marlin spike to 'ee, so I will."

She was trembling with fear and fury. She couldn't stay in that hot smelly cabin with him another second. She buttoned her breeches with shaking hands, struggled to open the door and ran. Her heart was still juddering with distress when she emerged on deck and she was achingly close to weeping. She could feel the tears rising in her throat and pricking her nose. She needed to hide away and cry out her grief the way she'd done as a child whenever she was beaten. But there was no privacy aboard ship, no hidden corners, no larders or cupboards, no quiet fields where there was no one to see her except the corn or the cattle. Ships were hateful places, chock full of hateful people and she'd got to go on living on this one until they put into port and she could escape. "Please God," she prayed, "put us into port soon. I know I didn't keep my side a' the bargain last time but I'm on my own now an' I got to look after myself and this baby an' if I can't jump ship, I don't know what'll become of us. For Thine is the kingdom, the power and the glory, for ever and ever."

THEY SAILED east for the next two weeks and never went near a port. In fact, the frigates were kept so busy that there was no time to think and very little time to sleep and they even had to take on provisions at sea. The Admiral was fidgety with impatience, sending every available frigate to keep watch at every likely meeting place. The *Amphion* went to Funis, where nobody had anything to report and they couldn't go ashore even if they'd been able to enter the harbour because it was full of Musclemen and their ships; to Malta, where they stayed outside the harbour and met up with one of Admiral Ball's frigates at sea and, to nobody's surprise, were told that they had nothing to report. Then they went to Toulon, where nothing was happening and to Koroni, where nothing was happening, and then back to Malta for the second time, where they met up with their own fleet but didn't sail into harbour, and finally the entire fleet took sail to Alexandria, which lay hot and stinking in the full glare of the Mediterranean sun and couldn't be visited. It was springtime by then and as hot as summer at that latitude and Marianne was mightily uncomfortable in her heavy jacket with the baby swelling her belly further and further with every passing day.

I *must* get off this ship, she thought, pausing in her labours to rest her back, I *must*, I just *must*, or I shall have to hide away in the hold and have the baby there, all in among the rats a-scuttling and scrabbling about and the bilge water stinking to high heaven and I don't know what-all, and what will become of us if I has to do that I dreads for to think. Her thoughts were scuttling and scrabbling in panic. It was all very well for Peg and Moll to promise they'd help but what could they do? They were women dressed as boys and they didn't know any more about birthing a baby than she did. If she was home in Portsmouth, she would have her mother to help her and probably old Mother Catty as well, for she helped with all the babies. But what was the good of thinking about that now? She was here, in this prison of a ship and all on her own. That was the truth of it. And she would have to go on with it all on her own with her shipmates giving her the oddest looks and Johnny Galley ignoring her and everything as bad as it could be. Oh, if only she could jump ship.

THEY STAYED outside Alexandria until the Admiral had satisfied himself that the French were not about to attack the place and that there was no sign of them in the Eastern Mediterranean, then he sent orders that they were all to sail back to Malta. The order renewed Marianne's hope and set her planning again. If he would just let them into the harbour, just once, even for an hour or two. That was all she needed. It lifted her spirits quite wonderfully to see the island again, its familiar stonework, the colour of honey under the spring sun and all those houses embedded in the hillside, and the old fortifications solid as rocks and the dome of the cathedral shining pink. As soon as she could slip away, she went below, took her purse from her ditty bag and tied it round her thickened waist under her breeches. They were bound to take on water, if nothing else, and now she was ready. She climbed back on deck, excited and determined, prepared to obey all orders to the letter provided they were going to take her into the release of that harbour.

It was an aching disappointment to discover that, yet again, they were going to stay at sea. "What's the matter with him?" she said to Peg as the no two of them stood by the capstan awaiting orders. "We got a fair wind. We could be in and out in less time than it takes to shake a lamb's tail."

"In, I daresay," Peg told her sagely, "but 'tis the getting out what worries our Nelson. He likes to weigh anchor the minute he hears news and if that wind was to be against him in that pertic'lar harbour, what it is at the moment what you got to allow, he couldn't move so much as an inch, not no how, there bein' onny the one way out."

"So here we'm stuck an' here we stay," Marianne grumbled, "what I don't think much of."

"Aye," Peg said. "That's about the size of it. Patience is a virtue at sea."

"I en't got no patience," Marianne said. "I gone past that. An' I en't got no time neither."

"There's a boat a-coming," Peg said, looking towards the harbour. "Very grand affair. Maybe 'tis news."

They watched as the grand affair was rowed to the *Victory* and a grand looking gentleman in a cocked hat was piped aboard. Marianne was saying her prayers again. Please God let it be something what'll take us into harbour. Just for an hour. That's all I need. One hour. Please God, for Thine is the kingdom. But then eight bells rang, and it was time to go below for dinner and they couldn't watch any longer.

There *was* news, but it didn't help Marianne in the slightest and it infuriated Lord Nelson. The French fleet had given him the slip once again and was back in Toulon. It was, as he told Captain Hardy, enough to try the patience of a saint. But saintly or not, he had to endure it. That afternoon, he set sail for the French coast prepared to resume his long, long watch.

The weeks passed in their enervatingly familiar way. The frigates were sent on one reconnaissance after another and all to no purpose. They took on fresh supplies of water and lemons at various watering holes, none of them ports. They sailed and watched, and the weeks went by. And then history suddenly repeated itself. The frigate *Phoebe* appeared, flying the message that the enemy were at sea.

"This time," his gunners told one another, "we shall catch the beggars and see 'em off once an' for all."

Frigates were sent to watch all the vantage points. The *Active* reported seeing a French fleet of eleven of the line, seven frigates and two brigs heading south-south-west with all sails set. Three supply ships joined the fleet and transferred their goods at sea.

The wait went on. The Admiral's impatience was acute, the gunners grew tetchy, and Marianne was in a fever of fear and frustration. Then news came that put Nelson in a temper.

Villeneuve's French fleet had been joined by six Spanish ships under the command of Admiral Gravina and the now combined and formidable fleet, totalling at least eighteen sail of the line, had passed unhindered through the Straits of Gibraltar and were on their way to the West Indies. There was nothing for it but to gather the British fleet together and give chase, for now it was Jamaica and the sugar islands that were under threat. He wrote a farewell message to Admiral Ball to keep him informed of the turn of events.

"My lot is cast," he said, *"and I am going to the West Indies, where, although I am late, yet chance may have given them a bad passage and may give me a good one: I must hope the best."*

Then he sent a sloop to Barbados to forewarn them that he was coming and to request an embargo on all ships in port, so as to prevent news of his approach reaching the enemy, and on the evening of 11 May, he sailed through the Straits of Gibraltar and out into the Atlantic.

Marianne was quite heartened to be sailing past the rock. "Then we a-goin' home," she said to Peg. "We must be, don't 'ee think? An' not afore time."

It was a profound shock to her when they continued west instead of heading north round the coast of Spain, and a worse one when Moll told her where they were really going. "Is it far?" she asked, her mouth trembling.

"'Tis half way round the world, accordin' to Johnny Galley," Moll said.

"An' how long's that a-goin' to take?"

"Months," Moll said. "Accordin' to Johnny. Even if we gets a fair wind. He's a bad lot but he knows what's a-goin' on."

"I can't go half way round the world," Marianne wailed. "How can I jump ship if I'm goin' half way round the world? 'Twill be the death a' me."

But her friends couldn't console her or give her any hope of a different outcome. "What's to come will come," Moll told her. "An' that's all there is to it. We've all got to make up our minds to it."

You en't carrying, Marianne thought, looking at her friend's weather-browned face and thinking how hard it was. You'd say different if you was. She put a hand on her belly and rubbed the place where she could feel her baby squirming under the skin. You'll be born in the hold, you poor little thing, she thought. That's what'll happen to 'ee. And it seemed most unfair to her. It was bad enough that she had to accept such a punishment, but she'd reneged on a solemn bargain, so she had to admit she deserved it. But to punish her baby along with her was cruel beyond belief. Oh, if only she hadn't given in to Johnny Galley.

CHAPTER 12

Jem Templeman enjoyed his passage across the Atlantic. "This is the life!" he said to Tom, as the two of them stood by the ship's rail, chewing tobacco in their customary way and watching the vast blue-green sea as it rolled away from them towards the distant horizon. They'd been sailing for more than a fortnight, and now they were scudding along before the famous trade winds, making good time, eating and drinking well and with very little work to do. The sun warmed them by day and the moon lit their passing by night and now and then a school of dolphins arrived to keep them company, curving sleek, blue-black and joyous from the white foam frothing at their bows. After their long, enervating battle with the winter storms of the Mediterranean, they were as warm and idle as lords.

Tom was growing a beard. He scratched the irritating stubble on his chin and grinned at his friend. "What did I tell 'ee?" he said. "I knowed we'd be a-headin' west. We shall see some sights in the Indies, you mark my words."

Jem grinned at him. "If we don't meet up with Johnny Frenchman on the way," he said.

"No fear a' that," Tom said. "Johnny Frenchman's on the run an' don't mean for to be caught."

And long may it continue, Jem thought, although he didn't say so for fear of being thought a coward. He just leant on the rail, chewed his baccy and looked out at the rest of the fleet as it sailed formidably all around him, letting the sight of it lift his spirits.

"No," Tom went on philosophically, "we shan't see Johnny Frenchman, till we'm in sight a' land an' he can make a bolt for it if we gets too hot for him. You mark my words, he en't one for a fight. More of a cut an' run man is Johnny Frenchman. We shall catch him come the finish an' give him such a trouncing he won't darken no doors ever again, like we done to the Danes at Copenhagen. Now that *was* a battle an' no mistake."

There was something about the tilt of his head that made Jem envious. He knows what he's talking about, he thought. That's the voice of experience. "You were there?" he said.

"I was," Tom said, with a modestly understated pride. "Wasn't a gunner in them days, mind you, only a powder monkey, but 'twas hot work I can tell 'ee. I seen men blowed to bits afore my eyes. But we won through come the finish and came home with a deal a' prize money. Which is what we'll do when we've trounced Johnny Frenchman, you mark my words. You can buy your lady a new bonnet. Make her sweet again."

Jem shrugged. "She'll have forgot what I look like," he said lugubriously.

"Not if you comes home with a pocketful a' silver," Tom told him. "Makes a deal a' difference does a pocketful a' silver."

It was hurting Jem to realise how completely *he'd* forgotten what *she* looked like. He could only remember her hair although he was pushing his brain hard. "Ah well," he said. "'Tis all over now. Too much water under the bridge."

"Or over the ocean," Tom grinned.

That made them both laugh. He's a good mate, Jem thought. He'd stick by you, come what may. The thought was cheering and washed away his annoyance at not being able to remember Marianne's face. But he couldn't help wondering how she was and what she was doing. She *was* his wife when all was said and done.

∽

THE *AMPHION* WAS in the van, under full sail and less than half a league behind the *Victory*, and Marianne was down in the hold of the ship, looking for a dark corner where she could birth her baby if the worst came to the worst. It was a dank and fearsome place and it stunk to high heaven, for the bilge was sour after so many months at sea. The orlop deck had been bad enough because that was immediately below the gun deck and directly above the hold and the stench had risen into her nostrils through every crevice and with every movement of the ship and besides that it was painted red which made her think of blood and men being brought down there to have their arms and legs cut off. But at least in the hold it was quiet and empty, and nobody was likely to die there, and it was very dark for there were no candles alight, although there were sconces on the bulkheads. Providing she made no noise — could you birth a baby without making any noise? — she could keep hidden well enough. I'll bring an old jacket down, she planned, and hide it in the flour sacks and then I'll have something to wrap the poor little mite in to keep it warm. It made her feel better to be planning and she climbed back to the orlop deck pleased to have made her decision. But she was so engrossed in her thoughts that she didn't hear the footsteps coming down the companionway until the surgeon was standing before her.

"What's this?" Mr Murgatroyd said, scowling at her, his eyes sharp in the half light. "Have you been in the hold, boy? Well let me tell 'ee, there's no food for you to steal down there."

Marianne tried to gather her wits and find a suitable excuse for being where she was. "Please, sir," she said, "I come down to find you, sir. I was wondering if you needed any more loblollies."

"No, I don't," the surgeon said. "And if you'd wanted to ask you should have spoken to your lieutenant. There was no need to come lurking down here. Be off with 'ee. I don't hold with boys lurking below decks and especially fat ones."

She went — quickly — before he could start thinking of punishments. But she'd found her place and, bad though it was, it would do. It would have to.

The long chase continued, and they made good time, which her shipmates said was a fine thing and would buck the Admiral up no end. The baby grew and wriggled but stayed where it was. Her belly was now so big she was teased about it at every meal and called "Fatty" and "Pudden" and told she ate a deal too much and, when she didn't answer, she was pushed and slapped by her mocking messmates until her back was sore and arms were bruised. Johnny Galley served her very small portions, scowled at her if she dared to look at him and never said a word to her.

As the days passed, she worked more and more slowly and found it difficult to stand through the service of a Sunday and for most of her time she was wretched with fatigue. But she made what preparations she could. When her messmates were skylarking in the rigging, or mending their clothes, or sitting about listening to ghost stories, she found a quiet corner, sharpened her knife, cut her brother's old shirt into two baby-sized pieces so that she could make a long gown. With its roughly cut edges it didn't look particularly elegant and it was badly sewn together, for she only had a sailor's tough thread, but it was a gown so at least the child wouldn't be left naked, and what was left of the shirt would make clouts to use to clean herself with when the poor little thing had been born. Finally, on a quiet forenoon watch when the ship was skimming along and nobody was looking, she crept below and hid the gown and the clouts among the flour sacks. Then there was nothing more she could do but wait.

The sea was endless, the days were endless, the weeks passed endlessly, and nothing happened. Then they woke one morning to find that they were being followed by a foreign ship that looked like a merchantman.

Johnny Galley told his messmates it was an enemy privateer "what'll report back to the Frenchies. You mark my words."

"Better not come within gunshot, if that's the style of it," they said, "or we'll give un what-for."

But the ship stayed well out of range of their guns and, after tailing them for two days, it disappeared as suddenly as it had appeared, and they were on their own again.

"'Tis June now seemingly," Peg said, as they were scrubbing the decks one salty morning. "Or so the lieutenant was a-saying. Third a' June accordin' to his reckoning. We must be there soon, surely to goodness. We been sailin' for weeks."

Marianne was feeling out of sorts that morning. Her belly was as taut as a drum-skin, her titties were sore, her back ached, her legs ached, her head ached and, if she'd been left alone, she would have stayed in her hammock and slept the morning away, so she grunted and went on scrubbing. What was it to her that it was June? One day was as uncomfortable as all the others now. But Moll sat up on her heels and looked out across the sea. "We got company again," she said.

There were two sizeable merchantmen tacking towards them, one behind the other, British merchantmen, broad in the beam and low in the water, carrying full cargoes. By the time the three girls had finished scrubbing and emptied their buckets over the stern and stowed them neatly away, the first ship was alongside, and the captain had come up to the quarter-deck ready to speak to her.

She was a day's sail out of Georgetown, so her master said, carrying sugar, and yes, there *was* a French fleet in the Caribbean, although he couldn't say where. The news was welcome, limited though it was, and was signalled down the line towards the *Victory* at once.

"There you are," Peg said to her weary shipmate, as the parley went on, "we shall see land tomorrow. Think a that. An' not a minute too soon, you ask me. Now you'd best make yourself ready. We shall be sent ashore for fresh water first thing, you mark my words, an if you'm a-goin' to jump ship that's when you must do it. Johnny Galley can fix for you to be in the first boat. He owes you that at least."

Marianne looked across at the master of the merchantman in his jaunty black cap and his jaunty black jacket with its fine brass buttons winking in the sun and tried to get her mind to accept what she was being told. There was a nightmare unreality about this moment now that it had come. If she were truthful, she would have to admit that she didn't want to leave the safety of the ship, especially if it meant finding her way around a foreign land full of foreign people. What if they couldn't speak English? What would she do then? How would she earn a living with this baby weighing her down? And where would she birth it? And what would she do when it *was* born? Where could she go when she was so far from home and there was no one to help her? Oh, she mourned, as she listened to the slap of the waves against the hull and watched the jaunty buttons shine, what's to become of me?

But however frightened she felt, they were heading for this foreign land at speed along with the rest of the fleet and nothing she could do or say or think would stop them. She rolled out of her hammock the next morning tired to her bones and dragged up on deck like a weary old woman. The sky was a drama of blazing red and gold, the way it so often was at daybreak in this part of the world and, silhouetted on the horizon, was a long smoke-grey smudge.

"Barbados is that," Moll told her as they collected their buckets, "Accordin' to Johnny Galley. Where the sugar comes from. Land at last, eh, my lubber?"

The smudge resolved itself into an island as they did their chores. By the time they'd been down to the gun deck and eaten and cleared their breakfast, they'd sailed close enough to see that it was a green island, that it had a range of low hills heavy with foliage, and that everything about it was sumptuously coloured. It was ringed by long pure-white shining beaches and the inshore waters were such a dazzling green that the shadow cast by their sails was as blue as a midnight sky. Despite her foreboding, Marianne was touched by how beautiful it was.

They had to work the ship quite hard to make progress with very little inshore wind, but Marianne watched their approach whenever she could. Soon, she caught sight of a long grey wall, protectively stony against the rich colour of the sea, and not long after that she saw a group of small fishing boats heading out towards them, very scruffy looking boats with stained sails and two-man crews naked to the waist and as brown as any men she'd ever seen, with hard bold faces that made her flesh shrink with fear. A strong scent of flowers drifted to her across the water and she could see headlands to port and starboard but there was no sign of the harbour until they came about and suddenly, there it was, a huge wide expanse of easy water edged with respectable looking houses, almost like Portsmouth; so like in fact that she was cheered by the sight of it and began to feel that she might find a place for herself on this foreign island after all. Then there was no time for anything except retrieving the baby's gown and tying it round her bulky waist under her jacket and then obeying orders.

By mid-afternoon, the harbour was forested by English masts but there was no order to go ashore and pick up supplies. The captain was rowed off to the *Victory* and returned two bells later to talk to the bosun but still no order came. Marianne was so tense that it was giving her pains in her belly and as bells were rung and the first dog watch wore away and they were still waiting, the pains got steadily worse. By the time the order to go ashore was finally given, they were so severe it was hurting her to stand. But she struggled into the bum boat and, by breathing hard through the height of the pains, she managed to row with the rest and presently they tied up alongside a busy quay. Not Portsmouth. Oh very definitely not Portsmouth. The cobbles under her feet were the same hard mounds and the warehouses that faced her were built in the same neat-windowed style, but there all similarities ended.

For a start, it was unbelievably hot. The sun pressed down on her head and shoulders as if it were a lead weight. And although she could see one or two men who looked as though they might be English in their brown jackets and their cloth hats, there were foreign people everywhere, most of them brown-skinned and talking in a sing-song English she couldn't understand, barefoot men stripped to the waist pushing laden carts, women in cotton gowns, with their heads tied up like puddings in huge folded cloths, standing behind trestle tables offering the most peculiar looking objects — she couldn't tell whether they were fruits or vegetables — bunches of curved green things like scimitars, things with spiky leaves, brown lumps that looked as though they were made of wood, bark and all.

The next pain gripped her as she was wondering at them and by then the lieutenant had jumped ashore and was barking orders in his peremptory way, telling them all to look lively and pointing at the direction they were to take. But they were unsteady on their sea legs and it was taking them a little while to find out how to walk on dry land again, so they staggered about and joshed one another and said it was worse than bein' tiddly and didn't take much notice of him, which made him stamp with temper.

"Look chearly, you lazy lumps," he shouted. "We ain't got all day."

They gave him a mocking cheer and went stumbling after him

towards the warehouses and at that Peg glanced across at her silent friend and indicated with a toss of her head that she was to get off quickly in the opposite direction.

It was time and Marianne knew it, even though she also knew it would be impossible for her to run. But it was time just the same. Her shipmates were all on the move and there was a huge cart passing to give her cover, so she had to make the effort. She gathered her strength, took a sustaining breath and walked off as quickly as she could, across the bumpy discomfort of the cobbles and away from the quayside, pushing through the crowds into a narrow alley between two rows of dusty buildings, heading off blindly without the least idea where she was going.

The heat of the sun was making her feel dizzy, and the crush of so many strange people exhausted her and there were flies everywhere, crawling on her arms and clouding about her face. When the next pain began to grip, she had to stop and lean against the nearest wall or she would have fallen to the ground. She wanted to lie down somewhere quiet, where there wasn't anybody about, to stop walking and just give in to the pain, but she knew she daren't do it and that she had to keep on walking. She wiped the sweat out of her eyes and made another straining effort, dragging one foot after the other, moving almost without will, panting and exhausted, pausing while the pains gripped and then struggling on again.

Presently, she stopped to catch her breath and realised that she'd left the crowds and stalls and dusty houses behind and was standing on a narrow pathway with wooden shacks on one side of her and a field full of huge stalked plants on the other. There was nobody about except for a group of small solemn children, who were standing very close together, watching her and whispering to one another. Should she walk into the field and lie down there? No, the crop was too thick and forbidding. Should she go to one of the huts? No, not that either, for what could she say, and what would she do if they turned her away? She gazed about her, bleary eyed with pain, and caught a glimpse of a tall stone building some way off in the field. It had a rounded top and looked like a windmill. Maybe she could hide there, somewhere behind the building, where no one would see her. She stumbled on, panting and gasping in the hot dusty air.

It *was* a windmill and it stood in a sizeable clearing but there were so many workmen coming and going that she stayed where she was, hidden by the huge stalks of the crop. They were formidable-looking men, barefooted and naked to the waist and wearing trousers that were so stained and tatty, they were more earth than cloth. Their backs streamed with sweat and they were walking beside wooden carts piled high with the mounded stalks of the crop and pulled by pairs of oxen. How could she possibly sneak past such a crew? And yet, she had to lie down. Dear God, she *had* to lie down.

Several men came out of the mill together, and then another laden cart arrived that would give her cover, and for a few seconds, there was a scurry of activity and nobody was looking her way. She half walked, half ran until she was alone behind the mill. Then she had no more strength left and sank to her knees on the dry earth. Whatever was to happen to her now, there was nothing she could do but endure it. The next pain was so strong, she lay on the ground and groaned under the pressure of it.

Pains and minutes passed, the sun beat down on her sweating head, the flies crawled all over her face and up her arms, she could hear the workmen talking in their sing-song way and a bird giving a harsh croaking call, over and over again. I'm at the end of the world, she thought, and there's no one to help me. Now there was no time and no place, only the pain and the heat. When a face moved into focus a few inches from her eyes she registered that it was there but couldn't find the strength or will to speak to it.

There was a voice speaking somewhere nearby. "He a ship boy."

"She no he," the first face said. The voice was low and gentle.

"She a wo-man. She birthin'a baby." Then it spoke directly to Marianne. "Don' you worry, chil'. We here for you. We look out for you."

Hands were lifting her; she was being eased out of her breeches; someone was wiping the sweat out of her eyes; she knew she was lying on a cloth of some kind and that it was much softer than the baked earth. She tried to find the words to thank them, but the next pain was so bad she could barely breathe, and speech was impossible.

"You wantin' to push now, honey?" the face said.

"Push?" Marianne said, wondering what she was talking about — but even as she wondered she knew she *did* want to push, and she wanted it badly.

Such effort, such heat, such pain, and that calm face coming and going, murmuring encouragement. "You doin' well, honey. I see de head. You push good."

And then a rush and a slither and she knew that the child was out in the air and she could catch her breath and stop pushing. She was so totally exhausted she couldn't move. It was over and that was enough. She lay with her hand on the cloth and her eyes shut, limp with relief, as the flies flicked against her face and the strange bird tore the air with its harsh foreign call. She was too tired even to look at the baby.

Presently, the kindly face reappeared and asked if she was ready to push again. She pushed obligingly, feeling glad that there was so little pain this time but puzzled because the child was born, surely, so there shouldn't have been any need to push. Then she came to herself and remembered that she hadn't seen this child nor heard it cry and she stirred herself to sit up and look for it.

It was lying on a rush mat some distance away from her and it was a small pale baby boy lying perfectly still with his eyes shut. There were two women crouching on their haunches beside him, looking at him but not touching him. "Please," she called, "Let me see him."

They picked up the mat between them and carried the baby over to her, moving gently but not speaking. The familiar face bent towards her as they laid the child, mat and all, across her belly.

"De life ain' come to he," she said sadly.

The words were so chilling that Marianne couldn't bear to understand them. She put out a hand to stroke the baby's head. Oh such a small, vulnerable head. "Open your little eyes," she begged. "Look at me." But the baby's eyes were too tightly shut, and she knew with her reason that he would never see anything. She looked up at the kindly face above her. "He en't dead," she said. "Please say he en't dead. He can't be dead. I onny just birthed 'un."

"I sorry, chil'," the woman said. "De life ain' come to he."

Marianne put one finger into the baby s white, curled, limp hand. She was crying now, the tears rolling down her cheeks and dripping off her nose. "He en't dead," she wept. "He en't. I only just birthed 'un."

It was growing dark in that abrupt and total way she had come to expect in this part of the world and the field was rustling. The two women stood up and lifted Marianne to her feet, supporting her one on either side. It upset her to realise how feeble she felt.

"You come sleep now," the second woman said to her. "We look after he."

They were leading her into the darkness through the great field. She could smell dust and sweat and the sickly-sweet smell of the crop and above her head, the sky was full of sharp bright stars. Everything was unfamiliar and unreal as though she was walking in a dream. I shall never sleep, she thought. Not after all this. But they'd reached a round hut and were ducking through the entrance into a room with an earth floor. It was lit by two smoking rush lights and there were several straw pallets on the floor. They led her to the nearest one, smiling at her, and she was glad to lie down on it.

I shan't sleep, she thought, and slept at once.

NELSON'S STATE room aboard the *Victory* was golden with light because all the wax candles had been lit. The Admiral was entertaining the two most important men in the island, Admiral Cochrane, who was an old friend and whose flagship the *Northumberland* was lying in Carlisle Bay, and Sir William Myers, the Commander-in-Chief of the Army at Barbados. The three men had dined well and now it was time for Cochrane and Sir William to report.

"Your arrival is timely, m'lord," Sir William said, "for I received letters only last night from General Brereton at St Lucia and he sends the most specific news. He has seen the Spanish fleet. It passed Gros Islet on 28 May during the night, heading south."

The news was disconcerting to Admiral Nelson. Before he left the Mediterranean, all his most reliable informants had assured him that the French were heading for their own island of Martinique. But this new information had to be taken seriously. Brererton was an old friend and a reliable one, what's more, and if he said the French were heading south then there could well have been a change of plan. "How many sail?" he asked.

"Twenty-eight."

It was a formidable force, but it could prove unwieldly. "A very pretty fiddle," Nelson said, smiling at them, "although I don't believe that either Gravina or Villeneuve will know how to play upon it. And heading south, you say."

"Aye, sir. He supposed their destination to be either Barbados or Trinidad but as there is no sign of them hereabouts it seems more likely that they are headed for Trinidad and Tobago."

That was Admiral Cochrane's opinion of it too.

Nelson gave it thought, resting his chin in the palm of his hand.

"I have two thousand troops at Carlisle Bay," the general told him, "all primed and ready to embark."

The decision was made. "We will take sail for Carlisle Bay tonight," Nelson said, "and embark your troops tomorrow, General. Then, with God's grace, we shall head south and find our quarry."

CHAPTER 13

The sun was blazing through the doorway of the hut, as hot and hard as noonday. Marianne had no idea what time it was nor how long she'd been asleep, but that was of little consequence because her waking mind was instantly full of anguish for her poor dead baby. She lay on her back grieving and aching and feeling totally bereft. Yesterday morning, she'd been making plans to birth the little thing, she'd had his gown ready for him and everything, and now he was gone. It didn't seem possible or right, not after carrying him for so long and labouring so hard to bring him into the world.

After a while, she realised that she was lying under a rough blanket and that she was naked except for a thick clout tied between her legs. She was wondering what had happened to her clothes when a shadow made her look up at the door and there was her friend of the previous day, bearing a wooden tray with a wooden mug and a wooden bowl on it full of something hot and steaming.

"How you feelin' dis morning?" she said.

So it was morning. "I don't know," Marianne said, and began to cry again.

The woman took her hand and rubbed it. "You eat, chil'," she said, "you feel better when you eat."

That's exactly what Ma would have said, Marianne thought, and she picked up a spoonful of whatever it was and ate it cautiously. It was a sort of porridge but thicker than she had at home and eating it made her aware that she was actually quite hungry.

"You eat up every las' mout'ful," the woman said. "Build you strengt'."

"What is your name, ma'am?" Marianne asked, lifting another spoonful to her mouth.

"Looma," the woman told her. "Looma MacKenzie."

"My name is Marianne. Thank 'ee for what you done for me an' the baby." It seemed odd to be so formal with one another but Looma was pleased.

"I birth all de babbies," she said and added with pride, "I don' work in de fiel's. No, sir. I ain' no fiel' hand. No, sir. I birth de babbies an' I look after de sick an' I lays out de dead."

She's the midwife, Marianne thought, returning to her porridge. Like old Mother Catty. And she had a sudden yearning vision of her room in Mrs Catty's boarding-house and felt miserably homesick.

"Now you mus' drink dis," Looma said, picking up the mug and holding it out towards her.

Marianne peered at the mixture in it. It looked rather peculiar. "What is it?"

"Is to tek away de milk," Looma said, "Then you don' get de fever. You don't want de fever. I tell you dat. You drink it down real deep."

Marianne did as she was told, grimacing against the taste, but her wits were returning to her now and she was remembering the ship. "Where are my clothes?" she said.

"I get dem for you, by an' by," Looma told her. "Don' you worry 'bout dem. Dey been wash all nice an' clean an' dey been alyin' in de sun since daybreak."

They're so kind, Marianne thought, and she felt she ought to explain. "I must get back to my ship," she said, "Or she'll sail without me."

"De ship gone," Looma said, in her calm way. "All de ship."

The news took Marianne's breath away. "Gone?"

"Las' night," Looma said. "Dere ain' a ship lef' in de harbour. Dey all up an' sail away."

They can't have done, Marianne thought. She must have got it wrong. They can't all have gone. Not as quick as this. I'll go down to that quay and see for myself. It en't far.

She set out as soon as she was dressed, walking back along the same dusty path towards the distant streets of the town. They couldn't be gone. They just couldn't. But the town was changed. There was no doubt about that. There were no stalls and the narrow alley where she'd struggled against the crowds was deserted except for an old man squatting on his haunches smoking a foul-smelling pipe, and when she emerged into the strong sunlight on the quay, she saw at once that her new friend had been right. There wasn't a single ship of the line in harbour. Not a single solitary one. There were two fishing boats heading out to sea across the glittering water, but the fleet had gone. The shock of it was so dreadful, she felt as though she was being crushed under a great weight and sat on the nearest bollard, just as she'd done in Portsmouth all those months ago, to gather her thoughts. She'd lost her husband, what she'd never see again, and her baby, what never deserved for to die poor little thing, and her ship and her friends and she was miles from home and all on her own in a foreign country. The sun was hot on her black hat and strong on her idle hands. She couldn't begin to think what would become of her.

~

IN FACT, the fleet was anchored in Carlisle Bay, just along the coast and a few miles south-east of where she was sitting, and the husband she was so sure she would never see again was watching as Sir William Myers' troops were being embarked on all the sail of the line.

"We're in for it now," he said to Tom. The sight of so many uniformed men clambering up the wooden sides of those great ships was making his skin tingle with excitement. It was going to be a mighty battle.

"Looks likely," Tom agreed, watching as the muskets glinted in the sun. There was certainly enough tension aboard the *Sirius* to justify their opinion. Most of the gun crews had made up their minds that the battle was only hours away.

"I'd best go below an' check the bungs," Jem said. In seas as placid as these, they weren't likely to be holed below the water-line, but it was better to be safe than sorry.

"Aye. You'd best," Tom agreed, still watching. "Once he gives that signal we shan't have time to breathe." And he stroked his new beard.

NELSON WAS WATCHING the embarkation from the quarter-deck of the *Victory*. He and his secretary Mr Scott had been up since daybreak and all the necessary letters had been written and were ready to be dispatched, to the Governor of Dominica, to Tobago and Trinidad. Now they were three bells into the forenoon watch and he was eager to be off and on the hunt again. There was no time to be lost. A search through all the islands between Barbados and Trinidad would take all his navigational skill and use every frigate and sloop he had at his disposal and the sooner they got on with it, the better.

IN THE FRIGATE *AMPHION*, the crew were being dosed with quinine. The captain had given the order for it as soon his lieutenant had reported that one of the ships boys had been taken with a fever and left behind in Bridgetown.

"What sort of fever?" he asked.

"That I couldn't say, sir," the lieutenant said. "He was in a muck sweat as we were rowing ashore, but then he slunk off somewhere and disappeared."

The captain scowled. "I trust you made a thorough search?"

"High and low sir," the lieutenant lied. "Couldn't see hide nor hair of him." In fact, he hadn't noticed the boy's absence until they'd been rowing back to the ship and he'd realised that he was an oar down but he certainly wasn't going to admit that.

"Quinine for all hands," the captain decided. "Tell the bosun."

Johnny Galley was most aggrieved to be dosed for no reason. "I ain't afeard a' bein' took with a fever," he said. "Leastwise not the sort a' fever that young shaver's took."

His shipmates mocked him. "Since when was you appointed surgeon, Johnny?" they said. "Shame on 'ee for a booby. Take your physic like a man!"

He couldn't very well explain how he knew the fever was no threat to them, so he had to swallow the quinine and put up with it. He was caught in his own trap, to Peg and Moll's grinning delight.

Fortunately, the troops were now embarked and the order to sail was being given so he was saved from further teasing by a flurry of orders, but he was growling and surly as he went off to obey them.

"Serve him right, lecherous ol' varmint," Peg said, when she and Moll were in the rigging and safely out of earshot of their mates. "If it 'ud been up to me, he'd have had a double dose an' been as sick as a dog."

"I wonder how she's gettin' on," Moll said, busy with the knots.

"We ain't like to hear from her now," Peg told her, shaking out the sail. "She'm stuck on the island, poor soul."

"True enough," Moll said, gazing back at it. It looked very beautiful from a distance, with those white sands and that blue-green sea and the mountains such a rich green and so luscious. She watched it for some seconds, saddened to think that there was going to be a battle in such a gorgeous place.

"We allus said we'd jump ship if the battle came," she said to Peg, "and now look at us, sailin' right into it."

"No chance a jumpin' now," Peg said. "We just got to get on with it. Our fevered friend had the right idea, if you ask me."

"Aye, she had," Moll agreed, shaking out the last sail. "We might a left her behind with the baby an' all, but least she won't be blowed to Kingdom Come and that's something to be thankful for."

"I shall miss her," Peg said.

But there was no more time for talk, because the lieutenant was shouting at them to look lively, and there was work to do.

MARIANNE WASN'T CONCERNED about the coming battle at all. She had only one thought in her head and one need in her heart and that was to get back on board a ship of the line and sail home to Portsmouth. But how that was to be done when they'd cut off and left her was a mighty problem. She walked slowly back to Looma's hut feeling unexpectedly tired but churning the matter over in her mind. Bridgetown was a big harbour. A very big one. There was no doubt of that. So sooner or later, ships would put in there either to take on water or provisions or to get out of a storm. That was what harbours were for. Very well then, sooner or later, there would be a ship for her to board. All she had to do was watch out for it. I'll dress in my slops, she decided, and I'll go down there every single day, twice if I have to, and I'll take the first ship what'll take me. I shall have to prove to 'em that I en't jumped ship, or I shall be flogged round the fleet an' I don't want that. But that's what I'll do. There's plenty a' ships in the sea an' I only wants the one.

Somewhere to the right of her, the raucous bird was calling again *kaa, kaa kaa* as though it was mocking her.

"Never you mind kaa, kaa, kaa," she shouted at it. "I shall do it. You see if I don't."

NELSON SPENT the whole of that day sailing through the Leeward Islands, watching the seas for the French and keeping his own ships in a state of constant activity. He'd given the general order "Prepare for battle" as soon as they left the harbour and now, he was sending out his messengers, Captain Bettesworth to Tobago in the brig *Curieux*, Colonel Shipley of the Engineers to the nearest post on Trinidad, the *Sirius* to Dominica.

The news the captain and the colonel brought back was puzzling. They'd seen no sign of the French, but the *Curieux* had met up with an American merchant ship, whose captain told them he'd been boarded by a French ship just off Grenada, so they were obviously in the area.

As usual, Nelson made a rapid decision. They would proceed to the Bay of Paria in Trinidad. If his enemy was not to be found at sea then he would be lurking in a harbour and, as his informants had told him that Trinidad was where the French fleet was headed, the Bay of Paria was the most probable. He was aggrieved and disappointed when they arrived late that evening to find it calm and completely empty.

"We were misinformed," he said to Captain Hardy, scowling his annoyance. "We have wasted time and effort on a wild goose chase. I should have trusted my instincts and sailed north. One French ship off Grenada may well have boarded the merchantman, that I will allow, but one ship does not make a fleet. We will overnight here and head for Dominica at first light. The governor there may well have better information and he should have received my letter by now."

IT WAS EVENING when the *Sirius* sailed towards Dominica and the setting sun was a huge blinding disk, bright gold in a fiery red and orange sky. Beside its magnificence the island slept in a grey haze, shrouded and mysterious and silent. Jem Templeman was bewitched by it. There was something magical about it, something dream-like and otherworldly, as if the sky was on fire and the island was a living breathing creature crouching beneath it, lurking and quiet but exuding the strong sweet smell of spices that drifted out to him across the water. Everything about the scene was a lift to his senses. Flocks of small birds rose from the mist and flew like black darts across the blazing sky. The sea around him was speckled with golden lights, as if it too had been sprinkled with fire, although in the shadow of their sails it was the colour of ink and deep as death. He recognised it as a place where amazing things could happen and knew that the pull of it was as strong as a magnet.

"Imagine living in a place like this," he said to Tom. "All this colour an' all."

"'Tis a deal too hot for me," Tom said, practically, "an' a deal too full of fever. 'Twill look different to 'ee come the morning. Mark my words."

But the morning revealed the full impact of the great rain forests that covered the hills with their heavy foliage, steaming in the first heat of the day and now Jem could see that there was a little town alongside the harbour. Far from diminishing, the pull of the island was even more powerful than it had been the night before and it was much too strong to be denied.

"I'm goin' ashore to see the sights," he decided.

"You won't find any," Tom warned. "There's only savages lives hereabouts. I've seen 'em afore."

"Very well then," Jem grinned. "I shall go ashore an' see the savages."

"Madness," Tom said, but Jem was already on his way to the longboat. It was as if this island was something he'd been waiting for and if there was a letter being taken ashore, he was going with it.

So much had happened to him in the last two years that there were private moments when he felt he was being dragged along from one event to the next as if he had no will or purpose of his own. Life aboard ship was good, there was no denying that. He ate well and slept well and there was plenty of work to do, which was praised and appreciated by his shipmates, and he'd certainly seen the world, but he couldn't help feeling that there ought to be more to life than food and sleep and work and travel. Something extra and better. Something that would give it all some purpose. He didn't know what it was, but he was sure he could find it if he only had time to sit down and think for a minute. And wasn't this just the place to do it?

As they rowed to shore, he discovered that the little town was called Roseau, and it turned out to be a very little town indeed. The quayside was cobbled and ringed by sizeable houses, one of them obviously the governor's mansion because that was where they were taking the letter, and another that looked like a factor's house, but apart from that there was very little else. There was a cobbled road that led out of harbour and ran from one side of the town to the other, but all the other buildings were either wooden shacks or mud huts thatched with palm leaves and there were no shops or inns or stables and hardly anybody about. It was quiet and peaceful just as he'd expected, and that was what he needed, a place to sit in the sun and think. If he could find somewhere to sit, apart from in the dust.

He made himself comfortable on one of the bollards, took out his tobacco pouch and his pipe, filled it, working slowly and methodically, lit it with his tinder box and took the first rich mouthful, enjoying it to the full. Then he gave himself up to the inadequacy of his memory and the puzzle of his thoughts.

Two years ago when he'd first asked Marianne's father if he could come a-courting, he'd had a vague idea that what he wanted was a wife and children and a good job to support them all. He'd marched off to church on his wedding day feeling cock sure that he was getting what he wanted. He could remember that clearly. Feeling cock sure. Full of himself and how well he'd done. And yet it had all gone wrong, all of a sudden and without any warning. He still couldn't understand why. He knew he'd got drunk and that drink had addled his memory, but that didn't help him. He knew she'd been unkind to him and that he'd stormed off out of the house and gone to the inn to get away from her, but apart from that he had no other memory of the day at all. And here he was, sitting in the sun trying to make sense of things, without the least idea of how to go about it. And there was someone whistling. The sound made him irritable. How could he think when there was someone whistling?

It was a small brown-skinned boy who was ambling over the cobbles towards the governor's house carrying a hammer and a bag of nails. A carpenter's apprentice, Jem thought, and a very slow one. He watched as the boy picked up a paling that had fallen out of the white picket fence and proceeded to ease it back into position. It was one of the first jobs he'd done himself when he was apprentice to old man Henderson. He remembered standing in the street with his bag of nails and his hammer, while people hustled and pushed all round him and he had a sudden vision of Mr Henderson, standing with his legs astride, watching him and saying, "Don' 'ee pay 'em no mind, my sonny. You got a job to do."

He was a wise ol' bird, Jem thought. Him an' his sayin's. "One thing at a time" and "Order an' method" and "Make a list". We were always making lists. He could remember standing in the workroom, writing them. "Make a list, my sonny. Then you can be sure you've got things in the right order an' you can tick 'em off that of list one by one as you do 'em. Order an' method. Tha's the style."

Very well then, he would try a little order an' method and make a list. He'd have to do it in his head because he didn't have pencil and paper handy, not being much of a writing man. But what of that? He could make a list well enough without writing the thing down. All he had to do was work out what sort of a list it was going to be. Very well then, he would make a list of where he was and where he would rather be and see what came of it.

For a start, he thought, I'm a ship's carpenter and I would rather be a carpenter ashore an' my own master. That much was very clear. Second, I'm tired of bein' at sea, on account of 'tis always throwing us about — what no man would endure more than five minutes if he was in his right mind — an' I would rather live ashore on good firm dry land and never, ever be seasick no more.

Third, I got a battle to face and no stomach for it. Who wants to be blowed to Kingdom Come with a cannon ball? I certainly don't. An' if I lives through it, I would like to take my pocketful of silver an' leave the navy honourable.

Fourth, I'm tired of whores — what are all the same when it comes down to it — an' I'd like a woman of my own and a home for us both to live in. And it occurred to him, sitting there in that easing sunlight, with the steadying rhythm of the child's hammer in his ears, that he already had a woman of his own and that he'd been a blamed fool and walked off and left her. A woman of his own, who had good thick hair the colour of a ship's rope and good strong hands what were used to work and had walked along beside him on their wedding day, laughing and holding his arm. He could see her in her blue dress, sharp and clear as if she was standing before him with a bunch of flowers in her hand and the wind fairly bowling her along.

Then all manner of pictures began to fill his mind, the wedding breakfast and all those meat pies and custards, their room with its new counterpane and the furniture he'd made to please her, feeling so wild for her, he couldn't control himself because there'd been such an urge on him, and her stopping him, saying he'd hurt her. And he remembered his anger, feeling it all over again as he sat there calmly smoking his pipe in the sun, the terrible strength of it, because he couldn't believe he'd hurt her. Wouldn't believe it. That was more like it. Wouldn't believe it. And he'd gone on being angry with her all these months, telling everybody she was a harridan and a nagging wife, and convincing himself that she'd been making it up. But what if she hadn't been making it up? What if he *had* hurt her? Men *did* hurt their women sometimes. He knew that now for he'd listened to enough rough talk below decks about how women were "asking for it" and how they "liked" being hurt. Plenty of men hurt their women and they did it deliberate.

He could see her now, standing in the middle of the room with a trickle of blood running down her leg, the image so clear and detailed it made his chest ache with regret and yearning. He might have hurt her, even though he hadn't meant to. He probably had hurt her. I should have stayed there and let her talk to me, he thought, instead of rushing off to The Dolphin. That was a fool's trick. I ran off an' left her an' she was my wife. Well then, if I can find her when I gets home an' if she'll have me, what en't partic'ly likely given what went on 'atween us, I should like to settle down with her in a home of my own and treat her proper. That's what I'd like. Failing that I shall have to find someone else, what I'll choose for myself this time instead a' lettin' Ma suggest it. That was a damn fool thing to do, now I comes to think on it, for I didn't know a blamed thing about my Marianne beyond what Ma had told me. But then I done a pack a' damned fool things in them days, seems to me. He was uncomfortable with regret and guilt, which wasn't his style at all. Fifth, he thought, turning his mind to something else.

But he never got around to thinking what the fifth point would be because there was someone calling him "Ahoy there, Mr Templeman!" and his shipmates were waving and pointing to show that the longboat was going back.

"No peace for the wicked," he called, and stood up to obey orders. Four points were enough. They'd shown him the way he wanted to go.

As they rowed the longboat back to the ship, they saw that they'd got company. There was a sloop hove to alongside.

"Now what?" the rowers asked, as they climbed back on board.

"'Twill be a message," Jem said.

And it was. There'd been a change of plan. The *Sirius* was to stay in harbour and wait for the arrival of the rest of the fleet.

MARIANNE HAD BEEN WAITING for the fleet for over a week but even though she'd walked down to the harbour twice every day, there'd never been any sign of a ships at all apart from the fishing boats and she was heartily sick of seeing them. She did her best not to get disheartened, but it was difficult.

Looma was full of sympathy. "You want dey to come, dey don' never come," she said, as if she was a seasoned traveller.

"They must come soon," Marianne said. "Surely to goodness."

"We mek de supper," Looma said. "Tomorrow dey come, maybe."

Marianne was glad of her company for without her the days would have been intolerably long. She helped her to cook, cutting up her peculiar vegetables and rolling chunks of goat meat in her rough flour; she served the food in the now familiar wooden bowls; she even sat beside of one of her "birthing" mothers as the poor woman laboured and groaned through a long hot afternoon. But whatever she did, the ships refused to arrive.

"I'm beginning to think I en't meant to go home," she confided to Looma one idle afternoon, as the two of them were squatting on their haunches cutting up vegetables. And shrugged. "Perhaps 'tis just as well."

Looma might have had a poor command of English but she was shrewd. "Why you say dat?" she asked.

"On account of I stands to be flogged for desertion," Marianne explained, "even if I can find a ship to take me aboard. That's what they does to deserters. They only got my word I was ill. I can't be sure they'll believe me an' if they don't…"

Looma put down her knife, got off her haunches, stood up and straightened her skirt. "I see 'bout dat," she said. "You come wid me." And she walked off into the sugar cane, her spine straight with determination.

Marianne followed her, feeling very surprised. How could a slave do anything to stop her being flogged? "Where are we going?" she called, as she struggled through the harsh canes. That horrible bird was laughing again. *Kaa, kaa, kaa.*

Looma's voice echoed back to her. "You see presen'ly."

"What will I see?"

"You see de massa." Looma called back. She was picking up speed now, striding between the canes and Marianne was finding it hard to keep up with her.

"Who is the massa?" she called.

But they were too far apart for conversation and there was nothing for it but to follow where she was being led.

After what seemed a very long time, they emerged into a large clearing where there was a cinder path leading to the back door of a large stone house, a gentleman's house, built in the latest style, all white paint and neat, gleaming windows, with a green lawn spread out before it and flower beds edging the path full of bold red and yellow blooms.

Looma had paused to catch her breath, "What you name when you ship boy?" she said, when Marianne caught up with her.

"Matt Morris."

"I don' tell him you woman," Looma said. "He don' needs for to know dat. I tell him you ship boy wid fever. You unnerstand?"

Marianne understood perfectly.

Looma nodded. "Dis way," she said, and set off towards the door where she knocked discretely.

They were answered by a small girl in a servant's gown and a white cap and apron.

"How's you keepin', Corryanne?" Looma said, and the child nodded and smiled by way of an answer. "I's come for to see de massa."

"Dis way, if you please, Missy Looma," the child said, and led them into very large kitchen. To Marianna's wondering eyes, it seemed to be full of women all preparing food and all looking at her in a decidedly suspicious way. They reached a door that looked as though it led to a cupboard or a larder but no, when it was opened, she saw that they were facing a narrow staircase, which they climbed in almost total darkness until they reached a plain door covered in green baize.

The servant child gave a timid knock and was told to "Come in."

"If you please, Massa," the child said. "Missy Looma here."

"Show her in," the voice said, and the child stood aside so that Looma and Marianne could walk through the door. They'd emerged from dusty darkness into a blaze of white light that made them blink. Sitting at the centre of it was a man in a bob wig and a fine brown suit. He had a newspaper on the table by his elbow and he was drinking tea from a bone china cup for all the world as if he was one of the nobs.

"What's this then, Looma?" he said.

"If you please, Massa sir," Looma said, "dis here is a ship's boy what need you for to help him."

"Does he indeed?" Massa said, making a wry face as if he was amused. "And what is that to you?"

"I nurse he when he sick, Massa, sir. He tell you."

"Go ahead then, boy," Massa said. "Have a name, do you?"

Marianne told him her name and plunged into her tale, explaining that she was ship's boy on the frigate *Amphion* and that she'd taken a fever when they came ashore for supplies and been left behind. "I was too sick to walk, sir, an' that's the truth of it," she said. "An' now I'd like for to go back to my ship only I'm afeard they won't believe me when I tell them where I've been on account a' they only got my word for it an' if they don't believe me, I shall be flogged, sir, as a deserter."

"Um," Massa said. "And we don't want that do we, Looma?"

Looma was beaming broadly.

"Very well then, Master Morris," Massa said. "I tell 'ee what's to be done. You are to go back to the kitchen and wait there until I send for you. Tell Cook she's to feed you. And while you're stuffing your face, I will write a testimonial for you that will be a match for any captain alive. Now be off with 'ee."

"Aye, aye, sir," Marianne said and gave him a grateful salute.

It was a very good letter, addressed "To Whom it May Concern" and written in a strong bold hand to certify that Master Matt Morris had been on the MacKenzie sugar plantation on the Island of Barbados ever since being set ashore from the frigate *Amphion* of His Majesty's Navy, and that he had not returned to his ship on account of being overtaken with a great sickness from which he was now fully recovered. It was signed with a flourish, *John Stewart MacKenzie*.

When Marianne had read it, she read it aloud for a second time so that Looma could hear it. "John Stewart MacKenzie," she finished. "En't that your name too, Looma?"

Looma shrugged her shoulders. "Dat all us name," she said. "We his slave. He own we. He give we de name. We all MacKenzies."

Marianne didn't press her any further about it, for she could see it upset her. "'Tis a fine letter," she said.

"So," Looma said with great satisfaction, "I fix good, eh? Dey read dis, dey not flog you. Now you find ship, eh?"

If only I could, Marianne thought. Oh where *is* that ol' fleet? They must be comin' back soon, surely to goodness.

CHAPTER 14

The Governor of Dominica was an astute and persuasive man. There wasn't much going on in his corner of the Caribbean that he didn't make it his business to know about it. So naturally as soon as he received Lord Nelson's letter and knew that the admiral was hungry for news of the French fleet, he set about gathering information from every quarter. By the time the British fleet had anchored in Roseau Bay and he and Captain Hardy and the great admiral were sitting down to dinner in the dining room on board the *Victory*, he was as thoroughly informed as it was possible for him to be. He had heard from the garrisons at Grenada, St Vincent and St Lucia and could report that all three were safe and had seen no sign of the French. Better still he knew that the French fleet had anchored in the neighbouring island of Martinique, exactly as Nelson's Mediterranean spies predicted, and that a French fleet of eighteen of the line, six frigates and three brigs had been seen passing Prince Rupert's Head on 6 June, heading north.

It was demoralising news for Nelson because it confirmed that his original informants had been correct and that he *had* been sent on a wild goose chase.

"Had I not been given false information," he said, bitterly, "I should have been off Port Royal as they were putting to sea and our battle would have been over and done by now and fought, what is more, on the very spot where the brave Rodney beat De Grasse."

"Aye, sir," the governor sympathised. "So it would seem."

"They were heading north you say?"

"Aye, sir, that was my understanding of it."

Nelson sighed and turned to Hardy. "I am rather inclined to believe they are pushing for Europe," he said, "To get out of our way."

Hardy sighed, too, for it seemed only too likely and if that *was* the case, it would mean another long chase across the Atlantic, which would be arduous because provisions in the fleet were now parlously low. However, these were matters that could be attended to when their guest had gone. For the moment, it was necessary to be courteous.

"We will sail for Antigua at first light," Nelson decided, when he and Hardy were finally alone. It was well past midnight but there were decisions to be made. "We will make such repairs as are necessary there and transfer Sir William's artillery men back to the *Northumberland* and take on the provisions we need — or as many of them as the dockyard can provide. Then we must make haste for Europe. I fear we have lost a deal too much time already and I am loath to stay long in that fever ridden place. Our men are well, I believe?"

"They were well at the last count," Hardy told him.

"Then let us keep them so. I will send out frigates to St Kitts and Jamaica to make sure that they are safe and unmolested. Not the *Sirius*. She must make all speed to re-join Collingwood. I will write to him tonight. He will need every frigate in his command if he is to watch Cadiz *and* Cap Ferrol. The *Superb* to St Kitts, the *Amphion* to Jamaica because she will make better speed. I tell you, Hardy, I have been in a thousand fears that Jamaica might have been taken. That is a blow that Bonaparte would have been happy to give us, and it has been in my mind ever since we arrived. The governor thinks them safe, but I must make assurance doubly sure."

"What of Barbados?" Hardy asked. "Should we not make contact there?"

"I will send a sloop," Nelson decided. "It will be slow, but it is all I can spare."

~

THE NEWS that the French were on the run again spread through the fleet at first light to derisive laughter.

"Bravo, Johnny Frenchman!" Tom said to Jem, when they passed each other on the gun deck on their way to their stations. "What did I tell 'ee? I knew the beggars 'ud turn tail."

"I can't see us ever catching 'em," Jem said, stopping in his onward stride.

"Don't you believe it," Tom laughed. "We shall catch 'em come the finish, be they ever so slippy. You just see if we don't. Our Nelson's made his mind up to it an' when our Nelson's made up his mind to a thing there en't a power in the world will stop it."

"We're to join Admiral Collingwood," Jem told him. "Have 'ee heard?"

"Aye. Seemingly," Tom said and strode on.

The *Amphion* was the first to leave the harbour that morning and she put on full sail as soon as she was in open water and headed off with as much speed as she could contrive. Behind her, the harbour was a froth of activity, as one by one the ships of the fleet manoeuvred into position, ready to leave. The sloop *Mary-belle* was the last to sail and was soon left far behind by the onward surge of the mighty ships of the line. Her captain was sanguine about their lowly position, for hadn't they been entrusted with a mission to enquire into the safety of Barbados? And wasn't that honour enough?

Nelson sailed for Antigua caught between conflicting emotions. He was driven on by the urgency of the chase, partly because there was still a faint chance that he might catch the French before they sailed for Spain, partly because it was imperative to make up lost days if they had sailed already, yet he was reluctant to visit the island at all. He'd been there on several occasions when he was captain of the frigate *Boreas* and knew from bitter experience that it was an extremely unhealthy place, where malaria and yellow fever were rampant, and the death rate was terrifyingly high. But, as he said to Hardy, when the two of them were standing on the quarter-deck the next morning, "Needs must when the Devil drives." And Hardy smiled at him, for he knew that the devil that drove them both was duty and that neither of them had any option except to obey.

IT WAS early evening when they finally arrived at Antigua after two days at sea and the irregular hills of the island were richly green in the sunlight. To Nelson's sea-wearied eyes, the landscape looked even wilder than he remembered it, but he noticed that the cannons on Shirley Heights were still manned and ready to protect the harbour, and that the red-brick forts looked as solid and dependable as ever. Whatever else, the place was strongly fortified.

The next morning, a sudden rain dropped across the sea like a thick mist from a low blue-grey cloud, but there was so much work to be done the weather was of little consequence. He began to requisition supplies, to enquire into the condition of his ships, to discover what repairs their captains considered necessary and, above all, to gather news. He learned that the French had arrived in Martinique three weeks ahead of him and that they'd been in such poor shape they hadn't moved from the harbour for more than ten days. They'd put a thousand men ashore with sickness and, according to his informant, most of them had died. A frigate had arrived from France on the 31 May which had provoked a lot of activity and the fleet had sailed on 6 June exactly as the Governor of Dominica had told him. There was now little doubt that they were on their way back to Spain and that his guess that they would put in at Ferrol or Cadiz had been right. The sooner they were provisioned and ready to sail, the better. They would send the *Sirius* on ahead, wait for the return of the *Amphion* and the *Superb* and then they would set off.

ON THE ISLAND OF BARBADOS, it was a hot morning and Marianne was sauntering down to the harbour, eating a banana and enjoying the warmth of the sun. She'd grown so accustomed to disappointment that she'd given up rushing there. Now, she simply made sure her precious letter was safe in her jacket pocket, strolled down, sat on a bollard, watched the empty water for a minute or two, asked the harbour master if he was expecting any ships to arrive and when the answer was no, strolled back. It was such a surprise to turn out of the alley into the quay and actually see a ship anchored in the bay that she blinked with disbelief. Then she saw that it was a British sloop and that there was a bum boat tied up at one of the bollards and she strode off at once to the harbour-master's office to see what was happening.

"Come to check we're all safe an' well, seemingly," the harbour master told her, "with a letter from Lord Nelson what they're just delivering. They'll be back presently."

As they were. Four oarsmen and a lieutenant, who all looked mighty surprised to see a ship's boy waiting for them on the quay.

"My stars!" the lieutenant said. "Where have you sprung from, young feller-me-lad?"

By this time, Marianne was so used to her tale that she smoothed into it at once without so much as a blush. "I been on the plantation ever since I was took ill," she finished. "I got a letter here from the owner what'll prove it."

"Hop aboard," the lieutenant told her, "and you can show it to the captain. My stars but he'll be surprised."

It was ridiculously simple. One minute, she'd been ambling along the dusty path without any real hope of being rescued and the next she was sitting in the bum boat on her way back to the fleet. She would have liked to have gone back to Looma and thanked her and said goodbye, but that was out of the question. The pace of her life had quickened. She was travelling now, on her way to re-join the fleet and get home to Portsmouth. Had it not been for the fact that ships boys are quiet in the presence of their officers, she could have burst into song.

The captain was on the bridge when they pulled up alongside and he noticed the stranger immediately.

"What's this?" he said to his lieutenant.

"Found him on the island, sir," the lieutenant reported. "Name of Matt. Off the *Amphion*."

"Jumped ship did 'ee, boy?" the captain said sternly. "That's a floggin' offence I hopes you knows. Seems to me you'd best explain yourself."

By now, it was an entirely plausible explanation, especially with Mr MacKenzie's letter to support it. It was a most satisfactory moment when Marianne took it out of her pocket and handed it deferentially across to the captain. And an even better one when he squinted at it and turned it sideways and obviously couldn't read it.

"Um," he said, assuming a serious expression. "If this is the case, we'll take you aboard. We shall work you, mind, and you'll have to muck in where you can. Dismiss."

Marianne went off to obey her first orders feeling light-hearted with happiness. The off-shore breeze fluttered against her check, cooling and restoring; she could smell English cooking, what was salt beef if she was any judge of it; she was a boy again, and on her way back to the fleet.

During the next two days, she worked hard and obeyed orders so promptly that by the end of the first watch, she'd settled into the ship's routine as if she'd been sailing in her all her life. Even her shipmates were impressed, especially when she told them she'd served on the *Amphion*.

"'Tis a good ship, so they say," one of the old hands observed, as they ate their salt beef. "Good captin."

"Aye," she agreed. "So he is."

"You'll be going back there I daresay, once we'm in Antigua."

Marianne had been giving the matter thought since she'd come aboard, and she wasn't at all sure she wanted to be back with the people who'd known her when she was carrying. They'd be bound to wonder at the state of her, seein' how skinny she was, an' then there'd be a deal too much explaining to do. Besides which, she wanted to keep out of Johnny Galley's way. Besides which as well, if there was a battle comin' she wanted to be below the waterline, where it was safer an' she wasn't so like to be blowed to Kingdom Come.

"Well now," she said. "I en't so sure a' that. I'd like for to be a loblolly an' our surgeon had loblollies enough."

"We'll get Jacko to speak to Cap'n," the old man said. "If that's what 'ee wants, good luck to 'ce. Loblollies are worth their weight in gold come the fighting."

They made surprisingly good speed through the islands, giving Martinique a wide berth, "in case old Johnny Frenchman was to come out" but there was no sign of any other ship of any kind, except for fishing boats and they had a clear run. The wind was fair, the going easy, the food filling. It seemed no time at all before Antigua appeared on the horizon. Then the pace of their lives changed again for they were back with the fleet and the fleet was hard at work.

Marianne had never seen so many ships gathered together in one place, not even in Barbados and there'd been ships a-plenty there. The bay was full of them, ships of the line, frigates and sloops riding at anchor, bum boats skimming like water beetles between their great wooden hulls as they carried goods and messages from shore to ship; longboats transferring soldiers to a ship called the *Newfoundland*; ships running up signals, and so much coming and going after the calm of an empty sea, it made her dizzy to look at it.

As they sailed gently into the harbour, another ship passed them on her way out.

"The *Sirius* is that," her new shipmates told her. But she could read the name for herself.

"I know her," she said. "I seen her afore. Comin' out the straits a' Messina." And, as she watched the great ship dipping away from them towards the open sea, she remembered the moment in sudden and disturbing detail. They'd been a-huntin' for one of Collingwood's' ships — they'd had a message for her or some such — and she'd been as sick as a dog, retchin' an' heavin'. How long ago it all seemed.

~

"Now for Cadiz," Jem said to Tom, as they passed the sloop.

"My money's on Ferrol," Tom said. "He's sailin' north, don' 'ee forget, and that's the nearest port a' call."

"Mine's on Cadiz," Jem said. "'Tis a bigger harbour by all accounts an' he's known there. He's been lurkin' in that quarter these many months. It'll be Cadiz. You see if I en't right."

"You don't think we might catch up with him then?" Tom said and grinned. "I thought you was all for closing with the beggar."

"Can't see it likely," Jem told him. "If he left Martinique on the 6th, he's got too good a head start. Howsomever, if we do, we do, but as to closing with him, that's another story. We shall have to tail him 'til the rest catch up with us."

They were putting on more sail, the ship bucking like a horse as she took the wind. The chase was on, whatever it might lead to. Death or glory, Jem thought, and shivered.

As soon as the sloop had dropped anchor, the captain put on his best jacket and announced that he was going across to the *Victory* to deliver his report. He was so full of importance that Marianne wanted to laugh at him. He en't got a thing to report, she thought, for there'd been nothing happening on the island, an' he'd soon have found that out. But there he was making an occasion of his mission. How these men do love to be important, she thought, remembering the saucy midshipmen throwing their weight about aboard the *Amphion*, and the lieutenant barking orders and expecting everybody to jump to and obey him. How they do carry on about how powerful they are! I never seen no woman carry on like that, never in my life. But then, now she came to think about it, a woman had no power to speak of and never laid claim to any, so she wouldn't. She remembered her mother for ever toiling over the washtub or bending over the ironing, rubbing her back against the ache, and she yearned to see her again. I wonder how she is, she thought. I must write her a letter. I en't writ to her for ages. 'Twill be the first thing I do when I can come by pen and paper.

She came by it sooner than she could have imagined and in the most satisfactory way. The captain returned two bells later, looking pleased with himself. He'd got her a job as a loblolly on the *Victory*, no less. "I spoke to Mr Beattie, the surgeon, and he has need of every loblolly he can command." A bum boat would take her across at six bells. She was so excited by the news, she could barely contain her feelings. The *Victory* she thought, Nelson's flag ship. Now that's something to tell Ma an' no mistake. But she stayed calm and thanked the captain for his kind offices and got on with her work as well as she could until the time came for her to leave.

It was an undeniable thrill to climb the high wooden sides of Nelson's great ship and to step aboard as the latest member of his crew, and an even bigger one to see the great man himself standing on the quarter-deck. Now he *is* powerful, she thought, glancing at him. He can send us all in to battle with just one word. Yet he looked the meekest of men, with his empty sleeve and his pale thoughtful face, standing there talking to Captain Hardy and another officer as quietly as if they were in an inn at Portsmouth. Then she realised that someone was looking at *her* and she glanced round and saw that it was a formidable-looking bosun and that brought her back to her own world with a jolt. There was a lanky looking boy standing beside him shuffling his feet and grinning at her.

"This here is Josh," the bosun said, what'll show 'ee the ropes an' so forth. You're to go along a' him an' do as he says an' no larking about, mind."

As if I would, Marianne thought. I en't a child. But of course she *was* a child now she was a boy again, so she would have to put up with it. The lanky boy ambled off towards the companionway, so she followed.

"You been a loblolly afore?" he asked, looking back at her over his shoulder.

She wasn't going to confess her ignorance. "'Course," she said. "Many's the time."

"He's a good ol' feller," he said looking back at the quarter-deck. "Tha's him along a' Lord Nelson. You has to do everythink he tells you, mind. He don't stand no nonsense. But he's a good ol' feller. Never saw a man so quick at hacking off a leg. Don't matter how much blood there is. He has 'em held down and he's on 'em like a hawk. Three hacks an' 'tis done. You wait, you'll see it."

Marianne wasn't at all sure she wanted to see anything so brutal, but she couldn't say so now she was a boy again. "I'll 'spects I shall," she said, trying to sound nonchalant. "Where's my station?"

He'd led her to the lower gun deck. "We'm here," he said, stopping between the last two guns. "Near the companionway, see. Best place. On account a' we has to be quick a-gettin' down to the orlop when we'm wanted. That's your bunk an' that's where you stows your ditty bag. We scrubs the orlop through first thing first dog watch. An' mind you does everything Mr Beatie says, or he'll have yer guts fer garters. I seen him one time—"

But his tale was cut short by the sound of the anchor chain. They were under way. "Hey up!" he said, instantly losing his stern expression and becoming a child again. "We'm sailin'. Let's go up an' see."

I got here just in time, Marianne thought, as she followed him back on deck. And she felt mighty pleased with herself.

CHAPTER 15

That second Atlantic crossing was as uneventful as the first one had been and every bit as fast. They were on short commons because supplies were low, but Marianne didn't mind a diet of salt beef, plum duff and figgy dowdy, not now they were on their way back home — and they must be on their way back home soon, surely to goodness. They'd been at sea for more than two years.

Josh would keep talking about the battle, in his horrible ghoulish way, gloating about what a lot of blood they'd see come the fighting and how many limbs would be hacked off, but the weather was fair, the going was good and apart from scrubbing the decks down in that stinking hold, there was little to do below, which was just as well for it was a hideous place and as dark as a dungeon. Having been out in clear air and strong sunshine for so long, she'd forgotten how vile the smell of the bilge could be. If there was a battle, it would be a nightmare place to have to work. But she'd made her choice and now she must stick with it.

Apart from the ghoulish Josh, the other four loblollies were a friendly lot and usually cheerful. When they were four days out, they spotted timbers floating on the water and they were all instantly sure that they must have come from a French ship.

"Which just goes for to show they ain't in good order, not doin' repairs in mid ocean," one of them said. "We shall blow 'em out the water when we catches 'em, you see if I ain't right."

Marianne looked at him pityingly. You won't blow anyone out the water, she thought, you silly little boy. All you'm goin' to do is see our men what've been blowed to bits brought down to Mr Beattie to have their arms an' legs hacked off. And she sent up a private prayer to God not to let it happen. Just send us all home, she begged, if 'Ee don't mind. I've took my punishment now. For thine is the Kingdom, the Power and the Glory.

Then, since there was nothing else she could do about it, she pushed it out of her mind and concentrated on settling into the routine of the ship. Even when she had to get up at five bells at the start of the last dog watch, she did it willingly, especially if it was another warm day. She scrubbed the weather decks until they were white and clean, rolled up her hammock as soon as they piped "up hammocks", was first down to the mess deck when they piped "Nancy Dawson", and whenever she was at leisure, she stood by the ship's rail and watched the sea and the sky. It was a good life and she wasn't going to waste a minute of it by being scolded for being slow about her work.

When they'd been sailing for seven days and she had a week's wage to her credit, she went to see the purser and bought two sheets of paper, a pen and a small quantity of ink in a rather battered horn, so that she could write to her mother. It was the oddest sensation to be writing home after all the things that had happened to her, especially as the most important ones couldn't be talked about. But she wrote what she could and chose subjects that she thought would be entertaining.

We are sailin aceross the Aterlantick Oshun, what is very big. You can sail here for weeks and never see land. I do believe we are on our way home, what I shall be glad on, on account of tis now two yeres since the last time I seen you. I seen two dolfins today what are very big fish. They kep us company for four leagues. Wem in the doldrums at present, what means we en't moving on account of there en't any wind. Lord Nelson is all of a fidget he is so cross. He don't like being becalmed on account of he wants to catch up with Johnny Frenchman.

After a while her stories began to flow more easily, and she wrote an edited version of her sojourn on Barbados, explaining that she'd been left behind by the bum boat and had had to live there — *in a mud hut sleeping on the bare earth with the slaves imagine that Ma* — until the next boat came along. She wrote about the brightly coloured birds and what a dreadful screeching noise they made, about the sugar cane — *what's like great trees you can hardly see the tops of you would never think tis sugar* — and how the slaves worked from dawn to sunset cutting it down with great curved knives — *what could cut you in half with one swipe you'd be afeard to see them* — about the huge snake she'd seen — *what could swallow you alive in one gulp.* As the stories got more colourful and she read them through, she realised she was embroidering things and telling tall tales the way all sailors do, but she was enjoying it too much to alter it and besides, would be a wicked waste of paper if she were to discard it and she couldn't abide waste. So the days passed, and the correspondence grew until she'd covered both sheets of paper and there was only a corner left. I'll keep that, she decided, in case they tell us we're a-goin' home.

Despite her sea-going tendency to exaggeration, she was absolutely right about one thing and that was Nelson's impatience. Being becalmed was a torture to him. It had been agony enough to chase the French to the West Indies, but chasing them home again was ten times worse because he was beginning to be afraid that he wouldn't be able to find them once they were in Spanish waters and that the battle he was so determined to fight would elude him once again. But what could he do about it, beyond what was already being done?

On the last day of June, when he was just off the Azores, he sent the *Curieux* home to Portsmouth with his personal mail and dispatched Captain Sutton in the *Amphion* to Tangier Bay, firstly to find out whether the French had entered the Mediterranean, and when that was done to deliver letters to the British Consul at Tangier asking for supplies of bullocks, oranges and lemons to be made ready for the fleet, and when every errand had been completed to rendezvous with the rest of the fleet at Cape Spartel. Then he made plans for as many eventualities as he could imagine.

As soon as they knew they were sailing for Tangier, Peg and Moll made plans of their own. Neither of them had any doubt that the battle was only weeks away and the sooner they got out of the way of it, the better. As soon as their watch was over, they found a quiet corner on the gun deck and talked the matter over. They still had the money they hadn't spent the last time they went ashore back in the Indies and good strong purses to carry it in. It wasn't much but it would suffice.

"We *must* jump now," Moll said, "or we'll be caught still aboard when the battle starts an' I ain't having' that."

"Not in Tangier though," Peg decided. "'Tis a fearsome place for the fever is Tangier, an' we don't want that neither. Not if we can help it. Asides which, there ain't the ships to take us home and I doubt there'll be anywhere for us to hide. 'Tis all Musclemen thereabouts. No, we'll wait till we gets to Rosia Bay. That's the place for us. If he means to take on supplies, he's bound to go there. Pray for a fair wind and no sign a' the French."

TOM AND JEM were discussing their future too, out on the deck of the *Sirius*. They'd met up with Admiral Collingwood's fleet, according to their instructions, and delivered their letters and now they were off Cadiz, watching the seas for the French, like every British ship in the area, and seeing nothing but fishing boats.

The endless watching and waiting was beginning to get on their nerves.

"There are times," Jem confessed to his old mate, "when I just wants this battle to start and be over an' done with. 'Tis no sort a' life just waitin' for it."

"Met a feller at Copenhagen said the self-same thing," Tom told him, adding gloomily, "blowed to bits he was."

"Aye," Jem said, "That's the trouble. We waits an' waits an' complains a-waitin' an' then we gets blowed to Kingdom Come."

"What will 'ee do when 'tis over?" Tom asked, shifting direction. "If we comes through, what I hopes an' prays we will, we shall get a handsome bonus, all this time at sea an' then a battle."

Jem considered. "If I still had a wife," he said, "which I doubts, on account a' she'll have forget about me long since, but if I still *had* one I'd rent us a house an' furnish it all fine an' dandy an' settle down to a peaceful life as a master carpenter, in my home town, what I should ha' done all along if I'd had a ha'pporth a' sense. What about you?"

"I could get *me* a wife, I s'ppose," Tom said stroking his beard, "if I could find a woman what 'ud have me. Don't much reckon to settlin' down though. That's a deal too tame. I got itchy feet an' that's the truth of it. I likes to be off a-seein' the world. But a wife to come home to now an' then would be dandy."

"Where the devil are they?" Jem said, scowling at the empty sea. "All this way an' all this time an' not a sign a' the beggars. 'Tis enough to try the patience of a saint."

"We shall find 'em once our Nelson gets here," Tom told him. "You mark my words. If anyone can find 'em Nelson can. He's made his mind up to it."

~

IN FACT, the great Admiral was in sight of Cape Spartel and in a state of miserable depression. There was still no sign of the French fleet and, as his gloom deepened, he grew more and more convinced that he was never going to run his enemy to ground. He might as well give up hope, take his long-deferred leave, pass the command to his old friend Collingwood and go home to Emma. In the quiet of his empty stateroom, he was writing a letter to her, with his painstaking left hand, telling her how dearly he loved her and how much he wanted to be at home with her and Horatia at — *our beloved Merton.* But there were other letters to compose too. The first was to Collingwood telling him how miserable he was — *at not having fallen in with the Enemy's Fleet* — and warning him that the time was fast approaching when he would pass the command of the fleet to him and return to England — *there being little of any consequence I can do here.* The third and last was to the Admiralty in answer to their last instructions. It was hard to know what to tell them when the news was so bad, and his view was so negative. But he began valiantly, describing their long voyage back to Europe.

Our whole run from Barbuda, day by day, was 3,459 miles; our run from Cape St Vincent to Barbados was 3,227 miles; so that our run back was only 232 miles more than our run out. Allowance being made for the latitudes and longitudes of Barbados and Barbuda — average per day, thirty-four leagues, wanting nine miles.

It was excellent seamanship, but it didn't detract from the fact that he also had to report that he'd had no sight of the enemy in all that time and that consequently, no action had been fought. Disappointment and weariness weighed him down. He had come so far and striven so long and all he had to report was failure. What was the point of struggling on? Or of vowing not to set foot ashore until the battle was fought and won? It seemed to him now, sitting there alone in the depths of his misery that it had been vainglorious to have taken such a vow, the worst kind of presumption and foolishness even to have considered it. No matter what he did or where he went, the French eluded him. When he finally put down his pen to seal his letters, he was so miserable that even the thought of being back at Merton couldn't lift his gloom. Nevertheless, and no matter what he might be feeling, there were still matters to be attended to, and he must bestir himself and get on with his duties. The fleet had to be fed and watered. The *Amphion* was waiting for him at Cape Spartel and there was just a faint chance that Captain Scott would have better news for him.

Negatives again. There had been no sign of the French fleet at all, although they'd scoured the seas for them. They could report that they were not in the Mediterranean, which was some comfort because it meant that a watch could be set at the Straits of Gibraltar and there would be no more wild goose chases to Alexandria, but it was demoralising news no matter how much their demoralised Admiral tried to make the best of it.

"I will provision the fleet for four months at sea," he said to Hardy, "and then we will sail north. I will meet with Collingwood and Bickerton and take reports from them and unless there are indications to the contrary we will join the squadrons off Ferrol or Ushant. If there is no action there, I will hand over command to Collingwood and head for Portsmouth. It is a hard decision to have to make but I can see no other course."

So, having taken delivery of all the meat and fruit that Tangier could provide, which was little enough in all conscience, he set sail for Gibraltar and Rosia Bay, to be sure his ships were fully provisioned, just as Peg had predicted.

TO BE SENT ASHORE to take on supplies was exactly what the two girls wanted. It would mean landing on a quayside crowded with carts and traders and that would give them plenty of cover when the time came to run. In fact, they got even better cover than they could possibly have expected, and it was provided by none other than Admiral Lord Nelson.

His gloom was now so dark and all-enveloping that he had decided to break his impossible vow and go ashore. Earlier in the day, he had written another letter to the Secretary of the Admiralty informing him of his intention to relinquish his command. Then he put on his best uniform and took the long boat to shore. He would find his land legs, dine with the governor and discover what news he could. Then he would go home.

The sight of him caused a commotion on the quayside. Within seconds, people were rushing in from all sides to greet him and cheer him. All eyes were focused on their hero and the crush around him was so great it was almost ridiculously easy for Peg and Moll to slip away unnoticed. By the time the bum boat was finally loaded, and the lieutenant was looking for the rest of his crew, they were long gone.

"Damned boys!" he said. "What are they playing at? They should've been here helping to load up and man the oars, not gone running off. I shan't wait for them. They'll have to come back on the next boat, that's all. I have enough to do without wasting time on stupid boys."

"Off tom-catting, I shouldn't wonder," Johnny Galley said, grinning at him.

"I'll have their guts for garters," the lieutenant said furiously, "and they needn't think I shan't report 'em. Could be a flogging matter, could this, an' we ain't had a good flogging for months."

Johnny Galley raised his eyebrows. He didn't hold with flogging boys and especially for tom-catting.

"Do 'em good," the lieutenant said. "Make men of 'em."

But the boys were already in the nearest slop shop and halfway back to their original sex, buying old skirts, jackets and bonnets for themselves, in a state of exquisite excitement.

"We'll keep our sailors' slops," Peg said, framing her now decidedly feminine face in a rather battered straw bonnet, "In case we has to work our passage. We could buy one a' them shawls and make a parcel of 'em. What do 'ee think?"

Moll was still marvelling at how easy their escape had been. "What a stroke a' luck ol' Nelson a-coming out like that," she said. "Who'd ha' thought it?"

THAT EVENING, Nelson dined with the governor, caught up with the local news and hardened in his determination to return to Portsmouth. The next day, while the bum boats were still ferrying provisions, he wrote to Emma to tell her he was coming home and that he should be with her in two or three weeks — *given a fair wind*. Then he sent out orders that all mail from the fleet was to be made ready for collection and, once it had all been gathered in, he dispatched a cutter post haste to Portsmouth to deliver it. After that, it was simply a matter of giving up hope and preparing himself for home. Whatever was to happen now was in the lap of the gods.

IT WAS RAINING in Portsmouth when the postman arrived, and Mary Morris was complaining to her old friend Lizzie Templeman. "Dratted weather," she said, rubbing her back. "That's five days' rain on the trot. Five days' rain non-stop an' how I'm supposed to get the washing dry I do not know. 'Tis enough to try the patience of a saint."

"Can't command the weather, my lover," Lizzie told her, "an' that's a fact. We just has to put up with weather."

The room was hung with washing steaming in the heat of the stove and the two women were taking a dish of tea to rouse their spirits. "All this steam," Mary complained. "'Ten't good for a body. I'm forever hackin' an' coughin'." Which was true enough for she was coughing as she spoke. The first knock their postman gave was lost in the noise she was making. But he was a stolid young man and knew he had to knock until he was answered.

"Letter for Mrs Morris," he said, holding it out. "Come in this mornin' on a cutter, so it did."

Rain, laundry and coughing fits were all forgotten. "'Tis Marianne," Mary cried, holding out her hand for it. "Give it here quick. Where's my purse, Lizzie? Oh quick, quick."

The purse was found, the money paid, the letter opened. Lizzie was most impressed by it. "My stars!" she said. "Will you look at the size of it. She must ha' been writing it for months. Can you read it all?"

It was read aloud and with great pleasure, twice, to make sure they'd got it right.

"Snakes what could eat you alive," Mary said. "Imagine that."

"You notice she don't say nothin' about my Jem," Lizzie said and sighed. "I'm beginning to think I shall never see him again. All these years. You'd ha' thought he'd ha' sent me a line or two. Just to know he was still alive. I means for to say your Marianne's writ a book. I wouldn't ha' hurt him to write a line or two. I means for to say."

Mary wasn't paying much attention. She'd heard the complaint before and even though she sympathised there was nothing she could do to help. "There's a postscript writ up the sides," she said, noticing it. "Perhaps that's about him." She patted her friend's arm. "She'll find him come the finish, Lizzie. Never you fear. She'd made her mind up to it."

"What does it say?" Lizzie said as Mary turned the paper sideways. But Mary was screeching. "She's coming home, Lizzie. Look what she says: *We are in Gibraltar. We are coming home. I shall see you in a week or two.*"

THEY WERE LONG impatient weeks and, after the first of them, the two women walked down to Portsmouth Point every day to see if there were any arrivals. But it wasn't until the 18 August that there was any news and then it fired the town quicker than gunpowder. There were two ships of the line anchored at Spithead, the *Victory* and the *Superb*.

"Praise be," Mary said. "Now I shall have her home at last."

But the day passed and there were no boats arriving at shore, only a bum boat that had been sent out to pick up letters from the Port Admiral and when that came alongside the quay, it came with the news that the ships were in quarantine "on account of they put in at Gibraltar where they got the yellow fever".

"Oh for pity's sake!" Mary said. "And how long are they to be kept waitin' out there?"

"No good askin' me," the boatman told her. "I don't make the rules. I'm only the poor beggar what's the messenger. That'll be up to the Port Admiral."

"Well he'd better make his mind up sharpish," Mary said, glaring at the poor man. "That's all I got to say. Keepin' 'em waiting out there after all the time they been away. 'Tis a scandal, so it is."

The next day was Sunday and to nobody's surprise, it was raining again. Not that a spot of rain could deter the people of Portsmouth. The ramparts were crowded throughout the morning and every single place that could command a view of the harbour entrance was packed with people waiting to catch a glimpse of their hero when he finally came ashore. Mary and Lizzie were pushed and jostled whenever they tried to find a space and Mary's temper was worn to shreds long before dinner time. But she was determined not to be put off by silly crowds, no matter how pressing they were, and she and Lizzie came back to push their way to a viewpoint as soon as they'd fed their families. This time, they were determined to stay where they were until the crews came ashore.

It was past seven o'clock before Nelson's barge was sighted heading for the quayside and the great crowd cheered it every foot of the way, waving their hats and shouting themselves hoarse. Then there was so much pushing and shoving that Mary was afraid she was going to be end up in the sea.

"Why don't you look where you're going?" she yelled at a man who was running straight at her.

"I knows where I'm goin', ma'am," he yelled back. "I'm follerin' Lord Nelson to the commissioner's office to give him one last cheer. Tha's what I'm doin'."

"Blamed fool," Mary said. "He could've had me over."

But the crowds were thinning, which was a relief to her, and after a few more minutes there were hardly any people left on the quayside at all and those who *were* still standing there were obviously wives and relations waiting for news of their menfolk. It was dark and cold, and they were all wet.

There was a sailor walking towards them, heading towards the barge.

"Wait there," Mary said to Lizzie. "I'm going to ask that feller what's what. I shan't be a minute."

That feller was damp but courteous. "No, ma'am," he said. "There won't be no one else comin' ashore this time a' night. We only come out for Lord Nelson, you see. Everyone else is to wait till morning. That's the style of it."

It didn't please her at all but there was nothing she could do about it. "They come all this way," she grumbled to Lizzie as they trailed home, "and then they got to wait till morning. I don't see the sense in it."

"Be morning afore you knows where you are," Lizzie tried to commiserate.

"It 'ud better be," Mary said, as they rain dripped off the end of her nose. "I've had enough a waiting."

CHAPTER 16

Marianne was woken at four o'clock that Monday, at the start of the morning watch. Normally, she would have growled out of her hammock like everyone else but this time she got up at once, ready and eager, dark though it was, for this was the day she was going to jump ship. She had everything planned. She would do her work as quickly as she could, have her breakfast and pack her belongings in her ditty bag and then she would ask for permission to go ashore and see her parents. Now that Nelson had been rowed off in his barge to report to the Admiralty and see that Lady Hamilton of his, they could hardly keep everyone else on board, even if they wanted to, and especially if Portsmouth was their home town. They'd let her go sooner or later, they were bound to, and then she'd walk straight home and change into her woman's clothes and take up her old life and have done with all this seafaring — even if she hadn't got a husband to live with and it would mean going back to her father's house. The one thing she wasn't going to do was to stay aboard the *Victory*, sail out to a certain battle and put herself in danger. Peg and Moll had been right: if there was a battle coming, you jumped ship and got out the way of it. 'Twas the only sensible thing to do.

She had a disturbing moment when she asked permission because the lieutenant told her she was to find Mr Beattie and ask him, "being you're one of his boys" and Mr Beattie was stern.

"You may go ashore," he said, "but on one condition. We have a battle ahead of us, as you know, and I shall need every pair of hands once we come under fire. Every single pair of hands. I trust you understand that. Very well then, I must have your word that you will return to the ship as soon as you see the signal that we are about to sail. The bum boats will be sent out to bring all crew members back on board, but you must make it your responsibility to keep a daily watch. Do I have your word?"

It was painful to have to lie to him because he was a good man and she admired him, but it had to be done. "Aye, sir," she said. "You do, sir."

"Then you have my permission," the surgeon said. "Don't let me down."

Then it was just a matter of seeing the purser and persuading him to give her some of her pay, which he did somewhat grudgingly, warning her not to drink it all in one go, and waiting for the bum boat to take her ashore.

Two hours later, she was in her mother's kitchen. It was a fine August day bright with summer sunshine and she'd been blown along by the same lively wind that had scudded her out of the church on her wedding day. The force of it lifted her spirits quite wonderfully and by the time she got home, her cheeks were red, and she looked so fit and strong and brown-skinned that her mother squealed with pleasure at the sight of her.

"Oh my dear life, child," she said, "how well you do look." Then she burst into tears. "Don't 'ee mind me," she apologised, wiping her eyes on her apron. "'Tis just… I means for to say… I thought I'd never live to see you again, an' last night when we'd been waitin' all day and no sign of 'ee, I thought… an' now here you are. Oh my dear heart alive."

Marianne threw her arms round her mother's shoulders and

hugged her for a very long time, standing there in that familiar kitchen with the smells of new baked bread and newly prepared starch sweetening the air around her and the tears running down her brown face. Oh it *was* good to be home. But hadn't she known it would be?

"Now," she said, "I'll just get changed into my old clothes. Still in the closet, are they?"

Her mother didn't answer. She dried her eyes and took down her shopping basket from its hook on the wall. "We must go an' tell your father," she said. "He said to be sure to tell him the minute you come home. An' here you are."

"What now?" Marianne said. "Can't he wait for me to get changed?" She really didn't want to go rushing off to the wheel-yard in her sailor's slops.

"This very minute as ever is," her mother told her. "I promised him."

"What about the laundry?" Marianne hoped, looking at the baskets full of clean bed linen. "En't you goin' to make a start on it?" If Ma was ironing, she could slip away and get changed in no time at all.

But her mother waved her work away. "That'll keep," she said. "I can't be doin' with laundry at a time like this. Come on." And she opened the door and bustled them both out.

They walked through the narrow streets to the wheel-yard arm in arm, looking for all the world like a proud mother with her sailor son. Passers-by smiled approval, knowing that this stocky boy with his weather-browned face would have come from one of Nelson's ships, although one or two of the neighbours they passed who'd known Marianne when she was a girl looked at her somewhat askance. What a difference clothes do make she thought, smiling at their bewilderment, and she wished she'd had time to change and could have greeted them properly.

The wheel-yard was the same as she remembered it, smelling of wood shavings and piled about with bundles of spokes and rows of hubs and lengths of new wood, and her father and her brother Johnny were hard at work in the midst of it. They'd just eased a red-hot iron rim onto a cartwheel and were dousing it with buckets of water, tapping it tight as it cooled, their brawny arms and intense faces half hidden by rising steam. This wasn't the sort of work that could be left, not even to look up and wave a greeting, and Marianne knew it. She and her mother waited patiently in the doorway until the job was done. But the minute her father stood up and straightened his back, Marianne smiled towards him. She could still remember how foolish he'd been when she'd enlisted but he was still her Pa.

"Lo, Pa," she said, "still makin' your wheels then?"

"Well bless my soul!" her father said. "'Tis Marianne as ever is. Look 'ee here Johnny, if this en't your blessed sister turned up again. You was right, Mother. You said she'd be here." Then he wasn't sure how to greet her because she was standing in front of him looking so exactly like a boy that it made him feel confused. In the end, he thumped her on the arm. And at that Johnny thumped her between the shoulders. It was just like being on board ship.

"Where's my breeches?" Johnny asked. "You've never left 'em behind."

Marianne had forgotten all about his breeches but remembered them now, left behind in her old ditty bag on the *Amphion* when she went ashore to birth that poor baby. Not that she could tell him any of that. "You an' your breeches," she said, making a joke of it. "I got better things to think about than your breeches." And was thumped all over again.

Mary thought it time to intervene. "Leave her be, you great gawks," she said. "You'll do her a mischief."

That made Marianne laugh. "This en't nothing, Ma," she said. "Not compared to what goes on aboard ship. They thumps you about all the time on board ship."

"Well if that's the truth of it I'd rather not hear it," her mother said. "Come on." And she gave Marianne's arm a tug. "We'm off to Mr Templeman's, Jack, to buy a pie for our dinner," she explained. "We got somethin' to celebrate."

Marianne wasn't sure she wanted to see Mr Templeman just yet, but her mother gave her no choice in the matter. She took her arm and marched her off towards the pie shop, chattering all the way. But when they reached the door, she stopped and put her hand over her mouth in some dismay.

"Lawks a' mercy, child," she said. "What am I a-thinking of? You won't want to see 'em in them clothes. I quite forgot."

"'Ten't just the clothes, Ma," Marianne told her. "'Tis worse than clothes. 'Tis what they must think of me with Jem running off to sea like that."

"Why, what would they think of 'ee, child?" Mary said, patting her arm. "'Tweren't your fault. He was drunk, that's the truth of it, or he'd never have done such a blamed fool thing. Drunk an' silly. Come on. They'll be glad to see you home."

Which they seemed to be, for Lizzie Templeman, who was behind the counter serving the pies, and dusty to the elbows with flour, came out into the shop at once to kiss her and hug her and tell her how glad she was to see her, and her husband was equally welcoming.

"Pleased to see 'ee," he said in his shy way. "No news a' Jem, I daresay?"

They were both looking so hopeful it pained her to have to disappoint them. "No," she said, "but weren't for want a' trying. Truly it weren't. I asked for him at every ship I could find at every port we come to, over an' over, and I couldn't find a soul what had heard of him. Not one single soul. I *did* try."

Mr Templeman smiled at her sadly. "You done your best," he sighed. "You'm a good gel."

"'Tis a great fleet," Marianne explained. "That's the size of it. You never see so many ships. *Scores* an' scores of 'em. 'Twould take a month a' Sundays to ask 'em all. 'Tis like a great forest when

we're all in harbour, all them masts. Biggest fleet you ever saw."
She was swollen with pride just thinking of it. "But I can tell 'ee,
he's on one ship or another. Bound to be. You can depend on it.
An' when this battle's over, they'll all come home. You'll see. 'Tis
only chasing Johnny Frenchman what's kep' us at sea so long.
Once we've caught up with the beggar an' fought him an' beat
him, that'll be the end of it an' he'll come home. You'll see."

Then she realised that all three of them were gazing at her
with their mouths open.

"What's all this about a battle?" her mother asked. "You never
said nothin' about no battle. You said the Frenchies cut an' run. I
remembers a-readin' of it."

"And so they did, Ma," Marianne said, "on account of they're
lily-livered cowards, every man jack of 'em. Took one look at us,
so they did, and cut off quick. But they'll have to stand and fight
us come the finish. The Admiral's set his heart on it and when the
Admiral's set his heart on somethin' it'll come about sure as fate.
He's off a-telling the Admiralty so this very minute." She was
bragging with the best now and enjoying it hugely. "Oh yes, Ma,
there'll be a battle come the finish. Don't you make no mistake
about that. An' when it comes 'twill be a mighty big battle. A
mighty big battle. We shall see 'em off good an' proper."

"Well if that's the size of it," Mary said, "Thank the Lord you're
home an' out of it. That's all I got to say."

But Lizzie's face was crumpling with distress and seeing it
Marianne realised that her bragging had taken her too far and
that she'd spoken out of turn because Jem was still out there in the
fleet somewhere.

"He'll be killed as sure as fate," Lizzie said. "They gets killed
like flies in battles."

"Not your Jem," Marianne tried to comfort. "He won't. You'll
see. He'll come home large as life an' twice as handsome. They
don't kill carpenters on account of they couldn't keep the ship
afloat without 'em."

But Lizzie was too near tears to listen to her. "Sure as fate," she said. Perhaps it was just as well that her husband was in the shop, for he knew what to do. "What was it you was wanting, Mrs Morris?" he said, turning their attention to trade. "A nice pie was it?"

They chose a meat pie, which he promised them would eat tasty and Marianne carried it home in their basket with a cloth to cover it against the dust of the street. She was still feeling ashamed of herself for bragging and upsetting poor Lizzie Templeman, but there was nothing she could do about it now. This is what comes a' wearing these slops, she thought. The sooner I gets into my old clothes, the better.

"Oh Marianne," Mary said, looking at her as they battled against the wind, "It is good to have you home."

She was to say it so often as they set the table and served the pie that Marianne got quite sick of hearing it, true though it obviously was. She'd grown tough while she was away, that was the truth of it, and she didn't like to be fussed over. When they were eating their pie, the entire family together as if they'd never been apart, she launched into the story of the great cutlasses the slaves used to cut the sugar cane and how they could slash a man in half with one swipe. She'd chosen the tale partly to entertain them and partly to show them how tough her life had been, but she'd barely said more than a dozen words before her father leant across the table, winked at her and dropped a spoonful of salt on her plate.

"You don't believe a word I'm a-sayin', do 'ee, Pa?" she said.

"I believes the odd one here an' there," he told her. "Only I en't so trustin' as your ma. I heard too many old salts a-spinnin' yarns."

"Is that what I am then, Pa?" Marianne asked him. "An old salt?" She wasn't sure whether to feel flattered or affronted.

"Don't you pay him no mind, child," Mary said, scowling at her husband. "He don't know nothin' at all, stuck there in that of workshop a' his. I believe you."

"Thousands wouldn't," her husband said. And that made Marianne laugh aloud, and the moment passed.

"Did 'ee get my letters?" she asked her mother, when they'd eaten in silence for a while.

"Oh them letters," her father said. "I should just say she got 'em. She been a-readin' 'em non-stop ever since they come. We knows 'em by heart, we does."

Marianne grinned at him. "Then I don't need to tell 'ee nothing for you knows it all-a-ready," she said.

"Oh, yes, you do," Mary told her, "on account of I wants to hear it all again. Did those ol' snakes really swallow you alive?"

"Not me, they never," Marianne said, grinning at her father. "They knowed better'n to try an' swallow me, don't 'ee worry. I'd ha' choked 'em. But they was mighty big." And she held out her arms to show the length of them. "Boa conscriptors they called 'em, but don't ask me for why."

That afternoon, when her father and brother had gone back to their wheel, her mother pulled her long-suffering face and returned to the ironing. "I'll just get these things done an out the way," she said, an' then I'll run the iron over your proper clothes an' you can get out a' that rig an' be yourself again. I can't be doin' with you talkin' about battles an' lookin' like a boy all the time. It sets my teeth on edge."

"You don't have to iron *my* clothes, Ma," Marianne told her. "I can wear 'em as they are. I don' mind creases."

But her mother was having none of it. "The very idea," she said. "An' have you out an' about all creased and anyhow. What would people think? 'Twon't take me more'n a minute. You take a little stroll round the town an' pop in an' buy us some more ale at The Dolphin and by the time you gets back 'twill all be done for 'ee an' I can have my gel back again."

There was no point in arguing, as Marianne could see from the set of her mother's jaw. She simply had to do as she was told and take another wind-buffeted stroll through the town which wasn't what she wanted to do at all. 'Tis such a small place, she thought disparagingly, as she passed the ancient beams of The Duke of Buckingham, a stuck-in-the-mud place, the sort a' place that just goes on and on and never changes. 'Tis only me what's changed. She stood on the cobbles and watched as a carriage and pair passed by and was saddened to think that the greatest change of them all was the one that had left no sign and could never be talked about. And suddenly and without any warning, standing there in the strong sunlight and the full power of the wind, she had the most wrenching memory of her dead baby, so small and pale and never alive, and before she could prevent it her eyes were full of tears. She had to turn in to Peacock Lane before anyone could see her for fear of what they would say, for you don't expect to see a ship's boy standing in the street blubbing his eyes out.

This won't do, she told herself, quite crossly. You're dressed like a boy so act like one. And she went striding off towards The Dolphin to buy the ale, making the most of her rolling gait and deliberately being as much of a boy as she could.

Which was perhaps just as well, for whom should she see booming his way out of the dark door of The Dolphin but Tom Kettle with his peg-legged companion and, being a shrewd man of business, Tom Kettle recognised her at once.

"Well dang my eyes if it ain't young Matt," he said. "Come back on the *Superb* have 'ee?"

"No, sir," Marianne told him. "I'm on the *Victory*." The pride of being able to claim such an honour dried her tears in the instant.

"Ship's boy, are yer?"

"No sir, I'm a loblolly."

"Are you, bigod!" Tom Kettle said, plainly impressed. "Then you're worth your weight in gold an' that's the truth of it. I allus knew you'd do well fer yourself. Didden I say so, Peg? First time I clapped eyes on 'ee I said 'That boy'll do well. Strike me if I didn't. Good luck to 'ee, boy. You got some sterling work ahead of 'ee once that there battle begins."

His words stirred Marianne to the strangest emotion. It felt like homesickness. But that couldn't be right. You don't feel homesick for a ship, do you? And specially when you've only just left it an' come ashore an' you got no intention a' going back to it. You feel homesick for your home. That's what the word means. But there it was, pulling her guts with yearning, strong and unmistakable. There was no doubt about it: she was missing the ship and her shipmates.

It troubled her all the way home because it was such foolishness. 'Twas as if she was still a loblolly, which she most certainly was *not*. I must get back into my proper clothes the minute I'm home, she decided. The sooner I'm done with my old life and I've put it behind me and forgot it, the better.

ONCE HE KNEW he was in command, Admiral Collingwood began to organise his forces. He was a patient man but a determined one and he meant to make sure that Villeneuve's fleet was located and then penned in harbour until he could send a message to his old friend requesting him to return to them and lead the battle. There wasn't a captain in the British fleet who didn't know how low their Admiral had been when he left them. They were *his* captains after all, who'd dined with him on the *Victory* at regular intervals all through their long chase, and none knew him better, nor admired him more. When Admiral Collingwood sent out a message requesting them to dine aboard the *Royal Sovereign*, they accepted his invitation at once. Like him, they felt the time of reckoning was long overdue.

He outlined his plan to them in some detail. He intended to dispatch his ships, two by two to every likely harbour and the rest in line to pick up signals and pass them on. The watchers would work in pairs so that their vigil was constant and when they saw any arrivals or any significant activity, they would flag it back to the next ship along the line. A squadron would be sent to guard the Straits of Gibraltar to make sure that there was no possibility of the French slipping through in to the Mediterranean, the rest would watch the harbours.

"We have several advantages over the French," Collingwood told them, "as you well know. We are excellent navigators and have given proof of that in the commendable speed with which we crossed the Atlantic, our gunners fire at twice the rate of any Frenchman, be he never so well trained, our ships are copper-bottomed, which we've had cause to be thankful for over the last two years, and we have Mr Popham's new signalling method, which ensures that our messages are promptly sent and quickly passed on. I mean to make full use of it." And then remembering the words with which Nelson always involved his captains, he added, "How say you to that?"

They thought it an excellent plan and said so. "We've let the beggars elude us for far too long," Captain Scott said. "Time they were brought to book."

So the paired ships were sent off on their guard duty. It took a little time before they were all in position, but the watch was kept as soon as they arrived off shore. The *Sirius* and the *Euryalus* were sent to Cadiz, which pleased Jem, because, as he said, "I've knowed the beggars would come here, all along."

"I hope they prove 'ee right," Tom said, "for I tell 'ee, I'm sick to the teeth with all this hangin' about."

AUGUST WORE AWAY and eased into a golden September. The British ships prowled the Spanish coast and blocked the Straits of Gibraltar, waiting and watching. The *Victory* and the *Superb* rode at anchor at Spithead, waiting for orders. Nelson, having reported to the Admiralty in person, recovered his spirits at Merton in the peace of the countryside. It was a quiet interlude which none of them expected to last for long.

Marianne spent her time helping her mother with the laundry and the housework. She found it mightily boring after the drama of the seas and it took her a long time to get used to wearing skirts again and even longer to accustom herself to ale instead of grog. One evening, after nearly three weeks of her new dull existence, she was so homesick for sea-going company that she dressed herself in her sailor's slops, while her parents were safely in the kitchen, and sneaked out to The Dolphin for a pint of grog and an hour or two of sailors' talk. It was the best evening she'd spent since she came ashore. For a start, she was greeted royally by a gunner called Taffy who recognised her as "one of our loblollies" and from then on, she sat in the midst of the crew, singing with the best until it was late at night and she was smitten by conscience and said she had to get home "or my ol' woman'll have somethin' to say."

"Keep a weather eye out for the signals," Taffy advised her. "'Tis my view of it we shall be sailing in a day or two."

His shipmates mocked him. "You been a-sayin' that ever since we dropped anchor." But he was undeterred. "You mark my words," he said.

She did mark them. They echoed in her dreams. *Sailing in a day or two* and then I shall be left behind, she thought, as she tossed in her truckle bed, with nothin' to do except clean other people's clothes and drag about in skirts.

And then suddenly, everything changed. Lizzie Templeman came knocking on their door early one morning, breathless with excitement, to tell them that another ship of the line had arrived and was lying at Spithead "alongside the other two".

"The captain come ashore first thing," she reported. "I seen him with my own eyes. And they say he's gone to Merton for to see Lord Nelson. What do 'ee think to that?"

"They've found the Frenchies," Marianne told her. "That's

what's happened as sure as fate. They've found the Frenchies an'
he's come for to tell him so." She was caught up in such emotion
she could barely contain it all, excitement and fear because this
battle was coming and it would be terrible, jealousy because her
old shipmates would be there to see it and she wouldn't, shame
because she was going to skulk away here in safety instead of
going with them where she really ought to be, and that terrible
ache of yearning because they were the bravest men she'd ever
met and they were going to their deaths. "I'll go down to The
Dolphin, Ma," she said, "An' see what I can find out."

The inn was crowded with sailors, all drinking but all oddly
sober, talking quietly among themselves, their faces stern.

"If you please, sir," she said to the nearest seaman. "Have they
found the Frenchies?"

"What's it to you, gel?" the man said, quite crossly. "'Tain't
none of your affair. You cut off home and leave well alone."

Marianne was ruffled to be treated so rudely. You wouldn't be
talking to me like that if I was in my boy's clothes, she thought,
and fought back at once. "My brother's a loblolly on the *Victory*,"
she said. "He sent me down for to find out. He wants for to know."

The tone changed. "If that's the size of it," the sailor said, "you
tell him to get hisself down here quick as he can. The bum boat's
a-comin' an' we shall be off an' gone within the hour. Tell him to
look sharp, or he'll miss it."

Oh no he won't, Marianne thought, as she ran home. He'll be
back afore you can down that ale a yourn. She was still running
when she reached home, and she didn't stop until she was in the
back bedroom and pulling her ditty bag out of the closet. By the
time her mother followed her into the room, alarmed by the rush
of her arrival, she'd already got her breeches on.

"Land sakes, child," her mother said." What *are* you a-doin' of?"

"I'm goin' back to sea, Ma," she said. "It *was* the Frenchies. They
got the bum boat a-comin' to pick us up."

"Us?" Mary said. "What are you on about? You're not goin' on no bum boat, surely to goodness. You've come home. You've left 'em."

Marianne was pulling her jacket over her head. "I'm goin' back to 'em," she said. "It's no good you goin' on. I've made my mind up to it." She started to plait her hair in the old familiar way, her length of tarred string between her teeth.

To be told such a thing put Mary into a panic. "Child! Child!" she said. "Think what you're doin'. This en't a sea trip, they'm off to fight a battle. You said so yourself. You could get killed."

The plait was tied and neat. She was ship-shape and orderly and quite herself again. "I know that, Ma," she said calmly, putting on her shoes. "But I can't stay here. I got a job to do. Mr Beattie's dependin' on me."

"Well then let him. He's got other boys. He don't need you."

"'Twill be a big battle, Ma," Marianne said, putting on her black hat. "It's been a long time comin' an' he'll need every hand he can get. He told me so when I asked for leave."

Mary tried a straight entreaty. "Please don't go," she said. "Please. For my sakes. I couldn't bear it if you got killed."

But she was wasting her breath. Marianne's head was full of powerful images, of the gun deck and the gunners testing their cannon, of Mr Beattie in his terrible orlop deck waiting for the wounded, of Nelson, calm and commanding on the quarter-deck. That was where she belonged, on that beautiful ship, where she was duty-bound to be and where she was going. She was beyond thought or argument, already on her journey. In a moment of instinctive pity, she stopped to kiss her mother's cheek, then she ran out of the door and out of the house.

CHAPTER 17

Nelson arrived at The George Inn in Portsmouth early the next morning and promptly set up his headquarters there as he usually did when he was in that city. News of his arrival spread with the speed of a gunpowder trail. Within an hour, the streets were clogged with carriages and thronged with excited crowds, most of them admirers who had come to cheer him and wish him God speed but some sightseers, come in a more ghoulish way to take "one last look at him afore he goes."

Lizzie Templeman arrived at Mary's house just before midday. She was appalled to find her old friend in tears and angered when she heard of Marianne's foolishness. "What's got into the gel?" she said. "'Twas one thing to go huntin' for our Jem — you could see the sense of *that* — but there's no need for this, surely to goodness. Didn't 'ee tell her?"

"Over an' over," Mary wept, "an' she never took a blind bit a notice."

"I'm off to see Lord Nelson an' wish him Godspeed," Lizzie said. "Shall 'ee come with me?"

"What's the good a' that?" Mary said. "He won't make her come back to me, now, will he?"

"No," Lizzie agreed, "but I tell 'ee one thing. If anyone can beat the Frenchies and keep his men safe while he's a-doin' it, he's the man. I means for to go and give him a cheer. 'Tis the least we can do. Come with me, my dear. He's a good man an' 'twill cheer you to see him."

So Mary was persuaded and put on her bonnet and shawl to join the crowd. It was a chill, calm afternoon with very little wind and the ships at anchor in the harbour lay still as if they were sleeping. But the streets were raucous with people all jostling for the best view and shouting the latest news at one another.

It wasn't long before a neighbour came pushing her way through the throng to join them. "Come to see him off, have 'ee?" she said. "That's the style. You got to see him off, I means for to say. I said to my Sidney, I said, I mustn't miss this. Got to see our hero off to sea. I means for to say. An' he said — my Sidney I mean not Lord Nelson — *Well, now Molly Simmons, I s'pose I shan't see you till he's took ship then.* That's just typical of my Sidney. Well you know what he's like, Mary. No sense a' hist'ry. Never has had. I means for to say, we can hardly let him go off to sea with the battle comin' an' all an' not be here to cheer him. The very idea! That's the trouble with my Sidney. He don't think. Never has done. I said to him only yesterday, I said…"

Lizzie took Mary's arm and edged her out of the way. A garrulous neighbour would be just the sort of person to say something foolish and upset her and Molly Simmons was renowned for letting her tongue run away with her. "We'll be better off over here," she said. "Better view."

There was a stir at the edge of the crowd and somebody shouting. "He's gone out the back door. This way! Come on!" Then the horde of people moved as one entity and Mary and Lizzie were carried along by the tidal rush with all the others, willy-nilly. Their hero had tried to make an unobtrusive exit from the back door of The George instead of pushing his way through the crowd in the street. He'd been seen of course — there were too many eyes looking out for him — and was being followed down the narrow alleys of Penny Street and Green Row towards the bathing machines. It wasn't long before they'd caught up with him and surrounded him, some with tears in their eyes, some falling to their knees, cap in hand to call out a blessing on him as he passed. Others offered him their hands and were touched when he told them he wished he still had two arms so that he could shake hands "with more friends". Many wept. It was an extraordinary, emotional progress. When they reached the steps by the bathing machines, the crowd broke ranks and pushed their way onto the parapet, ignoring the sentries who were trying to hold them back, anxious to watch him every step of the way. There were renewed cheers and cries of "God bless 'ee, sir." And then he was descending the step towards his barge, alone and serious, and there wasn't a woman in the crowd who wasn't crying.

"Such a fine good man," Molly Simmons said, pushing in between her neighbours. "I means for to say, when you think what's ahead of him, poor soul, off to fight them pesky Frenchies, no wonder he looks peaky. They say 'twill be a fearsome battle. This could be the last time he sets foot on English soil, think a' that. I means for to say, the last time we shall ever see him again."

"Don't talk morbid," Lizzie said fiercely, trying to check her. "You don't know what's to come no more than any of us."

"Quite right," Mary said, glaring at her neighbour because she was too near tears to do anything else. "No point meeting trouble half way. If 'tis coming, 'tis coming, and we'll face it when we must, that's my opinion of it. Meantime I'll trouble you to keep *your* opinion to yourself."

Molly Simmons blushed, suddenly remembering that Lizzie had a son in the fleet. "Time goes on, that's the trouble," she said apologetically. "You sort a' loses track. Seems only yesterday we was all at your Jem's wedding. Such a pretty wedding. All them flowers an' all." But her neighbours had turned away from her and were pushing their way out of the crowd.

"How can she say such things?" Mary wailed. "Don't she have any sense at all?"

"Let's go home," Lizzie said, taking her arm. "We've seen him go an' he's on his way an' there's nothing to be gained by staying here."

～

SHE WAS RIGHT. At that moment, Nelson was sitting in the barge beside his old friend Captain Hardy, being rowed out to his flagship. From time to time, he waved his hat to the crowds still cheering along the shore and smiled as some of them ran down onto the beach and waded into the sea to follow him as far as they could. It had been such an extravagant display of affection he was still moved by it.

"I had their huzzas before," he said to Hardy, "I have their hearts now."

～

ABOARD HIS FLAGSHIP, the gunners were standing ready to give him a thirteen-gun salute and the rest of the crew were on deck, lined up and ready to greet him as he was piped aboard, Marianne among them, surreptitiously watching the barge as it slid across the milky water towards them, oars dipping in unison. From time to time, she glanced up at the poop deck, which was full of politicians and statesman and such like waiting to dine with the Admiral, and a very grand lot they were in their fine hats and their fine coats, their silk stockings and their buckled shoes, standing about as if they were posing for their portraits and talking to one another in their loud plummy voices. They didn't impress her in the least. We shan't see the likes a' you around when the fighting starts, she thought, looking up at them. You'll be long gone by then. She was swollen with pride to think that she would be at the battle alongside the gunners and the marines and all the valiant men who would be putting their lives at risk, while these sugared dandies were showing off their finery in London. It surprised her to realise how much she'd altered her opinion of the gentry now that she'd had a couple of years in the navy. There was a time when she'd have admired 'em. But not now. What we wants, she thought, is a good strong wind from the right quarter so that we can set sail. You'd be off to shore pretty quick then.

But there was no wind until the following morning and then it was too slight to be very much help to them. Nevertheless, they weighed anchor and set sail along the Channel as well as they could. At first, they hugged the coast, watching as the fashionable holidaymakers in Lyme and Torquay stood along the promenades in the sunshine to wave to them. When they reached Weymouth, the wind became foul and it was only by Captain Hardy's exemplary seamanship that they avoided being blown into the town. But when the wind turned fair again, they continued to Plymouth, where they were joined by the two ships of the line that were waiting for them, and from there they sailed on to the Scilly Isles where they met up with the *Decade*, who was on her way back from Cadiz bringing Nelson's old friend Sir Richard Bickerton home on leave because he was too ill to continue in command. *Victory* hove to so that he could come aboard, which he did although he was obviously very unwell, and the news he brought from Spain was as welcome to Nelson as he was. Collingwood had the French fleet penned in at Cadiz, the Straits were so well guarded there was no possibility of any ships slipping through into the Mediterranean and there had been no battle, as yet.

"If you have a fair wind," Sir Richard told his old friend, as they said goodbye to one another forty minutes later, "you will be in time. God go with you."

His news spread through the ship within minutes of his departure. Marianne wasn't at all sure how she felt about it. Like so many of the men on board, she felt it would be a good thing when the battle had been fought and was over and done with but even so… hadn't she been standing on this very deck no more than a few weeks ago praying to God not to let it happen? And now, she was sailing towards it and it was coming as sure as fate.

Early the next morning, when she was on her way to the heads to empty her bucket, she met up with the gunner called Taffy and, because the battle was still on her mind, she asked him how long it was going to take to reach Cadiz.

"Depends on the wind," he said, shifting his wad of tobacco from one cheek to the other. "Given a fair wind we could be there in a fortnight, if 'tis foul, will take longer. But don't 'ee fret, my lubber, we shall get there sooner or later. The Admiral's set his heart on it."

"Aye," she said. "So he has."

What was coming would come no matter what she thought about it but, foolish though it was, she thought about it constantly. She simply couldn't help it for it seemed too terrible that these men would be killed. At least young Josh wasn't being quite so ghoulish now that the reality of seeing bloodshed was so close and that was a blessing. But it *was* getting close — no one could deny it — and the closer it got, the more she dreaded it.

IN THE QUIET of his stateroom with Secretary Scott to assist him, Nelson was writing letters, one to the British Consul at Lisbon to keep him informed of events, and the other to Admiral Collingwood, urging him to ensure that all his ships were fully provisioned and supplied with water and begging him on no account to acknowledge his arrival. "I wish to arrive unbeknown to the enemy and would not have you salute or hoist colours, even if you are out of sight of land." Then having made what preparations he could, he sent the *Euryalus* on ahead with his mail and began to draw up a plan of battle.

JEM TEMPLEMAN HAD BEEN FULLY PREPARED for this battle for over a month, the bungs made and in position, masts and timbers inspected and repaired wherever repair was necessary, every task no matter how large or how small completed at once and to the best of his ability. He was full of unleashed energy, secretly afraid of this coming fight and yet excited by it and eager for it too, unable to be idle, prowling about the ship as the ship prowled along the Spanish coast and the signalmen passed on any information that could be gathered and the watch kept a careful eye on Cadiz. There was now a combined French and Spanish fleet in the harbour and the ships were in plain view. Watchers from the crow's nest claimed they could count them and if their reports were correct, it was a formidable force — fifteen Spaniards of the line, and twenty-four French ships, four with 80 guns, fourteen with 74s, five frigates and two-gun brigs. The gunners on the *Sirius* maintained that the Spaniards could be discounted on account of they'm poor seamen and worse gunners but even so, thirty-nine warships was a sizeable fleet, even for Nelson to tackle.

"Time he come an joined us," the gunners said. "He'll know what's to be done with the beggars." But there was no sign of his arrival yet, so, for the moment, all they could do was keep watch and to note that the Frenchies were showing no signs of coming out.

Like everyone else on the *Sirius*, Tom and Jem were so tense they could barely stand still, even when they were standing by the rail chewing baccy. They fidgeted from foot to foot, spat more often than was necessary and swore at everything, from the food and the ship's boys to the French and the weather.

Tom's emotions were in such a turmoil, he was beginning to have superstitious doubts about the whole affair. "I can't help a-thinkin' of that ol' Count Carry Cho Lo," he said, gazing lugubri-ously at the French masts massed in that distant harbour.

"What ol' Count Carry Cho Lo?"

"Neapolitan prince," Tom explained. "Don't 'ee remember? Old Amos told us about him in the Bay a' Naples that time. Nelson hanged him from his own yard arm and buried the beggar at sea an' he came back to haunt him. Dead as a doornail, so Amos said — don't 'ee remember? — standin' up in the water with his white hair trailing an' his eyes still open. What if he was an omen?"

"I don't hold with omens," Jem said, "an' specially not afore a battle. I got enough on my plate without omens."

"But what if—" Tom persisted.

"You ask me," Jem said, spitting a long stream of tobacco into the sea, "It's high time them lily-livered beggars come out and faced up us and took what's a-comin' to 'em. I'm sick to the innards waitin' for the beggars. If Nelson was here, we'd be after 'em quick as a flash."

But it wasn't until 25 September that Nelson finally met up with Collingwood's fleet, on a balmy evening when the peaceful smell of the orange groves was wafted out to sea as if to greet him. Several days later, he too saw the French and Spanish fleet in Cadiz harbour and estimated them to number thirty-three, writing in his journal that night: *It is believed that they will come to sea in a few days. The sooner the better.* But unfortunately, the balm of the last few days had brought an almost total lack of wind power and neither fleet was going to sail that day or the next. The 29th of September was Nelson's forty-seventh birthday and, as a battle was still obviously out of the question, he threw a party instead and invited all fifteen of his commanding officers to join him on *Victory* to be wined, dined and entertained — and, when the celebrations were over, to be shown his plan of attack, which they unanimously approved.

The next day, the wind blew fair and tension aboard the British ships increased by the hour, for now surely the enemy would come out. But still nothing happened and although the wind continued fair, the French stayed where they were and refused to move. Nelson's frustration was even more acute than that of his men. He knew that some action was needed to break the tension or tempers would begin to flare. He sent a squadron of frigates, the *Sirius* among them, to cruise as close to the harbour mouth as they could get to see if they could tempt the combined fleet out, and a second squadron of 74s to a point, ten miles east, to guard against any attempt to cut and run into the Mediterranean. Then, since there were still many more ships with nothing to do, and crews that needed occupation, he set sail for a rendezvous point ten miles out to sea. The wind continued fair but still nothing happened. The frigates couldn't tease the French out of harbour no matter how tantalisingly close they sailed. There was no French shipping heading for the Straits. Tension rose no matter what Nelson tried to do about it. In fact, the one and only good thing that came out of their long fidgeting vigil was that other ships of the line had time to join them, one from Gibraltar and five from home.

Then, at last, on 18 October, there were signs of action. A look-out on one of the frigates reported that troops were being embarked on the French ships of the line and that the Spanish ships had got their top-sails up. The next morning, to Nelson's great relief, the combined fleet began to get under way. As soon as the news was flagged to him, he ordered a general chase in a south-easterly direction and signalled to his fleet to prepare for battle. It was a bright clear day but with little wind and by the end of it, only twelve of the Spanish ships had managed to get clear of harbour and were tacking northward dogged by two British frigates. But the battle was now imminent, and the decks were cleared for it.

That night, Nelson snatched a few quiet moments to compose a letter to Emma.

My Dearest beloved Emma, the dear friend of my bosom,

The Signal has been made that the Enemy's combined fleet are coming out of Port. We have very little wind, so that I have no hopes of seeing them before tomorrow. May the God of Battles crown my endeavours with success, at all events I will take care that my name shall ever be most dear to you and Horatia, both of whom I love as much as my own life, and as my last writing before the Battle will be to you, so I hope in God that I shall live to finish my letter after the Battle. May Heaven bless you prays your

Nelson and Bronte

THE NEXT DAY, the rest of the combined fleet gradually emerged from the shelter of Cadiz and by daylight on 20 October Admiral Blackwood sent a signal from the *Euryalus* to report that all thirty-four enemy ships were out of port. By then, the weather had changed yet again, and it was pouring with rain, but *Victory* hove to so that Collingwood could come aboard to report. He brought Captains Duff, Hope and Morris with him, for they were the three who had been passing Blackwood's messages from ship to ship down the line and they knew better than most what the present position was. After their visit, Nelson spent the day on *Victory's* poop so that he could watch the weather and would see Blackwood's continuing signals as soon as they came in.

Now, the two great fleets were manoeuvring for position, Nelson determined to cut off his enemy from the Straits and to lure him so far out to sea that it would be impossible for him to retreat to port, Villeneuve endeavouring to find the most advantageous position for the battle he could no longer avoid. That evening, Nelson sent a message to his captains detailing the signals that should be used during the night. If the French were heading south towards the Straits, they were to burn two blue lights together every hour, if they were moving westward, they were to fire three guns, quick, every hour. Whatever else, his old enemy was not to be allowed to slip out of his clutches again.

So the night watch began, and the crews took themselves to their duties or retired to snatch what sleep they could. On the dark gun deck of the *Victory*, Marianne rolled herself tightly in her blanket because the thought of what was to come was making her shiver, and said her prayers and tried to sleep, and on the open deck of the *Sirius*, Jem and Tom, smoking together for what they both knew would be the last time before the battle, looked out over the night-black water and saw the ominous glow of the lamplight from the stern-cabin windows of thirty-four enemy man-of-war.

CHAPTER 18

I t was such a gentle dawn. Not a rough breaking of day but a
gradual shimmer of expanding light over retreating darkness.
Everything about it was calming and beautiful, from the pale lilac
clouds drifting in a sky the colour of woodsmoke to the soft
breeze playing the sails and ruffling the quiet swell of a green sea.
Seasoned mariners like Nelson and Hardy knew that the swell
would mean a storm later in the day, but the breeze was almost
exactly right. It would give them enough power to manoeuvre
into position for the battle but be insufficient for the French to
make a run for it back to port. To Marianne, carrying buckets
down to the orlop deck ready to scrub Mr Beattie's table, it was a
good omen and she was cheered to feel it against her face.

The crew were up and about long before first light, dressed,
fed and ready for action, and Nelson was ready alongside them,
standing on the quarter-deck in the familiar undress uniform he'd
worn ever since they left Portsmouth, the four stars of his Orders
of Knighthood that were embroidered on the left breast of his
jacket glinting in the half light. All decks were cleared for action;
furniture had been taken from the cabins and stored in the hold;
the midshipmen's berth in the after cockpit had been cleared and

the space made ready for the wounded; the nets were slung ready to catch falling splinters; the gun ports were open; cooks had prepared what food they could before they had to put out the galley fires and leave the gun deck; marines had made sure that their cutlasses were sharp and their muskets primed; gunners had stripped to the waist, bound kerchiefs round their heads to stop the sweat dripping into their eyes and provided themselves with plugs of gun-cotton to block their ears; ship's boys had carried buckets of water down to the gun decks and set them by the scuttlebutts ready for use when the gunners needed to quench their thirst; Mr Beattie and his two assistants had sharpened their knives and saws; the entire ship from Nelson down to the newest recruit was in a state of implacable readiness. The orderliness of it all was reassuring and calming, even to Marianne.

At twenty minutes to seven, Nelson sent out his first signal of the day, saying that the order of sailing was to be in two columns, each ship "to engage her opponent". His captains already knew what had to be done for this was the order of battle he'd shown them on his birthday, so the columns began to form up immediately, Nelson leading the northern column in *Victory*, Collingwood heading the southern one in the *Royal Sovereign*. When both columns were ready, Nelson sent the signal: *Bear up and steer east*. Then they set sail towards their waiting enemy.

They were still too far out to see the French fleet but, as they progressed, the watchers on the quarter-decks began to make out the tops of their masts, rising like black trees against the skyline. Towards mid-morning when the clouds had cleared, an autumnal sun was shining, and the sea was a rich dark blue, the enemy sails came into view. Now it was possible to see what an enormous fleet they were, for they stretched along the horizon for miles. Even a novice like Marianne could see that it was a huge distance and her heart contracted with fear at the thought of all those guns and how soon they would be firing. *Please God*, she prayed, *don't let anyone be hurt*. But that was a foolish request and she knew it, so she amended it to *Please God don't let too many men be hurt* as they sailed on towards that terrible, waiting, death-dealing line. The breeze was so light it was hard to make much progress, so their long advance was achingly slow. They were taking an hour to cover a mile and a half and, as Jem said to his old friend Tom when he was working through the gun decks checking that all his bungs were ready and in place, "we could walk there quicker".

"Can't command the wind, my ol' lubber," Tom said, "an' that's a fact. We shall get there come the finish, depend on it."

As he was speaking, six bells were struck to mark the fact that it was eleven o'clock and the military bands, which had been standing ready on various quarter-decks waiting for the signal, began to play their martial music. On *Victory*, they gave a spirited rendering of the National Anthem followed by *Rule Britannia* and *Briton's strike Home*. On the *Sirius*, they played the sailor's hornpipe. There was instant pandemonium on the gun deck as the gunners leapt to the dance like dervishes, hooting and yelling.

"Come on," Tom said to his friend. "Let's see if you can still cut a caper."

Jem had no desire to cut anything at all. He was too full of apprehension to be leaping about. But he could hardly say no, when they were all jumping like fleas, so he joined in and after a second or so, he found that he too was dancing like a madman.

They only stopped when the music changed to *Rule Britannia* and by then they were out of breath and dripping with sweat. "My dear heart alive," Tom said. "That *was* a caper an' no mistake."

"Done us all good," his mates said. "Just what we was a-needin' of. Let off a bit a steam like. We might not have the legs for it when this day's over."

"How close have we got to get afore we takes up our positions?" Jem asked, as Tom peered through the gun port at the distant ships. He didn't know much about naval engagements, except that the two sides took up positions facing one another before they began firing.

Tom threw back his head and gave a roar of laughter. "Close!" he said. "There's a fool question. We don't take up no positions, my lubber. We sails till we can't go no further without ramming the beggars. Then we blows 'em to Kingdom Come, straight through the stern and out the other side. What you'm a-goin' to see today, my friend, is the Nelson touch, what en't never been beat yet an' won't be beat today."

The others roared their agreement. "That's the style of it, young Tom. You'll see, Mr Templeman."

They can't mean it, Jem thought, appalled by what they were saying. Surely to God. If we just keep going, we'll be shot to ribbons as soon as the French are in range and we won't be able to do a thing about it because our guns will all be pointing the wrong way, out to sea instead of at the enemy. It was the most foolhardy plan of action he'd ever heard of. And the most idiotic. And the bravest. Oh well and away the bravest. It was making his stomach shake just to think of it.

"Must get on," he said gruffly, and walked away.

NELSON WAS on the poop deck when the band on *Victory* began to play and his mood was lifted by hearing music too. "Do you not think," he said to Captain Blackwood, who was standing beside him, "That there is one more signal wanting?" And when Blackwood nodded and seemed in agreement, he said, "I'll now amuse the fleet", and sent a midshipman to fetch John Pascoe, his signal lieutenant.

"Mr Pascoe," he said when the lieutenant arrived, "I wish to say to the fleet *England confides that every man will do his duty.* You must be quick, for I have one more signal to make which is for close action."

Mr Pascoe took note of the signal but asked leave to suggest that the word *expects* should be substituted for *confides*, explaining that the first word was in the signal book and that the use of it would save seven hoists.

The suggestion was accepted. "That will do," the Admiral said. "Make it directly."

So the signal was sent and passed along the columns. Its effect was electrifying. Some crews gave it three cheers, others shouted "Aye, Aye sir!" and waved their hats towards the flagship. Jem, looking across the water at the towering hulks of their enemy, found he had a lump in his throat.

The French fleet were now in full view, boldly painted in scarlet and white, and black and yellow, and the crews on the *Victory* and the *Royal Sovereign* knew they would be coming under fire within minutes. Captain Blackwood and Captain Prowse were rowed back to the *Euryalus* and the *Sirius* ready to take command when the bombardment began, Nelson ordered his last signal, which was for close action, and his crews hardened their sinews to endure whatever horrors were coming in the last twenty minutes of their approach.

Marianne was down on the orlop deck trimming the lamps when the French opened fire and the sudden roar made her jump. My dear heart alive, she thought, that was close. But Mr Beattie and his two assistants were standing calmly by the table and although all the loblollies looked at one another in trepidation none of them said anything so she got on with the lamps and tried not to show how frightened she was. Seconds later, they heard the splash of a cannon ball that had missed its mark and fallen into the sea beside them, and then there was an uproar of sound as more guns fired and the ship shuddered as it took the shots and they could hear the crack of a great timber immediately above their heads and knew that the mainmast had been hit. The guns were still firing when their first casualty came staggering down the steps dripping blood, a great splinter of wood sticking out of his arm.

Mr Beattie dealt with him at once. He took his largest pair of pincers, pulled the splinter from the man's arm in one heaving movement and tossed it in a bucket. Then, since there were two more injured men being carried down the steps by the marines, he handed the first man over to Marianne telling her to bind the wound "tightly, mind" and turned his attention to the new arrivals. The first man had a shattered arm — even from where she stood in the shadows, Marianne could see white bones sticking out of the gory mess of his flesh — and he was grey-faced and speechless with shock. He didn't even say anything when Mr Beattie told him the arm would have to come off but lay on the table meek as a lamb come to slaughter, took the gag between his teeth and turned his head away from the agony that was coming. Marianne and the other loblollies watched in horror as the two marines held him down and Mr Beattie cut off his arm with those appalling knives and that terrible saw. Even then the man didn't scream or call out, but his groans were worse than screams. They seemed to come from deep inside him and were low and terrible as if they were being torn out of him with every cut. It made her ache to hear them. But there was no time for pity. No time for anything except the job in hand. The stump had to be bandaged and there were more injured men staggering down the companionway, slipping on the blood-smothered steps. Dear God, she thought, as she bandaged the grey-faced man as gently as she could, if 'tis like this down here what must it be like on deck?

It was a shambles, for once the French had found their range, they pounded the ship without mercy. Their sixth shot went through the main topgallant sail, then there was a short silence, then seven or eight enemy ships fired simultaneously and accurately. The mizzen top-mast was shot clean away, the sails were riddled with holes and a round shot, flying hot across the quarter-deck, hit Nelson's secretary Scott and tore him into unrecognisable pieces. The deck was covered with blood and guts and bits of flesh and bone, and before Captain Hardy could divert him, Nelson turned to see what had happened and knew who'd been hit, saying "Is that poor Scott?" But there was no time for pity, even here among friends. Two sailors were already shovelling the remains into the sea.

From then on, the fire was hard and accurate and there was nothing anyone aboard the *Victory* could do about it. They weren't close enough yet to come about and aim their own guns, and there was so little wind that they were a sitting target, moving with agonising slowness or merely shifting on the swell. They drifted for the next ten minutes and took more and more casualties until the cockpit was full of injured men.

But at last they were close enough for Nelson to give the order to port the helm and the ship hauled to starboard and the gunners on the leeward side could fight back. They were passing under the stern of the *Bucentaure*, which was a three-decker and Villeneuve's flagship, and the broadside went through her cabin windows and straight along the gun decks, smashing the guns and causing carnage among the crews. The air was full of black smoke and flying splinters of wood, which fell like rain on everyone on the quarter-deck. Now the battle proper had begun.

As *Victory* hauled to starboard, she came within range of the *Redoutable* and the *Neptune*. Hardy saw at once that she had no hope of breaking through and sailing between them but would be forced to run into one or the other and turned to ask Nelson which it should be.

"It does not signify which we run aboard of," Nelson told him. "Take your choice."

Minutes later, they collided with the *Redoutable*. It was a glancing blow and the *Victory* rebounded from it with little damage, but her yardarm was caught in the *Redoutables* rigging and the two ships were locked together as they drifted before the wind. The gunners on the *Victory* now had clear targets on either side, pounding the *Santissima Trinidad* to port while they smashed in the *Redoutable*'s sides with their starboard guns. By this time, the following ships of the column were manoeuvring into position and engaging the enemy too. The air was full of flying debris and the smoke from their guns massed like clouds about them obscuring the targets they were trying to hit. The fight was hot and unstoppable now.

The *Sirius* was between the *Heros* and the *Santissima Trinidad* and firing broadsides at both of them. The noise of the guns was so incessant, it was a continuous ear-battering roar. Jem had gone beyond excitement and even beyond fear, so the noise no longer stirred his senses or shook his belly. He was working automatically, plugging holes and making what repairs he could with such calm that it was as if he was back in Portsmouth working in Mr Henderson's wood-yard, as if his old master was standing beside him saying. "Don' 'ee pay 'em no mind, my sonny. You got a job to do." There was no battle, no death, no blood, no pity, no fear, just a job to do — and another, and another. "Order an' method. That's the style. One thing at a time."

ON THE *VICTORY*, the quarter-deck was under grenade attack and musket fire from sharp shooters on the *Redoutables* three tops, which, being a mere forty-five feet away and locked in position, were perfect places from which to take aim on the *Victory's* upper decks. The British marines returned fire from the poop deck and several of the French musketeers had been injured, although as both ships were lurching in the swell, and both were partially obscured by smoke, taking accurate aim was difficult. Even so the quarter-deck was a dangerous place to be.

Nelson and Hardy paced up and down the quarter-deck together keeping watch over the battle and ready to give such orders as were required. Hardy had reached the wheel and was walking back to the hatchway when he became aware that he had taken his last few steps on his own and, turning, he saw that Nelson had been hit and was on his knees, at exactly the same spot where his secretary had been killed an hour earlier. He was trying to support himself with his left hand, his fingers splayed against the deck, but as Hardy watched, his arm gave way and he fell on his side. There was instant movement towards him, first a sergeant-major of the marines and then two seamen who bent to lift him, and then Hardy himself. At first, he was reassured to see that Nelson was smiling but when the Admiral spoke, his words belied the smile.

"They've done for me at last, Hardy," he said, looking up at his old friend.

The words struck chill. "I hope not," Hardy told him.

But Nelson was stoically adamant. "Yes," he said with appalling calm, "My backbone is shot through."

"Cover his face," Hardy told the sergeant-major brusquely. "The men mustn't see this."

A handkerchief was found and draped over Nelson's face, which he took patiently. Then the seamen lifted him and prepared to carry him below.

ON THE CROWDED ORLOP DECK, Mr Beattie had over forty patients waiting for attention and the place was dank and dark and stinking of bilge water, blood, sweat, vomit and shit. When he saw yet another officer being carried down the stairs, he was removing a shattered leg and was tired to his bones and bloody to his elbows, so he shouted to the bearers to take him to a forward position on the port side and to mind how they handled him, but otherwise paid him little attention. Marianne barely glanced at him. She was holding a beaker of lemonade to the dry mouth of one of the wounded, and the poor man was shaking so much it was hard for him to swallow. But within seconds someone started yelling for Mr Beattie, calling his name and shouting, "Lord Nelson is here!" and at that she turned her head and looked at where they were pointing and there was the wounded man being carried through the cockpit in his familiar coat with its embroidered stars. Oh my dear heart alive, she thought, not him too. Mr Beattie finished his operation, handed his patient over to his assistant, and walked towards the bearers, treading carefully along the crowded deck so as to avoid the spread-eagled limbs of his patients, his face grim. "Fetch a sheet," he said to Marianne as he passed her, "and follow me."

The two bearers were still struggling through the throng and now the purser was running towards them too. He and Mr Beattie took Nelson away from them and carried him gently to one of the midshipmen's berths. He seemed confused by the change-over. "Who is carrying me now?" he said.

"Beattie, my lord," the surgeon said, as they laid him gently against the bulkhead, "and Mr Burke."

As soon as he was in position, the two men began to strip him, removing his blood-soaked jacket and setting it aside, then his shoes and stockings and breeches, which they handed to Marianne. There was a miniature portrait of Lady Hamilton worn like a locket on his chest and that was removed too.

"Doctor, I told you so," Nelson said, gazing ahead of him as if he couldn't see. "Doctor, I am gone." He seemed confused, as if he didn't know where he was or who he was speaking to. But then he paused and gathered his strength. "I have to leave Lady Hamilton and my adopted daughter Horatia as a legacy to my country," he said speaking directly to Mr Beattie. His voice was so low that Marianne could barely hear him.

Another injured man was being put down beside him, this time an unconscious midshipman with a terrible head wound which was bleeding profusely. One of his bearers took hold of Nelson's discarded coat and put it under his head as a pillow. But appalling though the young man's injuries were, all eyes were on Nelson and Mr Beattie, Nelson so pale and drooping and breathless, Mr Beattie examining him as gently and thoroughly as he could, taking his pulse, checking the bullet wound in his back and asking him to describe his sensations. His account of them was movingly unemotional. He said he had no sensation in the lower part of his body but could feel a gush of blood every minute within his breast and acute pain in that part of his back where he'd been shot. "I felt it break my back," he said, looking at Beattie and added, "You can do nothing for me."

The chaplain had arrived and was kneeling beside him, at a loss to know what to do or say.

"Fetch some lemonade for him to drink," Beattie told him quietly, "and make a paper fan to give him what air you can. He will find it hard to breathe."

The chaplain was so near to tears he could hardly speak. "Can I do nothing else for him?" he said.

"No, sir," Mr Beattie told him. "The shot is lodged in his spine. There is nothing to be done: He is dying."

"I'll get the lemonade for 'ee, sir," Marianne said to the chaplain, trying to comfort him, but the poor man was too full of grief to hear her and the sight of his stricken face was making her want to weep too, so she walked off quickly to the nearest barrel. It didn't seem possible that Nelson was dying. How would they fare without him with the battle still going on and nobody knowing the outcome?

It was worrying Nelson too. As the minutes laboured past, he asked again and again to see his flag captain, but even though Mr Beattie sent one messenger after another, Captain Hardy didn't appear, and Nelson began to fret for him saying that he was certain he must be killed. Eventually, a midshipman with a flesh wound to his arm came down "with a message for the Admiral" and was escorted to where he lay, propped up against a pillow and covered by his sheet, struggling for breath. The young man was overawed to be in his presence and stood silent for far too long until the chaplain urged him to proceed. Then he took a breath and made a short formal speech.

"If you please sir," he said, "circumstances respecting the fleet require Captain's Hardy's presence on deck, but he sent to tell you, sir, he will avail himself of the first available opportunity to visit your lordship." Then he saluted and turned on his heel and fled, before he could disgrace himself by weeping in front of his commander.

The minutes dragged by. Nelson's struggles for breath became more acute and more obviously painful. The chaplain rubbed his chest in an effort to ease him and the purser sat with one arm under the pillow to support his head but nothing either of them did made any difference. Death was hauling him in by slow agonising degrees, as the guns roared over his head and his shipmates screamed under the knife and his ship shuddered with the force of its own guns. From time to time, they could hear cheering and the latest arrivals reported that another enemy ship had struck her colours and surrendered. But it wasn't until three o'clock in the afternoon and an hour and a half after Nelson had been shot, that Hardy's stocky figure finally appeared on the stairs and he came stooping into the cockpit.

Although he was now finding it extremely painful to breathe, Nelson questioned him at once. "Well, Hardy, how goes the battle? How goes the day with us?"

Hardy brought good news. "Very well, my lord," he said. "We have got twelve or fourteen of the enemy's ships in our possession. Five of their van have tacked and show an intention of bearing down on us." And when Nelson looked concerned, he went on, "I have therefore called two or three of our fresh ships round us and have no doubt of giving them a drubbing."

Nelson's voice was little more than a whisper. "I hope none of *our* ships have struck, Hardy."

"No, my lord," Hardy reassured him. "There is no fear of that."

The two men looked at one another in the lamplight. "I am a dead man Hardy," Nelson said. "I am going fast. It will be all over with me soon."

THE BATTLE and the agony continued. In the cockpit, the work was endless. Mr Beattie and his assistants dealt with the injured three at a time: seamen or marines were called at regular intervals to remove the dead, among them the grey-faced man and the wounded midshipman. The chaplain and the purser stayed by Nelson's side and never left him for a second, fanning him to give him air and rubbing his chest to try and ease his pain. Marianne fetched lemonade for anyone who needed it, cleared up vomit, cleaned her patients when they soiled themselves, and struggled on until her back was aching with the sheer physical effort of it and her eyes were hot with unshed tears. And above their heads, the gunners fought on, sometimes firing such a volley that it shook the sides of the ship so that Nelson called out, "Oh! *Victory*! *Victory*! How you distract my poor brain!"

It was after four o'clock and the first dog watch had begun before Hardy appeared again and this time, he was able to tell his old friend that he had won a brilliant victory. He couldn't say for certain how many enemy ships had been captured because it wasn't possible to make out every ship distinctly, but he could answer for fourteen or fifteen.

Nelson was struggling for breath and in such severe pain, he didn't have the strength to do more than urge his captain to anchor. But the watchers round his bedside could see he was pleased and, now that they were paying attention to what was going on beyond the cockpit, it was plain that the battle was nearly done, for although they could hear guns they were in the distance.

Nelson was stirring and making another effort to speak. "Come nearer to me," he said to Hardy and, when his old friend stooped towards him, he whispered, "Don't throw me overboard, Hardy."

"Oh no," Hardy said, appalled that he should even think of such a thing. "Certainly not."

"Then you know what to do," Nelson said. Every word he spoke now was making him catch his breath with pain but there were things that had to be said. "Take care of my dear Lady Hamilton, Hardy. Take care of poor Lady Hamilton." He panted for quite a while, looking up at his friend, then he said, "Kiss me, Hardy." And Hardy knelt beside him and kissed his cheek.

"Now I am satisfied," Nelson said, and his voice was so low and broken it was almost impossible to hear him. "Thank God I have done my duty."

The watchers around him stayed perfectly still for several minutes, not wanting to disturb him because he seemed to be drifting away from them, but eventually Hardy bent towards him and kissed his forehead and at that, he stirred and tried to look around him, saying "Who is that?"

"It is Hardy," his captain said.

This time there was no recognition — only muttering. "Thank God... I have done... duty. Thank God... done my..." Over and over again. Hardy went back to his duties on the quarter-deck, Mr Beattie returned to his patients, the loblollies to their lowly work. The muttering went on, getting weaker and weaker. Mr Beattie came back to the bedside at short intervals to check for a pulse. The muttering went on. Then, at a few minutes after half past four, breath and muttering stopped together, and the surgeon pronounced that Admiral Lord Nelson was dead. It had taken him three hours to die.

It seemed appropriate to the watchers that the gunfire had stopped too.

CHAPTER 19

The silence that followed when the guns stopped firing was such a relief that it made Marianne shake. After such a long ordeal, it was impossible to believe that the battle was over. But it was. The silence roared that it was. There would be no more wounded men hauled down those blood-drenched steps, no more screams of agony, no more dead men being carried away, no more knives. Then she realised that there were other quieter sounds on that nightmare deck that she hadn't heard when the guns were pummelling her ears, that the wounded were groaning and weeping, that there were feet running about on the deck overhead, that the ghoulish Josh was sniffing and wiping his nose on his sleeve, that somebody was saying his prayers. But she barely had time to take it all in before Mr Beattie cut into her thoughts and began to give orders.

"You and you," he said, pointing at Marianne and Josh, "empty the buckets. The rest of you scrub this deck and see the stairs clean." And, as they were all standing about looking stunned, "Jump to it! The battle may be over, but we've still got work to do." It was true enough for there were still dozens of men who needed his attention.

Marianne picked up one of the buckets that stood beside the table. It was extremely heavy because it was full of shattered arms and legs and awash with blood and filth of every kind. It sloshed over the edge of the bucket as she carried it up the companion-way, moving cautiously because the steps were slippery, and the ship was rolling. It must be a storm coming, she thought, as she emerged onto the gun deck and she stood beside the capstan for a few seconds to steady herself and catch her breath. The deck was still full of smoke, which was swirling about the guns and breathing out of the gun ports. Most of the gunners were slumped beside their guns in utter exhaustion, some with their heads in their hands and all of them blackened by gunpowder and sweat, but one or two were lying on their backs as if they were asleep — or dead. No please God, she thought, don't let them be dead. We've had enough men dead. For a brief moment, she wondered what had happened to Taffy, but there was no time to ask and, anyway, they were in no state to answer questions, so she looked away, took a sustaining breath, picked up her burden and struggled up to the quarter-deck. The sight that battered her there was even more terrible than the orlop deck had been.

She had emerged into an evil-smelling, unfamiliar sunset. There were thick clouds of lavender-coloured gun-smoke drifting inshore and the air was so heavy with the smell of hot metal and spilt blood that it made her gasp for breath. The deck was covered in blood and debris, and although there were several crewmen working with shovels and brooms to clear it, they were slipping in the filth under their feet and struggling to keep their balance for there *was* a storm coming, with a strong wind blowing and a high sea running. But when she'd fought her way to the rail to empty her bucket, she saw, with a shock of horror, that if the deck was a shambles, the sea was much, much worse. It was a sullen bottle-green, as if the battle had drained it of all proper colour, and it was full of unspeakable debris, bloody arms and legs, drifting corpses, great spars of wood and lengths of rigging, even live men struggling to stay afloat among the wreckage, their wet heads black in the half light, their arms flailing. Some way out, there were two long boats searching for the wounded and another was putting out from the black and yellow sides of the *Royal Sovereign*, while all around them, the shattered hulks of the great ships tossed at anchor, some of them with no masts at all, the rest with masts broken and rigging trailing and their sails shot full of holes. As she watched, one of the distant ships began to belch thick black smoke as if it was on fire. She tipped her bucket over the side, glad to let it go, and then she was suddenly overcome with sickness and had to hang over the rail retching violently, as the ship yawed and tipped towards the water.

With the speed of instinct, she felt the approach of the wave before she saw it, but even so, it was much too late to get out of its way. It was rearing over the rail, engulfing her, sucking her down, pulling at her so powerfully there was nothing she could do to escape it. And then she was under the sea, that awful, filthy sea, among the shreds of bodies and the corpses, and she flailed her arms in panic and rose into the air again, screaming in the roar of the water and more frightened than she'd ever been in her life. She knew she would drown if she wasn't quick, that she was on her own and that no one could hear her, that there were no long-boats anywhere near her, that she had to find something solid to cling to. Quick, quick, she told herself, afore it drags you under again. And she reared up in the water using her legs as if she was running as the wave dragged her away from the ship and she heard the roar of a great explosion. She knew the burning ship had blown up, but it was of no consequence compared to the terror of drowning. But then there was a ship's timber with a spar attached to it being washed towards her by the next wave and near enough for her to make a grab at it. With the last of her energy, she reached towards it, seized it and clung on.

It took her a very long time to get her breath back and by then she was too far away from the ship to call for help and the waves were pushing her towards the shore. Her jacket was ripped open, her hair had come out of its plait and was heavy with sea water and she was shivering with cold, for the sea was icy, but at least she was alive.

JEM SAW the ship explode as he was doing what he could to repair the mizzen mast. He knew it was a French ship and that it was called the *Achille* for he'd seen the tricolour when it first took fire and he'd watched the longboats head off to rescue the crew, or as many of them as they could, and had been lost in admiration for them, because he knew what a dangerous job it would be, but for the moment all his attention was fixed on the repair. There were carpenters hard at work all over the fleet, because the storm was coming on apace. They needed to get the storm staysails up or they would be in trouble and, like all the others, Jem knew that the sooner he got this mast fixed, the better. He was worried about Tom because he hadn't seen him since the action began, but even friendship had to make way for getting the ship in trim. There was work to be done.

On the orlop deck on the *Victory*, Mr Beattie had examined Nelson's body and was dressing it in a clean shirt. When Josh came panting up to tell him that Matt Morris had been washed overboard, he merely nodded and told him to go and fetch an empty leaguer. Matt was a good lad and he'd done sterling service that day but there were other matters that were more important than a boy overboard. The Admiral had to be provided with a coffin of sorts and one of the big water barrels was the best thing he could think of. When the leaguer had been brought down to him, he and his assistants eased their commander's body into its limited space. Then they filled it with brandy so as to preserve him, sealed it and Mr Beattie wrote his name on the side. "Admiral Lord Nelson died at Trafalgar October 21st, 1805". After that, they turned their attention to their waiting patients. There was work to be done.

≈

THE BOY OVERBOARD WAS DRIFTING, clinging to the spar as the waves pushed her towards the shore and the smoke cloud. Sometimes, she was aware of what was going on, but sometimes she lost consciousness for a few seconds and came to her senses fearful that she could have lost her grip and fallen into the sea and drowned. But her clinging hands were locked in position, frozen by the cold. Even when she saw the fishing ship bobbing towards her through the cloud, she couldn't unclasp them to wave, although she tried as hard as she could. She couldn't call out either. It was as if her throat was frozen too. She couldn't wave, and she couldn't calk, she could only drift. Please God, she prayed, let them see me.

≈

THE SANTA MARIA belonged to two local fishermen, Juan Carlo and his brother Sandro who, being weather-wise, had come out to lift their nets as soon as they saw that a storm was on its way. The great fleets could fight one another day and night for all they cared, but nets were nets and they couldn't afford to lose them. It wasn't easy to get their bearings in all that smoke and they had no intention of running aground on the shoals around Cape Trafalgar, so they headed south-west until they were through the cloud and could see their landmarks again. It came as a great surprise to them to see a woman's body lying across a chunk of wreckage a few yards away from them, her breasts white in the green water and her long hair drifting across her face. Sandro took one look and crossed himself.

"*Madre de Dios*," he said. "*Es una sirena.* It's a mermaid."

"What of it?" Juan Carlo said. "It's a dead one whatever it is."

But then the figure stirred and seemed to be trying to sit up.

"*Madre de Dios*," Sandro said again. "It *is* a mermaid. A live mermaid, Juan. Think of that. Maybe we should catch it. We could put it on display and charge people to see it. What do you think?"

"I think we should find our nets," his practical brother said, "and leave mermaids to the waves." But then the mermaid was turned on her side by the next roller and he saw that she had legs and was human. "It's a wench," he said, and decided to rescue her.

It took their combined strength to haul her into the boat because they had to do it wreckage and all as her hands were so tightly attached to the spar, and once she was out of the water, she was shivering so much, what with extreme relief and extreme cold, that she couldn't tell them who she was or what she was doing at sea, not that they could have understood her if she'd tried. Juan found a spare sail and wrapped it round her like a blanket and at that she managed to say "Thank 'ee kindly."

"Foreign," Juan said to his brother. "That's never Spanish she's speaking. And I never knew a Spanish woman who would wear breeches. That's altogether peculiar. Let's get that net lifted before the storm comes."

Now that he'd got this foreign creature on board his boat and knew she wasn't a mermaid and wasn't likely to earn them any money, Sandro was losing interest in her. "This is all very well," he said, "but what are we going to do with her?"

"We will give her to Mama," Juan told him, gazing out to sea. "She'll know what to do." He had a great respect for his mother and thought her a very wise woman. Then he grinned. "She's brought us good luck whatever else," he said, "for there's our buoy. Now we can get the catch aboard."

It was dark by the time the nets had been lifted and they were within reach of the shore and by then the stricken ships were lighting their lamps. To Marianne, gradually easing her fingers away from the spar and growing warmer under her improvised blanket, the sight of them was cheering. It was such a pleasantly normal thing and it proved that her shipmates weren't too far away and that once the storm had passed, she would probably be able to get back to them. But to the men on board the fleet, the lamps brought a message of death and the most anguished despair.

It wasn't any time at all before they noticed that there were no Admiral's lights on board the *Victory* and the news spread from ship to ship that Nelson had been killed. Their grief for him was overwhelming. Men who'd spent four hours down in the heat and horror of the gun decks, fighting hard, wept like children to hear the news. "We have lost Lord Nelson," they said, and it seemed the worst thing that could have happened to them. And Jem, who'd just discovered that his old mate Tom had been shot and killed, wept too with his head on his knees and the tears rolling onto his breeches. We have lost Lord Nelson. Heaven help us all.

~

As soon as the *Santa Maria* had been pulled up on the darkening beach, Juan Carlos helped his speechless foreign girl out of the boat and led her up the beach path to the cottage he shared with his mother and his brother, while his brother followed behind carrying the wood. The sooner he handed her over to someone who would know what to do with her, the better. Rescuing her had made him feel quite valiant but now, like his brother, he was at a loss to know what ought to be done next.

His mother had no doubt at all. "She must be got out of those wet clothes this minute," she said, taking in Marianne's situation at a glance, and then she must be given something dry to wear and then she must have food and drink and a bed to sleep in. Go and get the truckle bed and bring it in here. She is exhausted, poor child. What a blessing you took her from the sea and brought her home to me. Come," she said to Marianne, leading her by the hand. "Sit by the fire."

Marianne couldn't understand a word she was saying, but she knew she was being welcomed, especially when she was led to the fire, so she nodded and smiled and shivered and said "Thank 'ee kindly," over and over again, wanting them to know how grateful she was. "Thank 'ee kindly. I'm beholden to 'ee." Her fingers were still marked by their long-frozen grip on the spar, white tipped and bloodless but ridged with red as if they were scarred; she was still shivering violently from time to time and her hair was so wet, it was dripping at every step she took, but Mama found a rough towel and was soon busy drying her, telling her to sit by the fire and removing her jacket while her sons were out of the room. An old patched chemise was produced and pulled over her head, a patched skirt replaced her sodden breeches, boots that were much too big for her were eased onto her chilly feet, and, by the time the two men returned with a small truckle bed and set it in the corner of the room, she was warm and respectable and rubbing her hair dry.

Outside, the wind howled round the chimney, the sky was full of dark clouds and a heavy sea was running, the waves crashing onto the beach with a noise like falling masonry. She knew that injured men were still suffering and dying out there on those battered ships, but she was here and safe, warmed by a fire and with another woman to look after her. Tomorrow, she would try to persuade somebody to take her back to the fleet but for the moment, it was enough to sit by the fire and count her blessings.

THE NEXT AFTERNOON, the storm began in earnest and it blew for three days. The rain was torrential, the sky perpetually dark, there was no possibility of anyone putting out to sea in such weather, and it took the combined efforts of all the survivors in the fleet to keep their damaged ships afloat. While her carpenter rigged up jury topmasts and a mizzen, the *Victory* was taken in tow by an old ship called the *Polyphemus*, but the seas were so rough that her captain had to cut the towing hawser for fear of being rammed. The prize ships were tossed about like corks, as the great fleet was scattered by the force of the waves. It was an anxious time.

Marianne wrapped an old sack round her shoulders to keep out the worst of the rain and went down to the beach twice every day, watching the weather and hoping it would clear. It pleased her to see that the fleet was still there even if she knew she couldn't get a boat to take her out to re-join them. She stood by the edge of that great sea, aching to be back aboard her ship, just as she'd done more than four months ago in the heat of the Caribbean. How life do repeat itself, she thought, rubbing the rain out of her eyes. But the thought was cheering. She'd got out of Barbados, so she could get out of Spain. 'Twas just a matter a' perseverance. Meantime, she helped Mama to sweep the floor and prepare the food, her clothes gradually dried so that she could wear them again, although she had to keep the chemise on too for modesty's sake. There was plenty of bread and fish to eat, and Juan chopped up the ship's timber and the spar and used it to build a blazing fire that kept them all warm in the evenings. The storm would pass. They always did.

On the morning of the fourth day, the wind began to drop, and two strange men arrived in a state of high excitement with some sort of news for Juan and Sandro. They stood in the doorway all talking at once and waving their arms about and, after they'd gone, Juan began to talk to Marianne, waving *his* arms about, pointing west and pulling at her sleeve to follow him. So she found her sack, draped it round her shoulders and went out into the damp air.

The beach was unchanged, the fleet was still there, but there was a pale sun shining and the sea was blue-green instead of that awful grey. Juan set off at a great speed glancing back from time to time to check that she was following and telling her things at voluble length that she couldn't understand as they walked west. It had better be worth it, she thought, for its a mortal long way. But when they'd followed the path round a small curved headland, it *was* worth it, oh it was more than worth it, for there was a British longboat pulled up on the beach and a group of British sailors, gathered round a huge driftwood fire. She could hear their easy familiar English from where she stood. She ran towards them at once, her spirits lifted by the mere sight of them and only stopped when she remembered that she hadn't thanked her rescuer. "Thank 'ee kindly, sir," she called to him. "I'm much obliged to 'ee."

He waved his cap and called back, but now it didn't matter that she couldn't understand him. She only had to join the company round that fire, and she would be on her way back to her ship.

The company round the fire looked up when she called out and one of them shouted. "Here's another of 'em, Mr Templeman."

The name stopped her onward rush. "Jem?" she said, looking at the group. It couldn't be Jem, surely to goodness, not after the battle an' all and when she'd been looking for him so long. "Oh my dear heart alive, is it you?"

And Jem stood up and left his shipmates and walked towards her. The sound of her voice had triggered his memory most powerfully. Reason told him it couldn't possibly be her, not here, not like this, his memory was playing tricks on him, he was dreaming it. But the closer he got to her the more sure he became. It was Marianne, there was no doubt about it, Marianne, wrapped in a piece of sacking and looking at him with the oddest expression on her face, wearing sailor's breeches and sailor's shoes, but Marianne, here on a Spanish beach. "Marianne!" he said and began to run.

To hear his voice was too much for her. She was caught up in a whirlwind of emotion, the shock of surprise, a five-day accumulation of suppressed grief and terror, and a quite extraordinary, overwhelming, unexpected happiness "Oh Jem," she said, "Oh my dear heart alive." There was a great pulse throbbing in her throat, and she put up her hand to steady it — and fell in a faint. He only just had time to run forward and catch her before she hit the ground.

When she struggled back to consciousness she was lying in his lap in front of the fire and he was holding her very close and stroking her hair and kissing her fingers. "Now that's better," he said, as she opened her eyes. "I can't have 'ee in a faint. My stars, 'tis the most amazing thing to see thee. I can't get over it."

She became aware that there were fire-lit eyes all around her, glinting as they stared at her, and she struggled to sit up. "Stay still," Jem said, putting his arm round her. "We en't a-goin' nowhere. Stay by the fire an' get warm an' let me look at 'ee. My dear heart alive, if this en't the most amazing thing."

"So who is he?" one of the sailors asked. "An' where's he sprung from?"

"He en't a he," Jem explained. "That's the beauty of it. He's a she an' she's my wife! My own dear wife what I never thought to see again. Can 'ee believe it?"

Happiness cradled her like a warm sea. She'd found him. After all these months and all that searching, after the horror of that dreadful battle with Nelson dying an' all, and being washed over-board an' lost at sea, after being becalmed and facing storms and losing her poor baby, and just when she'd given up hope, she'd found him. And he was calling her "My own dear wife".

"So what you doin' on this 'ere beach, gel?" one of the sailors asked, "An' in them slops? Tell me that."

"'Tis a long story," she said, smiling at Jem. Oh how good it was going to be to tell him. "I come to sea for to find my Jem, I took the shilling the self-same day as he done, an' bein' they don't take women aboard I had to be a boy."

Jem was stunned. "You mean you been in the navy all this time?" he said. "Across the Atlantic an' back again?"

What a triumph it was to be able to say yes. "An' looking for 'ee at every port we come to," she said.

His face was a study in astonishment. "My stars!" he said.

"You got a pearl there, Mr Templeman," one of his mates told him.

He was still struggling to take it all in. How she must love me, he thought, to follow me round the world. She'd never ha' done that if she hadn't loved me true. "My stars!" he said again.

"So you was aboard in the battle, was yer?" another man asked.

"I was on the *Victory*," she told him with enormous pride. "On the orlop deck. I seen Lord Nelson die an' a better, braver man you couldn't imagine." Then she was overwhelmed again and began to cry.

"Hush, my little lovely one," Jem soothed, cuddling her. "Don' 'ee cry. You're with me now. There en't a thing to harm 'ee. You're with me." How easy it was to talk to her and how much he loved her. She *was* a pearl, there was no denying it, a pearl of great price and he would love her forever.

But his shipmates wanted to hear her story and, as the weather wasn't quite fit enough for the long row back to the fleet, they built up the fire with more driftwood and gathered round its warmth to listen while she told them what had happened to her. Not everything that had happened, naturally, but the important things.

"An' here you are," Jem said, when the tale was done, "an' damn my eyes if you en't a giddy marvel. Tha's my opinion of it."

"Never heard the like an' that's a fact," his companions said. "An' to find 'ee here in this wild place, I means for to say."

The sun had risen in the sky and although it was still pale there were signs of better weather to come, a gentle breeze from the right quarter, the sea more blue than green, the waves tame, the clouds white, seagulls wheeling overhead, even a songbird trilling somewhere nearby. "Time we was getting back," Jem said.

They hauled the boat into the sea — one two six, one two six

— and Marianne hauled with the best. When they jumped aboard, she jumped too, neatly like the seaman she was, knowing that Jem was watching her and admiring her. And when they set off, she and her husband pulled on the same oar, sitting so close together he could have been holding her in his arms. She had never had such a happy journey.

CHAPTER 20

As the longboat creaked steadily on towards the fleet, the sea hissing at its prow, a small schooner called *Pickle* hove to alongside the *Royal Sovereign* with orders to wait for dispatches from Admiral Collingwood. The storm had taken all the admiral's attention for the last four days but, now that it was abating, he was eager to send news of the victory and of Nelson's death to the Admiralty in London. It was one of the most difficult dispatches he'd ever written, but it was done and sealed.

"Proceed with all speed," he said to Lieutenant Lapontiere, as he handed it over, and the captain saluted and assured him that not a second would be lost.

Now, Collingwood thought, I must attend to the wounded, who must be sent to the naval hospital at Gibraltar, and then I must arrange for such repairs as can be carried out while we are in harbour. It was going to be a difficult business sailing his great fleet and their prizes safely back to England and he meant to have them as sea-worthy as he could get them.

~

THE *PICKLE* MADE EXCELLENT TIME, arriving in Falmouth Bay at a quarter to ten in the morning on 4 November and Lieutenant Lapontiere hired a post-chaise immediately, made a flag pole from an old broom handle so that he could fly the Union Jack and a tattered tricolour as he travelled, and set off on his long journey to London. In ordinary circumstances, it would have taken him a week, but with determination and nineteen horse changes, he managed it in thirty-seven hours, arriving at the Admiralty at one in the morning on 6 November. There was nobody about and the city was shrouded in fog so thick that he couldn't see from one side of Whitehall to the other, even with a lantern held aloft to guide him, but not to be deterred, he knocked boldly and loudly, told the answering servant that he had despatches from Admiral Collingwood and was admitted at once. Within minutes, the First Lord was out of bed and at his desk to receive him. By three o'clock, the news had been sent to King George, Mr Pitt and all his ministers and the Prime Minister was up and about, being far too distressed by the news to go back to sleep. By first light, a special edition of a *Gazette Extraordinary* was on sale in the streets.

"It is with mixed sensations of transport and anguish," it said, *"That we have to report a glorious victory and a great loss!"*

The newspaper reached Portsmouth the following morning and was read by everybody who could get hold of a copy for themselves or purloin someone else's. Mary Morris and Lizzie Templeman read it in the pie shop and cried copiously.

"But what of Jem an' Marianne?" Mary said. "That's what I wants for to know. If they've shot Lord Nelson just think what they could have done to *them*. Anything could have happened to them. Any mortal thing."

"Your Marianne'll write an' tell 'ee, whatever it is," Lizzie said, "what I don't suppose my Jem'll even think of."

But she was wrong. Both their children had written to them and their letters were already on their way home.

THE FLEET TOOK sail to Gibraltar as soon as they had a fair wind and the first thing Marianne did after they arrived in Rosia Bay was to help the men she now thought of as "her wounded" to struggle down the gangplank and into the carriages that were waiting to take them to the hospital. It took all morning and the combined efforts of all the loblollies and both Mr Beattie's assistants and by the time the last man had been eased on his way, Marianne was so tired her back ached. She was standing on the quayside, watching the last carriage leave and thinking of dinner when somebody came up behind her and put a hand on her shoulder. At first, she was startled, then she turned her head and saw that it was Jem.

"My stars, Jem Templeman," she said, "you made me jump."

"Come an' see the town," he said. "You'm finished here."

Hunger pangs made her hesitate. "What about my dinner?"

"I'll buy 'ee dinner," he told her and jingled the coins in the pocket of his jacket. "Come on. 'Tis our leisure time."

So, since they were both officially at leisure, they walked into town. It was quite a jaunt, even though they had to be discreet and couldn't walk arm in arm as they would have liked, nor stop to kiss, which they would have liked even more. But for the moment, it was enough to be together, talking of their ships and their voyages, and enjoying one another's company. Marianne thought the town was a splendid place "with all them carriages an' all" and she ate a rather weird meal of rice, fish and onions and was hungry enough to enjoy it and drank so much wine, it made her head swim and declared she hadn't had such a day since Heaven knows when.

"Last time we ate hearty together was our wedding," Jem said, as they started their walk back to the quay. And then stopped, feeling too close to dangerous ground.

"Aye, so 'twas," she said and waited, looking at him steadily. The street was full of people and some of them were looking at them quizzically, as they stood facing one another on the cobbles, hesitating.

It was necessary to speak of it, painful though it would most certainly be. "I should never have left 'ee, Marianne," he said. "I know that now."

She considered him seriously. "No," she said. "You shouldn't have."

"I wouldn't leave 'ee now."

"Nor I you," she said and laughed. "Not when it's took me so long to find 'ee again."

There was so much he wanted to say to her. If only they weren't in such a public place. If he could kiss her, it would be easier.

"We could walk out again tomorrow," he suggested. "If 'ee'd like to. 'Twill take a deal a' time to make repairs. By my reckoning we shall be here a week or two at the very least. What do 'ee think to that? Comin' out, I means, not makin' repairs. We could climb to the top of the rock. 'Twould be more private-like up there."

She thought it an excellent suggestion. So the next day, they climbed to the top of the great rock where they ate a very British meat pie, had a fine view of the Straits and the distant coast of Africa and were pestered by a tribe of inquisitive monkeys. Not that either of them worried about monkeys. What was important was that they were far away from inquisitive human beings and could kiss one another at last, and whenever the spirit moved them, which it did with increasing ardour and frequency.

On the fifth day, a sea mist came up and the town was swathed in such a thick damp cloud that they could barely see one another when they were in the streets and they were still ribboned by swirls of mist when they'd reached the top of the rock. But that didn't worry them either. It just meant they were even better hidden and could kiss as long and as often as they liked.

When they'd finally kissed to a halt and had decided to find a suitable rock where they could sit and eat their pies, they fell to talking about the West Indies and what an amazing place it was.

"Some of them islands are…" Jem began. But then he had to stop because he couldn't find the word he needed. "Well, magic places, seems to me. Not magic like conjurors an' so forth. I don't mean that. Magic, like places where you face up to things, an' make decision, if you knows what I means."

"Yes," she said, remembering that poor baby. "I do."

"When we was in Dominica, I fell to thinkin'," Jem said. And then stopped again, because he was afraid he was going to make a confession and he wasn't sure it was the right thing to be doing.

She snuggled against his side, feeling glad of his warmth. "What about?" she encouraged him.

He put his arm round her and thought before he answered, because this *was* a confession. "About us, I s'pose, now I comes to think of it," he said eventually. "About how I meant to live my life if I come through the battle. I made a list of all the things I didn't like and how I'd change 'em if I got the chance."

"An' what did 'ee decide?"

"'Twas four things," he remembered, seeing the list in his head. "To take my pay and leave the navy honourable, what I certainly means to do the minute it can be done; to settle down on dry land on account of I'd had enough of sailing round the world; to be my own master an' work as a carpenter in my own town; and to find you an' see if…"

She leant back a little and looked up at him and waited.

He gave her a wry smile, feeling very unsure of himself. Confession was uncommon hard. But he'd come so far, he had to tell her now. "Well then, to see if you'd take me back," he admitted, "what I wouldn't ha' been surprised if you hadn't, bein' I left 'ee on our weddin' day, what was a blamed fool thing to do."

It was an apology and she recognised it and was glad of it for it would put things right between them. "'Tis all forgot now," she told him. "We been to the other side a' the word an' back an' lived through a battle an' seen Lord Nelson die — seems to me we got a right to live our own lives, wouldn' 'ee say?"

Oh he would, he would, and kissed her to prove it.

So their gentle courtship continued and although their need for one another soon grew into an ache that they couldn't satisfy out there in the open, they were happy to be together and to dream of the future.

WHEN CHURCH WAS RIGGED on their second Sunday in harbour, their captains told them that a state funeral was being arranged for Admiral Lord Nelson. It was no surprise to anyone in the fleet. "Quite right," they said to one another, nodding approval "Tha's what 'ee would expect." It felt like a justification of their efforts. And when Captain Hardy told his crew that six of them were to be chosen to carry the coffin and that a "sizeable contingent" of them were to walk in the procession carrying his flag, the nods became a cheer. It was right and proper. They were his men. They'd fought with him and suffered with him and some of them had died along of him and now they would carry him to his grave.

Later that day, the men who'd been chosen were called to the quarter-deck to be told the news. And among the "sizeable contingent" was Matt Morris, loblolly boy.

"What do 'ee think to that?" she said to Jem, when they met up again two days later.

He was looking saucy. "I think 'tis all very right an' proper," he said. "That's my opinion of it." Then he paused and grinned at her. "On account of I'm to be one a' the contingent too, bein' I'm a ship's carpenter. We can walk side by side. What do 'ee think to *that*?"

The idea delighted her. "What a thing to tell Ma," she said. "You an' me in the same precession. I wish I hadn't ha' sent my letter now."

"I wish I hadn't ha' sent mine neither," he said.

She looked at him in open astonishment. "You've never writ a letter!" she said. "My stars! I never thought I'd live to see the day. Your ma'll fall down in a faint."

Her teasing made him uncomfortable. "I can write well enough," he said huffily. It wasn't true. He'd had a terrible time of it writing that letter, what with the spelling being tricky and the ink smudging and getting all over his fingers and not having written for so long — but there was no need to tell her that. "'Tis just I've had too much to do for letter writin', on account a' bein' a carpenter an' all."

"I'll believe you," she said and added, "Thousands wouldn't."

"If you'm a-goin' to mock," he said, "I shan't tell 'ee what I said in it, what you'd like to know."

She held on to his jacket and reached up to kiss him, understanding him very well. "So what did 'ee say?" she asked.

He was mollified but only slightly. "Well…" he said.

She kissed him again. "Never mind well, what did 'ee say?"

"I told 'em we'd found one another, what I thought they'd like for to know, an' I asked Ma to find us a room for when we gets back. We shall need somewhere to live. Won't we?" It was a real question asked with some trepidation and Marianne was surprised and touched by it. Why he's shy, she thought. Who'd ha' thought *that*? Shy an' tender an' I thought he was a great rough critter, what 'ud hurt you soon as look at you an' then walk away an' join the navy. We've come a long way since them days, the both of us.

"Yes," she said, easily. "We will. We got to have somewhere to live."

"Then I'm glad I asked her," he said.

Seven days later, he heard that the *Sirius* would be sailing the following day, "what I'd rather she didn't on account of we shan't see one another again once we'm a-sailin', not till we reach England anyways, what'll be a blamed long time."

"'Twill pass," she comforted. "No voyage takes for ever, not even across the Aterlantic, an' we done *that* twice. We just got to have a bit a' patience, that's all, bit a' patience an' then we shall be home in our own town an' in our own room an' we can live as we please."

"Might take a bit a time afore I can get free of the service," he warned. "I'll have to stay till I've got me pay and me bounty and signed off an' so forth. I don't mean for to leave empty handed. Not after all this."

She understood that perfectly. "'Course you don't."

"You'm a-goin' to Portsmouth seemingly," he told her. "So you'll be home afore I am. But don't you go leaving without your full pay neither. We needs every penny we've earned."

"An' we shall have it," she promised. She wasn't at all sure how she had to set about claiming it, but it would be done, he had her word. "I wonder what Ma'll think to see us again."

THEIR LETTERS ARRIVED in Portsmouth in the middle of November to great excitement in both houses and, like her daughter-in-law, Lizzie was amazed that Jem had written. "I means for to say," she said to her husband, "our Jem writing us a letter. Wonders'll never cease."

Later in the day, she went down to see Mary Morris so that *she* could read the letter too and the two woman swapped letters and read them both twice, exclaiming at every sentence.

"Somewhere to live you see," Mary approved. "That's sensible. Once the fleet gets back there'll be sailors every which way, all a-wantin' rooms. Better to get that settled afore they arrives. He's got good sense your Jem."

"I'll go an' see Mother Catty," Lizzie said. "She'm bound to know somewhere for 'em. Then we can get it all set up an' lovely afore they gets back. You an' Jack'll give us a hand with the furniture, won't 'ee."

"And not hurt," Mary said, still thinking about the letters. "Neither the one a' them. Tha's the wonder of it. Not hurt an' comin' home safe and sound. How long d'you think 'twill be afore they gets here?"

"Could be any day," Lizzie said. "I means for to say the cutter's got here with the mail, so they can't be far behind. Oh I can't wait to see 'em again. D'you think we got time to make 'em a rug?"

In fact, their children were a very long way behind. They'd had to battle through two storms and, because she was severely dismasted and under tow, *Victory* had made very heavy weather of the journey. *Sirius* put in at Plymouth at the end of the month as Jem had predicted, along with several other ships of the line, but it wasn't until the 5 December that the long-awaited news of *Victory's* arrival broke in Portsmouth. A large ship under low jury masts was being towed in from St Helen's. Nobody in the town had any doubt that it was the *Victory* and the crowds came out at once, lining the streets at the sally port and the Blockhouse Fort, respectful and tearful, to watch the great ship and its great, brave, dead commander come back to port. Little was said, for what words would serve such an occasion, although the weeping grew to a wail when they saw Nelson's flag flying at half-mast. "A terrible thing," the watchers said to one another, "to be so brave and die so young."

But Mary Morris looked at the broken ship and wondered how soon it would be before they let Marianne come home.

She arrived four days later, in mid-evening and in a great rush, with her ditty bag over her shoulder, a huge smile on her face and her purse full of silver. Within seconds, she had swept her mother into her arms, kissed her entire family and announced that she'd left the fleet and been paid handsome.

"Where's that husband a yourn?" her father asked. "I thought you'd come a-howlin' in together."

"He's on the *Sirius*," she told him, "what have put into Plymouth. He'll be along shortly. Did 'ee find us a room, Ma? "And when her mother nodded, "How soon can I see it?"

"Tomorrow morning," Mary said.

"What about tonight?"

"'Tis too late," Mary told her. "And besides, we'll have to give 'em warning."

"First light then," Marianne said. "I've a great deal to do an' I wants to get on with it. I means to have it ship-shape and orderly afore he gets here."

Mary told Lizzie afterwards that it was like being in the middle of a tempest she was so quick and determined. "She was up an' gone afore we'd took breakfast," she said, when Lizzie came to call. "I never seen the like. She says it's to be ship-shape an' orderly afore your Jem comes home, what I don't doubt it will be the way she'm a-goin' on."

"Did she say when he was comin'?" Lizzie asked.

"Shortly," Mary said. And when Lizzie raised her eyebrows. "'Tis all we could get out of her. He's in Plymouth seemingly."

He arrived three days later, having travelled by stage-coach and, like Marianne, he was in a great rush to see his lodgings.

"'Tis Mrs Pennifold's in Farthing Lane," Lizzie told him. "Top floor back. Your Marianne's already there. She said she had to get it ship-shape an' orderly for 'ee."

He was on his way out of the shop. "Aye," he said. "She would. We've got a deal to do." And he ran all the way to Farthing Lane and took the stairs two at a time, his heart pounding. Now, he thought. Now. At last.

She was hard at work, sweeping the floor with a long-handled broom, but, as soon as she saw him, she threw the broom down and ran into his arms. And oh, such hungry kisses and such rising, breath-taking need. Their clothes were discarded piece by piece as they kissed, their shoes kicked into corners, and then they were tumbled into bed and holding one another tight, tight, in an agony of delight. Now. Now. At last.

"I shan't hurt 'ee, my lover," he promised.

"'Course 'ee won't," she said, kissing and kissing and thinking of the pleasure to come.

And how pleasurable it was after such a long wait. And it went on being pleasurable for the rest of the day and most of the night.

The next morning, they were both too tired to get out of bed but lay under their nice warm blankets and their nice new counterpane for a long luxurious time, cuddled together enjoying the peace and privacy of their room, lapped in contentment. Sunlight sliced through the shutters to pattern the counterpane with long bright bars, outside in the yard below them people were shouting at one another and laughing, and now and then they heard feet on the stairs, but inside the room, everything was quiet and orderly and entirely theirs, the furniture in place where Pa and Johnny had carried it in for her, their new shelves holding their new pots and kettles and dishes, the table and two new chairs standing ready for their first meal together, a new chest of drawers where she'd put her chemise on her wedding morning thinking she'd use it as a nightgown — and how foolish was that when 'twas a deal sweeter to wear nothing at all — their jug and washbasin waiting for use with a cake of soap in the saucer beside them, the trivet polished till it shone, coals in the scuttle, salt pot, tinderbox and spills on the mantelpiece, the fire set, their new rag rug placed foursquare on the polished floor beside it, with its bright red circle facing the hearth to keep out the devils. Home.

"I could stay here for ever an' ever," Marianne said, twining one of Jem's dark curls in her fingers.

"So could I, my lover," he told her, enjoying the way she was making his scalp tingle. "Howsomever, there's work to be done."

She went on twining his hair and supposed there was.

"I shall get up presently and light the fire for 'ee," he said, staying where he was, but planning his day. "After that we'll have our breakfast, an' then I'll go an' find me a workshop, an' I must see young Jonesy and get a sign writ to put outside of it, an' then I'll make a cupboard for our flour an' sugar an' such like an' a linen press for your clothes an' things, what I shall have to keep in the yard for a while to encourage trade — the press I means, not your clothes — but you shall have it here as soon as I gets my first order. You have my word on it. An' then—"

She laughed at him. "You got enough planned for a fortnight," she said, "Never mind a day."

"No peace for the wicked," he said. "That's how 'tis." And got out of bed.

He was busy all day and by the end of it he'd rented a workshop, ordered a sign for it and called in at his father's pie shop to collect his book of patterns.

"Do 'ee mean for to make furniture then?" his father asked.

"I means to turn my hand to anything what offers," Jem said. "I got a wife to support." And he was off again.

By the end of the first week, he'd made the linen press, put it on display in his workshop and taken an order for two more. By the end of the second, he had an order for a table and eight chairs from a wealthy lady called Mrs Tonbridge and was making doors for his old neighbour, the shoe-smith. By the end of the third, he had enough money in his pocket to buy a pair of geese to feed their families at Christmas. They ate it in the room above the pie shop and very good eating it made with apple sauce and roast potatoes and greens a-plenty and a roly-poly pudding to follow.

"That's one good thing about havin' a big oven," Mr Templeman said, wiping his forehead at the end of the meal. What with the fire and the rich eating, he was dripping with sweat and as red-cheeked as an apple. "Cooks up a goose a treat does a big oven."

"An' a son what treats us so handsome, don' 'ee forget," Lizzie said, smiling at Jem. "That's another good thing."

"Amen to that," Mary said, smiling too. "My stars but 'tis good to have 'ee home. An' doing so well too. Now you must tell us all about what happened to you when you was at sea, how you met up with one another an' what the battle was like an' everything."

"'Twould take a month a' Sundays," Marianne told her.

"Well then some of it," her mother said. "We en't heard a thing yet."

"We'll tell you the whole story from start to finish when we gets back from London," Jem said, eating the last of his roly-poly. "How would that be?"

Eyebrows shot up on every lace and both mothers spoke in unison. "London? What you goin' to London for?"

"Why, for Nelson's funeral, Ma," Marianne said, trying not to sound too proud and failing. "They say 'twill be the biggest funeral anyone ever saw an' we'm to be in the percession, a-carryin' his flag, along of all the nobs. Can't miss that now, can we?"

"My dear heart alive!" Mary said, much impressed. "When's it to be?"

"January the 9th," Jack Morris told her. "'Twas in the *Gazette* only yesterday with a picture of the funeral car. Very grand affair, built like the *Victory* with a prow an' a stern an all, only all done out in black a course. An' now you two'll see it. Imagine that. That *will* be a thing to talk about."

"We'm to go up the day afore," Jem told them. "They've give us our orders an' a chitty for the coach an' maps for to find our way about on account of London's a mighty big place seemingly, an' we've writ to the Belle Sauvage what's the inn where the coach will arrive, an' we've booked ourselves a room. 'Tis all arranged."

"My dear heart alive," Mary said again. "What a pair you are for adventures. If you'm a-goin' on a stage-coach Marianne, you must wear a good thick flannel petticoat. 'Tis mortal cold on them of coaches."

"If Mrs Tonbridge pays up in good time for her chairs, she shall have a mantle to wear," Jem promised. "She won't be cold then. She shall have a mantle and I shall have a greatcoat. How will that be, Mother Morris?"

CHAPTER 21

The outside seats on the Portsmouth stage were bitingly cold places to be on a January morning. The passengers huddled together for warmth, taking sips from their hip flasks and rubbing their gloved hands together, and those who had rugs wrapped them more and more closely around their shoulders, for the world they travelled was chill and bloodless, the sky pale with the threat of snow, the bare trees soot-black, the fields frost-white, the wind like a knife against their faces. Even in her new thick mantle and with her new thick gloves on her hands and her petti-coats wrapped about her legs, Marianne was shivering before they'd reached the Downs. Below her, the horses steamed and strained, their hooves clattering on the dark road, as the pole-chains clinked, and the coach rocked from side to side like a ship in a storm.

"I shall be glad to get to London," she said, snuggling into Jem's warm side. "'Tis mortal cold up here."

"Be there in two days," Jem encouraged. "That's all. Worse things happen at sea. Have some grog."

Marianne drank a great deal of grog on the first leg of their journey and that night, she slept very badly in an uncomfortable bed in a very cold bedroom. By the time they reached the Belle Sauvage on Ludgate Hill the following afternoon, she was chilled to the bone and feeling extremely sick.

"Chops by the fire," Jem said, as they limped into the inn. "That'll warm us."

"I hope so," Marianne said, fighting back another wave of sickness, "for I'm mortal cold." I shall need to sit quiet for a while, she thought, till this sickness passes. It was as bad as it had been on board ship that time and she could hardly run off and spew over the side in an inn.

The other passengers had decided to warm themselves by the fire, too, while they waited for *their* food to be served and now that they were all indoors and out of the weather, they fell into conversation with one another.

"Up for the funeral I daresay," one portly gentleman said to Jem.

Jem agreed that they were.

"A bad business," the man said. He was an extremely colourful person in a bottle-green jacket and a yellow waistcoat, and his face was as lurid as his clothes, his cheeks blotched scarlet with cold and his nose mottled purple. It gave Marianne another wave of sickness just to look at him. He gave his nose a good hard rub with his handkerchief and pulled his chair closer to the fire. "To lose our Lord Nelson," he said. "Terrible business. My hero, don'tcher know. A great man. I was saying so to Mrs Trotter only yesterday, was I not, my love?"

Mrs Trotter was an angular lady with a sharp white nose, small grey eyes and impossibly back ringlets. "You were, my love," she said. "You were indeed."

"My hero," Mr Trotter said, polishing his nose again. "A very great man." And he glared round at the assembled company as if he was daring them to disagree with him.

They obliged him by agreeing with him on that too and Marianne breathed through another wave of sickness and wondered what he would say if she told him she'd been there when his hero died.

Another traveller joined in, with his wife and two daughters listening beside him. "The fleet loved him, by all accounts."

"Aye, sir, Mr Yellaby," Mr Trotter said, "So they did. I was saying so to Mrs Trotter, only yesterday, was I not, my dear? The fleet loved him, I said."

"That is very true, my love," Mrs Trotter said, squinting at him down her long white nose and shaking her ringlets at him. "The fleet loved him. Those were your very words. And you should know, my love."

What with the grog and the cold and the sickness Marianne was beginning to feel tetchy. *You should know, my love,* she thought, crossly. Why, he don't know nothin' at all. Sittin here afore the fire sayin' things. We'm the ones what knows. He was *ours* not theirs.

"Ah yes," Mr Trotter repeated, "The fleet loved him. You can take my word for it." His voice was heavy with importance. "Mr Yellaby will bear me out on that. The fleet loved him."

Jem had been watching Marianne's thunderous expression and, now that he understood her so well, he knew he had to speak out before she did. "Aye," he said, looking at the two gentlemen. "You have the right of it there. We did."

There was a moment's startled silence as the import of what he'd just said sunk through the cold into their brains. Mrs Trotter's eyes grew round as pennies. "Are you in the navy, sir?" she said, looking at his uniform.

"Ship's carpenter, ma'am,"

She was agog for more. "Were you there when he died? Oh, do tell."

Jem answered her guardedly. "I was at the battle, ma'am."

Now they were all eyes and all attention and Mrs Trotter was full of admiration. "A great victory they say," she prompted.

"It was, ma'am, but a costly one. Our gunners did sterling service an' paid heavy for it."

That's right, Marianne thought. You tell 'em. They needs tellin'.

Now that he'd begun, Jem was unsure of himself, not wanting to brag of his part in the battle — it was all too raw and recent for that — nor to speak of his shipmates for that would make him think of Tom, which he certainly didn't want to do, but not wanting to let them go uncorrected either. Fortunately, he was saved by the arrival of the chops, which were borne in on an enormous platter, steaming succulently. So they left the fire and sat at their tables to be served and the moment passed. Although as Marianne struggled to eat what she could, which was none too easy given how sick she felt, she noticed that Mrs Yellerby and her daughters were casting surreptitious glances in Jem's direction.

"The sauce of 'em," she said, when she and Jem were on their own and trying to make themselves comfortable in a rather lumpy bed. "*Our Lord Nelson*. Did 'ee ever hear the like? He's *our* Lord Nelson, not theirs." She gave the pillow a furious pummelling.

"Don' 'ee pay 'em no mind," he advised. "We'm to walk in the percession, don' forget, an' they'll be standin' in the street."

She wasn't placated. "An' as to them silly gels, simperin' an' gigglin' an' carryin' on!"

"They meant no harm." Jem said easily.

"They was looking at you all through supper."

"An' a fat lot a' good it did 'em," he said, "on account of I only got eyes for the one woman, an' you'm her. Give us a kiss."

But she was still feeling sick and leant away from him. "Did you tell 'em to wake us in the mornin'?"

"Don 'ee fret," he said. "'Tis all took care of, every last thing. Now give us a kiss, for pity's sake."

"I en't in the mood for it," she said.

He felt rather hurt for it wasn't like her to push him away. "Why not?" he asked.

"On account of I'm cold and tired and I feels sick," she said.

"Too much grog," he said.

"Very likely," she said, crossly. "I'd like to take a rolling pin to this pillow."

~

WHEN THE BOOT-BOY came to wake them the next morning, Marianne's sickness had passed. There were frost ferns on the windows, the city's bells were jangling over their heads and they could hear traffic toiling up Ludgate Hill outside their window. Dark though it was, Marianne got out of bed at once, wrapped herself in her mantle and went to see what was going on, reporting to Jem that the street was full of lighted carriages all carrying people in black and all going the same way, which he said was likely to be to St Paul's. They dressed by candlelight exactly as they'd done when they were aboard ship, but with rather more room than they'd had on the gun deck, and Marianne said she was glad to be back in her sailor's slops, which seemed altogether more fitting for the day ahead of them, although she wore her chemise and her stockings underneath them because it was bitterly cold, and she'd had enough of being chilled and feeling sick.

They breakfasted on boiled ham, poached eggs and ale, which she managed to eat without feeling sick at all and which Jem said would set them up nicely for the day and then, map in hand, they set out along Ludgate Hill, towards Fleet Street, heading for the Admiralty. It was seven o'clock in the morning and the sky was still dark, but the streets bloomed with lanterns, attached to coaches that passed slowly and cautiously on their way to St Paul's, and held aloft by shivering walkers like Jem and Marianne who were all heading in the opposite direction towards Horse Guard's Parade and the Admiralty. By the time they reached the great open spaces of the parade and joined the crowd that was gathering there, the dawn was coming up and the dark sky was laced with blue light.

"'Twill be a bright day," Jem said and, as the sun rose and the troops and sailors and marines were marshalled into their positions, he was proved right. The great stone buildings all around them gradually lightened until they were a dazzling white, the sky enlarged into a high cloudless blue, the frosted grass under their feet was warmed green. Soon the horses that had been steaming and pawing the ground in the half-light were no longer monochrome shadows but had emerged into their full and natural colour, chestnut and grey and glossy black, eyes gleaming and harnesses glinting, and the assembled troops took on their uniformed colours too as they shuffled cold feet and waited for the order to march. Now, it was possible for Jem and Marianne to recognise their shipmates, who were wearing the clothes they'd fought in, and their officers, who were wearing full dress uniform, except that their waistcoats were black instead of white, and were standing about like everybody else waiting for orders. It made Jem think of the way they'd stood and waited as they sailed towards the French guns and the certainty that many of them would be killed. And now here they were in this huge crowded city, waiting to salute the worst death of all.

At half past eight, the great bell of St Paul's began to toll, and the Scots Greys rode off to lead the procession. Then the leading carriages pulled away and were eased through the arches into Whitehall one after the other. And they waited again. After what seemed an interminable time, the order was given for the coffin bearers to take up their positions outside the Admiralty and, as soon as they'd gone, the first minute gun was fired and out in the street a band of fifes and muffled drums began to play the *Dead March in Saul*. And they waited again.

"If we'm parted," Jem said, which we might well be with all these people, "go back to the Belle Sauvage an' wait for me there." He felt responsible for her in this great city and had no intention of losing her again. "You got your map an' it en't far from St Paul's."

Marianne promised to remember it, but then she fell to thinking. There was so much to think about, standing there on that great parade ground with the noise of the crowd all around her: the things that had happened to her at sea, the storms in the Mediterranean and the heat in Barbados, that poor little baby new birthed and lying dead on Looma's mat. The thought made her tearful, so it was just as well that the naval contingent was the next to be told to take up their positions. Movement was better than having to stand still and it would give her something to see, which would take her mind off all this troublesome thinking. As they emerged through the arches, she was taking everything in, noticing that Whitehall was lined with people, that the funeral car was in the road, with six black horses ready to pull it and that the coffin bearers were standing beside it on either side. The street was quiet except for the shuffle of hooves, the wail of the fifes and the sombre beat of those muffled drums, for the watchers were standing bareheaded and in respectful silence.

Orders were given that the *Victory* contingent were to fall in behind the funeral car and Marianne felt a flutter of panic at the thought that she and Jem were to be parted. But she was obeying even while the thought was in her head, because she was a sailor and that's what sailors did, even when they were in the middle of a terrible battle and anyway, she knew what she had to do if she and Jem lost sight of one another. There was no need to worry. She could find him again at the Belle Sauvage. What was important was that this great man should be buried with his sailors around him to grieve for him. The bosun held up the bullet-riddled flag that they were going to drape over his coffin at the end of the service and the procession set off, very quietly and at walking pace, following the muffled drums.

It took a very long time to walk to St Pauls and the streets were lined with weeping people all the way and every window they passed was full of pale watching faces. There must be thousands of them, Marianne thought, and she remembered people saying it was going to be the biggest funeral London had ever seen and was swollen with pride to be part of it, following his tattered flag in the steadying sunshine.

The great cathedral was as crowded as the streets had been but here the light was provided by hundreds of torches that burned warmly in every sconce and by a huge chandelier that had been suspended immediately above the spot where Nelson was to be buried. The pews were full of men in splendid uniforms and women in full mourning, black plumes and all, but space had been left in the aisles for the war-besmirched men of the Admiral's fleet, although it took another hour before the procession was over and all the troops had arrived and were in position. But eventually the service began, and the choristers sang their opening anthem, "I am the Resurrection and the Life", their voices rising sharp and clear into the dome above the opened crypt.

What with the weariness of their long wait and the relative warmth in the cathedral after the cold outside and the endlessly booming homilies of one pompous churchman after another, Marianne lost interest in the proceedings after the first twenty minutes and was soon finding it hard to keep awake. If it hadn't been for the fact that she was on her feet instead of sitting in a pew, she would certainly have fallen asleep, as it was, she had to concentrate to stop herself from swaying and falling over. When the coffin was about to be lowered into the crypt and it was time for them to step forward with the flag, her eyes were closed, and she had to shake herself awake. But the flag wasn't placed over the coffin, as everyone expected, it was held up and torn in two, the rasp of its sudden ripping a distinct shock in the reverential silence that had followed the words of the committal. Puzzled heads turned to see what was happening and people near them watched as the lesser of the two pieces was torn and torn again, until it had been ripped into shreds, which were passed among the

Victory party so that they all had a piece. And quite right too, Marianne thought, clutching her own scrap of dirty cloth. He was *our* Lord Nelson, an' 'tis ours by rights.

THAT WAS Jem's opinion too when they found one another in the inn at the end of the day. "I'll make a frame for it," he said, when they'd had their supper and retired to their room, "an' we'll hang it over the mantelpiece for all the world to see."

"Home tomorrow," she said, happily. "Back to our own room an' our own comfy bed an' all our nice things. I tell 'ee Jem, these inns are all very well, but their beds are as lumpy as skillygalee an' that there chamber pot smells like a privy. I shall be glad to be home. Only thing is, I hopes we don't have to sit alongside a that Mr Trotter, for I can't abide the man. If I'd has to hear him talk about *our* Lord Nelson just one more time, I shall show him my flag and give him what-for."

"Then perhaps 'tis as well I've bought us inside tickets," Jem said. And was kissed as a reward.

"You en't feelin' so sick today," he said hopefully. And it was true, she wasn't. So he was kissed again. And again.

They had a much better night, now that the funeral was over, and it was an easier journey home and didn't take them anywhere near as long as the journey out had done, which pleased them both. Their inside tickets meant that they were out of the wind, even if the coach was damp, and they had clean straw under their feet, even if it soon got smeared with mud. As Marianne was dressed in her nice warm petticoats again and wrapped in her new mantle, she didn't feel anywhere near so sick as she had on the first journey, and Jem was happy because they had meat pies to eat and plenty of grog to keep them warm and their memories of the procession to entertain them.

"What a tale we shall have to tell when we gets home," Marianne said, passing the grog bottle back to her husband, after she'd taken a cautious sip. "I tell 'ee what, Jem, we must invite 'em all to supper. We could borrow some chairs, couldn't we, and buy some pies? An' then we can all sit round the table, what'll be a bit of a squash but not to worry, an' we can tell 'em every last thing about it."

"Well now," Jem said, looking mischievous, "as to that, I got a surprise for 'ee."

She was intrigued. "What sort a' surprise?"

"You'll see."

"What sort of answer's that?" she teased. "What will I see? You can't tell me half a thing an' not finish it. That en't fair."

But he put his finger to his lips and just repeated that she'd see. "Once we'm home, which should be in an hour or two, the way we'm a-goin'. I can see the Downs already."

"Husbands an' wives en't supposed to have secrets," she said, but then she had to stop because the words were reminding her of that poor baby again and making her feel ashamed. She was surprised by how much she'd been thinking of the baby while she'd been in London, but a' course that was on account of there'd been a lot of time for standing about thinking and on account of she'd been feeling sick and the last time she'd felt sick was when she'd been carrying. She was feeling slightly sick at that moment and it couldn't be because she'd been drinking too much grog because she'd taken care to drink as little as she could. Thoughts and questions were crowding into her head. What if she was carrying again? She tried to remember the last time she'd seen her courses. Back on the *Victory* afore she came home an' that was a fair of time ago. What if...?

Jem was drinking his grog and didn't notice how quiet she was. "'Twill only be secret for an hour or two, that's all," he said wiping his lips on the back of his hand, "an' then I'll tell 'ee. Patience is a virtue at sea."

IT WAS GROWING dark when they reached the Sally Port and by then, Marianne was feeling very sick and only had one thought in her head which was to go home as quickly as she could and light a fire. She strode off along the High Street like a boy, kicking her petticoats out of the way. But when she went to turn in at Farthing Lane, Jem put out a hand and pulled her to a halt. "You'm a-goin' the wrong way," he said.

"No, I en't," she said. "You've drunk too much grog, my lover. This is the way to Farthing Lane."

He was wearing his devilish expression. "Except we en't a-goin' to Farthing Lane," he said, "on account of I got somethin' to show 'ee."

"What sort a' somethin'?"

"Come with me an' you'll see."

It was a neat house in a terrace of neat houses, two storeys high and with a fine new door painted black. "My dear heart alive," she said. "You never means for to say we got a room here."

"Come an' see," he said, opening the door.

It was a beautiful, clean, empty house. The hall was painted duck-egg blue and there were two doors leading out of it, both painted white. "Which one is it?" she said, looking at them.

He opened the rear door and led her into a kitchen. It was such an amazing room and so full of good things it dried up her sickness in an instant. There was a table in the middle of the room with two stools beside it and the biggest dresser she'd ever seen along one wall with enough room on its shelves to store every single pot and pan and all the dishes she could possibly want. And that wasn't all. There was a huge stove for cooking with a trivet for kettles and irons, and a sink with a bucket underneath it, standing ready for use and, wonder of wonders, a copper set in the corner where she could wash her clothes. When she lifted the lid, there was even a scrubbing board inside. "My dear heart alive," she said. "We only needs our bed in the corner an' we could move straight in."

"Ah, but that's not all, he told her. "Come on." And led her to the front room, which was wide and empty with a window that gave out to the street. "What do 'ee think to this?"

"Two rooms," she said. "We shall live like lords."

Now, he was laughing because this triumph he'd planned was such a joy. "Now come upstairs," he said. "'Tis even better upstairs."

Which it was, for there were two more doors on the landing and the first led to a room that spread across the width of the house and had a fine fireplace and two windows, no less. "If we're thinkin' of a party," he said, "This here is the room for it."

"You've never took the whole house, have 'ee?" she asked.

"The whole house," he told her happily. "I've took it for a year. Spent my bounty on it. There's a coal cellar in the basement and a yard at the back. I'll show 'ee presently. The back room up here can be our bedroom, what's a good room, as you'll see, and the front room downstairs can be a workroom for my furniture where people can come an' see it in the warm, what'll help 'em make their minds to buy it. Now what do 'ee think?"

She thought it was perfect.

"A fine secret don' 'ee think?"

"Aye, so 'tis," she said, beaming at him. "I got a secret for you an all."

That surprised him. "Have 'ee?"

"What would 'ee say if I was to tell 'ee I'm carryin'?"

He gave a crow of delight. First a wife an' then a job an' a house an' now a child! "I should make 'ee a cradle," he said.

CHAPTER 22

I t was such a lark to set up home. Marianne had never had so much fun. To stroll through the streets on a bright afternoon, in her fine new mantle, with her fine new bonnet on her head and her pretty new boots on her feet, with money in her pocket and Jem by her side was an absolute pleasure, but to walk into all those fine shops, where she'd watched the gentry making their purchases when she was an envious child, and actually buy things for herself was nothing short of a wonder. There were so many lovely things to choose from too, because the town was full of sailors returned from the war, with money burning holes in their pockets, so the shopkeepers had made sure their shelves were full of temptation — blue and white china fit for an emperor, brass kettles and brass pots and warming pans — "Imagine one a' them in the bed at night!" — canteens of knives and forks and spoons all with the prettiest china handles, cushions and painted chamber pots and printed fire-screens — even turkey carpets, although Marianne felt she ought to draw the line at them.

"That 'ud cost the earth Jem," she said, fingering the pile longingly.

"Have one if that's what 'ee wants," he told her happily. "We got the money."

"We shan't have it long if we goes on spending at this rate," she said trying to be serious. It wasn't easy because she was bubbling with happiness and she really liked the carpet, but *one* of them had to be sensible. China and chamber pots and knives and forks were necessities, but a carpet was quite another matter.

"I'm earning, don' forget," he pointed out. "'Ten't just the bounty."

It was true. He opened his "show room" for trade every afternoon and it was always full of customers, some of them come to pass the time of day, but most of them sailors' wives come to buy new furniture with their Trafalgar windfalls. He had so many orders he was considering taking on an apprentice. "And," as he said to Marianne, "who'd ha' thought *that* when we was afloat."

But Marianne decided against the carpet, despite being tempted most strongly. It was too luxurious for the likes of her and Jem and, besides, it would look out of place under their new chairs, fine though they were going to be.

They spent the first four weeks in their new home happily filling their empty rooms with treasures, sleeping in a warm bed every night, loving whenever they felt like it and eating so well that Marianne said they'd end up as fat as pigs if they didn't watch out.

"Never mind pigs," Jem told her. "We'm livin' like lords, that's the way of it, an' I'm blamed if I can see a thing wrong wi' that. We've earned our money hard, bein' at Trafalgar, an' I work all the hours God sends, don' forget, an' so do you. We needs our grub."

There was only one problem in this new life of theirs and that was the cooking. Before they'd moved into the house, the most Marianne had ever done in the way of cooking was to bake bread and fry chops or bacon or a bit of liver in a frying pan over the fire. Now, she had to learn how to roast meat on a spit and cook pies and pastries in an oven and that took patience and a lot of mistakes, even though she had a hearty appetite to drive her on now that the sickness had passed. There was no doubt about the baby now. As February gave way to March, she was swelling visibly and her love for this little unborn vulnerable creature grew as her belly did. "You shan't die, my little darling," she told it, stroking her belly. "I won't let 'ee. You'll be born safe and sound, I promise 'ee. You'll be a good, strong, healthy baby and have a ma and pa what'll love 'ee and good food to eat and fine clothes to wear. My own little darling."

~

"WHEN WE GOIN' to give that ol' party then?" Jem asked one evening, when they were sitting in their new chairs in the kitchen, one on each side of the stove, digesting their supper. "Now you got the hang a' the stove, I means for to say, we ought to be sendin' invitations, wouldn't 'ee say."

In the joy of furnishing her house and carrying her child, Marianne had forgotten all about the party. She didn't tell him of course, for that would never do. "End a' the month," she said. "How would that be? After church of a Sunday?"

"'Course."

"An' we can tell 'em about the baby?"

"'Course."

"What'll please 'em no end."

So the families were invited and on the last Sunday of the month they walked back to the house as soon as church was finished and when they'd admired the new furniture in the "show room" were escorted upstairs into the best room for the feast. Marianne had built up a good fire in the hearth and set the table with all her fine new ware, china plates, knives and forks, pewter tankards and all, and very good it looked. She'd been cooking all morning, while they'd been in church praying for their souls, roasting a joint of beef, no less, and baking a selection of pies and pastries, concentrating hard in order to do the very best she could, so as to impress Jem's ma and pa. The kitchen smelt like a pastry cook's and most of the dishes had come out well — or well enough. Now the proof would be in the eating.

They were a happy company gathered around the table that afternoon. Mary and Jack were so proud of their daughter's cooking they praised every mouthful and Lizzie said she'd never ate a pie what tasted so good, not even one she'd made herself and that was saying something, and all four men clamoured for second helpings and drank so much ale to wash the meal down that Jem had to go out and buy some more.

"An' don' 'ee go joinin' the navy this time," his father teased. Which provoked a roar of laughter.

"He's got more reason to stay this time," Jack Morris said, "what with the house an' his work an' all. I never see a room so full of furniture as that one downstairs. There's different things in it every time I comes round. He's turned out quite a cabinet maker."

The skill of his carpentry was praised at some length, while Marianne cleared the dirty dishes and took them down to the kitchen. They were still talking about it when she came back upstairs.

"I seen a cradle in the corner last time I was here," her father said slyly, when she re-joined them. "Very pretty thing, all carved an all. Very pretty."

Marianne was busy moving the fruit pies from the dresser to the table, but she was aware that they were all looking at her, smiling and nodding and hopeful, and she realised that their expressions were far too pointed to be ignored.

"Well now, as to that," she said, setting the last pie in the middle of the table. "I'll tell 'ee when Jem gets back. On account of 'tis as much his news as mine."

"I knew you was carryin'," Mary said, triumphantly. "Didn't I tell 'ee, Lizzie?"

"You did, my lover," Lizzie agreed. "An' I said what a fine thing 'twould be."

"You did. An' so it is."

Marianne was put out for she'd been looking forward to telling them her news. "Then there's nothin' for to tell 'ee," she said. "Not if 'ee'd knowed all along, what you could ha' told me."

"Come here an' let me kiss 'ee, child," her mother said, "for 'tis the best news in the world."

"What is?" Jem asked, striding in with the ale.

"Our baby," Marianne told him scowling from within the circle of her mother's arms, "what they knows about seemingly."

"Then that saves us tellin' 'em," he said easily, putting the ale on the table. But then he saw the scowl and realised how hurt she was for he'd grown skilled in reading her expressions over the last few months, so he added, "We've plenty of other tales for to tell 'em, my lover, given where we've been and what we've seen."

"What you *can* tell us," his father said, "is how you two came to meet up when you was at sea, for you promised us the tellin' a' that months an' months ago, an' we've heard nary a word of it."

The thought of telling them that particular tale cheered Marianne up at once. "I'll tell 'ee when I've served the pies," she said, smiling at Jem, "an' when you've all got more ale an' are settled comfortable."

"'Tis a long story then," her brother said, as she served them.

"Aye," Marianne told him, settling into her chair. "Two years long. An' Pa will need the salt cellar for he won't believe a word of it, will 'ee, Pa? But 'tis as true as I sits here. I tell 'ee no word of a lie. It came about like this…"

ACKNOWLEDGMENTS

Admiral Sir Kenneth Eaton GBE KCB and Dr Colin White FSA FRHistS MA, historian and director of the Royal Naval Museum.

HEARTS AND FARTHINGS

BERYL KINGSTON

CHAPTER 1

The couple standing under the olive tree were kissing, he moving his mouth gently and languidly over hers, she holding his face tenderly between her hands, guiding and savouring. They were absorbed in each other, concentrating on their pleasure, and neither knew nor cared that they were being watched. They'd have been annoyed if they'd known but not very surprised, for the watcher was young Alberto Pelucci, the village nuisance, and everybody knew he was always to be found where he wasn't wanted. But Alberto was keeping very still, and they were in another world of pleasurable sensation, so the kiss went on. The setting sun mottled their ecstatic faces and their encircling arms with patches of gold, and as the slight breeze of evening stirred the grey-green branches all around them, the dappled shapes shifted and swam with the same luxurious rhythm as their kiss. To Alberto, sitting above them in the olive grove, they seemed to be sparkling with pleasure, their hair glinting as they moved, their flesh edged with fire. With the reasonable part of his mind, he knew that they were only Giulietta, who was really no better than the village whore, and her idle cousin Enrico, who'd never done an honest day's work in his life. But his senses were recognising them in quite another way. To his senses they looked like gods, and he was profoundly and tearingly jealous of them.

He'd never been able to understand why the village girls had always rejected him. He knew he wasn't much to look at, with his big nose and embarrassing lack of height, but he could love them so perfectly, if only they'd let him. But they never would. 'Run away and grow up, little baby boy!' they mocked. And when his brow darkened at their taunts, 'Doesn't he like it then? Run home to Mummy, baby! Little baby!' Always this terrible insistence on his lack of size, lack of years, lack of experience.

One day, he promised himself, watching the kiss as it started again, one day some girl somewhere would arch her body against his just like Giulietta was doing, would hold his face between her hands or wind her arms around his neck in the same beautiful abandoned way. Not here in Pontedecimo of course. In England. In his new life. Where he'd be a success, with a thriving shop full of happy satisfied customers and a grand new house full of the latest furniture, and a fine English woman to love him. Much better than Giulietta. A lady. With white skin and long fair hair. It would all be different in England. Nobody there would laugh at him behind their hands, or tell him to run away and grow up, or call him a pest, or beat him for the temper he couldn't control, or tell him that times were bad and that the youngest son would have to fend for himself. In England he wouldn't be a son, or the village nuisance, or stupid Alberto. In England he would be himself.

Now that the time for his departure was so very close, his emotions were in such a turmoil that he couldn't settle to anything. He couldn't eat and he couldn't sleep. He couldn't sit still for more than ten minutes and there was nowhere he wanted to walk. He couldn't even listen to the end of a conversation, particularly when he'd heard it all before. This evening he'd left the supper table before the meal was over, an unheard-of crime in the Pelucci farm, and had wandered off into the olive grove without even being aware of what he was doing. Excitement, fear, regret, hope and impatience boiled in his brain and set his body into continuous alert. The occasional stab of anxiety only made matters worse and certainly didn't cool him or stop the mill race of sensation that seemed to be sweeping through him at every second of the day and night. Tomorrow he would be on-board ship and bound for his new life. Tomorrow! Tomorrow!

He stood up carefully, dusting the seat of his trousers with the palm of his hands and looking down at the dry familiar earth under his feet. There was no sound in the village below him. It lay subdued under lethargy, almost without life. The donkeys in the low pasture were asleep standing up. The breeze had dropped, and even the leaves hung from the branches all around him, heavy and somnolent. It was all so dull, so crushingly dull. How could anybody live in such a boring place?

As he ducked under the low lintel of the farm door, he sensed his father's brooding disapproval even before he saw it. A glance at the table showed him that his two sisters had already left the room, and he felt a flicker of relief that they wouldn't be there for the row that was bound to break the minute he opened his mouth. Vittorio and Claudio had stayed behind with their father. All three faces were dark and disagreeable. I'm for it, Alberto thought, and comforted himself that this would be the very last scolding he would ever have to endure. Tomorrow, tomorrow, his mind sang. Tomorrow was freedom.

But tonight certainly wasn't. 'Where the devil do you think you've been?' his father demanded, leaning back in his tall wooden chair to send a look like a knife straight at his son's face.

'I'm sorry, father,' Alberto tried. 'I just had to get out. I felt stifled in here. I needed air.'

'That's your trouble my son,' his father said. 'It's always what *you* want, isn't it. *You. You. You.* Never anybody else. You're so full of yourself you never give a minute's thought to anybody else. You don't care how you upset people just so long as you get your own way!' The complaint went on in its well-worn, familiar fashion. Alberto shut his ears to it and focused his attention on two flies crawling across the bread board. One stopped halfway over, to clean its head, stroking itself with legs like black thread, delicately, first on one side of its head and then on the other. Alberto wondered if it could hear his father's voice droning on and on and on, and decided that it, too, had probably learnt the trick of not hearing sounds it didn't like or didn't need. The fly stretched out its back legs stiffly behind it, flicked open its wings and flew off. There was a pause in his father's peroration. Alberto looked up to see if a response was required, so he was paying attention when Vittorio weighed in to have his turn.

'You wouldn't have behaved like this when Mother was alive,' Vittorio said.

Alberto was stung and replied before he could stop himself. 'You leave Mother out of it,' he said, and now his voice was shrill. 'When she was alive, we were a family. I was welcomed at the table. I enjoyed being here. Because she wanted me here. That was enough.' To his annoyance, he could feel tears rising in his throat.

'Your mother spoilt you,' his father said testily, drawing on his pipe again. He'd forgotten to smoke during his outburst, so it had gone out. 'That's your trouble. You've been spoilt. I tell you, you'll need to mend your ways if you're going to get on in England.'

'He won't last five minutes,' Vittorio said. 'You'll see! I give him three months, and then he'll be whining back here for us to give him a roof over his idle head and put food into his stupid mouth.'

'You needn't worry,' Alberto shouted, 'I wouldn't take your precious food. I wouldn't come back here if I was starving to death.'

'Then you'll have to work,' Claudio said. 'And mind how you behave. If you go sloping off in the middle of a meal in England, they'll give you the sack, I can tell you.'

'The whole things ridiculous,' Vittorio said. 'We're simply squandering money on his fare. How will he ever get a job? He's got nothing to offer. Nothing at all. No brains. No effort. He can't live on dreams.'

'He thinks he can,' his father said, getting his pipe to draw, at last, and covering the bowl with his thumb to encourage it.

Rage swelled in Alberto's chest. They were talking about him as though he wasn't there, as though he'd gone already, making him feel insignificant.

'I'm here!' he yelled. 'I'm here! I haven't gone! I'm here! In front of you! You just talk to me.'

'Temper, temper!' Vittorio said, mocking him. 'You can't even control your temper. Look at you.'

'You treat me like dirt,' Alberto shouted. 'I'm your brother, damn you! Your brother! Treat me properly!'

'Behave yourself properly then,' Vittorio said, deliberately cold and very calm. 'If you act like a baby, you'll be treated like a baby.'

'Naughty! Naughty!' Claudio mocked. He got up from the table and advanced on his brother, grinning and enjoying the boy's discomfiture. 'Look at him, Father. He's crying. Cry-baby!'

'I'm not!' Alberto roared, furiously. But he was. He couldn't hold the tears back. He was shaking with fury and shame. 'Leave me alone, you lousy bullies.'

Vittorio joined his elder brother. 'And you think you're going to get a job in a foreign country. They won't even look at you, a snivelling little worm like you!'

'They don't like cry-babies in England,' Claudio said, tweaking Alberto's ear to emphasise his words.

The tweak was painful, but the taunt and the mocking expression were worse. Alberto seized the bread board in one hand and the bread knife in the other and lunged at his brother, beating him about the head with the board, weeping and shouting incoherently. Instantly, the kitchen was in uproar. Vittorio, trying to get out of the way of Alberto's attack, fell back against the great table, scattering the pile of used platters onto the stone flags. One rolled back under Claudio's foot and he lost his balance and fell backwards into the debris of the meal with Alberto on top of him, wielding the bread board like a man possessed. Their father put his pipe carefully on its rack, took off his belt and waded in to restore order, beating the thick leather thong onto Alberto's back. At the first blow Alberto leapt from his brother and turned to face his father, knife aloft and snarling.

'Granny Bianchi!' Vittorio screamed. 'Granny Bianchi come quickly! Alberto's murdering Papa!'

Granny Bianchi, Pina and little Maria were in the kitchen before he'd finished shouting, and Granny had taken the bread knife from Alberto's upheld hand almost before he knew she was there. 'Calm yourselves,' she said. 'Calm yourselves, you bad boys. When will you all learn to behave?'

'When this maniac has gone to England,' Claudio said, rubbing the side of his head. 'I should think he's given me a black eye.'

'And what have you done to me? Do you ever think of that?' Alberto said, still bristling. 'No, you never do.'

'Come away with me,' Granny Bianchi said quickly to Alberto, putting an arm around his shaking shoulders, just as she'd done so many times during his childhood. 'I've got a job that needs doing. Come along.' She turned to her son-in-law. 'Is the farm running itself now that you've got time to brawl?' she asked.

Alberto followed his grandmother out of the kitchen, thankful as usual for her authority and the speed with which she could calm them all down when their passions were running too high. She was the only person he would really miss when he left Pontedecimo, and he knew that he would miss her sorely, her strength and her good sense and her affection. Now the moment was approaching when he would have to say goodbye to her, and he didn't think he could bear it. They crossed the courtyard to the barn.

Alberto settled into the routine of milking, brushing the two goats, and putting feed in their stalls to occupy them while Granny Bianchi milked. He was calmed by the familiar work and the familiar sounds, the swish of milk into the pail and the steady chomp and rustle of feeding. Granny Bianchi rested her head against the warm flank of the senior goat and looked at her grandson.

'Off tomorrow then, my dear,' she said.

'Yes, Granny,' Alberto answered, suddenly overwhelmed by the misery of parting.

'I shan't see you again after tomorrow,' Granny Bianchi said, looking him steadily and lovingly in the eye.

It was too much. 'Oh don't say that,' Alberto pleaded. 'Please don't say that,' and he rushed towards her, arms outstretched.

Granny Bianchi turned on her stool to accommodate him, taking his head into her hands and down into her lap. 'Things must be said, my little Alberto,' she said sadly. 'I'm an old woman. I shan't last very much longer and I'm never likely to travel. Even if you come home to visit us when you're rich and famous, I shan't be here to see it. So we are really saying goodbye, you and I.'

Alberto was weeping now and quite unable to answer. Granny Bianchi let him cry for a little, then she wiped his eyes on her milky apron and brushed the thick damp hair out of his eyes. 'I've something to tell you Alberto,' she said seriously.

'Yes, Granny Bianchi,' he said, loving her more than he could bear.

'I don't know anything about London or England,' Granny Bianchi said. 'I don't really know anything about Italy, if the truth be told. Only Pontedecimo. But I know about human beings. And one thing I can tell you for sure is that nobody likes a foreigner. We don't trust somebody who's different. When your grandfather first brought me to this farm, *I* was a foreigner. *I* was different. I didn't fit in. I wore different clothes and I spoke a different dialect and people kept their distance. It was very upsetting and very lonely, but I learnt what to do about it. After a very long time, it's true, but I learnt. Now when you get to England you will be a foreigner. Different. And they won't like it. You must make it your business to stop being foreign as quickly as you can. Find out how they behave and behave like them. Eat the same food. Wear the same clothes. Speak the same language. Worship in the same church. But be the same. Then they won't be afraid of you and gradually they will like you. Have you understood?'

'Yes,' Alberto said. 'I've understood.' He kissed her solemnly, feeling that it was almost as if they were in church, and he was making a vow. He didn't really understand her argument, but he knew, with his instincts, that her advice was sound, and resolved to follow it. He had already thought himself halfway towards it anyway, because he was so determined that his life in England would be totally unlike his life in Pontedecimo.

AT BREAKFAST the next morning conversation was sparse, limited as it always was to the state of the livestock, the progress of the fruit, last night's milk yield and the morning's crop of eggs. Alberto drank his coffee slowly, savouring every sip, but he was too excited to eat.

Then the morning chores demanded all their attention and activity excluded speech, as it always did. Eggs and olives were packed for market, and the donkey was persuaded and coaxed until he finally allowed himself to be harnessed to the cart.

Granny Bianchi handed Alberto a bundle of food for the journey. 'Eke it out, my dear,' she said. 'Don't gobble it all up on the first day. You've got a long way to go.' Alberto was folded into her black serge embrace and kissed firmly. Her faded eyes were bright, but she didn't weep and neither, to Alberto's surprise, did he. After all the emotions of the past twelve hours, he felt numb, saying goodbye as if he were in a dream. His brothers kissed him on both cheeks and thumped his arms. 'You'll be all right! You'll see!' Claudio assured him and Vittorio said, 'Good luck! We'll be thinking of you.' Little Maria stood on tiptoe to kiss him, and said,

'Come back soon!' as though he were going on a holiday. Then only his father remained, standing apart, small and awkward in his earth-stained jacket, with his trousers tied at the knee ready for the day's work.

'You will write to us,' he instructed his son brusquely, as they embraced. His skin was rough and dry against Alberto's cheek, and as they drew apart the boy looked hard at the seamed, earth-brown face beside him. 'I will write to you,' he promised. Then he and Pina climbed into the cart and the family stood back ready to wave him goodbye. And the donkey wouldn't move.

Plainly the little animal was in one of his most cussed and intractable moods. They tried coaxing and scolding; they tried shoving and sudden whipping; they tried dangling hay a few inches in front of his nose. The battle rapidly became a combined effort by the entire family, and after fifteen minutes of useless heaving and shoving they were all hot and sticky and stupid with laughter. Then just as they'd almost given up hope, the donkey suddenly started to trot down the path, with the perfect sang-froid of his kind, exactly as though that was what he'd intended to do all along. Alberto, who'd been pushing from the rear, almost got left behind. He had to sprint after the cart and leap on board. His brothers gave him a cheer and that, finally, was how he left the house in which he'd spent the first eighteen years of his life.

He and Pina were laughing so much that he almost forgot to turn back for a last look. They'd reached the bend in the track before he remembered. A minute later and the farm would have been out of sight, hidden by the folded hills. It looked unreal, this house he would never see again, unreal and poor. Even at this distance, he could distinguish the broken stones of the doorstep and see how uneven the yard was. It was a higgledy-piggledy collection of stones, mud, wood, livestock and people. Yet distance had already given it charm. For a second, seeing it like that, he didn't want to leave it, but there was no stopping the donkey now. And anyway he'd made up his mind.

The trouble was he had made it up so quickly, on the spur of the moment, on impulse, and it ought to have happened after a lot of talk and thought and planning. They'd all been in the middle of a row and on the edge of violence. His father had been snarling at him, the buckle of that horrible belt already under his fingers, and Alberto had been yelling at them all. 'I hate it here! I hate every minute of every single day!'

It was Claudio's answer that had done it. 'Then why don't you leave?' he'd said.

'I will!' Alberto yelled. 'I will! I'll go to England! That's what I'll do. Then you'll all see!'

'Never on your life!' Vittorio had said. 'Don't make me laugh! *You* go to England. You're too lazy to walk to the village.'

He had walked down to Genova the very next day and booked a ticket at the shipping office, paying a holding fee with what little money he possessed and promising that his father would make up the rest the next time he came into town. Afterwards, toiling back home up the steep cobbled streets and the climbing hill tracks, he had been aghast at what he had done. He couldn't think why he should ever have said such a thing. It wasn't as if he'd been planning to emigrate, or even thinking about England. He hadn't. The idea had entered his mind at the same time as the words spilled out of his mouth. They were spoken and he was committed before he'd had a chance to think about it at all. And now his passage was booked. He climbed slowly, half hoping his father would forbid it, half dreading the row that he felt sure would follow.

To his relief, astonishment, and dismay, he was wrong. Pelucci was thrilled by his son's initiative. He approved and he praised. He said it was the first fully adult action of Alberto's life. They even drank a toast to him at supper that evening. From then on, the matter was settled and out of his hands. He was rushed along by the enthusiasm and excitement all around him, stunned, whenever he stopped to think about it, that the whole thing had only taken six weeks from start to finish.

~

It was mid-morning before they arrived in the Piazza de Ferrari. Crowds thronged the square, and the pulse and bustle and noise of so many voices and so much movement triggered Alberto's excitement again. As he helped Pina to lower the side of the cart, his hands were shaking.

'You'd better go now,' she said, 'or you'll miss the sailing.' She was looking at him with her mother's dark eyes from under her mother's strong eyebrows. The similarity between them made things difficult. He was suddenly shy and ill at ease, embarrassed by this final parting.

'Yes,' he said, but didn't move.

'Go now,' Pina said, giving him a little push. 'Camillo will meet you, don't forget. He'll look after you.'

This time Alberto didn't look back. He kissed his sister once, twice, three times and walked quickly out of the square, his gait awkward and his shoulders hunched because he knew she was watching him. Once beyond the approval of her eyes, he began to run, dodging the crowds and stumbling over the uneven cobblestones, down and down, towards the Porto Vecchio, the bay and adventure. He raced through the narrow caruggi heedless of the washing festooned above him that dripped water onto his head and shoulders. Ragged street urchins erupted at his pounding approach, squealing and cat-calling. Twice he cannoned into passers-by and couldn't even stop to apologise. By the time he reached the quay he was completely out of breath, charged with an excitement stronger than anything he'd ever known in his life, a sense of extraordinary elation.

The quayside was crowded with people, busy as ants and with as little apparent purpose. Behind him the fish sellers called their wares, raucous as gulls, and before him the quay was edged with gently bobbing vessels, great and small, tar-stained and tatty, or smart with new paint. Beyond the ships stretched the great free

Mediterranean, not solid and stolid like those implacable mountains, but warm blue-green, perpetually moving and as alive as he was. It was the natural path to all the change he needed and desired, and he knew, in the crowded, clamorous moment, that good things were surely waiting for him, a few days away, just over the water.

timeless
fiction

If you sign up today, you'll get:

1. A free historical fiction novel from Agora Books

2. Exclusive insights into timless fiction, as well as the opportunity to get copies in advance of publication; and,

3. The chance to win exclusive prizes in regular competitions.

Interested?

It takes less than a minute to sign up.

You can get your free book and your first newsletter by visiting

**www.agorabooks.co/
timeless-fiction-newsletter**

Printed in Great Britain
by Amazon